Beloved Castaway

**Center Point
Large Print**

**This Large Print Book carries the
Seal of Approval of N.A.V.H.**

Beloved Castaway

KATHLEEN Y'BARBO

CENTER POINT LARGE PRINT
THORNDIKE, MAINE

This Center Point Large Print edition
is published in the year 2010 by arrangement with
Barbour Publishing, Inc.

This book is a work of fiction. Names, characters,
places, and incidents are either products of the
author's imagination or used fictitiously. Any
similarity to actual people, organizations, and/or
events is purely coincidental.

The text of this Large Print edition is unabridged.
In other aspects, this book may vary
from the original edition.
Printed in the United States of America.
Set in 16-point Times New Roman type.

ISBN: 978-1-60285-682-0

Library of Congress Cataloging-in-Publication Data

Y'Barbo, Kathleen.
  Beloved castaway / Kathleen Y'Barbo.
    p. cm.
  ISBN 978-1-60285-682-0 (library binding : alk. paper)
  1. Large type books. I. Title.
  PS3625.B37B45 2010
  813'.6—dc22
2009038934

DEDICATION

To Robin Tompkins,
the bird who now flies free

And of some have compassion,
making a difference:
And others save with fear,
pulling them out of the fire.

JUDE 1:22–23 KJV

PROLOGUE

New Orleans
December 27, 1814

A thick fog hugged the Vieux Carré, and darkness shadowed the entrances to the meager dwellings on the Rue Genevieve. The city lay gripped in fear of the arrival of the Englishmen, its citizens biding their time behind closed shutters while Her Majesty's Navy stood practically on their doorsteps.

Truly war was upon them, and none could predict the outcome. Of late, those in power insisted that certain victory was at hand. Jean Gayarre knew otherwise, having just that morning brokered a deal that would provide the powder for weapons currently lacking the ability to fire.

Until the transaction was completed—and there were no assurances it would be—nothing stood between New Orleans and the British soldiers save blustery pride and empty muskets.

In spite of this, on this late December night, Jean Gayarre felt no fear, only a pressing sense of urgency like none he could remember. To be fair, he'd always hurried to Sylvie's doorstep, anticipation riding high in his mind. But tonight, something else compelled Jean to pick up his pace.

Could it be his time of reckoning approached? The Lord, once his friend and Savior, had been quite patient. Perhaps tonight a payment would be required for his sins, of which there were many.

Jean drew nearer to the river, where low-slung clouds played havoc with the senses and hid all but the nearest passerby from view. So much the better, he decided as he gathered his cloak, conspicuous for its heavy weight on the unseasonably sultry evening, and traversed the uneven banquette as close to the shadows as he could.

Tonight of all nights, Jean could not fail in crossing the city to see his Sylvie. Even the lying-in of his wife—a coincidence only God could have wrought in its irony—would not keep him within the confines of the gilded prison his money had built.

He'd left the carriage well concealed behind the alehouse, paying his coachman handsomely as he did every time he made the journey. Brushing past the servant at the door, Jean raced up the stairs to kneel at the bedside of the only woman he'd ever loved.

Three days abed after birthing a squalling but tiny baby, his lady love now lay pale and, without question, nearer to death's door than a woman of two and twenty should ever drift. In deference to the religion of his youth, Jean dared to petition the good and mighty Lord to save her.

Penance is mine for my sins, Father. Do not extract the toll from one so young, so naive.

For a moment, he considered adding an offer to exchange places with Sylvie, to barter her life for his death. Sanity prevailed, however, and he shook his head.

"The babe," Sylvie whispered in English.

"It is well and truly fine," Jean answered in the French he knew would provide Sylvie with more comfort. "The picture of good health and fine spirits, *ma chère*."

Jean spoke the words—lies, all—merely to savor what time remained. Had he told her the truth—that the infant bore less chance of living than she—the grief might have done her in. Better she went to her Savior believing her child remained behind than to arrive and find the babe crawling toward the gates of Saint Peter ahead of her.

"And a more magnificent child has never been born of woman save the one at whom I now gaze," Jean said, addressing the silk counterpane rather than look into the eyes of the woman who had once rivaled all of New Orleans in her comeliness while remaining a secret to all but him and a select few others.

If only he'd married for love rather than political expediency. If only his wife, who just tonight promised to be aboard the first packet bound for Philadelphia as soon as she recovered, did not this very night intend to bear him a child, as well.

If only . . .

No, he would not allow what could very well be the last remnant of their time together to be spent chasing the dust motes of lost wishes. A knock at the door shook his thoughts.

"The soldiers," the slave woman called, "they be a-comin'."

"Friend or foe?" he called. "English or ours?"

"Ain't no difference to me," came the answer through the closed door.

Nor to him. Neither English enemy nor American friend dared catch him here—his future depended on it.

Jean pressed his lips to Sylvie's, then recoiled in horror. Where moments ago, the breath of life had been present, now it was gone, and so was she. Along with her, God had surely taken his heart.

Making a decision he promised himself he'd never repeat, he snatched up the squalling infant and hid her beneath his cloak. As before, he would find Delilah.

Yes, his most trusted servant would have the answer.

CHAPTER 1

New Orleans
April 1834

Josiah Carter leaned against the rough brick of the warehouse and breathed deeply of the thick New Orleans air before continuing his journey. Nearly three decades in age, today he felt twice that. Perhaps the weight of his current situation could be blamed for it, but Josiah preferred to think not.

He touched the gold watch in his pocket and resisted the urge to check the time again. If all went according to plan, the great Hezekiah Carter of the grand Virginia Carters would be none the wiser. The old man might have the ear of the president himself, but he'd never muster the power to best his elder son.

Not again. Josiah would not allow it.

Inhaling the fetid air was unbearable. Josiah covered his nose and mouth with the thick fabric of his cloak and forced his mind to focus on tomorrow's sail. He ticked off the itinerary as he walked through the narrow alley bordering the docks. Barring the need to stop along the way to wait out bad weather, the *Jude* would make arrival in London by month's end.

Not soon enough to suit him.

Perhaps he might find the time to make a holiday of the trip. He smiled. Yes, a few days of leisure might be a welcome diversion.

Fool. Your father will never let you rest, not until he extracts his retribution.

Josiah shook off the truth of the thought and focused on another: Only a meeting with I. M. Gayarre remained before he could ready his ship to sail.

To his left, the newly renamed *Jude* bobbed at anchor, a former slaving ship and an abomination among vessels, yet for nearly a week since its departure from Cuba, his alone. At least it would be upon completion of the night's transaction. After taking receipt of Monsieur Gayarre's gold, Josiah would pay his debt to the *Jude*'s former owner and then flee New Orleans, never to return.

Josiah smiled at the thought. Gayarre was expected some time before daylight, their meeting arranged for dockside at the *Jude*. The Café des Artistes stood nearby, and a stop there seemed the proper choice to begin the evening's entertainment. Perhaps a pint and a hot meal would relieve the ache in his gut and accelerate the waiting. From his post at the café, he could watch the only avenue leading to the vessel.

Stalking past clusters of dockside roughs and

piles of empty barrels and rotting cargo, Josiah patted the dagger hidden within easy reach in the folds of his cloak. On a good night, the knife remained there; many nights ashore, however, it did not.

Bone tired and purposefully wearing his vile disposition, Josiah watched a dark-cloaked figure approach. Surely he would not be facing trouble so early in the evening. Why, the sun had barely fallen below the horizon, and the constellations were only just becoming visible.

"Announce yourself."

The figure continued toward him, small enough to be a child yet moving swiftly and seemingly unafraid. Framed in a circle of moonlight, the interloper stopped and raised a hand in greeting.

A pale, slender hand.

Slowly, the hand moved to the cloak's hood and pushed it away to reveal a heart-shaped face framed with an unruly mass of honey-colored curls. The woman, and she looked to be barely of an age to be defined as such, cast a glance at the empty alley behind her, then faced him once more. Full lips hidden partly in shadow curved into a frown.

A warm wind, blowing from the river, picked up a long curl and deposited it once more into place like a flash of liquid gold. Beauty within the shadows, he decided, meant a stunning woman in the light. His interest piqued. A connoisseur of all things beautiful yet owner of none, he deliberated the possibility of attaining this prize.

"Monsieur Carter?" Soft as a whisper and clear as church bells, the voice was barely touched by the accent of the French Creoles.

Unbidden, tightness rose in his throat. Had his father's men found him out and sent this siren to trick him?

"Who calls this name?"

He watched her shoulders heave beneath the heavy cloak and her fingers begin to tease at the fabric. "I am Isabelle Marie Gayarre, sole passenger on the vessel *Jude*."

Had she stood before the devil himself, Isabelle couldn't have been any more afraid. This man, this reputed infidel, held her very life in his hands. Should Captain Carter refuse to honor her payment of passage . . .

No, I shall not consider it.

She lifted her eyes to the blackness of heaven to offer up yet another prayer for courage, then braved a second look in Captain Carter's direction. He stood cloaked in shadows, a figure whose description she had memorized long before this meeting and whose associates spoke terror into her very soul.

Yet the Lord had led her to him.

The dark-haired captain edged slightly toward her, moving close enough to show the faintest outline of his aristocratic features. Too handsome to be the embodiment of evil, this one, yet she knew of his questionable character from those who spoke freely in her presence.

Watch yourself, Izzy. The mademoiselle's father says he is a desperate man.

The mademoiselle's father.

He was her own father, as well, though she rarely thought of Jean Gayarre as such, even though she saw his gold hair, pale green eyes, and fine, straight nose every time she gazed at her own reflection. Only her unruly curls and the fullness of her lips gave the slightest hint of the mother she had never known, but of whom her half sister Emilie had shown her paintings.

Isabelle blinked back emotion. No, she rarely thought of these things.

Gayarre and his hidden circle of friends, however, were never far from her mind. The secret society of powerful men, all from well-placed families in New Orleans or farther east, was another reason for fear.

The one who had purchased Isabelle and to whom she was due to be delivered held the ear of the president himself, Emilie had informed her. To be chosen by a man so wealthy and powerful would give Isabelle much power and afford her the privilege to live as a pampered pet in a gilded cage.

Though never spoken of in decent circles, the

term for this arrangement was *plaçage*. Isabelle knew it to be slavery, plain and simple. Mama Dell declared her a striking success and praised Jean Gayarre for waiting to place Isabelle with a guardian until her beauty held the maturity of a grown woman. Isabelle knew she would have been given up years before had the monsieur received enough gold to placate his conscience. She also knew she'd been spared that fate by One more powerful than Jean Gayarre.

All of this she knew thanks to the mademoiselle. Never would Isabelle give her most precious gift to any man save the one the Lord had created for her. Until such a time, she would risk death rather than submit.

Despite her prayers, concern nagged at Isabelle. She fumbled with the fine fabric of her cloak and worked to slow her breathing and collect her thoughts. She must convince Josiah Carter to accept payment and take her far from New Orleans. There was simply no alternative.

To that end, Isabelle moistened her lips and slid her eyes half shut, easily slipping back into the ways she'd been instructed.

Father, forgive me for this.

She allowed the velvet cloak to slide off her shoulder, catching the soft fabric with the crook of her arm. Beneath it she wore her finest cream silk-and-lace gown from Paris, the one she'd been instructed to wear upon the morrow.

A breeze heavy with dampness blew over her skin, dancing across flesh she preferred to cover. Although she still remained modest by the standards of others in her social circle, she nonetheless felt uncomfortable with the display.

"Perhaps you are surprised to find I am a woman," she said softly.

The captain produced a most fearful-looking knife from beneath the folds of his cloak and began to study it. Isabelle froze, too frightened to move and too confused to pray.

"Perhaps I *am* surprised," he said lazily as the blade glinted sliver in the moonlight. "How old are you, *woman?*" The last word he said mockingly, jabbing the knife into the air for emphasis.

"Four and twenty," she said as she watched the blade move with blinding speed. *Another lie; another reason to pray for forgiveness to the Father for things done in desperation.* If the Lord allowed her to live long enough, she'd see her twentieth birthday at the hearth of her new home in Clapham, southwest of London, come Christmas Eve.

His chuckle held much disdain. "Four and ten is the more likely age, although I'll not dispute the word of a *lady.*" He spoke the last word with disdain.

Determination welled up, and Isabelle squared her shoulders to face the captain with renewed purpose. Given the circumstances of her birth, she might be considered something less than a lady here in New Orleans, but upon her arrival in England, she vowed to honor the Lord with her sterling behavior and humble countenance. Isabelle Marie Gayarre would make her heavenly Father proud even as she tried with all her heart to forgive and forget her earthly one.

The letter of introduction tucked safely into her bodice held nearly as much promise as the deed hiding beneath the Bible in her trunk. Both would set her free; both were gifts from the mademoiselle. The fact that she could read them could also be attributed to that woman.

Indeed, Emilie Gayarre, who had sought Isabelle out a year ago, would be the one person she would miss desperately upon her departure from New Orleans. Perhaps, when sufficient time had passed, Isabelle would post a letter to her. Or perhaps Isabelle would merely disappear as planned.

Braving the shaking in her limbs to glide a step closer, Isabelle mustered up some semblance of a smile. "You expected to transport a man. On this, I have deceived you, and this grieves me."

"So you're grieved, are you?" The captain heaved a sigh and scratched his clean-shaven chin. "Indeed you are not what the booking agent led me to believe."

"The fault lies with me, sir." Isabelle tried in vain to read the expression on his shadowy features. "I intend, however, to fulfill the terms of my agreement. I assure you there will be little seen of me during the voyage."

His inelegant snort nearly ended the ruse. The laughter that followed only added fuel to the fire.

Stepping into the circle of light, Captain Carter regarded her with more than the appropriate amount of interest. Isabelle took note of his sneer, saw the flash in his steel gray eyes, and wondered if he would answer her with words or action. She prayed for the former while expecting the latter, all the while watching the weapon in his hand.

How much of the father's temperament had been passed on to the son? She'd heard Mama Dell whisper tales of this man's father, tales that if believed would bring the elder man to her doorstep on the morrow.

"There is already much to be seen of you," he said in a drawl surely acquired in his native Virginia. "I daresay you've placed your health in danger with that ridiculous costume."

Anger pure and strong pulsed in her veins, and she longed to answer his rudeness with a bit of her own sharp tongue. Only her faith in God and the knowledge that this man would indeed bring about her release from the bonds of servitude kept her from picking up her expensive skirts and running away.

"I vow I shall not be any trouble to you, monsieur." She gathered the velvet of her cloak tight around her neck and lifted her chin in defiance. "Barely any notice will be taken of me."

He continued to weigh the knife in his hand as he lifted his gaze to meet hers. "*Mais non*," he said evenly, "I rather doubt you would go unnoticed anywhere."

He spoke the challenge all in French, and his easy use of the language startled her. She'd been led to believe Mr. Carter's education left something to be desired. Heart racing, she watched the blade rather than the man.

There seemed to be serious gaps in the information she'd overheard. Her gaze traveled from the weapon to the face of the man who held it. Dark hair, silver eyes, and a handsome face. All these things she had anticipated, but his quick wit and ability to converse in a language other than his own were things she hadn't expected.

What else had she missed?

The captain quirked a dark brow in what seemed to be amusement. "Something wrong, Mademoiselle Gayarre?"

She shrugged and, in the motion, accidentally let loose of the fabric she'd been clutching. Her cloak fell off her shoulder and pooled once more in the crook of her arm.

To her surprise, Josiah Carter sheathed his

knife and reached to slide the velvet fabric back into place, brushing the skin of her arm with his fingers in the process.

A chill slithered up Isabelle's spine and lodged in her furiously beating heart. She looked past Captain Carter to focus her eyes to the murky darkness beyond.

"Look at me, mademoiselle."

He stood too close, this reputed infidel, and on his face he wore a mask of scorn. Isabelle bit her lip to stop it from quivering, then quickly recovered. "You doubt me, sir?"

"Perhaps." His expression turned neutral, and then the captain inclined his head toward her. "Perhaps we have friends in common."

What to say? "Perhaps we do. I'm sure a man of your quality has found many friends here. Likely we would find at least one we share."

"Perhaps what we share," he said slowly, "is enemies, not friends."

Oh dear. "I was merely making polite conversation, Captain Carter," she said, the words emerging from a place of unknown strength. "I have found that a man generally delights in speaking of himself." She paused to lower her gaze for effect. "Obviously, I've misjudged you. Forgive my impertinence."

Captain Carter inched closer and took hold of her wrist. Isabelle sucked in a deep breath and steeled herself for what she feared would come next, namely, the man's fist—or worse, his knife.

The man's lips moved close to her ear, and his grip tightened. Isabelle watched his hand graze the ivory handle of the knife sheathed at his waist. Without removing his gaze from her face, the captain grasped the weapon.

For an eternity, they stood in silence. Only the rhythmic pounding of blood in her ears gave her pause to realize time continued to move forward. While she prayed, Isabelle shifted her attention from the Virginian to the knife now in his hand.

"I prefer to hear you converse about yourself," Captain Carter finally said, again speaking the harsh words in fluent French, "for I'm sure you've quite the story to tell."

Much truth lay in those words.

Unfortunately, the son of the man who'd placed the highest bid on her virtue was the last one in whom Isabelle could confide.

CHAPTER 2

The captain lifted his hand, and Isabelle forced herself not to cringe when the knife loomed closer. Instead, she stared as she'd learned to do, offering a blank and impassive face to the hands that meant her harm. She'd seen the transitory nature of the ire of men, and prayed this one's temperament would be the same.

He felt anger at her duplicity; this she understood. She also knew she'd be answering to the Lord on the matter of her manipulation of the truth. As soon as the ship sailed, Isabelle intended to set that situation to rights.

If he wishes your virtue rather than your gold; what then, Izzy?

Unprepared for the thought, she pressed away the answer. To trade one sin for another would not serve the Lord. Simply, she would rely on God, and He would bring her home. Captain Carter would merely provide the means.

Captain Carter.

Isabelle watched the glittering edge of the knife move closer. With the care of a surgeon, the captain barely touched the tender skin beneath her chin with the point of the blade.

"Are you afraid, Mademoiselle Gayarre?" he asked in a rush of breath.

Fear does not come from the Lord, for our God has bested the enemy. "You may do me harm, sir," she whispered, unable to muster a more forceful response, "but my Lord will protect me."

Josiah Carter's face darkened, and he loosened his grip on her arm. Expressions of shock, distrust, and anger drifted across his features as quickly as fog dancing on the muddy waters of the Mississippi.

"Your *lord,* is it?"

The point of the knife pressed a notch closer to her skin, threatening and yet not deep enough to spill blood. Only by the strongest of wills did she remain upright and still, silent even in the face of abject fear.

"So you hold favor with someone of importance." He shifted to hold her closer against him. "Someone you serve and are either fleeing from or running to, I'd wager."

"Yes, 'tis true."

As soon as the words were uttered, Isabelle imagined she would feel the sting of the blade slipping a hair's breadth into her skin. Pride caused her to bite her lip and hold her silence, while prayer kept her from falling into the gaping chasm of panic.

His grip tightened once more. "Name this lord of yours, and be swift with the truth of your hasty departure."

"It is the Lord Jesus Christ I serve, Captain Carter." She enunciated each word with care, keeping her chin still as she stared at the man who held her at his mercy. "And it is He to whom I run."

"So you've bought passage to England to find the Lord God Almighty." He shook his head. "Do you take me for daft, woman?"

Isabelle dared the Virginian's wrath to lift her head in defiance. "I've bought passage to England to serve the Lord's purpose."

The man's eyes narrowed. Then he laughed. Of all the reactions Isabelle had considered, this evil chuckle had not been one of them.

"You serve the Christ by securing passage on the *Jude*?" He sheathed his knife and pushed her an arm's length away, still retaining a grip on her while he burned a slow stare down the length of her body. "Do you take me for a fool?"

She squared her shoulders. How could she explain what she did not completely understand? The Lord meant for her to board this man's ship and flee to a country more apt to turn a blind eye to a woman of dubious background; His purpose, she need not know.

"I take you for an intelligent man, Monsieur Carter," she said. "I only wish I had the words to explain why the Lord asks this journey of me."

"You're serious?"

She managed a nod. All the while, her prayers were being lifted toward heaven. *Father, Thy will be done.*

Carter grew more agitated, as if he had heard her petition for help. "You're no cowering nun, and I'd hardly call this"—he released his grip to brush a finger along the lace of her sleeve—"the garment of a cleric."

The distant clatter of horses' hooves broke the

silence. Captain Carter whirled Isabelle around and gathered her tight to his side. His angry glare turned to a watchful, blank stare as he cast a long glance down the empty alley. For a moment, he barely seemed to breathe. Slowly, he reached to his waist and palmed the knife.

"If I've been sent to my doom, Mademoiselle Gayarre, I shall take you with me," he ground out through clenched jaw as he slid the blade of the knife up his sleeve and cupped its ivory handle in his fist. "Now smile, ma chère, and perhaps you and I shall live to see another day."

"Smile?" Isabelle shook her head as the rhythmic *clop-clop* and the creak of wheels in need of attention moved closer. "I don't understand. Why would I want to—"

"Silence, woman."

Captain Carter ducked into the shadows and pressed his back against a crumbling brick wall. Beneath a weathered sign advertising the Dumont and Sons Warehouse, he pulled her to face him. Brazenly, he pressed her against him and rested his clean-shaven cheek against hers. With one hand pressed against her spine, he tangled the other in the curls at the back of her neck.

To the world, they looked like a happy pair out on an evening's tryst. To Isabelle, the view was much more ominous. Somehow in the hour's time since she'd stowed her trunk and walked the remaining distance to the docks, she'd managed to come full circle. She'd left the expectation of landing in a stranger's arms to the reality of doing exactly that.

Clop-clop. Rattle. Clop-clop. Rattle. The sound rolled closer.

Isabelle took a deep breath and let it out slowly, willing away the nausea welling deep inside her. Closing the door to her lovely yellow and white home on Burgundy Street, she'd made a vow to God to keep only unto Him and never compromise herself.

Clop-clop. Rattle. Clop-clop. Rattle.

What sort of woman broke a promise to the Lord so soon after making it? The fact that she'd had no part in initiating this embrace held little comfort. Nevertheless, she stood in the shadows with a man, hiding from the world with the son as she would have been forced to hide with his father on the morrow.

Surely the Lord had left her to her wits now.

Breathe, Izzy. God is still here, and He understands your plight. Breathe and wait for Him to act.

At the end of the alley, a horse and cart appeared. A dark figure held the reins, and another rode at his side. The captain's hand released her hair and shifted to turn the handle of the knife around. Cold against her skin, the knife's blade scraped gently across the back of her neck.

"Beauty in the shadows," Captain Carter whispered, "yet you'll not live to charm again unless you convince these gentlemen you're overcome by my presence."

She braved a glance into eyes covered in shadow and darkened by anger. "What would you have me do?" she asked, again saying words she'd vowed never to repeat.

His lips curved into a wry smile. "Put your arms around me." Woodenly, she obeyed.

"Tighter." He pressed her head against his shoulder, holding the knife flat against the back of her head and covering it with her curls. "I mean you no harm," he whispered. "Nor do I wish to be found out by those who approach."

Isabelle forced her breathing to settle into a slow inhale and exhale pattern, a gesture both automatic and difficult. As she did, she hid her face in the folds of the stranger's cloak. He smelled of soap and something else, a fragrance not entirely pleasant and, in a blinding flash just short of recognition, unreasonably frightening.

She knew this scent and hated it yet couldn't put its meaning to words. What was it, and why did it frighten her to the depths of her soul?

As she pondered the question, Isabelle lifted her head slightly and watched the intruders draw near. The scent continued to assault her, scraping against her mind just as the cold blade scraped against her scalp.

•••

The cart rolled nearer, and with each roll of the wheels, Josiah felt the coil in his gut twist tighter. He gave brief thought to bargaining with either God or the devil to bring him victory but could not decide to which he should turn.

Not that the Lord would have him. And the devil would only be jealous once he'd heard of all the infamous Josiah Carter had done since his break with the religion of his youth.

Better to depend on no one and save himself. His skills had served him well thus far, and he'd needed neither the minions of Satan nor the angels of the Lord to do the work.

With the eyes of a man trained for battle, Josiah surveyed the situation. The river lay at his back and the city ahead. On either side of the alley stood the Dumont and Sons warehouses, oversized brick buildings that offered no means of escape.

The girl in his arms would provide little cover should the men be outfitted with more than knives, but she might provide sufficient diversion to allow him to take the advantage.

After all, he'd certainly been distracted by her.

The two dark figures leaned together as if in conversation, then parted. One of them raised a hand in greeting but said nothing while the other seemed to cast a glance behind him to the covered load in the wagon. Still the cart rolled forward as the swaybacked horse plodded on.

Clop-clop. Clop-clop. Rattle.

A moment more and they'd be upon them. The time for action had come.

"Evening, mates," he said in the slurred voice of a drunken Englishman, "have you a pint for me and me love?" He turned the woman toward them, being sure to cast sufficient light on her lace-covered attributes. "She's a might thirsty, she is."

"Whoa there," a youthful voice called. The driver pulled on the reins and leaned back in the seat to accentuate the motion. The wagon slowed to a stop as the pitiful mare snorted a protest and pawed at the ground.

Josiah suppressed a smile. If, as he suspected, the driver was a mere boy rather than a grown man, he stood a much better chance of escaping alive.

And so did the lovely Mademoiselle Gayarre.

"Mademoiselle Gayarre?" the driver called.

Trapped. The word sprang to mind, and just as quickly, he disposed of it. Never could a sprite of a woman and two undersized lads take Josiah Carter. He'd not allow it.

CHAPTER 3

S o, mademoiselle," Josiah whispered, trying in vain not to inhale the sweet scent of jasmine permeating her curls. "You've betrayed me."

"I've done nothing of the sort," she answered. "This is—"

"Her sister, Emilie," the driver said. She lifted the cloak's hood to reveal dark hair swept into a fashionable style. "Now please unhand Isabelle so we may proceed to board the vessel."

Josiah loosened his grip but did not relinquish his hold. "We?" he asked as he scanned both ends of the alley for the escort this woman surely had lurking about. "I see none fit for boarding my vessel in this company, and the payment was for a single passenger."

"I cannot let my sister travel alone, sir," she said in the clipped tones of someone obviously used to giving orders. "It simply would not be proper." Sweeping her cloak aside, she handed the reins to the lad beside her and climbed off the wagon to extend a gloved hand in Josiah's direction. "Emilie Gayarre."

"And your companion, Madame Gayarre?"

"Mademoiselle Gayarre," she corrected as she turned to regard the shadowy figure on the wagon.

"And my traveling companion is Mademoiselle Viola Rose Dumont, a friend of my youth. Vi, do show yourself, dear."

Dumont? The name rang loud in his ears, along with a warning. *Flee this company, Carter. Flee while you can.*

The aforementioned female slid the hood away from her face to reveal a mass of dark curls and an ugly purple bruise across her right cheek, visible even in the dim light of the evening. "Pleased to meet your acquaintance, Captain Carter," she mumbled from the seat of the wagon, her gaze not quite lifting to meet his.

Josiah studied the woman openly, noting other signs of mistreatment in the dried blood decorating her lip and dotting the front of what appeared to be a pale blue frock. She certainly did not appear to have planned this trip, owing to the formal nature of what should have been a traveling garment. Had he not evidence to the contrary, Josiah might have guessed the woman was en route to a wedding at the cathedral rather than to a ship awaiting her at the docks.

"Does your father know of your intentions, Miss Dumont?"

Dark eyes widened, then shut completely. A second later the young woman recovered and offered him a weak smile, her partly swollen lip quivering. Her gaze fell on him a moment, then flitted past him to settle on the painted mural above his head, the advertisement for warehouses owned by the Dumont family. "I'm afraid you've mistaken me for someone else, sir. I have no father."

A lie and he knew it. Viola Rose Dumont was the apple of her father's eye. Two of the ships in the Dumont merchant fleet were named after the girl, and another half dozen had been sent to sea with her likeness carved into a figurehead decorating the bow.

He knew this personally, having been indentured to the elder Dumont aboard the *Viola* at the age of fourteen due to his father's fury over some minor indiscretion, long forgotten. Dumont had been fair but tough, a mentor in some ways and a scourge in others, demanding hard work and giving little compliment in return.

The first year had been the closest to the fiery pits of hell Josiah had come, the second only marginally better, but he'd learned to fend for himself quite well aboard the *Viola* and other Dumont vessels. Taking this woman aboard his ship would be the best way to draw his father's ire, given that his father and Dumont were thick as thieves and lifelong friends.

A sane man would end the nonsense and send the women packing. He allowed his gaze to fall on the taller of the Gayarre sisters, her ramrod straight backbone and pinched expression giving away the lack of courage hidden just beneath the blustery veneer of confidence.

Behind the imperious Emilie, the Dumont woman trembled visibly as she gathered her cloak to hide her face once more. This one held no pretense save the lie she told regarding her parentage, a character flaw that would not bode well for her should she make good her escape.

Finally, he beheld the exotic Isabelle.

Something about the woman set his well-honed sense of danger on guard and made him want to flee her presence. Something else bade him lean forward and push away honey-colored curls to whisper sweet words of comfort and assurance in her ear.

Good sense required he do neither.

"Take you responsibility for these women?" he spoke against the warmth of her skin. He felt her tense. *She feels fear at my touch. An advantage I must not lose.*

Eyes the color of the green seas off the Florida Straits regarded him almost without blinking. A storm brewed behind those eyes, of this Josiah felt sure.

In that moment, with his knees as weak as a baby's, he knew he would give chase to brave that storm and tame those waves. For this one, he would span the seas to do her bidding.

Herein, he realized, lay the danger. *It is I who feel the fear.*

Josiah covered the shock of his discovery with

anger. Had he the words, he would have lashed out at the fair-haired siren and her entourage, telling the vermin in petticoats exactly how he felt about taking women aboard the *Jude*.

Rendered mute, however, he settled for a glare that would have sent the worst of his crew scurrying below decks in fear. Unfortunately, his best work of intimidation went ignored among the feminine group.

"Don't just stand there gaping, Isabelle. You'll swallow a fly." Emilie's direct gaze gave way to a look of near pleading as she stared first at each of her companions and finally at Josiah. "Now shall we proceed to the vessel? We've a long voyage ahead, and I'm sure the captain wishes us to be settled aboard posthaste."

"Yes, of course," Isabelle mumbled. "Please release me," she added in a hoarse whisper.

Once again mute, Josiah allowed the beauty to extricate herself from his grasp. He watched in pitiful silence as Isabelle diverted her eyes and settled her cloak around her shoulders in a show of modesty.

Off in the distance, a deckhand sounded the quarter hour while a night bird called overhead. A short distance away, the *Jude* rocked at anchor, its crew oblivious to the distress of their captain. Overhead, Josiah spotted the constellation Orion, the North Star, and finally the Big and Little Dippers.

He sighed, his temper briefly under control. Peering at the stars tended to do that, albeit temporarily. It always had.

"Very well then. Shall we, Captain Carter?" the other Gayarre asked. "Please lead the way."

All he'd worked for rode on this transaction; all he'd become stood in the balance. Three women for his very soul. An odd thought, he realized, yet somehow fitting. Once the women were deposited on English soil, he'd be free of them, free to sail as the owner of the *Jude*.

He would be a man without a past, a man whose future stretched wide and inviting before him. To accomplish this, he merely had to deliver three women—three well-paying passengers, he corrected—across the ocean.

A measure of benefits against possible difficulties stood before him, and he weighed each carefully. "Payment has been made for but one of you," he said. "What say you to this problem?"

Again, the other sister stepped forward. "Arrangements have been made for our passage, sir," she said, not quite meeting his eyes, "although I fear you must collect your payment once we reach the shores of England. I've made a bank draft in the amount of—"

"Impossible." He slashed his hand through the air, waving away her objection. "I require payment in coin."

Slowly the woman reached into the folds of

her traveling garment. Josiah, always on guard, captured her wrist before it could disappear into the sturdy fabric. Isabelle gasped while the Dumont woman stared mutely. Only Emilie Gayarre seemed unmoved.

"I wish to offer payment of another sort," she said, staring up at him with dark eyes that regarded him with what looked like a mixture of disdain and fear. "May I retrieve it?"

Josiah nodded and loosened his grip on her bony wrist. Trembling fingers disappeared, then quickly reappeared formed into a tight fist. Without fanfare, she thrust her hand toward him and dropped something hard and cold into his palm.

A key.

"What need have I of this?" he demanded.

Unblinking, she met his gaze. "It opens the door to a house on Burgundy Street. Perhaps someday you will require use of it."

Josiah snorted in disgust. "Only gold and silver will pay your passage," he said.

"Done."

He gave her a questioning look, and the amount she offered nearly set him to hoping she meant it. "And where do you propose to find this sort of money, Mademoiselle Gayarre?"

"It is in an account newly opened in the name of my father and given to make a rather costly purchase." A look passed between the sisters.

"A certain Virginia planter made the deposit some months ago."

Virginia planter?

Josiah's mind reeled with the possibilities. But any number of planters lived in Virginia. What were the odds that this one, if he even existed, was the same one from whom he'd vowed to someday extract revenge?

Still, the possibility enticed him. While Isabelle Gayarre's gold would ransom the *Jude*, perhaps her sister's bank account would place the final nail in his father's coffin.

Both figuratively and literally.

"Captain Carter?" Isabelle's sister called. "Perhaps you should take the reins. If you're agreeable to our terms, that is."

Stifling a grin, Josiah gave the woman a curt nod. In what was possibly the most foolish of his decisions of the evening thus far, Josiah pressed past Emilie Gayarre to put his hands around Isabelle's waist and hand her into the back of the wagon. She landed easily on the mound of canvas, then quickly scampered away.

Forcing his attention away from Isabelle, he turned to offer help to her sister. Shunning his assistance, Emilie Gayarre climbed aboard and motioned for him to take the reins from the cowering Dumont woman.

Josiah gripped the reins and slapped them on the back of the pitiful excuse for a horse, urging the nag into a slow forward motion. This accomplished, he slid a sideways glance at the Dumont woman.

"She made a misstep and fell from the lower staircase at my home," Emilie said. "I feel just terrible about it, but with our concerns over missing our appointment with you, sir, we hadn't the time to repair the damages."

Damages? He cast another glance at the cowering female. Hardly the word he would have chosen, yet what business had he in caring?

Josiah leaned into the turn as he eased the wagon around the bend leading out of the alley. In a matter of weeks, England and these women would be behind him with the coast of Africa beckoning. How simple a life he aspired to, merely a ship loaded with cargo and a fair wind in his sails.

What cargo his hold bore, he hadn't a care. Anything that brought a profit; anything that kept the *Jude* and its crew at sea.

Liar.

Josiah cast a furtive glance for the owner of the voice. Who dared cast aspersions on his honesty?

He was many things—a rake and a wastrel, according to his mother; and a serious disappointment to God and family, according to his father—but as yet, he'd not stooped to dishonesty.

Yet you lie to yourself.

This time he knew from whence the voice came. It was his own.

The wagon rolled on toward the dock, and with each turn of the noisily squeaking wheels, Josiah fought the urge to curse himself for a fool.

Any cargo save this one, the horrific symphony seemed to declare. *Any cargo save this one.*

Any vessel save this one, Isabelle's senses screamed. *Any other means to flee.*

It was silly, this gnawing fear in her belly, brought on no doubt by the nearness of the infidel Carter and the surprise that her escape from New Orleans would not be made alone. And what of the mademoiselle and her companion? Why had a day so anticipated in the Gayarre and Dumont households ended in an alley where heretics and thieves roamed rather than in the glorious cathedral, home of the wealthy and pious?

And where among this confusion was Monsieur Andre Gayarre, the mademoiselle's brother? Had he not been betrothed to this woman who now rode among them? Did his hand spill the blood staining the fine lady's bridal gown?

So many questions.

"Isabelle, how are you faring?" Emilie called.

"I am well, thank you, mademoiselle," she answered.

Isabelle fixed her eyes on the blackness above,

preferring the nothingness of the night to the details of the day. It gave her some assurance that while the world seemed to spin in endless circles, ever changing and never certain, the Lord Almighty remained a sure, steady rock on which to stand.

The wagon rolled past a neat line of vessels, each bobbing at anchor with mast posts disappearing into the evening sky. Here the docks swarmed with activity, and the chattering of many tongues made understanding impossible. The occasional crash of wood against wood punctuated the constant sound of water lapping against the quay.

The scents were stronger than in the alley or back on Burgundy Street. Rotting timber and humid night air competed with the odor of many sorts of cargo and the stench of unwashed bodies to form a pungent mixture. Above it all hung the thick, wet scent of impending April rain.

Isabelle held her cloak over her nose and stared at the straight backs of the captain and the two mademoiselles while the wagon rolled and bounced over the rutted lane. Beneath the canvas cover, the cargo, presumably her trunk along with those belonging to the ladies, jolted, then shifted.

Something soft rolled toward her, and she attempted to push it away. To her surprise, it resisted.

She tried once more, placing the palm of her hand on the widest point of the bundle. This time the valise rolled backward and thudded against something hard.

"Ouch," a muffled voice cried.

Isabelle started, jerking her gaze to the women. Neither appeared to have spoken, nor did they seem to have heard the noise.

Shaking her head, Isabelle leaned her shoulders against the rough boards of the wagon and took shallow breaths of the rancid air. Obviously her imagination had bested her. Still, she stared at the canvas until the wagon rolled to a stop and the fancy folk began to climb out.

"Which vessel is yours, Captain Carter?" Isabelle heard Emilie ask. The captain answered, although what he said came and went before recognition could strike. Through it all, Isabelle watched the covered baggage for signs of life.

It moved. Someone had hidden in the mademoiselle's wagon. But who?

Isabelle reached for the edge of the canvas and lifted it slightly. At the realization of who lay hidden among the trunks, her heart began to pound, and she clutched at the sides of the wagon like a lifeline.

She'd been followed.

CHAPTER 4

"Mama Dell?" The name fell from her tongue in a whisper barely carried on the last of her breath.

Images of years spent with Mama Dell flitted by, each memory just beyond her touch and yet so near. *Walk like this for the gentlemen, Isabelle. Smile for the gentlemen, Isabelle. Above all, keep your silence about the gentlemen, Isabelle.*

The thoughts ripped a path of terror from her head to her heart, lodging in her belly. A wave of nausea followed as she fled the wagon. Only Emilie's hand on hers kept her from fleeing the docks.

"Delilah, you may come out now," Emilie called.

Isabelle's gaze danced from the wagon, to her sister, then back to Mama Dell. "I don't understand," she somehow uttered. "She works for *him*."

Emilie linked arms with Isabelle and turned her away from the wagon. "She never worked for him, Isabelle. She was *owned* by him."

"But she—"

"When I sent for your things, she returned with them." The mademoiselle leaned closer and

43

lowered her voice. "She is a child of God the same as you and me. How could I deny her the wish to accompany us?"

"But I'm not the only girl she's prepared to send off to—"

"Hush," the mademoiselle whispered as she leaned close and motioned to the dock where the captain stood in conversation with a rather sordid-looking character. "Captain Carter need not know our business."

Casting a glance over her shoulder, Isabelle watched Mama Dell climb out of the wagon and begin to smooth the wrinkles out of her dark skirts. "But, mademoiselle, she—"

"Isabelle, really," the mademoiselle interrupted, "we share a common father and a year's worth of company. Do call me Emilie."

She lowered her eyes to study the toe of her slipper. "It wouldn't be proper."

The mademoiselle placed a finger beneath Isabelle's quivering chin and lifted it. "Impropriety is what we're fleeing," she said softly as the captain stalked toward the gangplank and his gray-haired companion raised a hand to beckon them. "Vi, dear, join us, will you? It appears we shall be boarding the vessel now."

Mademoiselle Dumont slid off the wagon seat and followed Emilie while Isabelle turned her back on Mama Dell and placed one foot in front of the other. Each step she took, she knew, was a step toward the liberty she would find on the English shore.

She inhaled a deep draft of the rancid air and proclaimed it sweet as perfume. Awful as it was, this would forever be the scent of freedom.

Aptly named for the Catholic's patron saint of lost causes, the vessel *Jude* rocked at anchor among ships of a higher caliber. Gently tattered in the sails and in need of a carpenter's care, she rode high on the water with lanterns illuminating her deck and casting eerie shadows through the rigging.

"If you ladies will follow me, please," the older man said. "We've made a place for you below decks." He cast a rheumy eye at each of them, then shook his head. "Didn't expect there to be a female population aboard, so don't go expectin' nothin' fancy."

"I'm sure the accommodations will be quite suitable," Emilie said. "Please lead the way."

Again a peculiar scent, the same one she had noted on the captain, assaulted Isabelle. It meant something, this odor, something frightening. Pinpoint daggers of thought jabbed at her, frustrating any attempt at understanding.

A fresh breeze blew away the smell and danced around the hem of her cloak and the lace gown beneath. The first fat drops of rain plopped around her as she scurried to catch up with the group boarding the *Jude*. Two pair of roughly dressed deckhands, scarcely of age to leave home, gave her little notice as they pushed past her to hurry to the wagon and collect the trunks.

Other crewmen of a more advanced age had gathered in a tight knot at the forward bow. In contrast to the four young porters, each of the questionable characters stared openly. Several offered smiles, showing off the gaps in their teeth, while one took the greeting a bit further to offer a formal bow.

Isabelle ignored them as she had been trained to do by Mama Dell. *Your attention belongs to the one who pays for it, Isabelle.*

"To work, sluggards! Make ready to weigh anchor."

Starting, Isabelle turned to follow the sound of the booming voice. A deck above her stood Captain Carter, silhouetted against the sails. His dark hair blew wild in the gusty wind.

"Have you a wish to join them?" he called to Isabelle.

Rather than respond, Isabelle hurried to follow the mademoiselles and Mama Dell. The captain's laughter chased her down the dark hallway and skipped past the little group to echo against the rough wood of the cabin door. Isabelle huddled against the wall and picked her way carefully forward, following the dim light as it disappeared into the corridor.

"This way, ladies." The sailor lifted his lantern to illuminate the way. "It's a mite small but cozy. I warrant your things will arrive presently."

The door swung open to reveal a tiny cell, barely larger than the outdoor kitchen behind Isabelle's home on Burgundy Street. Unlike her kitchen, nothing indicated humans had trod there in ages.

"Really, sir," the mademoiselle protested as she surveyed the mess, "we cannot possibly be expected to—"

"You'll be goin' in without a fuss, ma'am, or it'll not be pleasant." He backed up his words with a sudden and surprisingly angry glare, reflected in stark relief against the sickly yellow light of the lantern. His face softened. "Captain says you're to stay here, and that's all I know."

The mademoiselle opened her mouth to protest, then obviously thought better of it and wrapped an arm around the Dumont woman's shoulder. With a nod to Isabelle and Mama Dell, Emilie ushered Viola into the small chamber as if she were striding into the French Theater for an evening's entertainment.

Isabelle deferred to Mama Dell and allowed her to enter next. Before she could follow, the sailor clasped a gnarled hand on her wrist.

"You'll be a-comin' with me, lass." He hauled her backward and slammed the door shut. "Orders o' the captain," he added as he turned the key and locked the women inside, then extinguished the lantern.

"I can't see, sir," she pleaded.

"Ya don't need t'see." He gave her arm a tug. "I know where I'm goin'."

Isabelle followed blindly as the sailor led her by the hand, stumbling on the hem of her cloak as she went down rough stairs and lurched painfully into dark, unseen walls on her journey into what seemed to be the deepest recesses of the ship.

Each step forward sent a shaft of fear into her heart, and each obstacle she struck gave her pause to wonder if her companion had become every bit as lost as she. Then she heard laughter, deep booming sounds that shook the very timber of the walls.

Ahead, a slice of light appeared in a slender, horizontal yellow line. When her guide stopped short and began to knock, Isabelle realized they'd arrived at a door. The laughter, she surmised, had belonged to Captain Carter. Perhaps his good humor would save her yet.

As soon as the door swung open, she found herself being thrust into the glaring light. All laughter ceased, and once her eyes accommodated the change, Isabelle discovered the reason.

Their trunks had been removed from the wagon only to be brought to this room where the contents had been strewn on the floor. One of the sailors, a fellow of middle age and large girth, held one of Emilie's lace camisoles in the air and waved it about as if it were a flag.

"Welcome, Mademoiselle Gayarre."

Humiliation swiftly passed as anger took its place. If not for the certain peril her complaint would bring, Isabelle would have cried out. Rather, she clamped her mouth shut against the torrent of words begging to be spoken.

Refusing to acknowledge the crude man, she shifted her attention from the sailors to their captain. Seated at a table made of rough wood, Josiah Carter held her small traveling trunk open before him. Another chair sat vacant nearby, a curiosity since the room seemed near to full with people.

A feast had been spread before the captain, and it appeared the group had partaken of much of it. Only the captain seemed to wear a hungry look.

"You wish to see me?" she asked. *Of course he does, Izzy. You haven't paid the man.*

But the money was in the trunk. Isabelle stared at the ripped lining and knew the coins were gone. Her heart sank.

That same afternoon, she'd carefully filled the lining with the coins that would pay for her passage to England and set the trunk behind the summer kitchen in the courtyard for the mademoiselle's messenger to find. The rest of her small savings, a pittance really, she'd sewn into the hem of her cloak. All of it had been done just as Emilie instructed.

Even now, with the eyes of the captain and several others watching, she could feel the weight of the coins pulling at the cloak. "You've opened my trunk," she said. "I trust you've found the amount we agreed upon."

To her surprise, Carter smiled. "I would have you properly greet my associate."

From the ragtag group assembled there, he indicated a dark-haired man of approximately her age. Despite the condition of his clothing, something about him seemed to speak of wealth rather than poverty, and of being ill at ease among the half dozen others sharing the room.

"Good evening, sir." She extended her hand, and the fingers that grasped hers were soft, lacking in calluses as if they'd been covered with gloves much of the time. When he smiled, a row of perfect white teeth spoke more clearly of his rank than his bland greeting.

The fact that no names were exchanged had not been lost on her. Isabelle recognized his type; she'd been warned about men like him. Another shaft of fear snaked up her spine and forced itself into her throat. *What if he demands more than coins from you, Izzy? How then will you pay for your freedom?*

"May I join my companions now, Captain Carter?" she muttered.

The Virginian spoke a few words in rapid-fire Spanish to the man, and they shared a laugh. Finally, the captain regarded Isabelle with a serious look.

"As yet, you and I have pressing business." He looked past her to the ill-disguised gentleman. "Shall we continue on the morrow?"

The man seemed to consider the question a moment before slowly nodding. Another round of quick Spanish followed; then one by one, the rough crowd drifted into the hallway. The last of their heavy footsteps faded away, leaving Isabelle standing in trembling silence before Josiah Carter.

"Sit," he demanded, standing to push the crude wooden chair in her direction.

Rather than accommodate him, she grasped the back of the chair with both hands to steady herself and regarded him impassively as she began to recount silently the words of the Twenty-third Psalm.

The Lord is my shepherd; I shall not want. He maketh me to lie down—

"Sit down!"

Stunned, Isabelle mutely obeyed. Beneath her feet, she could feel the roll of the deck as, outside, the squall's intensity increased. A furtive glance at the captain's face showed that his countenance mirrored the ferocity of the storm.

He leadeth me beside the still waters. He restoreth my soul—

The captain pounded a fist upon the table, and its contents jostled about. A decanter half filled with some dark liquid toppled and emptied its contents. "Upon my soul, Isabelle Gayarre, I shall have the answer I seek."

He leadeth me in the paths of righteousness—

"For all that is righteous," he shouted as he threw his chair to the floor, where it splintered, "I should have you keelhauled and hung upon the yardarm for attempting to defraud me. In my world, the penalty for deception is death."

Yea, though I walk through the valley of the shadow of death, I will fear no evil: for thou art with me—

"Where are you, woman? Awaken from your stupor and answer me."

Isabelle forced herself to blink as she watched the captain reach for a piece of wood from the remains of the chair. He pounded it on the edge of the table, then wielded it over his head like a man gone mad.

Thy rod and thy staff they comfort me. Thou preparest a table before me in the presence of mine enemies—

"I demand your attention," he said, his voice suddenly and eerily calm.

Rather than acquiesce to his demand, Isabelle

began to count the amber drops of wine as they spilled onto the floor.

My cup runneth over.

Suddenly the decanter of wine disappeared, swiped away by the hand of Josiah Carter. It landed in a heap of shattered glass. The remainder of the chair followed.

Surely goodness and mercy shall follow me . . .

"Follow me," the captain said as he pulled her to her feet.

"No," she whispered, unable to give a stronger voice to the plea.

Just as his colleague before him, Captain Carter began to haul her into the darkened hallway. Behind her, the yellow glow of the lantern beckoned while nothing but blackness stretched on forever.

Then something inside Isabelle snapped.

She jerked away from the captain's grasp and stopped short, her slippers still within the ring of light from the lantern. The hem of her cloak swung against the back of her legs, and she felt the coins shift. Mentally, she counted them, tabulating the cost of freedom should she have to cast her garment aside to escape.

But as she watched the fury cross Josiah Carter's face and saw his hand tremble when he reached for her, she knew no amount of money could save her now. Her only hope lay in the Lord.

I will dwell in the house of the Lord forever.

This thought gave Isabelle comfort as her control slipped away, giving panic and abject terror free rein. She began to scream.

CHAPTER 5

J osiah clapped his hand over the howling banshee's mouth and instantly regretted his action. At best, Mademoiselle Gayarre would but harm herself; at worst, her flailing arms and legs just might harm him, as well. All his shouting and flailing about hadn't worked one whit to cower the lass, and he knew he could carry on the ruse of playing the madman for only so long before it became tiresome. Better he try another approach.

"Be still," he whispered into her ear, "or the entire crew will think I'm in need of rescuing and come running."

To his great pleasure, his captive quieted herself, leaving only the heaving motion of her shoulders to show for her prior exertions. Wild eyes, barely blinking, stared at him.

"You are afraid." He offered a slow smile. "Or perhaps you are merely biding your time until you flee."

Her pleading look answered for her. Of course, fear would rule her actions. He notched up his smile and looked past her to the single window where only the faintest light penetrated the gloom.

"Mademoiselle Gayarre, should I choose to unhand you, I will require a promise." Satisfied with her weak nod of agreement, Josiah pressed on. "I insist you remain silent and docile, speaking only when addressed and making no effort to escape. Will you agree to this?"

Again, she nodded.

"In return you shall be treated with fairness and dignity, so long as you deserve it." Before he could act to release her, however, the woman had the nerve to sink her teeth into his hand. "By all that is holy, woman," he avowed to her retreating back, "dare you accost me?"

The only answer he received was the sound of footsteps trodding a brisk pace on the stairs. So she thought to escape?

Josiah chuckled and stood by the door to wait. A moment later the steps halted, and, save for the noise of the docks and the storm outside, silence reigned.

"Mademoiselle? *Ça va bien*?" he asked, knowing she was more than fine, although she might not yet realize the fact.

She also had yet to discover she'd landed in a trap, for the stair held no visible exit. The *Jude*'s former owner had outfitted the passage with an ingenious system of doors serving to confuse the uninitiated and conceal the unpleasant.

The hatch at the bottom of the stairs opened directly into a small yet comfortably furnished chamber of dubious purpose. Beyond the room lay the vast holding area where the African prisoners of war, set to become cargo, had once been quartered one against the other like hogsheads in a warehouse.

The image flashed through his mind, an imagined scene that, should he descend to the depths his father thought him capable, could one day become all too real. Faces peered at him from the shadows of the hold, differentiated only by variations in the color of their skin or the shapes of their faces.

Human faces. The odor of their misery still permeated the ship. A wave of nausea threatened. *Liar. You are not that man. You never were, and you shall never be.*

Slowly he pushed the thought out of his mind, replacing it with the problem at hand.

To exit the captain's meeting room through the stairwell, one must know the complicated process. The Gayarre woman would never manage it. Only he and two select crewmen, Harrigan and Banks, could manage the convoluted maneuver, and to prevent prying eyes from learning the secret, the passageway remained cloaked in darkness.

Perhaps he should leave the golden-haired woman to her own devices and make his way out of the room and the situation. A second, less-visible exit lay at his disposal. An opening into a corridor below had been hidden in a floor panel and covered by a seemingly immovable trunk. He could easily use it now to leave and send one of the crewmen to claim Isabelle Gayarre, thus ending the charade.

An amusing thought, indeed, but not a solution to his lack of funds. For that, he needed the cooperation of his guest. Until he extracted payment in coin, his ship would remain anchored in New Orleans. The longer the time at anchor, the greater the danger of his plans for William being thwarted.

Atop one of the trunks lay a document of ownership to a parcel of land and a dwelling of some sort in Clapham, the single item of value gleaned from the woman's trunk. He considered offering the certificate in return for cancellation of his debt—the *Jude* for some bucolic spot called Woodbine Park in Clapham, a quaint burg known for its do-gooders and zealots—but he knew it would be an arrangement most unsatisfactory to his creditor.

Only gold could settle the debt.

Josiah inhaled a deep draft of damp air and listened to the rumble of thunder as it rolled across the Mississippi. Shrugging the tightness from his shoulders, he turned to stare at his reflection in the pier glass.

The man in the mirror frowned. Josiah looked away.

Before landing in New Orleans, he had felt that the disconcertedness he was experiencing must be due to the unfamiliarity of the vessel and the nature of his mission. At the moment, he attributed the feeling to the fact that his prime means of escape now stood in peril.

Josiah sighed and studied the teeth marks on his palm. Unfortunately, leaving the woman to rot in the pitch-blackness of the vestibule was not an option. A second plan began to take shape.

"Mademoiselle," he called, easing the slightest bit of jocularity into his tone, "perhaps you'd like to join me before the river rats take notice of your scent."

A shuffling sound and a soft gasp gave the only indication of the lady's presence in the stairwell. Josiah leaned against the polished mahogany wall and stared down into the darkness.

Stubborn woman.

"I assure you," he added, "your safety is my utmost concern."

A most unladylike sound emanated from the darkness. "Should I be forced to choose, Captain Carter, I would prefer the company of the rats," she said, her voice quaking with either anger or fear.

Josiah preferred to think he heard fear. "As you wish."

He stalked away from the door and settled onto the single remaining chair. Propping his feet on one of the women's empty trunks, he crossed his arms over his chest and set out to watch for his guest's return. To help pass the time, he looked to the shelf in the corner, where part of his collection of books had been stowed.

Bypassing the King James Bible of his youth, a chronicle both amusing and slightly unsettling, he retrieved a well-worn copy of the memoirs of Vidocq, the French police agent, and turned to the first page. Two chapters later, he tired of the ruse.

"Enough of this nonsense!" he shouted as he replaced the volume on the shelf. "Appear forthwith, or I shall be forced to come down and fetch you myself."

He paused. "Or perhaps you prefer I send for your lovely traveling companions." Another pause, this one calculated for the maximum effect. "I would so enjoy an interview with each of them," he said, punctuating the statement with a chuckle before adding, "individually and at length, of course."

"That won't be necessary," came the small, uneven voice.

A moment later, Isabelle Gayarre stepped out of the shadows, her face showing equal parts defeat and defiance. She seemed to be having difficulty accustoming herself to the change in light, and leaned heavily against the wall, shielding her eyes.

Josiah gave no show of sympathy as he leaned over to kick at a small traveling case, then watched it slide across the floor to land at the woman's feet. She jumped in surprise and knelt to set it to rights.

If only she knew how little chance she had of actually being hurt by him. No, the sins of the father would not be visited on this son.

"I will be brief," he said. "I require payment as promised. Until such payment is delivered, you and I shall be at odds. Unlike the arrangement with your sister, I demand gold for your passage."

Before his eyes, the cowering lass stood, her backbone straight and her eyes shining. She cradled the case in the crook of her arm as it were made of pure gold. Her full lips twitched, and she looked as if she were about to say something.

Josiah congratulated himself. An unpleasant situation had been averted. The truth of her deception would now be told and his debt to the Spanish noble-brat be paid.

"Speak your mind, Isabelle Gayarre." He cast an offhand glance at the woman before turning his attention to the basket of apples on the table. "Settle this matter so that we may sail." He reached for the largest of the heap and polished it on the lapel of his frock coat while he glared at her. At least, he hoped he managed a passable glare.

"Sir," she replied as she seemed to watch the movement of the apple rather than meet his gaze, "I've but one thing to say before the matter is settled."

Josiah rested a boot on the chair and leaned his elbow on his knee. "Then proceed to enlighten me, mademoiselle." He took a large bite of the sweet red apple. "I await your every word of wisdom like a deer panting for a cool stream."

"You, sir," she said, enunciating each word as if he were a lad still in knee pants, "are a thief."

A thief.

Had she actually said the words her mind had so nimbly wrapped around? Isabelle's blood boiled and heated her skin as it rushed past her ears, rendering her both speechless and deaf. From the looks of the man, she'd said exactly that—or worse.

He choked and threw the remains of the apple against the wall. Pieces of red skin and white flesh exploded to cover the dark surface of the floor. An odd white fleck or two decorated his leather boots and spotted the hem of his black frock coat, but he seemed to resist any urge to wipe them away.

Josiah Carter stood in the midst of the chaos, a man obviously much aggrieved. A man whose wrath she'd grown tired of seeing. Still, perhaps she might have remained silent rather than risking the chance to speak her mind.

Watch him, Izzy. Pray for God to restrain his hand. Ask for protection; ask for peace.

Peace? From whence had that come? Surely there would be no peace between a man of Captain Carter's reputation and herself.

Isabelle waited for him to strike her, knowing the blow would come quickly once the captain digested her words. Like a fellow wrapped in the fog of a siren's enchantment, however, Josiah Carter stood transfixed. His fingers twitched, and his face darkened with what had to be rage. Still he did not move.

From nowhere, she felt words bubble into her throat and emerge. "This temper of yours, has it always been so fierce?"

For a moment, her question seemed to disarm him, giving her pause to search the room for a second exit. A cursory examination led her to believe she was well and truly trapped. Where, then, had her fear gone?

"I've been swindled, mademoiselle," he said, enunciating every word carefully. "Would you have me dance a jig in response to your duplicity?"

Duplicity? What sort of merriment did the man think to have with her? It was she who had been swindled, for the gold had obviously been spirited away before she arrived in the room. This charade must be Captain Carter's way of ascertaining the size of her fortune and her willingness to add more than the original amount to his coffers.

Well, she would have none of it.

"Captain Carter, you have been paid," she heard herself say as she held the box at arm's length. "This chest contained the amount you requested. There is no more."

"So your story remains unchanged." The rage on his countenance darkened. "And you saw to the disposal of this payment?"

Isabelle pointed to the largest of the trunks now lying opened on the floor. "I placed the traveling case inside that locked chest."

"And that is where I found it," the captain said. "It was empty."

"Empty?" She shook her head. "Impossible."

But was it? Looking into his angry eyes, she began to wonder. In a backward progression, she walked through the events of the afternoon.

Behind the kitchen at the rear of the house was a traveling trunk, a farewell gift from Emilie. Inside, Emilie had placed a few items of clothing and the deed to a home and a bit of acreage near Clapham.

Just enough room had been left to insert a small traveling case, the sort generally used to hold personal and toilet items but now used to hold gold pieces, before administering the lock that would prevent theft. An identical case had been left inside the bedchamber so it would appear that Isabelle had brought a new set of personal items to the house in anticipation of tomorrow's assignation.

The proper case, identified with a wax seal on its underside, had gone into the trunk in the designated spot. As a final insurance against theft, the trunk had been locked and sealed with the same wax used to mark the case. Evidence of the broken seal showed on the lock now lying in pieces at the edge of the pile of luggage. This meant the trunk had not been opened since it left Isabelle's sight.

At sunset, Emilie's messenger must have arrived to load the trunk onto the cart and deliver it to the dock. Obviously all these things had happened just as planned, for the luggage now stood before her, and the case sat in her hands. Surely the captain could prove nothing to support his assertion that he had not yet received payment for passage from her.

Once she showed him the proof, as evidenced by the red wax mark on the bottom of the box she now held, Captain Carter would most certainly have to apologize and release her. To that end, she explained the course of the afternoon's events, ending with the promise that the red wax seal on the underside of the case would prove beyond a doubt the story she told was true.

Through it all, Captain Carter listened impassively. Finally, at her conclusion, he nodded. "Show me this proof, mademoiselle," he said, "and perhaps I will believe."

Slowly Isabelle turned the case over and stared in horror. No mark showed on its surface.

It was the wrong trunk.

CHAPTER 6

The captain regarded Isabelle curiously. "Have you some concern with the case, Mademoiselle Gayarre? Perhaps you'd prefer another of these." He gestured in the direction of the spilled trunks. "But I assure you each has been searched with equal care."

Isabelle stared at the item in her hands, willing the crimson mark to appear, begging for time to fall backward and resume anew. Perhaps then she could form some sensible answer.

"But, I don't understand, I—"

A rip of thunder tore through the cabin, followed in short order by the flash of lightning. Outside, the squall had begun to blow in earnest; inside, the situation looked just as stormy.

The Lord hath his way . . . in the storm, and the clouds are the dust of his feet.

Silently she prayed for the Creator to lead her to the solution, to give her knowledge to solve this current dilemma. Then, realization dawned.

To her knowledge only three keys existed to the house on Burgundy Street. The first was in the hands of her sister, Emilie; Isabelle carried the second; and the third belonged to . . .

Isabelle allowed the trunk to fall to the floor, losing the splintering sound of it breaking as another peal of thunder echoed in the chamber. The captain added a string of curses, blending the noise of the storm outside with the one brewing inside.

"Mama Dell," she whispered when the captain finally fell silent. "She's swindled us both. Seek your information there."

"You speak nonsense," he announced. "Be plain with your answer, or say nothing more."

Isabelle lifted her gaze to meet his. "The woman Delilah has your answers."

Captain Carter seemed to consider her statement, leaving Isabelle to wonder whether he would take any action at all. Just when she'd given up hope, he turned and stalked to the edge of the dark passage.

"Harrigan," he shouted into the blackness.

When the elderly sailor arrived, the captain gave him instructions and sent him on his way. Slowly rotating to face her, the captain wore an expression that offered nothing of his thoughts.

His eyes narrowed. "If this is yet another deception, I'll hear of it now rather than later. Do you understand?"

"Sir, I've offered no deception save the decision to allow you to believe a man had purchased passage on your vessel. Beyond this, I have been nothing but honest with you."

Animosity radiated from his eyes, reduced to bare slits yet still visible in their silvery depths. Quickly, she averted her eyes, studying the toes of her slippers and the broken pieces of wood lying between them.

Be not overcome of evil, but overcome evil with good.

This verse from Romans had given her much cause to think and offered many opportunities for spirited discussion with the mademoiselle. While offering her heart and soul to the Lord had been relatively easy, agreeing to follow in the Christ's footsteps had been a battle of another sort, one where a clear victor had not yet been established.

Bless them that curse you, and pray for them which despitefully use you.

Although the man's heart wore a blackness she could feel, it was a heart created by God, knit in his mother's womb for a better purpose than frightening women and carrying on like a banshee.

Isabelle stared past the captain and began to

pray, allowing the Gospel of Luke to be her guide. Rather than ask God to save her, she asked the almighty Father to save Josiah Carter.

As if the captain sensed her purpose, he made a show of stalking to the table to pound his fist once more on its dark surface.

"Women shall be the death of me," he shouted as he kicked a broken piece of chair in her direction, narrowly missing her feet.

And unto him that smiteth thee on the one cheek offer also the other. . . .

Isabelle refused to flinch. Rather, she offered him a bland expression.

As if bored by her lack of response, Captain Carter settled one hip on the table and crossed his arms over his chest. The ship rolled quietly beneath their feet while the sounds of the storm blew louder.

The occasional shout of a deckhand and the clank of the chains split the silence. The Virginian seemed to notice none of this while each sound was magnified a thousandfold to Isabelle.

Finally, the sailor returned with a silent and sullen Mama Dell. The captain stared at the woman, starting at the brightly colored *tignon* tied about her head and proceeding to its end at the glove-leather slippers adorning her diminutive feet.

As if he knew of Mama Dell's penchant for making others bow to her will by intimidation,

Josiah Carter applied the same tactic to her. Had the situation not been so dire, Isabelle might have considered feeling a bit of satisfaction at the turn of events.

"Woman," the captain said slowly, an edge of menace in his voice, "what say you on the matter of Mademoiselle Gayarre's recent financial loss?"

In a rush of words, most of them unintelligible, the old woman professed ignorance to the situation at hand. "No traveling case has touched my hand this day," she vowed passionately, "and no gold has been found or taken."

"Interesting," the captain said slowly as he looked from Mama Dell to the old sailor. "Heard you the mention of a traveling case or missing gold pass my lips, Harrigan?"

"I did not, Cap'n," Harrigan answered with a shake of his head.

"He did not," Captain Carter repeated.

The captain approached Mama Dell like a panther stalking his prey, using his height to intimidate. To her credit, Mama Dell neither flinched nor shirked away.

"Save your skin, woman, and save me wasted time, as well. Speak what you know of this."

Ending the ruse, he centered his concentration on the older woman. Harrigan snickered, then silenced when the captain glared in his direction.

"I demand a response," Captain Carter said through clenched jaw.

Mama Dell stood motionless, defeated, then suddenly defiant. An irrational fear crept up Isabelle's spine as she recognized the look for what it had meant to her.

None dare take a stance against Mama Dell; the threat of the monsieur's wrath always carried warning enough. Dare she now believe the monsieur still stood behind the woman, even as the woman seemed bound to flee?

Mama Dell's features smoothed into a near smile. For what seemed like an eternity, only the heavy thud of rain against the wood boards above them broke the silence.

Isabelle gathered her cloak about her, knowing each second that ticked by brought her closer to either liberty or bondage. Either fate seemed preferable to the endless torture of waiting.

This she believed until Mama Dell looked at her. The collision rocked her to her toes. Hiding behind false bravado, she stared back at her former tutor, willing the veneer not to crack and the tears not to flow.

"From her birth I was charged with the care of this child. That care continues now, whether she realizes it or not."

"And the money she makes claim of?"

Mama Dell clamped her lips shut and refused to meet his gaze.

"I tire of this," the captain snapped. "Harrigan, fetch Banks to remove her; then see to our safety in the coming storm."

"Aye, sir." Harrigan strode out, and a moment later, another man wandered in.

"Banks, take her away," the captain said.

The old sailor wrapped bony fingers around Mama Dell's ample arm and gave her a tug. Isabelle stood in awe as the most contrary woman she knew followed the ill-garbed man out of the room like a lamb on a string. Had she not witnessed it herself, the image would have refused to form.

"Ye'd best tell 'im what ye know, if'n ye wanna save your hide," he said.

Mama Dell mumbled something and shook her head.

"Cap'n Carter's a fair man for th' most part, but he ain't patient by any stretch o' thought." Banks cast a quick glance over his shoulder at the subject of his discussion. "Beggin' the captain's pardon, sir," he added hastily.

Captain Carter gave Banks a curt nod as he watched the sailor and Mama Dell disappear into the stairwell. Down below, a door opened, and the sound of a scuffle ensued.

"The girl will never be free," Mama Dell shouted over the sound of Banks's protests. "*He* will see to it."

A second later the struggle ended. "All's well,

Cap'n," Banks called. "Quite the tart, this one."

The door slammed, leaving Isabelle to consider the words she feared were true. *The girl will never be free.* She took a deep breath of the thick, musty air and held it inside until her lungs threatened to burst. *He will see to it.*

Something inside cracked open, spilling bitterness into her soul as she released the breath and quickly took another. Isabelle knelt to rest her forehead on her knees, a curtain of hair covering her face.

Softly the tears began to fall, wetting the skirt of lace that had been intended as a bridal gown for the most unholiest of alliances—the union of a stupid girl born of the wrong parentage and an arrogant man born of the right one. What sins had her forefathers committed to have such afflictions visited upon her?

Be strong and of a good courage, fear not, nor be afraid of them: for the Lord thy God, he it is that doth go with thee; he will not fail thee, nor forsake thee.

The words of Deuteronomy 31, especially verse 6, had given her the courage to endure, then exit, her life of servitude. How like God that He would remind her of them now.

She let the words soak in, like the tears from her eyes, seeping beneath the skin to dry and leave no mark. Yet the mark of the Lord still felt new and fresh.

Her tears vanished and her heart less heavy, Isabelle lifted her head and peered from behind a curtain of curls to brave a look in the captain's direction. Without regard to her attention, he stared past her, obviously lost in his own thoughts.

His gaze swung to meet hers. Somehow words of assurance seemed necessary, and she made the attempt while brushing away the strands of hair blocking her vision.

"Before God, I promise you shall be paid for this voyage," she said quickly, grasping her knees tighter, "whether it is in coins recovered from my trunks or in bank vouchers delivered upon our arrival in England."

The money she'd just promised was meant to give her food to eat and to provide her with a start on a new life. Now that she had acquired additional traveling companions, the funds would be stretched even further. Still, offering them up in payment for passage seemed preferable to any other solution.

"Promises of payment will do me no good," he said slowly, obvious contempt moderating a voice much deeper in timbre than Isabelle had previously noticed.

"But I assure you—"

Captain Carter swept away her answer with a wave of his hand. "Before dawn, I've a debt to pay, and your pledge will not satisfy it." He paused and seemed to take note of the thunder's roar. "Nor, I fear, will it ransom my skin when the holder of that lien seeks restitution."

Fear not . . .

Strangely, she did not hold this emotion. Resignation took hold, tempered with the strength of her beliefs, and she rose to stand before him.

The Lord thy God, it is He that doth go with thee. . . .

Isabelle squared her shoulders and stilled her quaking knees, busying her hands with the removal of a particularly troublesome wrinkle in her cloak rather than show them unable to remain still. Words bounded forth and demanded she speak them while her heart fluttered and threatened to forsake her.

He will not fail thee, nor forsake thee.

Indeed. With God there would be a solution; He set her on this path, and He would not let her fail. Surely He had a plan, for she did not.

"Captain Carter," she said slowly, testing the sound of her voice against the battering of the rain outside, "you and I are at odds, yet I fear we must work as allies."

He gave her a sideways look. "Aye," he finally said, "sadly, it seems this is true."

"Then perhaps there is a solution."

A solution.

Josiah stifled a laugh. How in the name of all creation could this slip of a girl find a solution to a predicament that seemed to have none?

The situation lay before them plain and simple. Payment for the *Jude* would be required on the morrow, and this woman held nothing with which she could satisfy the note. Even if he could manage to buy extra time from the Spaniard, say in the form of a deed to an English house in one of the more pious sections of the countryside, the delay could well cost him his refuge.

For all Josiah knew, Hezekiah Carter's minions were nipping at his heels, as well. A day. That's all he'd been granted by his advance scouts. More than that and he risked being caught and returned to Virginia, a fate worse than death.

A fate not even worth considering.

Worse, he would not be hauled back to Virginia alone. For the boy and for himself, he could not let this happen.

Isabelle Gayarre made a discreet coughing sound, drawing his attention. Josiah looked her up and down. A fancy sort, this one, most likely with a home and servants and . . .

A solution most simple yet ingenious dawned bright. Someone somewhere would be looking for her—a father, a mother, maybe even a husband—and that someone most certainly would possess the means to secure her return.

No more than the mortgage on the *Jude* would be required. Of criminals and extortionists,

Josiah had no tolerance. After all, he'd been born of the lineage and carried the pedigree.

Business transactions, however, were another matter entirely.

He gave the fair-haired Isabelle a quick look of consideration. Given less-taxing time constraints, perhaps the two of them could have been more than erstwhile business partners—he the receiver of the funds and she the means of procurement—but alas, this was not to be.

Another crack of lightning split the darkness beyond the window-pane and crashed danger-ously close. A roar much louder than conventional thunder shook the walls and rattled the pier glass. Above decks, he heard the rush of footsteps and the shouts of men on watch, obviously shirking their duties to seek a drier haven.

"Ill-tempered weather, contrary women, and lazy fools will be the death of me," Josiah mut-tered under his breath, mentally adding a few choice curses to mirror his mood.

"Captain Carter?"

The woman reminded him of her presence less by the calling of his name than by the shifting of her position. She drew near, her face the mask of naïveté. Her proximity crowded out the broken trunks, the howling torrent, and even the thoughts of the world beyond the doorway.

"I would like very much to pray about this." Her lashes lowered, brushing cheekbones etched of the most glorious color and form. "Would you pray with me?"

Josiah froze. Seconds passed, and the walls quickly fell away as the Gayarre woman began to speak in a soft whisper as if conversing with a friend. Nothing existed but he and she. She had asked a question, made a statement that required a response, but his tongue turned to cotton, and his voice fled like his crew in the storm.

She required his help, or was it his cooperation? Perhaps his lot was to merely listen and agree. He'd known when she spoke, yet his mind had suddenly gone to mush. Bits and pieces of words stuck in his head as he stared, more watching her speak than listening.

A sea siren, this one, yet he could no more turn away than complain. Instead, he leaned into her voice and tried to concentrate.

Cooperation, yes, that's a word he recognized, and liaison also rang true. Perhaps a liaison, however brief and tempestuous, could make a glorious moment out of a grand mess. Perhaps this beauty from the shadows would indeed bring a bit of light to his darkness. Despite appearances, he was not a man given to the temptation of the flesh, but just this once, he might set aside his principles and his vow to be an acceptable example to his younger brother, William.

"And so, God, we ask Your help in this matter. . . ."

The reality of the situation intruded. Bedazzled, that's what she'd done to him.

She called aloud for aid, reminding Josiah of her assertion of belief in the powers of the Christ. He'd known too many who wore the mantle of believer only to cast it aside when the crown began to pinch—and he included himself in this number. Only fools kept to this sort of superstition, and while Isabelle professed to be an innocent, she looked to be no fool.

He, on the other hand, had studied at the university of the cold, cruel world. His professors were each of the men who'd attempted to rule him or worse, and his diploma lay not printed on sheepskin, but written in the scars on his back and burned into the hidden places of his mind. Nothing short of a miracle would erase either of these.

The last thing Josiah Carter would ever believe in was a miracle. Even God didn't have that much power.

Out of some long ingrained habit, or perhaps it was fear brought by the education of his youth, he hastened to apologize to the Deity in question. Perhaps He had the power, but He certainly hadn't chosen to exert it.

She spoke again, phrasing Josiah's name as a question and giving him cause to stare unabashedly. Perhaps behind the lace-covered image of a girl untainted was the reality of a woman trained to create this illusion. Indeed, in all his years, he'd not met a single woman without some measure of guile. Each wanted something from him, be it a night's pleasure, a day's entertainment, or his last name along with a babe or two for good measure.

Surely this one was no different; this far better fit his hypothesis.

"Do you so charm all the men in this way?" he asked, pretending to ignore the surprise on her face and the soft gasp that escaped from her lips before she continued with her prayer.

Her response shook him, even as the deck above shook with the footsteps of his crew. Had his calculations been off? Being wrong was something he refused to consider; behind the facade of religion lay a seductress lying in wait, seeking his very soul.

Little did she know that on more than one occasion he'd come close to selling his scarred and battered spirit to the devil. Only the sore condition of the thing and the fact he'd not tie himself to either man or deity gave rise to the explanation that his soul still lay somewhere in his possession.

Still, something about the woman made him want to lay bare the core of his being, spit polished and newly clean, for her inspection. Disgusted, he spat and wiped his mouth with the back of his sleeve while she continued her prayer.

Rubbish!

Yet he felt such a strong tug. Dare he consider the implications? Dare he hope a lost cause had found asylum? That a modern-day Jude might possibly become something worthy of the Lord's attention?

He waved away the possibility with a sweep of his hand, ending the woman's monologue before she could utter an amen and seal the deal with her Creator. Overhead, he heard more scurrying about followed by an increase in the commotion. He sighed.

Had he more time, he might replace the whole lot of them with a more suitable crew. Time, unfortunately, lay in short supply, as did his patience. Still, Josiah attempted a more gentle tone as he spoke.

"Please be seated, Mademoiselle Gayarre," he said, "and we shall make our plans."

The woman complied, lowering herself onto the last remaining unbroken chair in the cabin with the ease of a princess ascending her throne. When she'd settled her lace and finery around her and threaded her fingers together in her lap, she offered him a weak smile.

"I should like to ask you about your relationship with the Lord, Captain Carter."

Her statement stunned him. "I daresay He is as irritated with me as my earthly father," he said when he found his voice. "I've spoken to neither in years." Josiah gestured to the basket of apples. "Perhaps you'd like something more substantial before we discuss this solution of yours?"

The watch bell rang thrice, and Josiah checked the time. Strange, the ship's clock read barely past nine. He made a note to speak to Harrigan upon conclusion of his conversation with the mademoiselle. The crew, it seemed, was woefully remiss in its training.

"Actually," she said softly, capturing Josiah's attention once more, "I'd much prefer you see to the needs of my traveling companions than concern yourself with me."

Suppressing a frown, he gave her an even look. Obviously more posturing to take advantage of his sensibilities and arouse his compassion. If only she knew that what little compassion he possessed had left him so long ago he barely had memory of it.

He shook his head. "I warrant your friends are comfortable enough." While he'd not taken any steps to secure their comfort, he had not used all in his power to arrange their discomfort, either.

Josiah caught the scent of a peculiar odor, no doubt the wind blowing some of New Orleans's worst his direction. And yet it smelled strangely of . . .

Smoke. A sea captain's worse nightmare.

Someone pounded at the door. "Beggin' the

cap'n's pardon," Harrigan called, "but there's been a bit of trouble and—"

An explosion followed by a shuddering movement knocked Josiah to the floor. He scrambled to his feet and chased the words down the dark staircase, leaving his guest to fend for herself.

CHAPTER 7

Had the captain really left her alone? Isabelle shook off her surprise and raced for the small porthole, only to find that layers of grime prevented her from seeing through to the outside world.

Strange, though, how the window glowed with an eerie golden color that rippled and changed as raindrops trailed across the surface. Pressing her finger to the glass, Isabelle rubbed away a small circle, then a larger one until a most unexpected picture emerged through the streaks of rain.

Fire!

The golden glow formed and fashioned itself into an angry inferno already spiraling up the main mast of the brig *My Lady Mathilde*. Her bulwarks were ablaze, and her bowsprit lay in the path of the flames. Here and there, men jumped into the water, some coming so near to the *Jude* that it seemed they might land inside the cabin. The smell of smoke filtered uninvited into the small space, lifting and curling through the fresh air to dance a jig in Isabelle's lungs. She coughed and covered her nose with the fabric of her sleeve, offering but a small measure of comfort against the noxious haze.

A mighty creaking sound rolled through the room, and Isabelle watched in horror as the quarterdeck of the *Mathilde* collapsed and disappeared into the inferno, taking the mizzenmast with it. The flames increased, feeding on the seasoned timbers and sending showers of sparks into the air to dust the window like blackened snow.

Silhouetted against the furnace, a lone sailor held tight to the mainmast, his feet dangling inches above the inferno. While Isabelle watched in horror, the fire engulfed him, traveling past the sailor to steal away more of the mast until it had all but disappeared.

Isabelle blinked, hoping to erase the image, yet it remained firmly lodged behind her eyelids. While rain continued to beat against the vessel, the brilliance of the nearby furnace had swallowed up the lightning display.

Already the glass had grown warm beneath her palm. Anchored barely an arm's length away, the *Jude* would certainly be the next to feel the flames.

Isabelle backed away from the porthole and

cast a quick glance around the room. Another glow, this one not quite as bright, caught her eye.

The captain had left the door unlatched, and it now stood open at the base of the stairs. Stopping only long enough to retrieve the deed to her new home from the pile of rubble, she tucked the document into her bodice and raced out of the already-warm cabin.

Following the glow through the maze of passageways, she emerged onto a rain-drenched deck filled with shouting men. Above the din, one voice rang loud.

Captain Carter stood in the midst of the melee like a frantic general directing a war. To his right, a group of men tugged and pulled at a chain and wheel, while behind him, another pair doused the deck with water from the rain barrel. Harrigan stood alone on the quarter-deck, bellowing the captain's orders to a youngster perched high in the rigging.

Great tongues of fire licked at the wooden sides of the *Jude*, and from where she stood, Isabelle could see yet more of the crew working to keep them at bay with buckets hoisted up from the river. A giant bolt of lightning split the sky, casting an eerie moment of daylight over the scene.

The great Levee Steam Cotton Press provided a stark backdrop for the melee taking place at her doorstep. On the nearby dock, all sorts of persons raced about throwing water on the flames or carrying cargo ashore. Many others stood in clusters, obviously bent on viewing the spectacle rather than offering aid.

"Watch yourself, boy," she heard Harrigan shout.

Isabelle looked up to see the youth dangling upside down like a circus performer, his hands flailing about and one leg tangled in the rain-soaked rigging. Just above him, flames teased the topmost points of the mainmast and engulfed the fellow in intermittent clouds of smoke and ash.

"I'm a goner, sir," she heard him cry, his voice hardly deep enough to show him to be male rather than female.

A great explosion ripped through the burning vessel *Mathilde* and caused her to list toward the *Jude*. A fiery sail unfurled and draped itself around the *Jude*'s mainmast, taking a portion of the rigging and the young man with it.

Covering her mouth with her hand, Isabelle suppressed a scream as the boy scrambled to hold himself away from the flames while he fought to release his leg. Even from her spot on the deck, she could see the boy's situation had no good resolution. His position in the ropes made rescue difficult, and the smoldering flames of the canvas sail blocked the way.

Rain streaked her cheeks, mingling with tears Isabelle did not bother to wipe away. She sucked in a deep breath and instantly paid for it by a fit of coughing. Recovering, she covered her mouth and nose with her cloak and watched the flames dance nearer to the youngster.

A few more moments and the mainmast would ignite. When that happened, the elaborately knotted rigging would collapse. Only the wet conditions from the torrential downpour seemed to have prevented it thus far.

"Please, help me!" the boy cried.

Isabelle's gaze jumped from the boy to the flames, and finally to the distance between them. She stared down at the drenched mess her lace gown had become. If only she could throw off these female encumbrances and extricate the boy herself.

Sadly, she knew the truth. It would take a miracle. In desperation, Isabelle closed her eyes against the scene and began to pray.

Father, bring forth Your miracles and save this boy. Appoint someone to be Your hands and feet in this situation.

She took a deep breath and opened her eyes, casting another glance on the poor boy now dangling inches away from the fire. Her breath caught in her throat and choked off another cry.

If it's me You choose, Father, bestow upon me Your strength and favor, for without You this cannot be achieved. If You choose another, I beg You grant him Your favor and protection.

From nowhere, the captain appeared at the base of the mainmast. "Hold tight," he shouted to the boy.

His words to Harrigan and once more to the young man were lost in the whirlwind, but the old sailor's objections were clear in the expression on his wrinkled face and the waving of his hands. Against those objections, Captain Carter took hold of the ropes and began to scale the rigging.

Inch by inch, the captain climbed, ducking to avoid torrents of debris mingling with the blowing rain. "Cut her loose if you must, Harrigan," he shouted.

"Aye," the weathered seaman answered, bellowing the captain's command to the crew in clipped tones.

A jolt rocked the *Jude*, landing Isabelle on her derriere just as the wind gusted. Reaching without success for some purchase on the slippery wood, she slid against the deck housing and skidded to a halt in a most ungainly fashion some yards away.

Pieces of the tattered sail fell about her and landed in bursts of fire and smoke. A particularly large scrap of canvas, its edges black and curled, scalded her bare ankle while another attached itself to her cloak and began to smolder until she brushed it away.

"Away with ye, lass," a deckhand called as he

tripped over her feet and landed in a heap beside her. "Back in the hold with the women you go."

The women.

Isabelle stifled a gasp. Where were her companions? Did they fear the same fate as she, or hidden away in their cell, had they no knowledge of the calamity taking place above them?

Barely giving her a backward look, the crewman rolled to his feet and resumed his race for the forward bow and the knot of sailors gathered there. Isabelle watched them heave to and haul something dark and glistening over the rails onto the deck.

Could it be the anchor? Isabelle's breathing sharpened, as did her hopes. In the midst of this firestorm, had she taken her first permanent step toward freedom?

Overhead, the youth began to scream. Climbing to her feet, Isabelle limped forward and looked up into the rigging in time to see the boy's flaming shirt plummet to the deck and land in a steaming heap in a puddle of rainwater. Thankfully it appeared the boy had thrown the garment off in time to avoid burns, although he still hung precariously by one leg.

Flames roared near while the rain continued to beat against the wood and rope. At any moment the whole intricate fretwork of rigging could join the neighboring inferno and collapse. This could very well set the ship ablaze and cause a chain reaction among the ships docked so close together on the crowded wharf.

Wedged nearest to the source of the blaze, the *Jude*'s fate seemed uncertain at best. Vague sounds behind Isabelle gave the impression that the other frigate's crew was swarming the decks in defense of their vessel.

The deck rocked beneath Isabelle's feet and jarred her aching ankle as she watched the captain progressing up the swaying mast. Against a wind that swirled in earnest, a giant wall of flames in the form of the *Mathilde*'s sail stood between Captain Carter and the young man. Isabelle could only duck the thick smoke and cough, waiting for the haze to clear so she could see the action taking place overhead.

With a burst of effort, Josiah Carter somehow managed to ascend the mast to stop within reach of the source of the conflagration. Unable to believe her eyes, Isabelle watched the captain reach into the fiery mess to tear away the sail and toss it into the river.

"Give me your hand, lad," the captain called as he batted at the smoke thickening around them.

Another streak of lightning chased across the sky and shone ghostly white on the faces of the young man and his rescuer. While Captain Carter continued to shout, the boy, bereft of his shirt and frozen in the tangle of damaged ropes, merely stared into the sky, rain washing over his face and down his narrow, soot-covered back.

A thread of rope loosened and caused the boy to plummet out of reach of the captain. He hung suspended halfway to the deck, too far away to be rescued by the captain, who seemed to barely maintain a hold on the swaying mainmast.

"Drop, boy," Harrigan shouted as he positioned himself beneath the dangling youth and batted frantically at the burning debris and raindrops blinding him. "I'll snag ye."

Captain Carter shouted something in encouragement, as well, but the lad continued to stare into the sky. "See 'em up there, Captain?" the fellow asked as he curled his body upward and grasped his knees with his hands. "Up there atop the mainmast."

His voice, almost angelic, carried eerily across the distance between them. Isabelle's gaze searched the topmost areas of the masts and rigging. Whatever the boy thought he saw, it remained hidden from view. Slowly, she focused a bit lower, centering her attention on the captain. An unlikely hero at best, he now stood perched to be just that.

If only the boy would allow it.

"There's nothing atop the mainmast save the rain and the threat of a decent fire." Captain Carter made another grab for the boy, holding his hand just beneath the flames. "Now reach for me so we both aren't done to a crisp."

"We ain't going to be done to a crisp," the boy answered. "They ain't gonna let it happen."

They.

Of course, the ethereal *they* of which the boy spoke had no existence in reality. Josiah had seen this sort of shipboard lunacy before, but never in one so young. Often the trail of lives lost or decisions ill made came full circle in times like this.

On many a deathbed had come claims of ghost-like *they*s, always invisible to those whom they had not come to claim. Josiah shook his head. *Rubbish.*

He watched the boy dangle like a horsefly in a spider's web for a second longer than he thought he could stand, then made one last grab for him. A decade prior, he might have gone onto the rigging after the fool, but age and good sense kept him firmly in place.

"Listen, Captain," the kid declared, "they're singing."

Singing? More rubbish.

"Hear you any singing, Harrigan?" Josiah called when he could manage his voice.

"I do not, sir," came the response from below.

"He does not," he repeated.

The boy ignored his statement and pointed toward the heavens, a senseless grin etched upon his freckled face as the flames danced closer.

"That one looks like me ma. A sight, she is. Hullo and g'day, fair one."

His words began to slur but did not slow. Instead, he seemed perfectly happy to carry on an animated conversation with the top of the mainmast while the inferno gathered about them.

Another alarm sounded nearby, and Josiah turned to see the flames jumping across the *Jude* to touch the quarterdeck of the frigate tied to the south. Instantly an orange glow spread across the aged timber, scattering the crew and engulfing the wheelhouse.

A glance toward the bowsprit gave him pause to believe the *Jude* would be soon set adrift. This much at least he could count in their favor.

The mainmast rode the weather and waves, lurching first to the north and then to the south. Josiah sighed and renewed his grasp on the blessedly sturdy timber, his mind too weary from the aggravation and his heart too jaded to be concerned for life or limb, be it his or his crew's.

Flames on two sides and neither the Lord nor the devil to beg for help. An all too familiar situation. "And one you can only blame on yourself, Carter."

Sparks danced about and mirrored Josiah's mood, while the young man's incessant chorus strummed at his concentration. Another man might feel sorry for the boy and the insanity wrought from such a harrowing experience.

Josiah Carter was not that sort of man.

"Harrigan, fetch four of your best men and something to stretch between you. I've endured this madness long enough."

The older sailor nodded and scampered away, leaving the captain to watch him go. "I swear by all creation, women and children will be the death of me," he muttered.

When he caught sight of the woman standing below, he mentally added a blistering oath. This time, he chose French as his language of delivery and made sure *she* heard every word. To her credit, the Gayarre woman turned her back on him and walked away.

"Ahoy there, Cap'n," Harrigan called. "Beggin' yer pardon, but this piece of sail here was the best we could do on short notice."

Josiah tore his gaze from the woman's back to see the foursome gathered below. Harrigan held one corner of a large canvas remnant while three other fellows of dubious strength carried the others.

He surveyed the spectacle, felt the heat once more on his back, and calculated the odds. Neither he nor the boy stood much of a chance should the motley lot below need to save them. Likely, the dry-rotted canvas would not hold. Nor could they remain perched in the rigging to await the flame's advance.

An odd thought dawned, and he turned to stare

at the dock. Cast in an orange glow, the market, the warehouses, the giant cotton press, and the city itself lay half hidden in the face of the flames and smoke.

The people who'd come to witness the conflagration, however, stood out in distinct relief against the hazy backdrop. Here and there, groups of men and the occasional pair or threesome of women watched in silence, some carrying children on their hips. A few milled about in circles, looking almost as if they'd missed their cue to enter the fiery scene.

Even from this great height, Josiah could see their faces. Young, old, frightened, amused, dark, light: each one looked as distinct to him as if he stood before them on a sunny summer afternoon.

Centermost in the crowd of onlookers stood a familiar figure dressed in a gentleman's finery, a man most likely just come from a performance of *Evadne* at the American Theater or perhaps a round of revelry at the Ball Paree et Masque in the Salle Washington Rue St. Philippe.

The gentleman leaned on his cane and tipped his hat, revealing a face Josiah visited only in a rare nightmare.

Hezekiah Carter had found him at last.

Cursing life and death all in the same sentence, Josiah turned to square his shoulders. Weighing the flames above him against the man on the dock, he made his decision.

"On my signal then," he called to the men below.

Positioning himself just beneath the rope holding the young fool, Josiah gave the rigging a hard yank and watched the boy go spiraling toward the deck. In a rush of movement, Harrigan and his men captured the lad in the sail.

The *Jude* gave a hearty lurch backward, sending Josiah's chin smashing into the mast. He felt his fingers begin to loosen their grip on the mast. Blood inched a crimson path down his shirt-front, mingling with the soot and grime already there.

When he gained his senses, he looked down to see the boy scramble to his feet, obviously unharmed. The sail, however, did not fare so well. Two of the men held pieces of the fabric, and two were empty-handed save shreds of torn canvas. As Harrigan had predicted, the sail had not held.

One of the men spirited the youth away, while Harrigan turned to offer a sign of approval to Josiah. "Ready yourself, Captain," Harrigan said. "Dunston's gone to fetch another canvas."

"Aye," he answered, breaking into a cough when a burst of smoke trailed past.

Above, another piece of sail had come loose from the *Mathilde* and danced about, teasing his head and shoulders with showers of burning fabric. Josiah brushed a smoldering ember off his shirtsleeve and watched as Harrigan and several men engaged in a heated argument.

There seemed to be a problem locating a replacement canvas. Harrigan called up to him, but most of his words were lost in the rumbling of the fire, now consuming ships on either side of the *Jude*. Without a fresh sail, there looked to be two ways out of his predicament. Neither appealed.

Either he could climb down the way he climbed up, or he could chance a ride down on the riggings. The mainmast, while still steady, held nothing in the way of support for a man descending to the deck, especially now that the *Jude*'s anchor had been lifted.

How he'd managed the upward climb baffled him. The rigging, on the other hand, looked every bit as insecure as the first choice. It held the added danger of small spots of smoldering ash threatening to spark into true flames at the slightest hint of a breeze.

At least the *Jude* had cleared the dock and begun sliding backward toward the headwaters of the river. Another few minutes and the vessel would be clear to make her turn.

Though not in the manner of his choosing, Josiah Carter and the *Jude* would be sailing away from New Orleans forever. The fact that Hezekiah Carter stood somewhere watching his escape was an added bonus.

"Make haste, Harrigan, for I've work to do," he called to his second in command.

"It seems, sir," Harrigan answered, "we've run into a bit of an obstacle."

Josiah clung to the swaying mast and watched a streak of lightning dance way too close. "An obstacle of what sort?"

Harrigan shook his head. "All we've got is the sails we need fer navigation. There's nothing to spare save a scrap or two for patches." He paused. "What would you have us do, Captain Carter?"

So that was how it would be. No escape from the fiery flames and nothing to catch him when he fell.

Josiah suppressed a wry smile. How very much like the end his father had predicted for him.

Glancing over his aching shoulder into the crowd, he looked for the familiar face. Hezekiah Carter, if he'd been there at all, had vanished from sight. Soon New Orleans would disappear, too.

Good riddance to them all.

A shuddering sound brought his attention back to the situation at hand; an action demanded to be taken posthaste. Should he die, he would have but few regrets; should he live, he would have to give serious consideration to the reason.

"So be it," he shouted into the storm.

Josiah released his grip on the mainmast and

grasped for a purchase on the rigging. Missing altogether, he lurched forward and felt nothing but air beneath his feet.

Odd, but he heard no splash when he hit the water. The only sound was silence, and the only sight murky darkness streaked with orange.

Breath that came so easily before failed him now, and his lungs began to ache. Through the void, a gentle voice whispered something in Josiah's ear. Something about compassion.

As the blackness overtook him, Josiah heard another voice. This one bid him to curse God and die.

With his last breath, Josiah refused. Then something caught him and thrust him back in the direction from which he'd come.

CHAPTER 8

Isabelle felt nothing but the boards beneath her feet as she careened blindly down the narrow passageway, the image of Josiah Carter's plummet into the water fresh in her mind. With the golden glow behind her now, nothing led the way save instinct and prayer.

And others save with fear, pulling them out of the fire. . . .

The verse from the book of Jude rang in her

ears as she pressed forward. She must find the mademoiselles.

Banging on door after door, she made her way toward the end of one passageway only to turn and go back. Time and time again, she repeated the process, searching in vain for the place where the captain had incarcerated her companions.

The captain.

Unless the Lord intervened, the man most likely would not survive his mission of rescue. From her hiding place behind the wheelhouse, she'd heard the shouts of approval when the young sailor dropped to safety. She'd also heard the man called Harrigan express the difficulty of bringing the captain down alive.

The sound of the crew pronouncing the man's imminent passing sent her feet flying. Should Josiah Carter perish in the fall as the crew predicted, the fate of all women aboard would be . . .

She couldn't bring herself to finish the thought.

Gradually feelings returned. Stabs of pain needled at her knuckles, and more than once, she doubled over to cough the black smoke from her lungs. Finally, she dropped to her knees at the end of yet another empty passageway and rested her face in her hands, tears scalding her raw, bleeding fingers as they rolled from her eyes onto the ruined lace fabric of her skirt.

And others save with fear, pulling them out of the fire. . . .

"But, Lord, I tried," she whispered as she rose and wiped the tears away. "I can't find them."

"Are you looking for the ladies, miss?"

Isabelle gasped and lifted her head. A small figure stood a few yards hence, silhouetted in the gentle radiance of a single candle.

"I frightened you," he said, his voice all too young for the age it held. "I'm sorry."

Upon closer inspection, the individual looked to be a lad of no more than a decade, wearing a miniature version of the trousers and flowing shirt favored by the captain and crew. But what would a boy be doing wandering the passageways of a ship in danger of burning to the waterline at any moment?

He held the candle high, casting a shadow on his full cheekbones and curious stare. Raven curls framed an oval face, and a pair of wide eyes the color of an angry silver sky stared back through a thick fringe of dark lashes.

Strange, but his presence bore some familiarity.

For a moment, Isabelle thought he might be an angel. Then he sneezed and wiped his nose on the hem of his shirt.

"Are you looking for the ladies?" he repeated.

Words failed. She nodded, hoping he could see her.

"They're fit and well." He paused. "You're worried. Don't be. Miss Emilie sent me to ease your concerns."

Isabelle shook her head and willed her voice into cooperation. Many questions materialized; she gave voice to only two. "Who are you," she mumbled, "and how do you know of my friends?"

The boy grinned and thrust a small hand toward her. She automatically accepted his greeting.

"I am William."

"I am pleased to make your acquaintance, William," she said, noting the warmth of his little hand and the confidence with which he carried himself. This was no average young boy. "And I am Isabelle," she added.

"So *you* are Isabelle." He seemed to appraise her for a moment. "Miss Emilie and Miss Viola have become my chums. Miss Viola is fearful quiet, but Miss Emilie knows many exciting stories of England. She speaks of you and your trip to England, as well."

"How nice. Please, will you tell me—"

"Did you know I'm to go to England, too? I've an education to see to, and there are folks who will care for me because I'm clever smart." Again he paused, seeming to study her for a moment. "I'm nine, you know. I'll be ten two weeks thence, and the captain says—"

The captain.

Images of Josiah Carter plummeting from the rigging flitted across her mind. "Where might I find my companions?"

"Oh, I'll see to them," he said, "if you'll see to the captain. I'm dreadful worried about him. He and Mr. Harrigan say I'm never to go above decks without one of them present, but what with all the commotion up there, I'm afraid they've all but forgot about me." He punctuated the statement with another bout of sneezing.

Isabelle collected her handkerchief and offered it to the lad. "William," she said slowly, "I shall require a visit with my friends first, please."

"And then you'll find the captain?"

Before she could nod in agreement, the boy had her hand in his and begun to lead her through the passageway. A few turns and they arrived at what looked like a dead end. "Hold this, please." He thrust the candle toward her.

She watched him run his little palm over the smooth wood, then sink his finger into a crack between the boards. A moment later, the wood shifted and groaned, and a narrow door swung open.

"How did you do that?" she asked.

With a shrug, young William retrieved the candle. "There are many secrets in this vessel, Isabelle," he said.

And you are but one of them.

"Isabelle," Emilie called. "Look, Viola, Isabelle has found us."

The room where the two women now sat bore little resemblance to the tiny cell in which they'd all been incarcerated at the onset of the voyage. In contrast, it held a table and two chairs, a pair of lamps attached to the windowless wall, and an austere but pristine set of bunks covered in blankets in a decent state of repair and cleanliness. At the moment, Viola huddled beneath one of them, unresponsive. Mama Dell was nowhere to be found.

Emilie rose from her bunk to kneel and envelop William in a hug. "I see you've met our friend William," she said as she straightened an unruly shock of his dark hair. "He's quite a young man, isn't he?"

Isabelle nodded, a thousand questions circling, yet none lighting long enough to be asked. Where was Mama Dell? Had Josiah Carter actually taken pity on the ladies and ordered their move to a nicer cabin? That image certainly did not fit. A tug on her cloak distracted her.

"So now that you've seen your friends, will you please fetch the captain?"

She met Emilie's gaze over the boy's head. Her head told her to deny his request; her heart thumped a furious agreement. "Yes, of course," she said.

William caught her sleeve, concern etched on his little features. "Promise me you won't tell him I sent you. He'll be fierce angry if he finds out I spoke to you."

Fierce angry. Yes, she'd seen that side of the man.

"But why, William?" she asked. "I don't understand."

"We're not to know he's about," Emilie said. "It seems as though his presence is quite unknown aboard this vessel." She paused and leaned closer. "I'm not certain our presence is remembered, either," she added in a whisper. "We've seen no one but young William since the fire."

Isabelle opened her mouth, but Emilie's look silenced her. "Go and see to the captain's safety for our friend, please," she said. "We'll wait here for your word."

"Of course," she whispered.

What made her turn and put one foot in front of the other, Isabelle couldn't quite define, although she knew it must be of the Lord, for she longed to stay behind in the safety of her friends' company. Yet despite her better judgment, Isabelle bade the trio good-bye and moved with certainty through the passageway to emerge onto the rain-slicked deck of the *Jude*.

All around her, chaos reigned even as the downpour abated. The *Mathilde* no longer stood at their right but rather looked to be drifting off the forward bow. The fire-consumed frigate to the left, however, seemed to be following them into the channel.

A half dozen men labored at cutting the *Jude* free, using all sorts of tools on the thick line stretched taut between the vessels. Alongside them, clusters of men tugged on ropes, working what remained of the sails into submission, while others raced along the rails, putting out fires with whatever water-carrying vessel they could find.

Harrigan stood at the wheel, pointing and shouting much as the captain had done a short while earlier. But where was the captain?

She cast about for a sight of the captain, only to feel the pinch of a hand on her arm. "Here's another one, Mr. Harrigan," a deep voice with the touch of an Irish lilt called. Isabelle stared up into the dark brown eyes of a man nearly twice her height.

Harrigan took a long look at her before shaking his head. "I thought we'd rid ourselves of the curse of females aboard."

A roar went up on the foredeck. "It looks as if they've cut her free," her captor said.

"Aye, indeed it does. You'd best join them at your post, Banks. I warrant the bosun will have need of your expertise."

The man nodded in agreement. "What would you have me do with the lady, sir?"

Harrigan glanced back at the docks as if gauging the distance to shore. "Fetch her aft and secure the siren t' the longboat," he finally said, disgust lacing his words. "I've little time t' worry myself with demons in skirts."

"Aye, sir."

The big fellow led Isabelle around the edge of the quarterdeck to aft where the longboat hung suspended from the rail. Racing to keep up with his long steps, she tripped on a loose board and landed in a puddle beneath the small vessel. Thankfully, the rain had stopped and only her vanity had been injured in the fall.

"I'm sorry about this, miss," he said gently as he settled her into a more dignified position and made quick work of tying the thick twine into an intricate knot, "but I warrant you'll be safer here than amongst that lot."

"I vow we shall all be safer, young Banks."

Isabelle jerked her attention toward the source of the statement. There stood Captain Josiah Carter in all his soggy glory.

Despite his soaked condition, Josiah thought Isabelle actually looked pleased to see him. He couldn't miss how her lower lip quivered before she spoke. How her eyes seemed to be filled with concern.

Or did he only imagine this?

"But, Captain Carter, I thought surely you must be . . ." She shook her head, seemingly unable to speak further.

"Dead?" he offered.

With a chuckle, Josiah reached for the length of rope securing her wrist to the longboat and began unwinding the knot. Throughout the process, he avoided looking into her eyes. "Yes," she whispered.

"I fear not, although for a brief moment, I thought it possible." He looked to the right and then to the left before addressing Isabelle again. "At least this is not my vision of heaven, though it does come close to my image of the other fellow's province."

" 'Tis a poor jest you made, Captain." The ropes fell away, and she began to rub her wrist. "And yet, better than I thought you capable of."

The woman's attempt at humor caught him off guard. So did the sudden fatigue that washed over him.

"What's this?" he finally managed to say as he leaned against the rail. "Do you not find me entertaining?"

"Truly, I can say until now I did not." Isabelle seemed to study him for a moment while absent-mindedly rubbing her wrist. "You're injured," she stated.

Josiah followed her gaze to the bloodstains on his shirt. "Merely a minor inconvenience," he said as he lifted his chin to show her the source of the bleeding. "Chin hit the mast; nothing more."

He'd not tell her that the true damage might come days later when fetid water from the cess-pool known as the New Orleans docks decided whether or not to fester inside the wound.

She moved toward him. Soft fingers brushed his forehead as she pushed back the wet tangles of his hair. "This must be attended to. I warrant you've other injuries, as well, given the height from which you fell."

"So you witnessed my descent?"

"Mostly," she said, "although I saw only that you disappeared into the water. How came you to be back on the ship again?"

How indeed? If he could explain the phenomenon of how he rose to the surface of the water, he might attempt to tell her. At present, however, he could not.

The vessel swayed, or perhaps he did. In either case, he found himself nearly upended before landing hard against the rainwater barrel.

"Complete the journey to the deck and remove your shirt so I can attend to you, Captain."

The sea siren fell to her knees, then yanked him down beside her and reached for the hem of her skirt. Honey-colored curls, damp from the rain, had escaped the confines of her scarf and lay plastered against the back of her neck. Another curl rested against the curve of her cheek. With care, he reached to touch it and missed when she ducked out of the way.

"Captain, you must remove your shirt forthwith else I will be forced to take action."

When he failed to comply with her order, Isabelle began to see to the removal of his shirt herself. Somehow in the middle of all that swirled around them, this woman expected—no demanded—her way with him.

Josiah sighed.

His head swam with the possibilities, none of which were within his ability to consider at the moment. Then there was the odd realization that the man who fell into the river was not the same as the man who now sat under the ministrations of the prettiest woman in New Orleans.

The old Josiah Carter would have declared a pox on propriety and done as he wished. This one, well, he couldn't quite place the why of it, but he knew there was a better way to be.

To live.

Odd, yet unquestioningly, he did know this.

Unable to put this new knowledge into words just yet, he aimed for a jest. "As appealing as I find you, dear, I'm afraid I must discharge my duties as captain before I can consider a—"

She slapped at the hand that came too near to hers. "Do not flatter yourself, sir. I seek only to make you fit once more to discharge those duties."

Isabelle yanked a strip of fabric from her torn petticoat and fashioned a bandage. Using rainwater from the barrel, she doused the cloth and began to dab at his wounds. The same foolishness that should have kept his mouth shut before did so now.

"Much as I am sure most ladies would seek a dalliance with one such as you, I am not of a mind to do so." Their gazes met as she gently touched the damp cloth to his chin. "Ever."

This time he managed to capture her fingers. "Do not say 'ever,' Mademoiselle Gayarre. Even you must admit that the Bible says to worry only about today."

Pausing, she met his gaze. "Indeed, it does, Captain Carter." She sat back on her heels and tossed the bloody bandage aside. "The Lord says tomorrow will have trouble enough of its own."

" 'Tis I who've found trouble," he admitted. "I cannot fathom tomorrow will bring more than this."

"Trouble, sir?" She leaned close, too close, and placed the cloth at his forehead. The sensation of cool water against his skin took away his breath.

So did Isabelle Gayarre.

Whether roughened by the smoke or the closeness to this woman, Josiah found that his voice now refused to cooperate. A good thing, indeed, for he'd probably said too much already.

She wadded his shirt and handed it back to him, then reached to dampen another strip of fabric in the rainwater barrel. As she settled back beside him to attend to a rather minor scratch on his forearm, Josiah looked past her to the flames.

Flames.

Fire.

The spell broken, Josiah clambered to his feet, then steadied himself against the wall of the wheelhouse. Another moment standing alone and he'd be fit for duty.

Or rather, another moment with Isabelle Gayarre and he'd be unfit for anything but enslavement by her.

Somehow he wrestled himself back into his shirt, though he knew he must look a fearful sight in the blood-covered garment. Rather than attempt to close the front of the garment, he let it hang loose, willing Isabelle to keep her distance rather than offer help.

"It's too soon to stand," she said. "You've injuries that may be more dire than those I've managed to bind up."

"No doubt this is true." He tested his sea legs and found them worthy. "Yet my ship will not pilot itself, nor my men fare well without their leader."

Isabelle nodded. "Fair enough, yet I fail to see how you cannot be more concerned with your own health. The distance from which you fell was . . .well, a lesser man might have . . ."

A greenhorn, brother to the young fellow who'd been caught in the rigging, sidled up to them, his face plastered in shades of bright scarlet. He stood fidgeting, dancing from side to side as he worried with the brass buttons of his too-large jacket.

"Yes," Josiah finally said, "have you a message for me?"

"Beggin' yer pardon, Mr. Captain, sir, but Mr. Harrigan has need of you upon the quarterdeck."

"Tell him I'll be about forthwith." He watched the boy scamper off in the direction of the quarterdeck, then returned his attention to the lady. "You were saying?"

His question seemed to take her off guard, but she soon recovered. "Forgive me for only now mentioning this, but you were left up there with no hope of . . ." A shaking hand pointed to the riggings, indicating the spot from whence he had taken his dive. " 'Tis a height from which most men would have perished had they plunged in the same way you did."

"And yet now I am here."

The statement, stark in its simplicity, stood as a reminder of the sum total of his ability to explain what happened in the moments after the young boy fell to safety. A voice spoke then, soft words that worked their magic, cleansing him and filling him with something akin to peace.

He remembered seeing the devil himself, formed strangely into the person of his father, or perhaps he merely heard him. In either case, his next memory was that of being plucked out of the river, drenched but breathing.

True enough, the fire he fell through had

touched not a hair on his head. It was as if somehow he had been pulled from the fire and saved by divine intervention. Those were the words spoken to chase away the demon. Something about fire. If only he could recall.

Rubbish.

The whole thing was pure rubbish. Or was it?

"Mr. Captain, sir?" The young boy again.

He turned and waved him away with a threatening gesture, then returned his attention to the lady. "Have you further questions, Miss Gayarre?"

She smoothed her skirts "Perhaps this is not the time to inquire, but I must wonder what you intend to do with me."

More than one answer occurred to him; he decided to stick to the safest of the lot. "Once we're on our way, I'll have your things brought down, and you may join your companions in their cabin."

"Mr. Captain, sir?"

This time, the boy stood a good distance away, too far to be frightened by him. Harrigan caught Josiah's eye, and a smile dawned on the old man's face.

"But if I could just have a word with you, Mr. Carter," she said, "I'm sure I can explain how the money—"

"Not now." Josiah turned and walked away; he'd already left his post unattended at the sight of the sea siren, and it irked him to be reminded of the fact. It also irked him to be reminded that while it appeared he'd left the docks of New Orleans relatively unscathed, there would soon be at least one man, the owner of the ship, giving chase.

Two if his father was informed William had sailed with the vessel.

Josiah tried to curse and found himself strangely unable to do so. He stalked across the quarter-deck and brushed past Harrigan to take the wheel.

His second in command gave Josiah more than a moment's observation, studying him like a bug under a lamp. "Say it not, Mr. Harrigan," he stated, "and there will then be no cause for your release from duty."

" 'Twill be a fine day when you release me from duty, Mr. Captain, sir," he whispered.

Josiah ignored the comment to look into the heavens. The rain had ceased, and a sliver of the moon shone above the clouds. With luck, their voyage would be much less eventful than their stay in port.

"How fare the masts and sails?"

"Sturdy and fine as a warm wife on a cold night," Mr. Harrigan reported.

Was that a chuckle he heard from the seasoned mariner? When Josiah turned to look, his second in command gave him his back, seeming to search the river's edge for something of

114

importance. Yet Josiah found it impossible to ignore the shake of the old man's shoulders.

"And the rigging, Mr. Harrigan?" he asked in an attempt to steer the conversation into a more professional realm.

"Trussed up tight and looking quite well." He gave Josiah a sideways glance. "Considering what she's, ahem, I mean, what *they've* been subjected to."

Irritation rose. He ignored it.

Isabelle Gayarre wandered into his line of sight. He ignored her, too; at least he made the attempt. Behind him, Harrigan began to laugh in earnest.

"Do you wish to include me in your jest?"

"Jest?" Harrigan shrugged and feigned an innocence Josiah knew he hadn't possessed in four decades, possibly five. The old man studied him openly. "She made quite the impression on you, lad."

A thousand rebukes boiled and churned inside, none of them worthy of the anger just beneath the surface. "*She,* Mr. Harrigan?" he asked, lacing each syllable with venom as he spoke them. "And to *whom* might you be referring?"

Again Harrigan pretended virtue. "To *whom?*" he echoed.

"Are you now deaf as well as daft, old man?"

The sailor laughed heartily, clutching his sides until tears ran down his wrinkled face and he looked to be in pain. Just as Josiah had determined to run him through with the point of his blade at the earliest opportunity, Harrigan took a robust breath and allowed a moment of silence. He cast a glance at Isabelle, leaning innocently against the rail, then caught Josiah looking in the same direction. Their gazes met.

"Did you suppose I meant the *girl* when I said *she?*" Harrigan asked.

Another round of laughter split the short distance between them. This time he chose not to answer. Who else could the fool mean?

"I was speaking of the *mast,* Captain." He pointed to Josiah's chin. "The *mast,* that's the *she* what made the impression on yourself." Harrigan sobered, but only slightly. "You should have Cookie finish dressing the wound and any others you and Miss Gayarre found, or you'll soon find more misery than even that one can give you." He paused to touch Josiah's sleeve. "And this time I *am* talking about the girl."

CHAPTER 9

The Reverend Hezekiah Carter, late of Richmond in fair Virginia, stood stock-still in the midst of the milling throng as the *Jude* slipped from its moorings. The night air smelled of bitter smoke and unwashed bodies, and wisps of clouds rolled across the orange sky.

Hezekiah's first impression of the scene unfolding on the river below was one of irony. All those years of warning Josiah and now this. Surely his son from his vantage point aboard the former slaver saw a preview of his eternal destiny.

"First the water and now the fire." Hezekiah shook his head. "Lord, Your mercies are wondrous to me. Thank You for saving my son. If only he appreciated the—"

Someone bumped him. A hand reached beneath his cloak. A second later, the ruffian fell, a victim of Hezekiah's practiced skill with a walking cane. Hezekiah stepped past the fallen wharf rat.

"I only look like an old man," he muttered. "May God have mercy on your rotten soul."

His gaze searched the burning river for Josiah's vessel but found only a scene worthy of Dante. Perhaps among the smoke and flames, his firstborn had met his match.

Hezekiah sighed. Pity to lose a son, even a lost one, to the flames. He turned on his heels and made his way through the crowd toward the Dumont warehouses on the southernmost bend in the river near the cotton press. From there, he knew he could find some measure of privacy and perchance see his son's sails among the many floating about.

Halfway to his destination, he cast a look around him and took note of the mass of humanity packed together. "Poor folk with nothing better to watch than the destruction of lives."

Would that he could reach just one or two of the lost souls here. Alas, his had not been the lot of an evangelist. His flock, large in number and with pockets well lined, preferred their Sunday morning sermons padded with drivel and sweetened with promises of good fortune.

If only he could preach the coming doom to the folks back in Virginia without losing his shirt and the fine parsonage they'd built him last year. Mary did love that home, and she'd busied herself filling the rooms with many fine things from their home in the country.

No, better to leave the soul saving to one more qualified. Hezekiah had been called to do grander things for God.

He completed the climb to the levee at the warehouse and covered his eyes against the brilliant orange glare. All seemed lost, again reminding him of the inscription described by Dante. "Through me you enter into the city of woe . . . ," Hezekiah quoted as he watched a brig explode into flames that seemed to touch the clouds. "All hope abandon, ye who enter here."

Then he spied the *Jude*, her mainmast charred and her foresail torn. She cut hard to the right and seemed to glide among the wreckage with her safety insured. Close enough now to see her deck and the crewmen scrambling about, Hezekiah searched the vessel until his gaze landed on its captain.

There he stood, bold as the day he took on the neighbor's rabid spaniel and seemingly no nearer to good sense or restraint. Rather, he stood at the quarterdeck, spyglass tucked under his arm. Slowly, Josiah lifted the spyglass and aimed it toward the warehouse. He seemed to be scanning the levee, searching.

Hezekiah straightened his back and rested both hands on the cane. Soon the whelp would see him. A pity his suit coat was black. He took a step away from the shadows and dared his son to find him.

There. Josiah lowered the spyglass. He'd found him.

Remaining still took great restraint, but then, Hezekiah had perfected that trait over time. A man too quick to act often found himself sorry. As the vessel slid between two burning hulks, Hezekiah moved farther down the levee. Once the *Jude* cleared the blockage, her captain returned to view.

Hezekiah considered lifting a hand in greeting, then thought better of it. Josiah, however, fashioned his own greeting. He pointed to Hezekiah, then spit in the water. Then he began to laugh. Through the rumble of the fire, the cracking of the timber, and the screams of those in and out of the fire, came the laughter of the one Hezekiah had once called his pride.

A better man might have gone after the young pup, but Hezekiah preferred to let his son suffer whatever fate the Lord had for him without a parental audience. And the heavenly Father would surely dole out a punishment equivalent to the crimes his elder son had committed.

To be certain, Josiah Carter would try the patience of any father, heavenly or otherwise, but stealing his brother like a common highwayman surprised even Hezekiah. Mary was behind the scandalous act of fetching William from the nursery, but what his dear wife did not figure was that Hezekiah would discover the crime.

By doing nothing, he'd allowed it, of course; but then Mary was nearly as dear to him as the Lord Jesus. Perhaps he had been a bit too insistent that young William be educated at home rather than being sent away for schooling as Josiah had.

He knew of several excellent schools in the New Orleans and Charleston areas. No doubt, Josiah had arranged for William to board at one of those, using the monies Hezekiah deposited into Mary's household account. At this moment, his men were combing the campuses of these venerable institutions to locate the nine-year-old.

None save his few trusted men would know Hezekiah had found the boy. It did no good to cause an uproar over a matter so trivial. When he deemed the time right, he would impart the information. In the interim, sending a man to keep tabs on the boy would suffice.

What neither his wife nor his eldest son could fathom was that Hezekiah's worst fear was that William would lose his faith and his way just as Josiah had. Tracing the rebellion back to its origin, he knew it stemmed from sending the boy away rather than dealing with his disobedience at home.

Now Josiah boasted with pride that he would have none of the God of his youth. The God of Hezekiah Carter.

Did he not see that the very same God whom he disdained would one day judge him? Did he not further see that a father's duty was to loosen the bonds of the enemy from his children in whatever manner he must?

Watching the sails of his son's ship glide through the fiery inferno untouched gave Hezekiah an uncomfortable feeling of respect. While other ships succumbed to the flames, the *Jude* seemed to dance through them, mocking the danger. Very much like its captain, that ship. Perhaps sending the boy to sea at a tender age had been the proper move. Better he learned a trade than embarrass the Carter family by sowing his wild oats in full view of the good citizens of Hezekiah's church.

A burning vessel floated into the path of the *Jude*, and Hezekiah pushed past a pair of foul-smelling citizens to keep the ship in sight. Holding his breath, he prayed the larger vessel would not send his son's ship into flames.

Not that he held any concern for the pitiful excuse for a sailing ship or its crew. Like as not, it and the men aboard were doomed. No, his only hope was that Josiah not meet his end until he'd met his Maker on the field of battle and succumbed to His authority.

A pity that bowing to authority had never been Josiah's strong suit.

A pity, too, that Hezekiah hadn't had the privilege of awakening Josiah from whatever place of squalor he'd bedded last night to tell him he'd been followed and found. That much satisfaction he would have liked. But at least Josiah now knew his father had found him.

The *Jude*, unfurling her sails to pick up speed, made way for the southernmost bend in the river. Soon the vessel would be out of sight.

No matter. A swift vessel, and Hezekiah had ready access to several, would catch the *Jude* before daybreak.

A dark figure, compact and full-bodied, bustled

toward him in the shadows. A female, he discerned.

"Oh, mercy, there you are, Monsieur Carter. It's just awful. Plumb awful. I got out soon as I could. Them men, they tried to keep me on that old ship, but I said, 'No, I'm Mama Dell, and I won't be held against my will, I won't.' "

"Delilah?"

The woman barged into the circle of light, arms flying like some pitiful broken windmill. Upon reaching him, she halted and leaned into a wheeze that sounded like a death rattle.

When she could manage a breath, she straightened and began her odd arm motions again. This she combined with strange jumping, a disconcerting dance in the moonlight.

"You got to stop him, Monsieur Carter. You just got to stop him."

Hezekiah took a step backward lest Jean Gayarre's slave woman was either contagious or murderously mad. For extra precaution, he reached for his handkerchief to cover his nose and mouth while gripping his cane.

"Make sense, woman." He shook his head. "What or who is awful, and be specific."

"The boat. The womenfolk." Her gesturing changed as her eyes went wide. "There 'tis. Right there. Stop them."

Hezekiah looked over his shoulder. He cast away the consideration she might be carrying some vile contagion and decided she'd merely lost her mind. "The fire? Yes, I'm sure we're all aware of it."

"No." She halted her motions to give him an imploring look. "The boat. That one."

He caught sight of his son's vessel veering to starboard to bypass another fiery hazard. "The *Jude*?"

She nodded in a most inelegant manner. "He took 'em all, monsieur. I tried, but I couldn't do nothing but save myself."

"Woman, what are you babbling about? Whom did my son take?"

"I'm sorry, monsieur. I tried to keep her safe for you. I know you bought her fair and square from Monsieur Gayarre, but she done slipped off. She's smart like that. And the boy, oh my, but he is—" Another coughing fit halted the woman's babbling.

Meanwhile, Hezekiah attempted to make logic of the woman's nonsense. "Are you saying my son Josiah has taken Isabelle? Jean's Isabelle?"

The woman cowered as she nodded.

He took a step toward her, brandishing his cane. "But I don't understand. How did this happen? How is it even possible?"

"I don't rightly know."

Hezekiah raised the cane higher. "And the boy to which you refer. Who is this?"

"Master William," she said. "He's with his

brother. Well, no, last time I saw him he was with the Misses Dumont and Gayarre. The other sister, Miz Emilie Gayarre. The lady from the big house."

A feeling akin to lightning zigzagged across Hezekiah's mind and caused him to take two steps back. The roiling in his gut followed on its heels. The cane he affected as both fashion and protection became the only thing keeping him upright.

"But Viola Dumont and Emilie's brother, Andre, were to be wed today. I missed it, pressing business, but surely the women cannot be aboard that vessel if there was a wedding."

"Oh, I saw it all, I did." Delilah shook her head. "He done hit her right there on the cathedral steps. Said he didn't like the color of her dress. Miss Emilie saw it, too, and I guess she had enough of her brother's ways with the women-folk. He's mean, that one. I heard tales from the girls about him."

So the *Jude* had become an escape for more than just Josiah. "Impossible," emerged from his lips. But as he said the word, he knew he could be wrong. Very wrong.

"Lower your weapon, *señor*, or I shall send you both to your rewards."

The speaker stood behind him and some distance away. Hezekiah marked his thick Spanish accent and excellent command of the language as an interesting combination. Like as not, he would be able to identify this man even if he never saw his face.

The slave woman remained frozen in place, clenching and unclenching her meaty fists as if she might burst into motion at any moment. To her right, the river glowed orange, casting an odd shade of color to that side of her face.

Hezekiah watched Delilah's eyes dart between the two of them and judged he would have no help from her should things go awry.

"Sir," Hezekiah began, back straight and fingers wrapped around the head of his cane, "I am a man of God and a gentleman. Certainly you do not intend to hide your face like a common criminal. Reveal yourself so that we might conduct our business as men of reason and intelligence."

"That's right," the slave woman said. "This man, he knows the president, he does. You don't need to treat him like that."

"Hush, woman," he hissed.

Out of the shadows behind Delilah came a man dressed in a dark overcoat and top hat. He raised his fist to the slave and knocked her to the ground. Hezekiah watched without reacting. Where there were two, most likely more would be found.

He was good and well caught in someone's trap.

Delilah moaned and rose to her knees. Hezekiah shot her a warning look. Better she fear him than betray him further.

A boom resounded from the river below, but Hezekiah resisted turning to seek its origin. Like as not another frigate or sloop had met the Mississippi River bottom. He refused to believe that vessel might be the *Jude*. The Lord would not be so cruel as to take William. Not today.

"The man Josiah Carter, he is your son, no?"

A statement, rather than a question; thus Hezekiah remained silent.

Hezekiah held his handkerchief over his nose as much to alleviate the stench of smoke and foul air as to cover his expression. The stranger remained impassive.

Tiring of the game, Hezekiah took a calculated risk by rapping his cane on the levee. "Step into the light, coward, and address me properly."

Delilah gasped, but he spared the fool no attention. From the corner of his eye, Hezekiah saw three men approach. "You, sir, *are* a coward."

The shadowy figure waved a hand to stop the men's approach, then said something to them in rapid-fire Spanish. His minions faded into the shadows, although Hezekiah entertained no thoughts that they'd retreated any farther than out of sight.

"Better men have died for saying less." The slender figure of a well-dressed, dark-haired man stepped into the circle of light. "You are fortunate that my concern is not your life but rather for the ship your son has stolen from me."

The man's command of English was impeccable, and Hezekiah assumed the stranger was either educated here or made his living in the city. From the cut of his clothing, he did quite well at whatever enterprise employed him.

"Josiah Carter is no son to me. Not anymore." Hezekiah pounded the levee with his cane. "And if it's revenge you're looking for, you'll have to stand in line behind me to get your chance."

"So you intend to go after him?" The man drew near, then gave Delilah a withering stare before turning his attention back to Hezekiah. "Perhaps you and I should discuss this further." He paused. "Alone."

CHAPTER 10

Walk faster, woman," Hezekiah barked as he prodded the slave woman forward with his cane. "I daresay a man of my age shouldn't have to wait for a woman of yours."

Delilah swiped at the sweat on her brow with her handkerchief and trotted on a half step ahead. Despite the coolness of the April evening, the woman continued to complain of the heat until finally they reached the Rue Royale.

"Cease your talking," he said as he climbed three steps and raised his cane to knock on the door of Jean Gayarre's redbrick home.

A moment later, he settled on his favorite settee in the front parlor, a cup of coffee balanced on one knee and a remedy for his present troubles on his mind. The slave woman stood beside the fireplace, obviously rethinking her complaint of excess heat in order to seek it from the roaring fire.

He took a moment to study Delilah, allowing his mind to slide backward to a time when she was a great beauty. Had it really been nearly three decades since this woman had held court at the balls and fetes so popular in the early days?

Hezekiah felt Delilah's eyes on him and turned to stare until she looked away. There was a time when she'd earned the right to look so boldly in his direction. Unfortunately, that right had been lost some years ago when he took his bride home to Virginia.

For all his faults—and Hezekiah was painfully aware that he had many—straying from the marriage bed had not been one of them. He took pride in his faithfulness and set himself on an elevated pedestal from which he looked down on those of lesser virtue. It was a right he'd earned.

Boot heels rang out on hardwood floors, and Hezekiah sat a bit straighter. Delilah froze, her eyes roaming the room with the wild look of a cornered animal.

"Settle yourself, Delilah. You're here to be of help to us, remember?"

The slave woman nodded and adjusted the brightly colored tignon that covered hair the color of dark honey. She cast her gaze toward the pattern on the rug.

"Hezekiah, my friend, to what do I owe the—" Jean Gayarre stopped, seemingly unable to propel himself completely into the room. Face as white as the starched collar that hung loose around his neck, his lips tried and failed several times to utter intelligible words.

"You look unwell, my friend," Hezekiah said. In truth, Jean looked more than unwell. He looked as if his next visitor might be the undertaker.

"What is *she* doing here?" Gayarre finally managed to say.

"Come in and sit down, Jean." Hezekiah gestured toward a particularly gaudy Louis XIV armchair with his cane. "I've a bit of news and some serious business to discuss."

Somehow, the piteous man stumbled forward and landed in the chair. "I'll need a drink, won't I?"

"The doors, Delilah." Hezekiah waited until

his command had been carried out before shaking his head. "A drink may help you, old friend, but it will not help the situation."

In truth, his friend's years of drinking told a story written across the pale skin of a once-handsome face and in the trail of sins that followed him like a pitiful pack of mongrel dogs. The demon rum had ruined more than Jean Gayarre's past. It looked to be placing a pall over his future, as well.

A rustling of skirts told Hezekiah the slave woman had settled somewhere behind him. As much to keep her in his sight as to release the pent-up irritation he felt at the mess that had been made of his carefully constructed plans, Hezekiah rose and began to pace.

The room was small, as fit the narrow city brownstone, but its furnishings were worth a king's ransom. He stopped beside the pianoforte and plinked out a few notes from a hymn that had been plaguing him.

How sweet the name of Jesus sounds in a believer's ear! It soothes his sorrows, heals his wounds, and drives away his fear.

Drives away fear? Hezekiah sighed. Perhaps he'd best leave off any remembrances of Mr. Newton's music until he could live up to the words.

"I daresay you didn't arrive on my doorstep to entertain me with a sonata," Gayarre said as he stretched his legs and crossed them at the ankle. "Perhaps if I'm to abstain from drink, you will abstain from procrastination. And you can start by telling me why she is in my parlor."

Hezekiah turned away from the pianoforte but did not allow his gaze to fall yet on Gayarre. Instead, he watched Delilah carefully. On her face he saw no sign of fear, only the practiced look of one trained not to show an interest in her surroundings. "There was to be a wedding. Did it take place?"

"So you've heard."

Delilah stared back, her guarded expression turning insolent. Had he the energy to turn from the pressing issue at hand, he might have upbraided the woman. He settled for a stare that promised as much.

"I've been given a version of the story, but I prefer to hear yours, Jean," Hezekiah said.

"Most unfortunate, actually. The Dumont woman should be horse-whipped." Gayarre paused and let out a long breath, then scrubbed at his face with what seemed to be shaking hands. Finally, he lifted his head to stare past Hezekiah. "It's my understanding the bride-to-be took offense to a suggestion Andre made regarding her wedding attire. I was not party to the discussion, but apparently she was not of a mind to marry that day."

"And where is Miss Dumont now?"

Jean shrugged. "This is not my concern."

Hezekiah took up his pacing once more. "And your daughter, Emilie?"

Another shrug.

Pausing to consider his words carefully, Hezekiah inclined his head toward his old friend. "Perhaps your wife has knowledge of her whereabouts?"

The words propelled Jean from his stupor and his seat. "What sort of question is that? You know as well as I that—" He pinched his nose and sank back into the chair. "No," he said slowly, "I am certain Mrs. Gayarre has no knowledge of Emilie's location, nor Emilie of hers." Jean turned his attention to Delilah. "For that matter, the girl has little knowledge of Mrs. Gayarre at all, given how young the girl was when her mother left our home forever."

"As I assumed." Hezekiah gestured with his cane toward Delilah. "This woman claims to have seen both Emilie and Miss Dumont this very evening."

Gayarre's only reaction was the lifting of one brow. "Together?" At Hezekiah's nod, Jean leaned forward. "You know more than you're telling me."

"This is Delilah's story to tell, Jean." Hezekiah paused to consider the volatile Frenchman's possible reaction to the news that his daughters were together and fleeing the city. "Perhaps," he said slowly, "it would be prudent for you to fortify yourself before hearing it."

"Fortify myself?" Another lifted brow, another sigh. "Something tells me the effort will prove futile. Forge on with your story, Delilah."

The slave woman repeated the tale she'd told Hezekiah on the docks, embellishing here and there with details left out in the first version. At the mention of Josiah's name, Jean closed his eyes, but otherwise he sat quietly until she finished. Finally, he opened his eyes and nodded, then turned his attention to Hezekiah.

"Tell me, my friend. When did you learn of this?"

"Only tonight as I watched the *Jude* sail away."

A long moment passed. "So," he finally said, "our children have flown the nest together."

"It appears so."

"And you had no knowledge of this?"

Hezekiah straightened his shoulders and stared down the man who'd saved his life more than once. Had they not shared a common background with more adventure than misadventure, he might have used the cane to let the Frenchman know how little he appreciated the question.

"No," he said. "I knew only that my elder son wished to provide a different education for his brother than he received. I was a day away from hauling both of them home."

"A day away and yet such a different outcome had you acted sooner." Jean rose and turned to Delilah. "What part did you play in this, I wonder, *Mama Dell?*" Delilah opened her mouth to speak, but Jean silenced her with a look. "You are confined to the quarters here until further notice. Do you understand?"

The woman's upper lip quivered as she nodded.

"Then be gone, and do not use the excuse that you know not how to find it."

A quick pleading glance at Hezekiah preceded her out the door.

Silence hung thick until Jean strolled to the pianoforte. The man sat himself at the keyboard and began to test the chords.

"Show me again what you were playing, Hez."

Hezekiah complied, all the while watching Jean, whose eyes were once again shut tight. In this close proximity, Hezekiah could smell the alcohol and knew the only reason for the calm Jean displayed was the effect of liquor. Once the rum ran its course, Jean Gayarre would prove dangerous.

It would not be the first time.

Jean's fingers began to copy the notes, moving slowly at first, then embellishing the simple melody with flourishes of chords. Grace notes, his wife had told Hezekiah. Those notes that while not expressly included by the composer were nonetheless pleasant to the ear.

"Tell me the words, Hez."

"How sweet the name of Jesus sounds in a believer's ear," he said. *"It soothes his sorrows, heals his wounds, and drives away his fear."*

The Frenchman's fingers halted. "I tire of this." He swiveled to face Hezekiah. "How shall we solve the problem of our children?"

"I fear you'll dislike my solution, my friend," Hezekiah said, "but I know of only one way to catch the *Jude*."

Jean rose and pitched forward, then righted himself. "Lead on."

Hezekiah stepped into the hall and called to the cook. "Strong coffee," he said, "and hurry. And have the carriage brought around."

"My father's going nowhere but to bed tonight." Andre Gayarre took the stairs two at a time as he stormed the hallway toward Hezekiah. "What purpose would you have for taking an old man out tonight?"

Hezekiah noted several things about the younger Gayarre. Other than the angry red scratch that ran across Andre's right cheek, he was a near replica of his father at that age. He could not help but think of how like Jean Gayarre his only son had become.

The lone difference came in the way the tempers were displayed. While Jean satisfied his rage by taking what he wanted and ignoring good sense, Andre was known to pound his out on whatever poor female had the displeasure of making his acquaintance.

Tonight that temper seemed to have surpassed the danger level. His right fist was bound in fresh bandages, attesting to an unfortunate choice of some sort, likely striking an object harder than the fool's head.

Andre halted before Hezekiah, barely acknowledging his father's presence. "I asked a question, sir."

"Sit down." Hezekiah gestured toward the nearest chair and waited in preparation of the younger Gayarre's protest. A servant carrying the requested coffee cowered in the hall, and Hezekiah motioned for her to enter the parlor. She eased past Andre, her expression akin to a beaten dog confronting its tormentor.

The younger Gayarre gave the woman no notice. Rather, he puffed out his chest and drew himself up to his full height. "I prefer to stand."

"Suit yourself." Hezekiah accepted the tray from the terrified servant, then poured a cup for Jean. Without warning, Hezekiah whirled around and landed a blow against the back of Andre's knees, sending the arrogant fool sprawling to the carpet.

At the sound of his father's chuckle, Andre scrambled to his feet. He took two steps toward Hezekiah, who stood his ground.

"No whelp of a pup is going to best me." He

looked askance at Andre. "Better men than you have tried and failed."

"Yet your own son succeeded." The arrogant man offered a smirk. "At least, that's what I managed to discover from my various contacts down at the docks. I understand he's captain of the *Jude* now. I believe that vessel, vile as it looked, slipped safely out of the fire this evening with a lad aboard. You have a younger son of, oh, a decade in years, do you not?"

Opening his mouth to respond, Hezekiah decided better of it. Andre Gayarre would serve a purpose, but only if carefully manipulated.

Jean set his cup down with a clatter and climbed to his feet. "Did your contacts tell you, my son, that your *sister* was also aboard the *Jude*?"

Hezekiah wanted to add that both the man's sisters were aboard but decided against it. No sense muddying the issue with semantics. Getting the job done was primary, and as much as he hated to admit it, sending Andre Gayarre after Josiah might make a better plan that the one he'd settled on. First, however, he must make the younger Gayarre believe the idea was his.

"Some contacts you've got," Jean taunted his son. "Like as not they know more about what goes on in the back rooms and bars." Andre's silence told the tale, as did Jean's cackle of laughter. "Still not able to find that bride of yours, either, are you? Well, she's aboard, too."

A moment before the men came to blows, Hezekiah stepped between them. "Settle this tomorrow, gentlemen. Tonight, I shall require the use of your carriage."

Jean's brows rose once more. "For?"

"I'm an old man, and I refuse to walk to the Dumont home when you have a perfectly good carriage to take me there."

Andre shouldered his way past his father and strode to the door. "If anyone is paying a visit to the Dumont home tonight, it is me."

Hezekiah suppressed a smile. "I must protest, lad. I—"

"You have no grounds to protest. Your son is the cause of this unfortunate situation." Andre paused to shout for a servant to fetch his hat and cloak. "And I, sir, intend to be the solution to it."

"As you wish," Hezekiah said, "but I will accompany you." When the fool turned to protest, Hezekiah raised his cane. "You underestimated Miss Dumont, to your disadvantage. I urge you not to do the same with me. Unlike the woman, I will leave more than a mark on your face."

"A minor misunderstanding, I assure you," he said calmly. "Once I secure the fastest ship in the Dumont line, I shall catch up to the *Jude* and remedy the situation."

"How?" Hezekiah said. "By finishing the job you started on the cathedral steps? And do not think you will harm a hair on my son William's head, for you will not live to hurt another should any injury befall him."

Josiah, as well, although his fate may best be left to the whims of his heavenly Father rather than to me.

The younger Gayarre ran the back of his hand across his cheek and glowered at Hezekiah. Without a word, he turned on his heels and strode to the door.

Hezekiah made to follow then stopped short to turn around. Jean Gayarre sat slumped in his chair, seemingly studying the pianoforte. "Are you with us, Jean?"

The Frenchman shook his head. "Tell my son I'll have a traveling satchel at the ready when he returns from the Dumonts. It will contain plenty of funds to finance this venture."

"Of course, but—"

"There's one more thing." Jean rose and walked toward his desk, then pulled down the family Bible from the bookcase. "See that Emilie gets this. There are letters inside. She will know to whom they are to be delivered."

Hezekiah took the Bible and held it against his chest. "Yes, of course, but aren't you going to accompany us?"

"There will be no 'us,' old man." The door

opened once more, and Andre walked across the parlor to snatch the Bible from Hezekiah's hands. He attempted to hand it back to Jean. "This is useless aboard ship."

The elder Gayarre straightened his shoulders and stared at his son. "My mistake, Andre, was in loving you too much to discipline you. That is about to change. Hezekiah can attest that I have already seen to the legalities should I meet an unfortunate illness or accident, or should something happen to your sister."

Andre looked confused; then amusement colored his features. "Is that so?"

"It is. Go and find your sister, and you will be rewarded handsomely, but only if she returns in good health and with this Bible and the letters it contains." Jean glanced at Hezekiah, then returned his attention to his son. "You depend on me, Andre. Without me and my money, you have nothing."

CHAPTER 11

Isabelle tore a strip of cloth from a petticoat most would call far too precious for binding wounds, then set the ruined garment aside. A full three days had come and gone, and still the sailors wounded in the fire cried out for care. In the hold, fresh air and sunshine from above met murky darkness. It was a place to which Isabelle had grown accustomed, yet it was hardly fit for the sick. Thus far, not a man aboard the Jude had been lost to his injuries, although more than a few trod dangerously close to death's door. The vessel, near enough to seaworthy to proceed, aimed to the southeast and the open ocean.

The mademoiselle's delicate sensibilities and Miss Viola's traveling malaise prevented the ladies from attending to the ill for very long, leaving Isabelle and two cabin boys to do the work. The scent that Isabelle had first noticed in the folds of the captain's cloak was magnified a thousandfold here. She recognized it as the smell of death and the dying; it hung in the air like Mississippi River fog.

She welcomed the mind-numbing exhaustion that came with binding wounds and wiping brows. What Isabelle hated was the suffering she could not ease.

Without training or supplies save the meager contents of a box discovered in the darkest corner of the hold, Isabelle found her only recourse to be prayer and distraction. Here, she could forget the bounds of polite society, constraints that only loosely held her even then, and tend to those in need without fear of reprisal.

Counting the number of patients proved fruitless, for as soon as one left, two more arrived.

In all, Isabelle estimated twoscore and ten members of the crew had suffered in some way.

The worst injured of the lot was the obstinate Mr. Banks, who declared in the first hours of their voyage that he'd not be nursed by the likes of a woman. Bad luck, he stated, had followed the females aboard ship, and he intended to steer clear of any worse fate than the busted leg and sore head he'd received.

What Isabelle hadn't the heart to declare was that the leg he claimed merely busted was most likely ruined beyond repair, and his burns were such that any fellow of a lesser constitution would not have survived. Something about the incorrigible seaman appealed to Isabelle. While his stubbornness might very well be the end of him, he professed a loyalty to captain and ship that could only be admired.

If jumping ship to rid the place of women would bring Mr. Banks and the others back from the brink upon which they now teetered, Isabelle would gladly have taken the plunge. Alas, there was little she could do now save to keep her distance and read the scriptures over each soul who didn't chase her away.

She cast about for her Bible and found it tucked beneath a coil of rope. There a sliver of light cast a fretwork pattern on the old boards. The words of her heavenly Father beckoned, and Isabelle rested against the ropes to oblige her need for comfort in this most horrible of places.

"Are we not yet t' open water, miss?"

Isabelle looked up and placed her finger over the sixth verse of the fourth Psalm to hold her spot. "You're speaking to *me*, Mr. Banks?"

The older fellow sent a hard look past her, then added a reluctant nod. "I'm just askin'," he said. "Don't make a fuss of it."

"Forgive me. Yes, we're more than three days gone from New Orleans. Mr. Harrigan says the Straits of Florida are soon ahead." Gathering the Bible up along with her skirts, Isabelle moved past the sleeping patients to settle nearer the man's pallet. "Perhaps you'd like me to read to you."

He gave her a scornful look. "I'm no babe in the nursery."

The man's skin, already pale, had gone ashen, and his eyes wore a tired look. A scowl twisted thin lips. His very countenance dared her to answer.

"Of course you're not. I merely, well . . ." She cast about for a better way to phrase the statement. "I merely wished to practice my reading skills and wondered if, well, you might oblige me and listen awhile."

Banks looked doubtful. "I'm not much on that sort of thing." His shuddering breath echoed in the chamber. "I reckon if you read quiet-like you won't bother me much."

"Of course."

Isabelle began where she'd left off. " 'There be many that say, Who will shew us any good? Lord, lift thou up the light of thy countenance upon us.' "

"Aye, now, there's a fine thought."

She looked up to see the old man's scowl had softened. "What's that?"

"The light of thy countenance." He shook his head. "What does that mean, do ya think?"

Isabelle pondered the proper response. "I'm not qualified to state for certain, sir, but the words give me certain comfort."

"Aye. Read it again, would ye?"

Her throat raw and raked with smoke, Isabelle longed to deny his request. Yet a man hungry for the Word should never be refused, so she complied.

"Enough, sailor. The lass is done with her reading for tonight."

She found the source of the familiar voice at the opening to the hold, a man in silhouette with the lamplight circling his face like an inappropriate halo. The captain's tone brooked no complaint, and his stance indicated he would bodily remove her should she tarry in the hold.

"Tomorrow then, Mr. Banks." She gathered her skirts and Bible, then rose. Josiah had not moved, nor had he softened his expression. Well, then, upsetting his good mood would not be an issue.

Isabelle knelt once more and set the Bible beside the aged sailor. "Mr. Banks, would you like me to leave this with you?"

The old man blinked hard, then looked up as if stunned. "Truly?"

"Truly." She laid her hand atop his. "Before I go, may I pray for you?"

"I don't rightly know." He rubbed his bald head with his bandaged hand. "Nobody's ever asked me that, but I reckon it can't hurt."

"Miss Gayarre, you're stalling, and my patience is wearing thin. These men need their rest."

She cast a glance over her shoulder in a weak attempt to placate the captain, then bowed her head and prayed for the injured man and for the eternal salvation of all those aboard the *Jude*. "Me, as well, please, miss," she heard as she finished.

Isabelle opened her eyes to see the fellow next to Mr. Banks had leaned up on his elbow. She had thought the man, a victim of a nasty fall from the mainmast, to be comatose at best. Now he smiled.

"Those stories remind me of me mum back in Linconshire, they do." He swallowed hard. "It's a fine day when an aching head can see home again."

"Aye," another called. "A fine day."

"Wonderful." The captain's boots echoed against the wooden floor. "You've turned my crew into babies longing for their nursemaids."

Isabelle looked up to find him towering over her, his boots a mere finger's breadth from her hand. She'd done it now. Her zeal for the Word had surely caused her to be banned from this place for good.

Please, Father, no.

The captain stared down at her for an interminable length of time. As Isabelle grew more daring, she broke her gaze to scan the hold. Every man who'd shown the slightest interest in her readings was now prone on his pallet, feigning sleep.

Except Mr. Banks.

When he caught her staring, the old man had the audacity to wink.

"Father," she said, eyes downcast, "You say in Your Word that You hear the prayers of Your people. Hear these men tonight, and listen as they pour their hearts out to You. Give them peace and rest. Amen." She paused, then opened her eyes. All around the hold, she heard the men adding their own amens.

Thank You for the words, Father. And for holding the captain at bay.

"Miss Gayarre, I must insist," the captain said.

"Tomorrow then," she said as she gathered her dignity and rose. "Please mark any passages that interest you, Mr. Banks, and we shall discuss them."

Due in equal parts to fear of the captain and her training as a courtesan, Isabelle walked across the uneven boards with a straight back and a smile. The captain might have won this battle, but she had a weapon that Josiah Carter seemed unable to use: prayer.

As she swept past the guards posted on deck, Isabelle's smile grew more genuine. The men on this ship needed the Lord's Word; they were hungry for it. Perhaps that need extended to the captain.

She would keep him in the forefront of the Lord's attention until such a time as he submitted to the Father's instructions. That settled, she made way to her cabin and her pallet beneath her half sister's bunk.

By now, Emilie would have begun her evening preparations for bed. Perhaps Miss Viola, as well. Isabelle picked up her pace; she would be needed. Emilie never could manage to brush her curls without snarling them. And Miss Viola would need treatment for her wounds.

"The damage a man can inflict," she whispered as she made her way slowly down the darkened passage without aid of a lantern.

"I beg to protest."

The captain again. She turned but caught sight only of his silhouette as he moved toward her.

"The damage a woman can inflict," he said, closer now.

Something touched her. She flinched.

"Take it," Josiah said. "It's your Bible. You left it in the hold."

Isabelle leaned against the wall. "That was my intention, sir. Mr. Banks expressed a need of it."

"Banks has as much need of it as I." He fairly spat the words, such was the passion in his voice.

"I beg to differ, Captain." She kept her voice gentle, tender. "We have all fallen short and have need of the Lord."

Silence.

Above, the great sails caught a fair wind and slapped against the mast. The boards creaked in protest, and the ship lurched to starboard.

Still no comment from its captain.

"Forgive me if I offend. 'Tis not my intention." Isabelle paused. "I'm nothing but a woman and a slave, but I am a child of God. He welcomes all who but ask."

A chuckle. "Ah, lass, if only it were that simple."

The words, Lord, what are they? How shall I explain?

The ship gave a mighty shudder, and Isabelle leaned into the wall to stay upright. Far as she could tell, the captain never moved; a testament to his life at sea, she supposed.

"Again, forgive me, Captain Carter, but it is just that simple. God doesn't wish complicated sacrifices or special rituals. He only asks that you give Him your heart. Nothing more."

He inched closer. "Well then, there's the trouble. It's impossible for me, Isabelle. Absolutely impossible."

The ache in his voice hurt her heart. "But, Captain, please understand. God—"

"No."

He was near now, too near, yet he kept sufficient distance for propriety. Isabelle forced herself to breathe.

Forced herself to remain still.

Forced herself not to reach for the Bible he held.

"Miss Gayarre, I cannot give my heart to God, you see. I have no heart left to give."

She thought a moment, then dared a response. "I warrant that's not entirely true."

"Have you been speaking to my mother?"

Isabelle smiled. "See, you're capable of making jest. A man without a heart cannot find humor, nor can he express it."

"You've convinced me," he said. "Perhaps I have a heart, after all; it is merely underused."

Braving a move away from the wall, Isabelle shifted positions to bring herself nearer to the weak light in the corridor. "I have the cure for its underuse," she said casually.

"I would hear this cure."

" 'Tis simple, actually." The vessel shuddered, and Isabelle reached for the wall to steady herself. "Our mutual friend Mr. Banks is quite ill. Worse, I would wager, than any other man in the hold."

A grunt told Isabelle the captain was still listening.

"He needs care that Cookie and I cannot provide."

Another grunt, his face impassive.

"Mr. Harrigan says there is an island a day's sail from here."

The captain shifted positions. "Aye, that would be Key West."

"Then we should take him to Key West." Before Josiah could protest, Isabelle continued. "To keep him from the care he needs would mean certain death."

"Impossible." He gathered the Bible to his chest. "To sail in the direction of the key in this vessel would be a fool's journey."

"How so?"

"Perhaps you've failed to notice, but this vessel is older than Neptune's teeth. A decent breeze could blow her off course."

"Not with an able captain at the helm." She offered the captain a genuine smile. "And prayer."

"Am I to understand you expect me to do both?"

Isabelle reached out to touch his sleeve. "Perhaps I could relieve you of one of the duties."

Josiah placed his hand over hers. "Dare I

hope your talents include a background in sailing a vessel of this size?"

She looked up into eyes that were shadowed by the dimness of the corridor. "It does not."

"Then I shall take on that duty." He lifted her hand to his lips, and Isabelle closed her eyes. "Providing you take on the other."

"Yet I have every confidence of your ability to pray, as well." Isabelle opened her eyes when her fingers brushed the captain's lips. "Won't you consider it?"

A strange look came over him, and he took a step back, releasing her hand.

"Captain?"

Josiah let Isabelle go without comment, as much from embarrassment as from irritation. What was it about the Frenchwoman that set his tongue wagging at the most inopportune moments? And what was it about that Bible of hers that made him want to keep it, savor its contents, rather than return it? He had one on the shelf in his cabin that never saw use. Why this one?

The knowledge of his curiosity set him aback, for he'd only thought to hold the ancient leather-bound tome as a threat. Funny how the fact that she owned it made all the difference.

Harrigan took the news of their change of course without comment, a blessing considering that Josiah would be hard-pressed to admit why he allowed the woman to convince him to take the risk. As he strode toward his cabin, however, Josiah felt something akin to the moment he met Isabelle. Neither that incident nor this was particularly pleasant, yet he knew from some spot within his being that both were parts of something that had been set in motion and could not be stopped.

Josiah threw open the door, startling the cabin boy as he turned back the bedcovers just out of the circle of lamplight. Setting the Bible atop the table, Josiah shrugged out of his coat and sighed. The rustling continued behind him, surely a sign the fellow was attempting to earn his pay.

"Cease, boy." He leaned his head against the wall and closed his eyes, exhaustion falling like rain over his head and shoulders. "Leave me be."

"Can't I stay here tonight?"

Josiah whirled about to see his brother tucked happily into the captain's bunk. To his amusement, the lad had stolen all the blankets as well as Josiah's best nightshirt and pillows.

"There can only be one captain on this ship, Sir William," he said. "And it is not thee but me."

William rose and stood atop the bunk, the nightshirt pooling at his feet and a pillow in hand. "Then we shall joust, Sir Josiah," he replied, pillow in hand.

The pillow flew, and Josiah returned it forthwith, purposefully missing the boy. Soon the war was on, culminating in two damaged pillows and a settling of feathers around the cabin.

"Like as not, young William, you will best me one day." Josiah lifted his brother into the bunk and climbed in beside him. "But today is not the day. Now off to sleep with you, and no complaints. I am still the captain and can banish you to the brig if I wish."

"There's no brig on the *Jude*," William said as he tunneled under the pile of bed coverings.

"Then we shall have to build one together."

"Tonight?" He made a dive for Josiah's sea trunk. "Aye, mate. I'll fetch the treasure."

"Treasure? I hardly think so." Josiah ruffled the boy's hair. "Tonight, I suggest you close your eyes and make your plans."

"But I really have—"

The boy bounded off the bunk, but Josiah was too fast for him. "Enough, lad," he said as he returned him to the nest of bed coverings, "else I decide to toss you and your treasure overboard."

William's giggles soon became soft breaths of slumber as he fell asleep with Josiah's best cloak for a pillow. With nothing soft upon which to lay his head, Josiah climbed to his feet and began to pace the outer ring of the lantern's yellow glow.

In the center of the light, Isabelle Gayarre's Bible taunted him from its place on the table. It

154

beckoned to him, as did the insistent voices that told him to leave it alone. Ultimately, his inability to take direction led him to sit at the table and pull the Bible near.

"What say you to an infidel such as me, God?"

And others save with fear, pulling them out of the fire.

Josiah shook his head. Fear? Men such as he, with a fast ship and strong sailors at his bidding, merely laughed at the emotion. Yet almost in spite of his command for them to lie still in his lap, Josiah's hands reached for the Bible and opened it to the book of Genesis, at the beginning. "Aye, the part where the world is built. Doesn't apply to me, now does it?"

He closed the Bible and rose, catching his heel on the rug. The room tilted, and his forehead hit the floor. Something heavy, most likely the table, landed on the backs of his thighs.

"Josiah?"

"I'm fine, William," he said as he lifted his head to push his hair from his face.

He struggled to turn over and push the table away. Thankfully, no candle had been burning atop it tonight, or he'd have been incinerated.

Then he saw it. The Bible.

It lay on the floor a small distance away, open to an ornate print of some ancient soul and a colorfully decorated page with an inscription across the top that stated he had found John, chapter 16. Leaving the book where it lay, he rose to right the table and chair. William had drifted off to sleep once more, leaving the room silent save for the seaman's lullaby of waves lapping against the hull and wood creaking with the wind.

Josiah stepped over the Bible and went to his sea chest. Perhaps a soft something or other from the depths of the trunk could be fashioned into a decent pillow. He found a pair of trousers and a summer weskit and wadded them into a ball. At least his face would be protected from the lumps in the moss-filled mattress.

Closing the trunk quietly so as not to disturb William, Josiah crossed the room with a plan to secure his own spot on the bed. He knew from past experience that the nine-year-old was as active in slumber as in his waking hours, and he'd soon have to fight for the real estate that was his own bunk.

Better to make a pallet than to meet the floor unexpectedly, he decided. He managed to wrest a single blanket from the cache his younger brother had wadded about him, and he laid it on the floor beside the bed. As he rested his head on the makeshift pillow, he rolled to his side and realized he had a view of two items: the chamber pot and the Bible.

"No mercy for a sailor tonight, eh, Lord?"

Josiah sat up and pushed the chamber pot

away, then stared at the Bible. Perhaps a peek inside would break the spell and grant him sleep.

He approached with care and slid the leather volume toward him. The book of John, chapter 16, beckoned.

"Jesus answered them, Do ye now believe? Behold, the hour cometh, yea, is now come, that ye shall be scattered, every man to his own."

Scattered. That surely described his life. He'd been scattered to the winds nearly since his earliest memories. Nursemaids, schoolmasters, and an apprenticeship before his beard hairs had begun to grow. Aye, scattered; every man to his own.

Josiah looked up at the ceiling and the swaying lantern. Had God heard him? Did the heavenly Father know of his feelings? Surely not. He skimmed down a few lines and began reading again.

"These things I have spoken unto you, that in me ye might have peace. In the world ye shall have tribulation: but be of good cheer; I have overcome the world."

Despite his intentions to the contrary, Josiah continued to read, completing the book of John all the way to the end, then beginning again at the first verse. By the time he reached chapter sixteen once more, the words were swimming through his tears.

CHAPTER 12

Wild waves of emerald green licked the edges of the craft and sent sprays of salty foam across the deck. Lightning snaked across the sky and teased the clouds, turning them from orange to purple. In a few hours, the sun would rise. A few more than that and the southernmost tip of Florida would be in sight, leaving nothing but the Atlantic Ocean and Great Britain ahead once Banks was deposited on dry land.

But first came the matter of navigating the reef. Much less daunting a task than the one he'd just taken to navigate the salvation of his soul.

Josiah sighed. There would be time to contemplate the ongoing wrestling match over his eternal destiny. For now he must concentrate on the challenge ahead.

For so many reasons, it was right to seek help for Banks in Key West. Yet for so many more, it was very wrong.

Florida seas were much like a woman. Surface beauty often sheltered hidden snares, and a man could be none too careful with either.

Josiah knew all too well the danger both held, but at the moment, he set his concentration on only one: the Florida Straits. If the wind held, they'd sail beyond the graveyard for vessels by sundown. If it changed, as the fickle trades were known to do, they'd be hard-pressed to see the sun rise tomorrow aboard the *Jude*.

"It's a fair clip, this breeze, aye, Captain? What are the odds we'll navigate the maze today?"

Casting a glance behind him, Josiah watched Harrigan approach. The first mate eyed him with anticipation of an answer that Josiah knew would not come. He'd keep his concerns to himself and give none cause for concern.

"You know as well as I that a sail through the straits is never safe. You're a praying man, Harrigan, so perhaps you should ask Him."

His first mate chuckled. "Already did, sir. Aye, it's a dandy squall we'll be meeting up ahead," Harrigan said. "Biggest I've seen in many a year this late in the season. We're in for a battle getting this tub through the straits without meeting the wreckers."

Josiah pulled the spyglass to his eye to study the wall of wind and water ahead. No change, though he knew that. Yet he'd hoped.

"Just now in the hold, I saw Miss Gayarre," Harrigan said. "She mentioned a missing Bible. Something about wanting to read stories to the men."

Josiah kept the spyglass resolutely fastened to his eye. In the distance, the black clouds rolled about and the sea boiled and foamed. The scene mirrored the turmoil in his heart last night.

"Perhaps you've seen this missing Bible?"

Slowly, Josiah lowered the spyglass to his side. A nice trap Harrigan had laid, yet a trap could only work if the prey took the bait.

While the *Jude*'s bow plowed on through waves that warned of the upcoming storm, Josiah turned his attention to Harrigan. "How fare the injured, Harrigan?"

Harrigan ducked his head and studied the backs of his hands. "Tended with care by Miss Gayarre."

A bit obvious mentioning the woman again. Josiah frowned. "That job belongs to Cookie."

"She's assisting him still, I believe, sir," he said as he adjusted to meet Josiah's glare, "and doing a fine job of it, I understand. Has the men listening to the Good Book."

Josiah clutched the spyglass. So, Miss Gayarre had continued to go about the business of turning his infirmary into a hospital for lost souls, even without her Bible.

"You know, Harrigan, when the crew took up their manners and left off their cursing, I was pleased. What passes for acceptable amongst men isn't always appropriate for the delicate ears of women and children. But now . . ." He paused to steady himself against the roll of the deck. "Now that she's beginning to turn my men into a passel of preachers, I'm, well, I'm displeased."

"Displeased?"

The amusement in Harrigan's voice touched a nerve. "Aye. *Displeased.* Have you an issue with this?"

"No." He chuckled. "It's just that in days past you might have used a stronger word to describe your feelings on the matter, sir. If I do say so myself, it looks like Isabelle Gayarre has had a positive effect on the *Jude*'s captain as well as on her crew."

Harrigan must have read his expression, for he gave Josiah a most displeased look. "Miss Gayarre is a good woman, and it would behoove you to remember that, sir." He cleared his throat and set his face toward the rising wind. "The *Jude*, she's fit and fine with fresh sails and sturdy timbers. No evidence we brought her out of a fire."

And others save with fear, pulling them out of the fire.

Try as he might, Josiah failed to turn his attention from the woman to the storm. More needed to be said on the subject of Isabelle Gayarre. "So, she's bewitched you, as well, Harrigan?"

"Bewitched?" Harrigan chuckled. "Oh, Miss Gayarre? Hardly, sir. It's the light of the Lord shining through those eyes. That's what makes her so"—he paused, and Josiah met his gaze—"*interesting* is the word, sir."

Josiah swallowed hard. "Take the watch, Harrigan," he said before turning on his heel and making good his escape. "Fetch me in ten minutes. I shall be visiting the sick. They'll need to be told to batten down in anticipation of the coming storm."

"Already done, Captain." Harrigan wore a look Josiah didn't like. To say so would only invite teasing or discussion, and he had little time for either.

"Then I shall inspect the hold to see that your instructions have been carried out."

He found Isabelle in the hold, once more at the side of a sailor, one Francis Rentrain, carpenter's apprentice from Lyon. The man was quite suddenly gravely ill from his burns, Cookie had reported, and the chances of him seeing the end of the voyage were slim. Even a view of the infirmary at Key West seemed unlikely. Lying in his hammock, Rentrain seemed to have one foot on the other side already.

The vessel jolted to leeward, and Josiah braced himself. The stench of the room made him want to flee, but Isabelle seemed not to notice.

Rather than make his presence known, Josiah stood in the shadows and listened while Isabelle asked Francis questions about heaven and his future. The words came straight from the verses he had read last night, Josiah soon realized, but spoken in Isabelle's lilting voice, they seemed to hold more meaning. He heard the man sob and thought perhaps he was done for.

"*Félicitations*, Monsieur Rentrain," the Gayarre woman said. "*Nous verrons l'un et l'autre dans le ciel un jour.*"

"*We will see one another in heaven one day.*"

Josiah's breath froze in his throat. The very thing he'd read about until the wee hours of the morning had happened in his hold. This man, a mere carpenter's apprentice, had accepted the proposition of eternal life as offered in John. A proposition Josiah still held in consideration.

Last night, with the words of the prophet John before him, Josiah felt a tug toward the things of heaven. Today, in the light, he was no longer sure.

No, he could not—would not—become his father, a man certain of his eternal destiny and determined to take everyone else with him by force if necessary. If shunning acceptance of the God of Hezekiah Carter meant missing out on his heavenly reward, so be it.

And others save with fear, pulling them out of the fire.

"No!" Betrayed by his own voice, Josiah stepped from the shadows. "Monsieur Rentrain, how are you feeling today?"

The man was pale beneath his cocoon of blankets and bandages. He said nothing but fixed his eyes on Isabelle Gayarre and smiled. Then, slowly, he drifted off to sleep.

"A word with you, Isabelle."

She seemed not to hear. Rather, Isabelle inclined her ear to the wounded man, then lightly pressed her palm to his chest. A gasp escaped her lips.

"*Mais non.*" She regarded Josiah, eyes wide, then attempted to rise. "The monsieur, he is with Jesus."

"What?" Josiah stepped forward to steady the woman.

"Monsieur Rentrain, God rest his soul." She slipped from his grasp to lift the man's blanket over his head, then fell into Josiah's arms and began to cry.

He held her, unable to muster words of comfort. Instead, he rested his chin on the top of her head, wrapped his arms around her, and asked God to do the job.

"I've never watched a man die, Captain," she said into his shoulder. "I'm sorry."

You'll get used to it, he wanted to tell her. Rather, Josiah remained silent, sparing her the knowledge that all the world was not like her safe and secluded existence in New Orleans.

Isabelle's sobs subsided and became a whimper. Josiah whispered words of comfort against the softness of her hair and, in a moment of insanity, kissed the top of her head. She lifted her face to stare into his eyes, and the lunacy continued.

Moving without volition, Josiah pressed his lips against the wetness of her cheeks, first one then the other. Tasting of the salt of her tears, he softly touched her lips with his.

It was a chaste kiss, as if he had never kissed a woman before this moment. Had he any good sense left, a hasty exit and a vow to avoid Isabelle Gayarre's presence for the rest of the voyage would have been in order.

As he had none, he stood stock-still and held the woman in his arms.

"What's this?" Mr. Banks called from his hammock. "Is the bloke a goner?"

Isabelle broke the embrace to address the older man. "I'm afraid our loss is the Savior's gain, Mr. Banks."

Josiah fisted his shaking hands. Cookie appeared at the opposite passageway and gave him a salute. The best Josiah could do in return was a tilt of his head. To move, to respond to anything other than what had just transpired with the woman took more strength than he had.

Word spread among the sick, whispered through gasping breaths and spoken in strong voices until all seventeen of them knew they'd lost a member of their company. Cookie rapped on the floorboards with his fist, and all went silent.

"What with the storm coming and Apprentice Rentrain's passing, I say we make haste to pray."

Several sailors spoke up in agreement. Others nodded.

"Captain, would ye do the honors?" Mr. Banks asked.

"The honors? Well, I, um . . ."

He caught Isabelle looking at him and clamped his lips shut. *All right, Lord, if You're who You say You are in that Bible, give me the words these men are needing. In case You haven't noticed, there's a storm brewing out there. Would You get us safely to our destination?*

"I suppose I could say a few words," Josiah said.

The captain praying? Yet the captain's speech was beautiful, an eloquent plea to God to carry Monsieur Rentrain across the heavenly threshold and to bring the *Jude* through the storm. When Josiah whispered his amen, tears stood in his eyes.

Isabelle offered him her handkerchief, but the man looked at her hand as if it contained a snake. Tucking the linen square back into her sleeve, Isabelle braced herself against the wall and waited for the ship to right itself.

He kissed you. Isabelle blinked hard as the realization hit her. *And you kissed him back.*

"Return to your cabin, Miss Gayarre," Josiah said. "There's a storm coming, and we'll not be needing to concern ourselves with the women."

Isabelle turned her attention from thoughts of the kiss. "May I fetch young William? Like as not, he'll be afraid."

Josiah paused a moment, then nodded. "First, a word with you."

"Of course."

He moved near, and she flinched. Odd, but this man's presence seemed to bring with it a need to protect herself.

"Miss Gayarre." He spoke her name gently yet with a veiled threat of some unnamed consequence should she not pay proper heed. "I will not have my ship turned into a floating church house and my men into a passel of parsons. Do you understand?"

She looked up into eyes that told her he only half meant what he said. His expression told her not to try his patience; a soft, insistent urge to do so won out.

"No," she said as she stepped past him into the passageway. "I don't understand, Captain Carter. Is it the Bible reading you object to, or the prayer? For unless you were suddenly transported elsewhere and replaced by your twin, you recently entreated the heavenly Father on behalf of dear Monsieur Rentrain."

The captain followed on her heels. "That was

for the deceased, Miss Gayarre, and an entirely different matter."

Isabelle stopped and turned on her heels, and Josiah nearly slammed into her. "I fail to understand two things."

Recovering, Josiah shook his head. "And what two things are those?"

"First, what is the difference between one prayer and another? Each time are we not speaking to the heavenly Father? And second, how can you be so blind, Captain Carter? Did the Lord not work a miracle in snatching you from death in the midst of the fire? Can you not fathom that perhaps God has some use for you yet?"

Josiah opened his mouth but said nothing. He looked away. Either her words had reached their mark or the captain was intent on ignoring her.

A shuffling sound was followed by the appearance of a young man in the corridor. Red-faced, he spared Isabelle a nod before turning to Josiah. "Beggin' the captain's pardon, but Mr. Harrigan has need of ye on deck. Said to tell ye the thing ye suspected has happened."

The boy's look of panic struck a similar feeling in Isabelle's heart. The captain, however, looked nonplussed as he absorbed the news.

He placed his hand on the boy's shoulder and looked into the lad's eyes. "First, help any man who is able out of this hold. Those who cannot move of their own volition must be secured in hammocks," he said in a calm and deliberate voice. "When this is done, go back and tell Mr. Harrigan I'm on my way. Tell him to call all hands to their stations and prepare for battle."

"Aye, Captain," he said on the run.

Josiah turned to Isabelle. "Shall I escort you to your cabin, Miss Gayarre?"

She hid her trembling hands behind her back. "Thank you, Captain, but that won't be necessary. I shall go and warn the ladies of the coming storm. William, too."

He looked, what? Grateful? Surely not. Thus far she'd not managed to do a single thing correctly in his eyes.

"Have you undertaken rough seas before?"

Was he serious? Obviously Mama Dell hadn't found time to inform the captain of the background of his passenger.

She settled for a simple "No," then listened intently as Josiah explained what was to come and how to safely ride out the storm.

"And keep William below decks," he said. "Sometimes he forgets I am the elder brother." He looked away, then returned his gaze to Isabelle. "You're not a fragile woman. I'm uncertain as to whether I could say that of your traveling companions. I feel you must know that this passage through the straits is dangerous at best."

Isabelle managed a nod.

"But now, with the storm atop us and the wind shifting, well, even the most practiced mariner will have only a slim chance of surviving to sail again."

Thankfully, he was kind enough not to remind her that their trek through troubled waters was solely her fault. Had she not entreated for Mr. Banks's care, the *Jude* might be plodding along in deeper and safer waters.

"Then I shall pray for that slim chance." She touched his sleeve. "I don't believe the Lord saved you only to allow you to be taken now."

He cleared his throat and stared at her fingers until she pulled away. "I am not concerned for myself, Miss Gayarre. I am most concerned for the welfare of my crew and passengers. To that end, I must insist you return to your cabin now and prepare the others."

Isabelle turned to follow the passageway to her cabin, and Josiah fell into step beside her. Glancing up at him, she noted he looked a bit nervous.

The hallway tilted, and Isabelle felt a rush of water over her slippers. She paused to get her bearings, then picked up her skirts to jump over the growing puddle.

"One more thing, Isabelle." He caught her elbow and gently pulled her to a stop. "The kiss."

His use of her first name caused the breath to

catch in her throat. "Yes, I understand." She gulped down her fear to focus on the captain. "You acted in the height of emotions, and it won't happen again."

"No," he said slowly, "not exactly." Josiah leaned toward her with a most serious expression. "Actually, Isabelle, it was—"

Wood splintered. A rush of cold water poured between them. Isabelle fell backward, and Josiah slid from her reach. Salt stung her eyes and burnt her tongue as she gasped for breath.

Isabelle went under and blindly grabbed for the first solid thing. It was Josiah.

Both hands around her waist, he slung Isabelle over his shoulder and lifted her out of the water. A moment later, he deposited her on a dry patch of decking.

"Go now. See to my brother," he shouted as he sprinted off in the opposite direction. "Wait. First I ask a promise."

Isabelle turned to see him standing on the opposite side of a small breach in the hull. "Yes?"

"No matter what happens, see to his education, Isabelle," he shouted over the roar of the storm, "and keep him safe from my father!"

CHAPTER 13

Isabelle grasped for something solid to hang on to as the planks beneath her feet sent her reeling, the dim lantern light casting only a small circle of light and leaving shadows all around. She held tight to the edge of a heavy barrel and stared at Josiah Carter. Much as she longed to be of help, to somehow offer service to thank him for not tossing her and the ladies out on their ears, practicality weighed hard.

Still, what power did she, a woman born into slavery, have against any man?

"What you ask is impossible, Captain," she said. "I have no power to care for William or for anyone else, and I certainly cannot keep him from your father should the man require I give him over. It is only by the grace of the mademoiselle that I am released from my own bondage."

Josiah reached her in a moment's time and grasped her hand, anger flashing in eyes that reflected the lantern's glow. "I see."

Her fingers crushed by his grip, Isabelle bit her lip but said nothing. The captain seemed to study her a moment while the storm raged outside. Water flowed into her slippers and dripped from the boards above them to dampen the captain's shirt, but Isabelle refused to look away.

Suddenly, the barrel beside Isabelle rocked, and Josiah steadied it with his free hand, bringing him inches away from her. Above them, the lantern remained steadily fixed to the ceiling joist, its flame dipping only slightly with the jolt.

"You have no power?" Her words, yet when Josiah Carter spoke them, they sounded cruel, mocking. "Look at me," he commanded.

Isabelle complied, a habit born of her training at Mama Dell's knee. *Do as the gentleman bids you, Isabelle.*

But this was no gentleman. A vein throbbed in the captain's temple, and Isabelle settled her gaze upon it.

Finally, he released his grip and took two steps away before whirling about. "You, Mademoiselle Gayarre, are a hypocrite." He leaned close. "Yes. I said you are a hypocrite." Closer still. "Perhaps this God you speak of cares not for His children as the Bible states? Perhaps He does not give the power to those who believe as you stated to those in the sickroom. Perhaps it was all a lie."

Isabelle blinked hard and tried in vain to keep her focus off the captain. His shirt now clung to wet skin, and water dripped from the captain's hair onto his shoulders. The storm raging outside suddenly seemed small and far away.

Cold seeped into her bones and lodged there. "I did not lie to those men nor to you," she

173

finally managed through chattering teeth. "It is the Lord who will save William. With prayer, He can save us all."

A clattering of feet above them told Isabelle that soon they would no longer be alone. The shouts accompanying the approaching men gave her pause to wonder if they were celebrating or sounding the alarm. She gave up a silent prayer for the latter.

Josiah swept the back of his hand across his brow, then shook off the water. "Perhaps if we survive this storm, you and I can discuss at length how He manages such feats. Until then, I will leave the praying and the care of my brother in your hands."

A trio of seamen poured into the room, stomping into water that splashed and splattered, nearly dousing the lantern the largest of the three held. Curses were followed in quick succession by mute silence.

"Mr. Harrigan sent us t' see to the patchin'," the lantern holder said.

The captain pointed to a breach in the hull, and without a word, the man hung the lantern on a hook and set to work. The others followed suit, their eyes averted. Isabelle felt the attention nonetheless.

"Leave us, mademoiselle. Lash yourselves together. William will show you how." Anger fled the captain's face, replaced by a tender expression. "Protect my brother until I can see to him myself, and take him to your home in England should I fail to return to claim him."

Isabelle tried not to think of the implications of his statement. "I shall."

He extended his hand to grasp hers. "Thank you. Now hurry along" was a whisper falling against her ear as he released his grip and brushed past to supervise the trio.

Isabelle complied quickly, struggling against the rocking of the sea to make her way up the stairway. Above her, men shouted, and the wind blew in hard gusts. She should see to the sick, but first she must find William and the ladies.

Into the depths of the vessel, she went, the lamps long ago extinguished to allay any hazard from fire. Her fingers traveled as fast as her feet, tripping across rough boards and slipping over knots and square pegs to reach the corridor leading to the room she shared with the ladies and, of late, the boy.

Dark as night was the path to the stateroom, and calling out proved futile. Finally, Isabelle located the latch and pushed just as the ship darted southward. Falling into the room, she skidded across damp floors to land at someone's feet.

"Isabelle, do take care." Emilie helped her to her feet. "There's an odd layer of seawater in the room. I cannot account for it save perhaps seepage from the window there, but William says it's not a good sign."

Blinking to adjust to the gray light, Isabelle cast about for the boy. She found him huddled with Viola, two sets of eyes peering from above a cloak that Emilie must have laid over them.

Affecting a casual air, Isabelle peered at the boy and forced a smile. "I've just spoken to your brother, and all is well. He wishes us to lash ourselves to one another so as to have a better night's sleep. Might you help me with this, William? Your brother tells me you're mighty clever with knotting a rope."

The boy sprang to action, first locating a coil of rope, then fetching a knife from a trunk lodged beneath the bunk nearest the door. "I keep it hidden just in case," he said as he set to work cutting twine.

Emilie gave him a skeptical look. "Do stop teasing us."

"Not teasing, Miss Emilie." William paused. "A man at sea must always be mindful of pirates."

She nodded. "I see. Well, I certainly feel safe with you aboard, William."

He handed a length of rope to Isabelle. "I reckon we ought to take care of Miss Viola first."

Isabelle stretched the rope to its full length and made her way across the pitching floor to the bunk where Mademoiselle Dumont lay quiet

176

and still. Only her wide eyes moved, blinking furiously as tears streamed over her bruised face.

"All is well," Isabelle said, then felt the fool for having done it. All was most certainly not well, yet even on a storm-tossed sea, she knew the Lord held her.

Still, as lightning crashed and men shouted on the deck above, Isabelle wondered if perhaps God had forgotten for a moment that she belonged to Him.

"Miss Isabelle?"

She shoved her thoughts away and turned to face the boy. "Yes?"

"Someone's going to have to hold the ax since Josiah says I'm still too small to swing it. Will you do that, Miss Isabelle?"

"The ax?"

He dropped the rope and pointed to the chest. "I'll fetch it. A moment later the boy extracted a fierce-looking pickax that nearly toppled him before he could hand it over to Isabelle.

"Of course, I will," she said as she settled the tool onto the end of the bunk at Viola's feet, "but whatever is it for?"

"It's for if we sink." His lip quivered, and Emilie rushed to comfort the boy. Eyes the color of the elder Carter stared up at Isabelle. "Even if we're floating, we'd go down with the ship unless someone cuts a hole for us to escape through."

"Oh, now we don't have to worry about such a thing, do we Isabelle?" Emilie cast a sharp glance over the boy's head. "Remind the boy of just how lovely the weather is in Florida this time of year."

"Florida?" Isabelle shook her head. "I'm not sure I—"

"Yes, dear, remember? Just yesterday Mr. Harrigan mentioned we'd be in Florida waters soon. I'm sure William would be interested in what sort of weather will greet us once we're able to trod the deck again."

"Ah, yes." Isabelle gulped down her fear. "I'll tell you what I recall while you begin tying knots. How's that?"

"Let's all climb into Viola's bunk, shall we?" Emilie said. "It'll be much easier to accomplish the task, and our feet will stay dry."

Emilie climbed in first, cajoling Viola into a sitting position. William scampered up between them and went to work. Isabelle found a spot on the corner of the wildly pitching bunk and held on for dear life, painfully aware she did not belong as equals among these three.

In short order, the boy trussed Viola to himself, then began to work on Emilie's bonds. Isabelle stared at the rope, at the tiny hands working the slender coiled threads into a noose that slipped over the mademoiselle's head and came to rest at her waist.

While Viola continued to stare into space, Emilie and William turned their attention to her.

"Your turn," the boy said. Did his lower lip quiver a bit or was that her imagination?

"Do move closer, Isabelle." Emilie reached behind William to grasp Isabelle's elbow and gently tug. "It appears the ship is holding well, but we mustn't be lax in our watchfulness. Come closer, dear, and allow William to bind you to us with the rope."

Rope.

Shackles.

Inexplicable panic skittered up her backbone and sent Isabelle running for the door and freedom. Her slippers splashed through water that seemed to have inched higher. Still, she plowed forward.

"Where are you going?" This from Emilie, whose voice seemed to hold as much irritation as confusion.

"To see to the sick," she called, wilding crashing into the rough wood of the narrow corridor's walls.

When she reached the sick bay, Cookie was tending to a fellow whose injuries prevented him from being moved. In all, seven hammocks dangled from the ceiling joists and held men who awaited attention.

Isabelle made her way through water that thankfully no longer rushed past, stopping to see to each man. One wanted a prayer while another preferred to tell stories of days past. Isabelle listened until the fellow's words trailed off and sleep overtook him.

At least she hoped it was sleep.

Cookie caught her attention and motioned for her to join him. "This fellow here says he must speak to you. Name's Arnaud, Étienne Arnaud."

Isabelle affected a wide stance in order to remain standing on the rocking boards, then gazed into the face of a young man near to her in age.

She offered him a genuine smile as he told her his name. "*Bonjour*, Monsieur Arnaud."

"The time is short." Heavily lashed eyelids fluttered closed, then opened wide. "You must tell the captain," he said, his voice a hoarse whisper barely heard over the din.

Isabelle leaned closer, ignoring the stench of the dying man. "Tell him what?"

"The boy," he said. "I was sent to follow the boy."

Isabelle leaned away from the hammock. Her gaze found Cookie, who stood nearby openly watching. "What is this he speaks of?"

Cookie moved closer. "I know not, Mademoiselle Gayarre. Perhaps this one was after more than just work on the *Jude*. Other than a few men, none know of the lad's presence. Arnaud was not among those few."

She turned back to the sick man. "Tell me

more," she said in his native French.

"I am no sailor, mademoiselle." He looked past her and licked dry lips. "My employer is Jean Gayarre. 'Tis no small coincidence that you bear his name, eh?"

"Indeed. Have we any water for the gentleman, Cookie?" she called as she gave her attention back to Arnaud.

"Plenty, miss," he said. "Unfortunately it's all underfoot and filled with salt." He moved away to answer the call of a man on the other side of the hold.

She sighed. "Pray tell me, sir, what your association with Monsieur Gayarre has to do with passage aboard the *Jude*."

Eyes closed once more, he appeared lifeless, yet his lips began to move. "The monsieur has friends, powerful friends." He paused to take a ragged breath. "A transaction was detected. A large sum of gold coin. I was hired to find it and report its whereabouts to my employer."

Isabelle's heart slammed against her chest, and her throat threatened to close. "Did you find it aboard the *Jude*?" she finally croaked.

Again the eyes opened. They were blue, she noted. His nod was so slight that Isabelle might have missed it had she not been studying him intently.

"Is it still here?"

"The boy," he said with his dying breath.

Chapter 14

Hezekiah Carter awoke with a start. He sat bolt upright and tugged at the top button of his nightshirt. The constriction gone, he continued to feel as if each breath was precious.

A cold breeze, no doubt the cause of his interrupted sleep, drifted across the bedcovers and caused him to shiver. It took a moment for him to remember where he was.

New Orleans.

The panic returned, a gnawing, grasping fear that belied any faith in his Creator's sovereignty. Carefully measuring his breaths, Hezekiah eased back onto the pillows and closed his eyes lest his wife find him awake.

His wife. She had no idea her only surviving children were careening away from her in a tub that looked barely seaworthy. He'd hoped to wait until the pair—or at least their youngest —had been returned before burdening Mary with the tale.

"Are you unable to rest, husband?"

Rolling to his side, Hezekiah stared into the near darkness until the shadowed form of his wife became visible. "Aye. Forgive me for awakening you."

Her pale hand reached out to grasp his, and for a moment, silence fell between them. "Something is troubling you," she finally said.

How many times had he admonished his parishioners that confession was good for the soul? Perhaps it was time for both of them to heed that advice.

As husband, he must lead by example.

"Josiah has spirited away our William." He paused when he felt his wife's grip tighten. "I had him nearly caught, but now he's gone again. My men tracked the pair to New Orleans, hence our hasty departure for the city."

"I see."

"I regret I am not innocent in the matter."

Silence.

"I shall explain myself," he said.

"Yes." The soft whisper barely reached him. Still, she held tight to his hand.

"It has always been my desire to have a son who would succeed me in the pulpit. In seeking to avoid some of the, well, difficulties of raising our elder son, I thought to keep William close."

A sob tore through the silence.

"Trouble yourself not, Mary," he said. "I've taken steps to—"

"I meant only to avert William from the path his brother took," she said between sobs. "I feared. . . ."

Knowing the answer, Hezekiah yet asked the question. "What did you fear, wife?"

The long silence left him to consider that Mary may have fallen asleep. After a shuddering sob and a shift in position, she removed her hand from his.

"I feared he, too, would hate you."

"So you had your elder son steal him away? Woman, I fail to see how—"

"Yes, husband, once again you've failed to see."

Her vehement response stunned him. Never had his wife spoken so boldly. "Go on."

"William is a bright boy, full of promise, but so was Josiah. I could not face another son's banishment for things that were crimes only in his father's eyes."

Unable to remain prone, Hezekiah rose to light a lamp. Yellow light spilled into the room and filtered through the mosquito netting surrounding the massive bed to glint off his wife's tears. Mary was sitting, arms wrapped around her knees and her nightcap slightly off-kilter.

Hezekiah climbed back into bed and reached to straighten the cap, then drew his wife into his arms. She stiffened but did not protest, giving Hezekiah's heavy heart a greater burden.

If pressed to name the last time he had held his wife in a tender embrace, he could not.

Mary gathered the bed coverings around her as if she felt a sudden chill. "Husband, Josiah did only what I asked of him."

This news, while not completely unexpected, was quite disheartening. His dear Mary, wife of his youth and comfort in his old age, had thought so little of him as to conspire to spirit away his son.

What did you expect? The answer was one he had known for some time but never admitted aloud. To speak of his shortcomings to Mary would go far toward easing her pain and guilt. Hezekiah looked into her eyes, watched a tear roll down her familiar wrinkled cheek, and said nothing.

Anger shot through him, quickly chased by an odd measure of remorse. "I've sent someone after them," he said when the danger of admitting the full truth had passed. "In a few days, I suspect you'll be reunited with your son."

"Rather I be reunited with both sons." Her eyes dared him argue. "Josiah is as much your son as William." She paused. "He certainly has inherited more of your temperament."

The taunt chased him as he extinguished the lamp. "Jean Gayarre's instructions are to return William to me. I left Josiah's fate to his own choosing."

"You sent Jean Gayarre to fetch William?" Her laugh held no humor. "Unless he's reformed, I doubt Monsieur Gayarre could find his way downriver for all the alcohol in him. Pray tell me you didn't send a pathetic drunk after our son."

"Jean Gayarre is none of the things you allege, but no, I did not send him. His son has taken the helm and likely has already accomplished the task of wresting the boy from Josiah's clutches."

His wife clambered from the bed and raced to relight the lamp. The look on her face struck terror into his heart just as the sudden light pained his eyes.

"What sort of foolishness is this? Douse the lamp and come to bed." He turned his back to her and pulled the covers to his chin. "I've no further inclination to discuss the matter. You will be informed when your son returns. Now I bid you good night."

"Hezekiah Carter, have you no idea what you've done?"

Dare she speak thus? Hezekiah decided to ignore his wife's disrespectful tone, attributing it to duress. "Yes, I've set in motion a plan to right a wrong. When our son returns, I shall listen to your opinion of what William's future holds." He paused for effect. "I will, however, make that decision myself, and I'll tolerate no further meddling from you on the issue."

"No, you old fool. You've sent a murderer after an innocent child and a son who sought only to obey the wishes of his mother." She gave him no time to respond. "You don't believe me," she stated. "Ask Delilah. She's been in that family's employ since Andre was in the cradle. She'll attest to it."

The breath went straight out of him, and only with great effort did he speak. "How do you know of—"

"Of Delilah?"

The sharp words he sought became babble when pressed to his tongue. Rather than be thought daft, he pressed his lips together and affected a defiant stance. Carefully, he managed a nod and with further effort whispered, "Yes."

"I'm no fool, Hezekiah Carter. Your mistake was in assuming so." Mary moved closer, her fists clenched. "In all things, for the duration of our marriage I have deferred to you, with the education of William being the sole exception. Dare you to disagree?'

" 'Tis true," he said.

"Even when you banished Josiah, I held my tongue." She moved closer, her eyes narrowing. "I've received letters, as have you, professing admiration for the way you fill your pulpit."

His own fingers fisted. "Speak plain, woman. What are you suggesting?"

Never in all the decades he'd awakened next to Mary Carter had he ever seen such anger cross her lovely features. Even when he had sent Josiah away, she'd remained complacent, dutiful.

"What reaction, *Reverend* Carter, do you think the good people of our church will have once they find their esteemed pastor has been associating with murderers, drunkards, and women of ill repute?"

Hezekiah reached for his trousers and yanked them on. He'd not spend another moment under this roof under these circumstances. "Jesus associated with those people," he said, although he knew the defense to be a weak one.

Mary crossed her arms over her chest.

Odd, but he felt the need to bargain. "I have known Jean Gayarre since childhood. Would you have me walk away from him now?"

Her silence spoke volumes. "You've given this more than a little thought, haven't you, Mary?" His shoulders slumped as defeat sank in.

"I have."

"Then you know I am at your mercy." He paused, hating to ask the question yet knowing the answer. "What is it you would have me do?"

Angry waves tossed the two-masted sloop *Perroquin* as she eased away from the mouth of the river, then cut across the gulf in a southeasterly direction. The scene unfolding outside mirrored what was in Andre Gayarre's heart.

The *Perroquin* might be the fastest ship in the Dumont line, a Baltimore clipper only recently acquired, but her speed was balanced by her spare accommodations. Much care had been taken to see to his comfort, likely at the instruction of a worried Monsieur Dumont.

Threats made by Andre Gayarre were rarely forgotten and always acted upon, a fact the owner of Dumont Shipping had heard. Yet the silks on the bed and crates of provisions in his cabin did little to cause Andre to feel anything but fury at the thought of Viola Dumont and those who had helped her escape.

"And to think I trusted her."

But did he really? Andre took three steps forward, then halted. Did he trust anyone, really?

His sister, perhaps, at least until he discovered she'd been the one who had betrayed him. That wound cut the deepest. Deciding what to do about Emilie would be the most difficult element of his plan.

Viola's fate, he'd already decided.

And the idiot Carter? " 'Tis a sentence worse than death merely to be associated with the Carter name," Andre muttered. "Yet I shall do what I can to relieve him of that association forthwith."

A jolt sent him sprawling. Andre rose, cursing the skills of the fool at the wheel. Though he was more than qualified, he did not take command, preferring to leave such mundane chores to those whose temperament allowed for them. Perhaps he should relieve the dolt who now piloted the *Perroquin*.

No, his disposition was better suited to pacing. And to planning. Barring any trouble with the gale they now plodded through, their trajectory would take them across the Straits of Florida in a few short days. Surely the tub that Carter piloted would be in his sights soon.

A pity he'd nearly had to send the captain of the *Perroquin* to his death before convincing him not to take the coward's route around the storm. Valuable time would have been wasted going around a squall through which they could easily navigate.

In the end, the man had seen the wisdom of Andre's suggestion to plow through and take the shortest course. Like as not, the coward Carter would be limping along at the edges of the weather, losing time with each moment of smooth sailing.

The only concern Andre felt was the possibility the sloop might get ahead of the plodding vessel and miss the criminal entirely. No, he'd not think on it. His was on a mission that would brook no defeat, would make no mistakes.

The *Jude* would be caught. Viola would be his. So would revenge.

Andre scrubbed at his eyes and tried to keep from screaming. The creaking of the wood was destined to drive him mad if he listened to it another minute. It certainly conspired to keep him awake most of the night, and that was before the rain and wind had hit. Odd since he'd made his home aboard seagoing vessels most of his adult life.

He rose and resumed his route around the small cabin that passed for his home aboard the *Perroquin*. Seventeen paces to the north, twelve to the east, seventeen back to the south, and then twelve to the west. The pattern had been repeated since daybreak, although the past hour's trudging had become difficult at best due to the rolling of the deck.

If revenge had a cost, it was the time he spent in this jail cell of a stateroom. Then he thought of Viola Dumont, of the cathedral, and of the wedding that wasn't.

Fury boiled anew. How dared the woman defy him? Before he could exact revenge, he would see that she married him true and proper. Nothing vexed him more than a promise not carried out. And nothing fueled his anger more than a missed opportunity to fill Viola Dumont with a Gayarre heir and a Dumont grandchild.

Sweet would be the revenge, yet something stirred in him at the thought of a new life, a child of mixed Gayarre and Dumont blood. To his relief, the moment passed, and his thoughts cleared.

"A welcome payment for what I shall gain, this imprisonment at sea," he said as he steadied himself against the wall, then returned to his pacing.

The book Father thrust upon him lay buried in the trunk among the clothing and sundries he'd packed himself. Odd the old man would insist he give this book to Emilie and not something more personal. Despite his crusading sister and his father's frequent arguments on the topic of freedom and salvation, the pair had a strange affection that Andre did not share. It was as if he'd been judged to be like his mother, who had deserted the family, and been left to his own devices.

He glanced at the pier glass and caught his reflection glaring back. The fact that a mother he had no memory of could somehow cleave a wedge between father and son seemed at once patently unfair and strangely appropriate. Andre knew as a Gayarre he was born of mother and father, but as a man, he was not like the father who'd contributed to his birth.

No, he was nothing like Jean Gayarre. So, by default, indeed he must be like her.

Whispered stories of his mother often swirled in circles about his nursery like wisps of smoke from a dying fire. Even now, he could recall his nurse and others speaking of a woman who left not one child but two before she'd fully recovered from her confinement. Thus the question that went unspoken except in the back quarters of the Gayarre home was not why she left but why she returned.

Why, after a year away and no contact with

husband and daughter, did Madame Gayarre present herself on the doorstep at Rue Royale, then install her formidable person in the upstairs rooms as if she'd never been away? Why, when presented with the son and heir to the Gayarre fortune, did she wail with great sorrow and leave their home forever, a description that lodged in Andre's heart in childhood and rendered it cold and lifeless?

Andre sighed and commenced his trek across the shorter length of the stateroom. At least he knew his heart was dead and withered. Many men walked about without such valuable self-knowledge.

He needed neither the approval of his father nor the presence of his mother. This was fact. The Gayarre fortune, he did find necessary; thus his father's request would be carried out.

Still, the book and what it might contain taunted him. A moment later, he tore through the contents of the trunk and retrieved the Bible. He carefully lifted the seals from the letters with a penknife and began to read.

A commotion above caught Andre's attention and sent him hurrying up onto the deck. The wind drove sheets of rain toward him as he emerged to find a group of men setting the ship to anchor.

"What are you doing?" he called, but his voice was lost in the roar of the gale.

Then he saw it. The mainmast.

Or rather he saw where it would have been.

The splintered wood lay sprawled across the foredeck under a tangled mast of rigging and sails. Picking his way through the mess, Andre reached the group and pushed his way to the center.

The captain, a wretched skeleton of a man in drenched cap and spectacles, spied Andre and sidled up beside him. "We've got no choice but to anchor her until the storm passes."

The anchor splashed over the rail, chased by the thick, rusted chain like a mongrel after a bone. A moment later, the ship lurched, sending Andre sprawling against the man next to him. Like dominos, they fell, yet despite the wind and waves, the *Perroquin* held fast to her mooring.

Scrambling to his feet, Andre held tight to the rail and watched the sea boil and beat against the ship. He fisted his free hand and shook it toward the heavens.

A jumble of thoughts melted into pure, white-hot rage that blinded him to anything save the rumbling black sky and the pitiful vessel that slipped farther out of his grasp with every second that ticked by.

Halting now with the *Jude* so near to being caught was unthinkable. Someone must pay.

Someone *would* pay.

"I know you're frustrated," the captain called

as he reached the rail. "Like as not, we'll be on our way tomorrow."

Frustrated?

In truth, Andre would have preferred to send the old man flying into the gulf. Rather, he restrained himself in hopes the man's expertise might save his life. Much as he preferred to exact vengeance when vexed, losing the captain would not bode well for a man in a hurry. And he was nothing if not a man in an extreme hurry.

The thoughts that followed were dangerous at best, so Andre tucked them into the place he kept such musings. "How did this happen?" he asked through clenched jaw.

The old man started talking about weather and wood, but as he spoke, the words became angry darts shot into Andre's soul. The only way to stop the darts was to stop the words. And the only way to stop the words was to send the captain into the sea.

So he did.

CHAPTER 15

Was it possible God still heeded his prayers? Swiping at the errant raindrop that dared pelt his face, Josiah kept his gaze on the horizon and pondered the question. Unless he'd gone daft, there seemed to be a lessening of the gale and the slightest glimmer of sunshine to the southwest.

He aimed the vessel in that direction, steering away from the treacherous green waters of the keys. Much as he had hoped to save Banks, the crew and passengers of the *Jude* were not to be sacrificed in the endeavor.

If all went well, he could lay anchor in calmer seas and complete the repairs to her hull, then resume the voyage a few days hence. Thus far, he'd managed to keep the old tub afloat, and if reports were to be believed, the vessel had held together better than expected.

At least the rain had stopped, and the seas had calmed slightly. None were to relax, even he, but there was some measure of comfort in the fact all seemed well at the moment.

"Dare I hope the Lord has heard our prayers, Captain?" Harrigan inched into view and raised the spyglass toward the east. "A pity the reef lies between us and that land over yonder. What I wouldn't give for a good night's sleep on dry land tonight."

"In truth, a good night's sleep anywhere would be a welcome change."

"Then seek it. I'm of the opinion that a captain with no rest is a dangerous man."

Josiah chuckled. "Haven't you heard, Harrigan? I *am* a dangerous man, rest or no rest."

His second in command offered no response to the statement save a discreet raise of one brow. In truth, this man knew full well how dangerous Josiah Carter could be, a fact Josiah was neither proud of nor happy about.

Yet Josiah now concerned himself with reading a Bible and speaking, however tentatively, to God. What amusement his former crews would find in that.

A bolt of lightning zigzagged across the western sky, slicing across gray clouds and shaking his sense of peace. Perhaps the storm was not abating as he'd thought.

There was nothing to be done for it except to see to the safety of the vessel and those aboard. He would stand firm on his course and shake away the foolishness of wishful thinking.

"Have you a report on the repairs, Harrigan?"

"Aye, we're watertight and safe to travel. What seemed to be a nasty gash was a slight scrape." He paused. "The Lord has looked favorably upon us yet again."

The Lord has looked favorably upon us yet again.

Would that he could cling to that belief as tightly as Harrigan. Odd, but he found he truly wished it so.

With that thought bearing down hard on him, Josiah held tight to the wheel until the *Jude* sailed safely away from the outer reaches of the reef and into calmer seas. Despite his better intentions, the question of the Lord's favor continued.

Know that I am God. He'd read those words more than once in the hours he pored over the mademoiselle's text. *Seek and ye shall find.* That, too, had remained in his thoughts. For a third time, the question appeared in his mind.

This time he did not ignore the opportunity to respond. *Do You still hear the pleadings of this miserable sailor, God? Show me, then, if I may be so bold.*

Some might say their reprieve from certain doom was proof enough, but Josiah held out hope that the Lord, if He still cared, would do something more.

Something a bit grander.

Indeed, a miracle on the order of those recorded in Isabelle's Bible would certainly allay any concerns. Josiah looked up to judge the power of the iron gray clouds overhead, then revised his request.

I don't want much. Just show me You care.

A thought occurred, and he smiled. *God, if You're listening, would You redeem this vessel from the devil that seeks to claim it?*

"Captain, a word with you if I might." Isabelle Gayarre rounded the corner and nearly collided with Harrigan.

"Begging your pardon, Mademoiselle Gayarre,"

Harrigan said quickly. "I was just leaving."

"No, you weren't," Josiah called. "I was. Have the men lay anchor. She'll be safe here for tonight."

Harrigan gave him an odd look but said nothing. Rather, he sidestepped into position behind the wheel and barked the order.

While the business of securing the vessel for anchoring went on about them, Josiah met the older man's gaze. "I'll be looking for that good night's sleep, so see to the *Jude* while I rest, eh? Tomorrow, I'll fight the battle of the reef again."

"Aye, Captain." He smiled. "Top of the evening to you both."

Ignoring his second in command, Josiah sighed. A long night and longer day of fighting wind and water had him ready to do no more than find his pillow and seek the solace of sleep. Or perhaps, if his eyes did not fail him, he might open the pages of the Bible once more.

"I've neither the time nor the inclination for lengthy conversation, mademoiselle."

"Nor I." Isabelle fell into step beside him. "But I've news that will not wait."

When he continued to press forward through the throng of men working on deck, she boldly reached for his elbow and halted his progress. "Captain Carter, I beg you to listen. The coin with which I was to pay my passage may yet be aboard the *Jude*."

The captain's attention captured, Isabelle allowed herself to be steered away from the throng. Josiah led her around coils of rope and groups of men, one hand on her elbow. Men called to one another as sails were trimmed and the anchor readied to be dropped overboard.

William had schooled her on the names for each sail and the purpose for each man aboard. Never would she have dreamed that even a vessel such as the *Jude* would require so many men to keep her afloat and headed in the right direction.

His entertaining tales of Josiah Carter's exploits on voyages to exotic ports had filled the time between sleeping and caring for the sick. Seeing the man before her now, Isabelle wondered how much of the stories was true and how much had been cleaned up to make them fit for a young boy's consumption.

Over the days of their voyage, the captain had become much bolder in his questions to her about the Lord. What had transpired in the hold last night during the storm served to remind her that this was not an unintelligent fellow. Rather, his was a sharp mind. And she'd seen many examples of his courage and self-sacrifice for the well-being of his crew. If only she'd known this before she had boarded the vessel. Those who had spoken with Mama Dell about Josiah Carter had called him a dolt and a heathen. They were sorely mistaken.

The captain strode ahead of her, a confident man whose presence parted the way and caused even the vilest of the sailors to pay him tribute. Most backed away in what seemed to be fear, others in obvious respect.

His dark broad coat bore signs he'd worn it through not only this gale but also others. It had certainly been doused by the downpour, then dried upon his back. His white linen shirt had also seen better days, although it looked a sight better than the bloody one she'd pulled from his shoulders some days ago.

A flitting memory of that incident crossed her mind, and she had to blink hard to dislodge it. What had seemed necessity at the moment— seeing to a man whose injuries threatened his ability to command—now took on new meaning. Fingers across bruised and bleeding flesh had worked to bandage and heal, but they still carried the recollection of a touch that under other circumstances might have been more personal.

She curled her fingers into fists and willed away any thought of Josiah Carter in those terms. What sort of madness sent her musings toward such foolishness anyway?

Unable to look at the man directly, she lifted her gaze skyward and promptly caught her foot on something that sent her sprawling in a most undignified manner. Before she could scramble to her feet, a half dozen unwashed bodies came to her assistance. The throng parted as Captain Carter joined their company.

The act of reaching out his hand to her sent the men shuffling back. Josiah's fingers grasped hers and tugged, then to her surprise, he placed his hand at the small of her back and led her away from the obstacle course that was mid-deck.

"You are unharmed."

A statement she dared not dispute, for she did not rise from her fall unscathed. In addition to the damage to her pride, she'd also reveled for a moment in the feel of his hand on hers, the touch of his palm against her back.

Izzy, you are a fool. Stop acting like a brainless twit. This is a man who on most occasions you barely tolerate.

Still, seeing the captain through the eyes of his peers certainly gave her pause to wonder whether she, too, should feel a measure of awe and respect for him. Certainly the breadth of the Virginian's shoulders and the handsomeness of his face were not unpleasant to look upon. Nor did she believe he would always be at odds with the Creator.

No, there were signs he'd become acquainted with God's goodness and, in time, perhaps would join her in knowing His saving grace, as well. When that happened, there would only be one reason for keeping her distance from Josiah Carter, and that was her mixed parentage.

Even that did not have to be known, she reasoned. The thought sent a skittering of something unfamiliar up her spine.

Watch yourself, Izzy. There is always danger in deception, and the Lord's blessing is never to be found there.

She sighed. If the captain were willing to join her in the deception, it would be so easy to pretend they were like any pair.

So easy. And so wrong.

When they were sufficiently alone, Josiah halted. Even then, he scanned the passageway in both directions before turning his attention to her. Their closeness, the position of his body so near hers, brought back memories of their first meeting and, along with it, a strange feeling of butterflies in her stomach.

She placed her hand against the back of her neck and recalled the blunt side of his knife as the cold metal touched her there.

Watch yourself with him, Izzy. The danger now is to your heart, not your neck.

"Tell me how you suddenly have this knowledge, Mademoiselle Gayarre."

He'd reverted to speaking French, making her wonder if he sought to keep even the most casual of listeners from understanding. She related the tale of the dying man, keeping to the same language and pausing several times when commotions on deck warranted the captain's attention.

"So his last words referenced William?" Josiah said when she finished.

"Yes, at least I think he was referring to William. He said 'the boy.' "

Even in the shadowed light, she could see the troubled expression on the captain's face. "I cannot fathom what my brother would be doing associating with anyone aboard. He was commanded to keep to himself, and Harrigan knew I had no desire for my brother to mix with others. Too much danger in that."

Isabelle nodded.

Josiah moved close, balancing easily on the rocking deck. She, however, needed one hand to be pressing against the rough wood of the passageway's wall to keep her feet under her.

"Tell me again exactly who this man was and what he said."

She did, then waited for him to digest the facts. It was an odd statement, she knew, and nothing so far could explain it.

He scrubbed his hand over his face, then shook his head. "I cannot fathom the connection."

Isabelle shrugged. "Nor can I. William has said nothing of venturing forth from his quarters save to visit the mademoiselles and me."

A look crossed the captain's face, and one

corner of his lips turned up in a smile. He took two steps back, then returned to his spot before her and laughed out loud.

"Of course." His fingers encircled her wrist as he tugged her along behind him. "I've an idea where it might be."

"You do?" She followed the question with a yelp of pain when her elbow crashed against the wall. "Do slow down, Captain," she called.

When they turned the corner, Josiah paused and released his grip. Weak light filtered through the passageway and illuminated their path. Somehow, they'd circled about and were standing before the entrance to the captain's quarters.

Josiah threw open the door and stormed inside, leaving Isabelle to decide whether to enter or flee. "Come in and close the door," he commanded. "This business is private."

Heat flooded her cheeks as she complied. What sort of gentleman would speak thus to a lady?

Yet she was no lady.

As if he'd heard her thoughts, Josiah whirled around and stood facing her. "I trust you understand I have not lured you to my quarters to compromise your reputation, Isabelle."

Having seen his anger, she decided to try and spark his humor. "A pity, Monsieur Carter," she said. "You disappoint me."

The captain's odd look told her the joke had

fallen flat. Or rather had been mistaken as something altogether different that jesting.

"It was a joke." While she waited for a response, Isabelle stared past the captain to study the sparse quarters. Topped by a multicolored quilt in a log cabin design, the bunk was neatly made, and the single porthole was now clear enough so she could see the iron gray sky and whitecapped waves off the aft deck.

Her gaze moved to the floor, where a few odd feathers decorated the corner nearest the bunk. The sleeping spot held no pillows but rather something looking very much like a folded over-coat in their place, leaving Isabelle to wonder as to the provenance of the feathers.

She clutched the back of the lone chair in the room and watched as the captain lifted a sea chest as if it were a child's toy. Setting it atop the table, he threw open the lid and peered inside. A moment later, he began pitching out child-sized clothing by the handfuls until the floor was littered with it. Finally, he upended the trunk and sent it crashing to the floor.

The scene, vaguely reminiscent of her first hours aboard the *Jude*, made her shiver. To her surprise, the captain snatched a quilt from his bunk and tossed it to her.

"What's this for?"

He retrieved the trunk and sat it on the bunk. "You shivered," he said simply. "Now come and help me. I've an idea, but it will take two."

She moved slowly across the floor, the quilt draped over her arm. "Thank you, but it is not necessary," she said as she folded it over the end of the bed, then quickly stepped back.

Josiah studied her a moment before returning to consider the interior of the trunk. "Suit yourself." He reached inside and gave something a yank, then mumbled under his breath. "Isabelle, I'm in need of assistance."

Inching forward, she leaned over and looked into the trunk. A corner of the bottom had come loose, but Josiah was having trouble pulling it up any farther.

He gestured to the wall where several shelves were enclosed behind slats of wood. "See that mallet and chisel over there?"

Several items that could possibly be called tools decorated the shelves. The prettiest of the group was a lovely brass thing with a point on one end. It was definitely a tool, but whether it could be termed a mallet or a chisel she could not say. She reached for it, then contemplated what else to pick.

Kneeling, Isabelle spied the top of what looked to be a beautifully carved box. Upon closer inspection, she found the carving was actually a lovely painting of robed figures on a bridge done up in black and brown lacquer and burnished with gold.

Setting the brass object aside, she pulled the box off the shelf. It was heavier than she expected, and the weight of it combined with the rolling motion of the vessel sent her to the floor with a thud.

This was no mallet or chisel, she knew, but perhaps, she reasoned, it held one inside. Glancing over her shoulder, Isabelle could see that Josiah was still busying himself with tugging on the trunk's interior.

Isabelle smiled as a thought occurred. Perhaps it held the gold Josiah now sought. What a lovely surprise that would make for a man now uttering the oddest grunting noises.

She lifted the lid, oh, so slowly, to reveal a silk-lined top. The interior of the box was lined in dark wood and accented with what appeared to be ivory. Compartments were sectioned off, each holding some sort of exotic ivory object. She picked up one, an exquisite orb with a flat bottom and a top that came to a fanciful point. Leaves and swirls banded the center of the curious treasure, one of three exactly alike.

"Never mind, Isabelle. I've almost loosened this completely, and there seems to be nothing hidden beneath it." He paused. "What have you found?"

She jumped at the sound of his voice, and the orb went rolling away. "Oh, I don't know, but it's escaping me."

Setting the box aside, she dove for the ivory object before it disappeared beneath the shelf. Too late, she nonetheless slipped her fingers into the smallish space. The effort only succeeded in pushing the orb further away.

"Oh, no." Isabelle reached further past her knees, and again the aggravating thing slipped just out of her grasp.

"Isabelle?"

"I'm terribly sorry." She leaned forward to rest her ear against the floor and spied the ivory orb. "There it is," Isabelle said as she strained to press her fingers farther into the space.

A pair of boots stopped just shy of her nose. Isabelle looked up to see Josiah Carter towering over her. Gradually, she became aware of how she must look from his vantage point. For her ear to brush the ground and her ankles to remain covered, she had counterbalanced herself by . . .

Isabelle froze. If only she hadn't refused Josiah's quilt, she might have thrown it over her head and hidden. The only way out of the embarrassing position was to sit back onto the part of her that was now slightly elevated but thankfully covered.

Worse, her hand seemed to be stuck. In order to flatten herself completely to the floor, she would have to risk her skirt remaining put while her legs scooted. That would expose far too much ankle and possibly her calves, as well.

In all her years learning manners and deportment, Mama Dell had never instructed Isabelle about how to extricate herself from this sort of situation. Then again, there was little doubt Mama Dell never considered her star pupil might be caught in such a state.

CHAPTER 16

Entranced, Josiah stared at the woman, who lay prone on his floor. Well, not exactly prone. He cleared his throat, turned his back, then peered with care over his right shoulder.

"Mademoiselle Gayarre?"

Isabelle did not answer. Rather, she turned her head, presenting him with a rather mussed-up braid that had begun to come uncoiled.

"Begging your pardon, Isabelle," he said while struggling to keep from laughing, "but I believe I sent you to fetch a mallet and chisel. Did you find either?"

A muffled "No" drifted toward him.

"Pray tell me, then, are you seeking them beneath the shelf?"

He stepped over Isabelle to retrieve the lacquered Chinese sewing box. He'd fetched it all the way from the Orient thinking to have a brief visit with his mother before secreting William away. Now he stared at it rather than at the woman still motionless on the floor.

"The orb has rolled underneath," she finally said.

"I'm sure it will roll out of its own accord once the seas are sufficiently rough." He placed the box on the bunk. "I have my back to you, Isabelle, and I shall not turn until I have your permission. Do stand, please."

A rustling sound was her only response.

He studied the wall a moment longer, then cleared his throat. "Isabelle, have you accomplished the task?"

"I fear . . . I . . . cannot," she said.

"You fear you cannot?" Josiah took a deep breath and let it out slowly. "Woman, I've given my word that my back is turned. Is this not sufficient?"

"You misunderstand." More shuffling. "I would stand if I could, but I cannot."

The vessel pitched, and Josiah braced himself until all was right again. "Are you asking for my help?"

"No. It wouldn't be proper to see me thus."

Anther pitch of the deck, and this time he went tumbling. The sewing box landed with a crash, and so did Josiah.

Only the cause for the rough seas worried him more than the fact Isabelle had neither moved nor spoken. Surely the weather hadn't overtaken them so quickly. By his calculations, the storm had been moving to the west away from the *Jude*.

Josiah would see to that situation once he saw to Isabelle. He glanced over his shoulder, and, keeping care to look at the shelf and the pale arm disappearing beneath it, he crawled toward her.

"I fear I am well and truly stuck."

An idea occurred. It appeared the rocking of the vessel had shifted the position of the heavy furniture a few inches off kilter. "Perhaps there's a solution. If I were to put my weight against the shelf, then perhaps—"

"No," she said. "You cannot."

"There's nothing for it, then," he said. "I'll have to fetch a half-dozen or so strong sailors to help me."

He was teasing, of course, but the jest worked as he suspected. "I'll listen to your suggestion, Captain," she said meekly. "But I have one requirement."

"And that is?"

"Close your eyes."

He might have argued had the watch bell not rung. "Aye," he said as he climbed to his feet, "now let's get on with it." Moving into position in front of the shelf, he leaned his shoulder into the boards securing the shelf and pressed against them.

Isabelle managed to extricate her arm from beneath the bookshelf, her fingers still wrapped around the ivory thread barrel. "Thank you," she said as she skittered into a sitting position and covered her ankles with her skirt. She thrust the thread barrel toward him. "This belongs in the box."

Josiah cast around for the whereabouts of the sewing box and found it had slid into the corner beside the bunk. The silk-lined drawer had come loose, its contents now visible.

He blinked lest his eyes deceived him. Where once it held swatches of fabrics and pieces of trim, the drawer was now filled nearly to the top with gold coins.

"But how?" he whispered as he sank to his knees and lifted a handful of coins, then let them filter through his fingers. "When I purchased the box, it held sewing supplies. I warrant there was no gold within." He poured the money onto his bunk and began to count.

"Yet there it is." Isabelle smiled. "Perhaps the Lord wishes you to redeem this vessel from the devil who seeks to claim it."

Exactly the amount of gold coin he'd required of the mysterious I. M. Gayarre as passage to England. So the mystery was solved, or at least part of it.

Isabelle's words caught his attention. "What did you say?"

When she repeated them, he set the box aside. Why did the statement seem so familiar? *Because you made it first in your plea to God.*

213

Josiah found it difficult to speak. He rested his head on his fists and felt the floor rolling beneath him. While the seas were certainly tossing them about, the real battle, it seemed, was in his heart.

Dared he believe in the same God of his father, the God that Hezekiah Carter claimed would smite him should he dare to lift his countenance heavenward?

Something touched his shoulder, and for a moment he entertained the thought that perhaps the Lord had sent some angelic messenger to explain things for Him. He opened his eyes and saw Isabelle had closed the distance between them.

He did not deserve the grace she'd given him, the forgiveness obviously offered without reason. Despite the fact that he'd taunted her with a weapon, berated her, and behaved like a spoiled child in her presence, she still comforted him.

There was no logic to it. Yet after poring over the pages of her Bible, he understood.

But whosoever shall smite thee on thy right cheek, turn to him the other also.

Her hair had come unpinned, and she toyed with the repair of it with her free hand. It was all Josiah could do not to reach out and wrap a curling tendril around his finger. To lift the honey-colored strand to his lips.

Eyes as green as the Florida seas he would

soon master looked up into his. *Such an innocent, this one, and yet so wise.*

She removed her hand from his shoulder. Josiah captured it, laced his fingers with hers, and held it to his chest. To his surprise, she allowed the intimate gesture.

Josiah cleared his throat. "I must ask your forgiveness for my behavior at the outset of this voyage. I made accusations." He winced at the memory. "Suffice it to say I was wrong in many ways."

Isabelle's fingers tightened inside his. "There is no need to discuss this further. It is finished."

It is finished. The same words the Savior uttered. How strange he would continue to think of the Bible now. Yet the words he'd read kept bubbling to the surface as if they were part of something deep inside that only now could be felt and heard.

"You were robbed," he heard himself say, his voice husky and near to failing, "just as you claimed."

The deck rolled, and he slid sideways, crashing against the wall in a most undignified manner. Isabelle slid along with him, their fingers still entwined.

Josiah released his grip to gather her into an embrace. "Have I hurt you?"

She looked up, and her lower lip quivered. "No," came out as a soft whisper.

How he longed to kiss away that quiver. To seek her lips now would be a disaster, for his was a world where a woman's love was a liability.

Love? Was he daft? Men like him sought solace for a time, then sailed off to another port, another woman until time erased all the faces and names and left only an empty void with nothing to fill it.

Something stirred inside him, something foreign in nature yet deeply familiar.

"I will seek an answer as to how the funds came to be placed in this box. I will also exact redress for anyone involved."

Isabelle studied her slippers, which peeked out beneath her skirt. As he watched, she drew her knees to her chest, making sure to adjust the ample fabric to continue full coverage of her limbs. Wrapping her arms around her knees, Isabelle finally glanced in his direction. "Thank you," was her soft reply.

She felt this foreign stirring, too; he knew it, although he knew not how he came to the knowledge. The question before him was whether another had already claimed this sea siren.

"Isabelle?"

Green eyes blinked. "Yes?"

He paused to choose the proper words. "Is there someone waiting for you in England?"

"The mademoiselle has distant relatives," she said, "although I am uncertain as to whether

I will make their acquaintance. She did send letters of introduction, but . . ." Color flooded her cheeks. "I am babbling."

"Yes," he said with a chuckle. "One further question."

Isabelle nodded, and several of the curls she'd pinned up fell. "I shall attempt to keep the answer brief."

"Aye." He allowed his hand to touch the tendril of hair now, beyond caring about the propriety of it. When she met his gaze, he stated his question. "Is there someone waiting for you, someone to whom you have been promised?"

A shadow crossed her pretty features, and she seemed to be grappling for an answer. Just when Josiah thought she might crush him with her answer, she responded.

"There is no one I love."

He watched her face for signs of protest or discomfort as he wrapped the curl around his finger. When his palm touched the back of her neck, her eyes closed. There was nothing left to do but kiss her, so he did.

"As the lily among thorns," he whispered a moment later.

Her eyes flew open. "You've been reading my Bible."

"Aye, although 'tis not my first time to find solace in its pages." He paused to gauge her reaction. "Are you surprised?"

"Truthfully?"

Her smile was radiant, so much so that he could only kiss her again. His lunacy complete, Josiah nodded.

"I was told you were an infidel."

"Is that so?" Josiah leaned his head against the chamber's wall and gathered Isabelle to him. "And who told you this?"

She stiffened in his grasp. "This I prefer not to say."

Josiah chuckled. "A woman of mystery, I see. Perhaps I can cajole the information from you. I am, after all, captain of this vessel. I can have you thrown in the brig until your tongue is loosened."

Isabelle joined him in laughter. "There is no brig aboard this vessel."

"You've been talking to my brother."

"I have." She settled back against him. "He's an intelligent fellow, your brother."

"Aye. Yet he is not the object of our discussion, Isabelle."

She gave him an innocent look. "I must plead ignorance, then. Pray tell who the object of our discussion might be, Captain."

The vessel shuddered, and wood creaked, a sound that in a more familiar ship might not cause concern. The *Jude*, however, was yet untried and thus a source of mystery.

Much as he could wile away the hours thus,

Josiah knew the conversation must soon end. "I would return briefly to an earlier statement you made, Isabelle," he said, affecting an air, he hoped, of casual indifference.

"Oh?"

She shifted positions and studied her fingers until he touched her chin and directed her gaze toward him. "When asked if you were promised to anyone, you did not answer directly."

Guile was not her natural friend, yet Isabelle could practice it when she wanted. This much became quickly obvious. "Did I not?"

"You did not." His hand moved from her chin to caress her jaw. "I would have an answer."

Her throat bobbed as she swallowed hard. She either liked him very much or disliked him solidly. Either was possible, but only one did he hope for.

"What concern is it to you?"

How much more to declare? With the kiss, he'd already dangled his toes in the dangerous waters of love and affection. Dared he jump in full away?

"You are promised to one you do not love."

The statement was out. Now all that he could do was pray she refute it.

Isabelle turned her face to hide her expression in his palm. A moment later, he felt the first tear. "Yes."

Twin emotions of jealousy and rage filled him.

Jealousy over whatever passions she had shared with the unnamed man and rage that he would never deserve such a treasure.

Neither of them would.

Three words escaped his clenched jaw. "Who is he?"

The watch bell rang, and voices called from the deck above. He should to go his men, see to whatever situation was unfolding.

Yet here he sat, a hopeless sot in the throes of a love that would remain unrequited. He was, in short, a piteous fool.

"I am not who you think I am, Josiah." Her eyes downcast, she looked away. "I am only who I pretend to be."

What sort of statement was that?

To his surprise, she shifted position to rise up on her knees, bringing her at eye level with him. A new expression, one of determination or perhaps resignation, touched her delicate features.

The vessel shuddered once more, and Isabelle tumbled forward. Josiah caught her waist and held her at arm's length.

"Who is he?"

"Did you not hear me? I am not who you think I am." She grasped his shoulders and held on tight. "I was not born to the manor like you."

"Born to the manor?" His chuckle held no humor. "Born to the parsonage is more like it. Although it was a fine and elegant parsonage despite the fire and brimstone that was bandied about, I will admit that."

"Yes, I am sure it was." Her sarcasm was impossible to miss. "As was my gilded prison, although I assure you no fire and brimstone was ever preached within the confines of its silk-covered walls."

"You were held prisoner? Isabelle, I will have an explanation, and I will brook no merriment or folly. Give me the full truth."

She seemed to consider his command for a moment. "Know you the term *plaçage*?"

"I do." Realization dawned. "Isabelle, are you?"

"A *placee*? Yes, I am, or rather I was sold as one but made my escape courtesy of the *Jude* before my protector could seal the bargain."

"That would make you—"

"An octoroon." She stated the word with no distaste, only polite dispassion. "My mother, I am to understand, was a quadroon. A slave kept not to work the fields or polish the silver, but for her owner's comfort. She captured many hearts with her beauty, but she belonged to only one. I belong to him, as well. My mother should have been considered a free woman of color, but he would not allow it because he feared he might lose her. At least, that is what Mama Dell says." She shrugged. "Because my father could not bear to lose my mother, I was born a slave. The great irony is that he's lost both of us now."

The air went out of him and, for a moment, Josiah was unable to speak. What she stated with such ease should have changed everything.

It should have, but it did not.

CHAPTER 17

When he could force the words from their lodging place in his throat, Josiah gave voice to the only remaining question. "Who are these men, the ones who have bought and sold you like livestock? I will have their names and their heads."

"No." Isabelle's defiance startled him. Should someone offer him a measure of revenge against those who wronged him, Josiah knew he would have answered with a resounding yes.

At least it seemed the logical answer.

Again the vessel shifted and rolled. This time the watch bell sounded with greater urgency. Time was short. He must go. Yet . . .

"Isabelle," he said firmly, "I would have you kiss me again."

From her expression, he could see the change of subject confused her. "But I am—"

"A sea siren who has enchanted me beyond all understanding? Perhaps." He paused to smile. "But I prefer to think of you as a lovely woman whom God may have gifted me with. Now before I must see to my duties as captain, I will require an answer. The kiss, Isabelle? What say you?"

The change in her expression was swift. "You're asking permission *now?*"

"No," he said softly. "Consider it more of a warning."

This time when their lips met, it held the promise of a sweet beginning, a hope perhaps that the Lord would bestow on both of them the chance to find love regardless of the strictures of society.

After all, what was not immediately visible need not become known. Why, his hair was darker than hers by many degrees, and the skin on his arms grew much browner after he'd spent a few months at sea.

It was a conversation they must have, but not now.

Again the watch bell rang, leaving Josiah no time to tarry. "Duty calls, but I will continue this conversation once the storm has passed, and I will have those names. Are you injured from your battle with the bookshelf?"

Isabelle shook her head. "Nothing but my pride has been damaged," she said. "And it will heal, I am certain."

"Very well then." He surveyed the room and noted William's trunk. Tomorrow in Key West, he must purchase another. It wouldn't do for the lad to arrive at school and be thought less of.

In the meantime, he must find a hiding place for the coins. The trunk was no spot for secrets, nor was the sewing kit any longer. Should the dying sailor not be the only man who was involved in the heist—for this was obviously the same gold Isabelle brought aboard—then others were most likely bent on retrieving it.

The vessel gave a shudder, and Josiah took note. Theirs was no longer the safe harbor he'd predicted.

He dumped the coins back into the sewing box and set it in its place on the shelf, then secured the items with the safety boards. Later he would find a better hiding spot. At present, he had no more time to consider it.

"Have Cookie see to your arm, Isabelle. There may be damage that is not seen on first inspection." He moved to take her hand in his, turning it over to see a bluish bruise already staining her flesh. "There, it is as I predicted. Now heed my warning and take care. With the gale obviously changing course, I will need all passengers fit and healthy."

She pulled away to rub her wrist. "A compromise, Captain. I will see to the sick and, should Cookie be available, let him also see to me. Would that suffice?"

With a hasty nod, Josiah sprinted out the door. What he saw when he reached the deck stopped him in his tracks. Where once orderly discipline reigned, now the men seemed to race about as if no one was in charge. Once they caught sight of Josiah, they slowed their paces but still wore stunned expressions.

Josiah found his place at the wheel and nudged Harrigan aside. "A word with you, Mr. Harrigan," he said. "I see nothing to indicate an emergency."

His second in command had gone pale. "The report is not good, Captain," he said grimly. "The repair of the breach in the hull has not held, and we are taking on water."

"There's nothing to do but race for shore," Josiah said. "Give the order to lift anchor and unfurl the sails."

Harrigan shook his head. "We're doomed if we try to navigate the reef under such conditions."

"Yet we cannot sit and wait for the *Jude* to go under," Josiah countered. "Lift anchor and head for Key West. It is our only chance."

"Aye, Captain," Harrigan said.

As Josiah watched the old man shout orders to the crew, he had the chilling notion that until now he had never seen Harrigan afraid.

Redeem this vessel from the devil that seeks to claim it.

Josiah tightened his grip on the wheel and braced himself for the moment the mainsail would raise. Indeed, the gold coin that had been hiding in his cabin all along was an answer to this prayer. The subsequent storm, however, seemed to negate any thought that prayer might have saved them.

For now, salvation seemed to lie in the skill of the captain and the seaworthiness of the vessel. Fearing neither was sufficient, Josiah pondered the solution.

The sails caught wind, and the *Jude* jerked in response. While Josiah calculated the course, Harrigan reappeared on the deck. "It is as you ordered, Captain," he said, his wrinkled face flushed with the effort. "Every man not needed on deck is stationed below to see to the breach in the hull. I've also taken the liberty of seeing to the ladies and young William. Mademoiselle Gayarre was below with Cookie when last I left her."

Mademoiselle Gayarre. Were he to allow himself, Josiah knew he could easily step away from his command to seek the sea siren's company. All the more reason to sort out things once the vessel was safely to port.

"Well done," Josiah said. "Now, I've one more command. More of a request, actually."

Harrigan gave him a sideways look. "What is that?"

"Pray, old friend, and enlist those aboard who are willing to do the same."

He grinned. "Will you be joining us?

Josiah turned his face to the wind. "Aye, Harrigan, I believe I will."

"Will you now?" The aged sailor moved into his line of sight. "And would this be a prayer of dependence or desperation?"

" 'Tis both, I reckon."

Isabelle prayed aloud as she made her way into the depths of the ship where the ill waited on hammocks. Oddly, it was quiet down here, deathly quiet.

She cringed at the thought.

Already the bunk where the green-eyed sailor had slept was gone, no doubt folded up and put away in the rafters with the other bedding. She found Cookie tending to the sick.

"Welcome back, lass," he said. "Are ye ill or here to help?"

"I promised the captain I would allow you to see to a slight injury I've recently acquired. Then I mean to check on Mr. Banks. How does he fare, by the way?"

In short order, the cook pronounced her fore-arm fit but temporarily bruised, then sent her to the far recesses of the chamber where Mr. Banks lay still and silent. She approached on tiptoe, then realized the silliness of the gesture. Like as not Mr. Banks would not hear her should she plod forth wearing the captain's heavy boots.

He surprised her by opening his eyes as she

peered into the hammock. "You come to pester me again?"

Isabelle giggled. "I did."

"I should run you off, but I'm not of a mind at the moment," he said. "So instead I'll bid you top o' the . . . er . . . what is it?"

The old man's face had gone nearly as gray as his hair, and his brow felt feverish. As the hammock rocked with the vessel, she saw him grimace in pain.

She reached to steady herself. "I beg your pardon? Oh, it's near to midafternoon."

Mr. Banks drew a ragged breath. "Then top o' the midafternoon to ye, Miss Isabelle."

"Are you in pain?" She spied a bucket and fetched it, then tore a strip from her petticoat to use as a mop for his brow. "Here, I've brought water. Do you wish to drink first, or should I bathe your face?"

He grasped her arm by the wrist with a surprisingly strong grip. " 'For whosoever shall give you a cup of water to drink in my name, because ye belong to Christ, verily I say unto you, he shall not lose his reward.' "

Isabelle smiled. "Why, Mr. Banks, you've surprised me."

His free hand reached beneath the blanket to produce a book. A worn black Bible. "Mr. Harrigan brought this to me." His chuckle turned into a rasping cough that seemed to take forever to end. "I suppose old Harrigan figured I had more need of it than he," he finally said, "what with me a considerable measure closer to death's door than he."

"Now, now," she managed, unwilling to admit the truth of the old codger's statement.

"No need to humor me," he said. "And I do wish you hadn't ruined a petticoat just to mop my ugly mug."

She dunked the cloth into the bucket, then let the cool water soak the fabric until it dripped. "I'll not respond to such drivel," she said lightly. "Now open up and drink."

Mr. Banks complied, even allowing her to cradle his head while the water dripped off the cloth onto his tongue. As she held him upright, she could feel the fever, could smell the rot of his wounds, and her heart broke.

Don't you dare cry, Izzy. The dear man would be furious with you.

Isabelle distracted herself by reaching for the lantern and moving it to a hook nearer the hammock. "Would you like me to read?"

She reached for the Bible, but he yanked it away. "No."

"I'm sorry," she said as she laced her fingers behind her back. "I didn't mean to—"

"Hush now. I've got something to say. I'm old, so I'll forget if you keep up your talking."

The return of the crusty old soul made her

smile, but she hid the expression behind her hand. "Of course," she said. "Do forgive me."

He nodded. "The Lord and me spend a lot of time together down here. I've not much choice since those other fellows aren't good company at all."

Isabelle looked around at the hammocks, now numbering only four. In all but one she could hear snoring. She hated to consider why the fourth was so quiet.

"Is that so?" she said as she returned her attention to Mr. Banks.

The vessel rocked and creaked, sending Isabelle reeling back to slam against the wall. When she recovered and returned to the hammock, Mr. Banks seemed not to have noticed her absence. She, however, took great note of the headache beginning at the back of her skull.

Mr. Banks peered up at her through watery eyes, a serious look on his face. "I've decided the Lord is either daft or very forgiving."

The statement would have bordered on blasphemy had it come from anyone other than Mr. Banks. Isabelle held her peace and let him continue.

" 'Tisn't true. I know He's not daft, but there's just no good reason for Him to take notice of an old fool like me." A fit of coughing delayed him for only a moment.

Isabelle set the bucket down and folded the

cloth to rest against his forehead. Despite the cool temperatures above decks, the air inside was stifling. In addition, the stench in the small space had grown, and so had the noises from the deck above.

Someone had taken to ringing a bell with frightening regularity. Not being completely ignorant of the ways of seamen, Isabelle deduced this was not a good sign at all.

Mr. Banks had taken note, as well, and looked concerned. She grappled to think of something to say that might distract him. Then she caught sight of the Bible still clutched in his hand.

"So, are there any other verses inside that brilliant brain of yours, Mr. Banks?" she asked with as much cheer as she could manage despite the throbbing in her head.

"Oh, I don't know 'bout all that." He heaved a long sigh. "I just remember what comes to me. Sometimes it's in the Good Book, and other times I wake up with it in my mouth and I just have to spit it out."

Her chuckle was genuine. "What an interesting way to state things."

"Aye, but being new to this, I wouldn't know interesting from not, would I?" He arched his gray brows. "I'm a mite bothered by what I keep hearing lately, though."

"Oh?"

"Aye. I'm of a mind to tell you something I

read in the book of Luke." His eyes widened. "I skimmed it at first, but the words wouldn't leave me alone. Considering I don't believe I'm the messenger of anything but bad news, this has got me worried a mite."

"Oh, that's not true at all. You've always been quite kind to me," she said quickly.

"You're a sweet girl, Isabelle," he said. "But I know who and what I am, and for most of my life it's not been anything I'm proud of."

The dreaded bell rang again, and the ship lurched hard to the right just as the awful thing stopped its clanging. Isabelle fell back against the wall once more, but this time she managed to catch herself and keep from banging her head.

The hammock where Mr. Banks lay swung wildly for a moment, then slowed. When it stopped altogether, Isabelle removed the cloth and dipped it into the bucket, then reapplied it to his forehead. Before she could remove her hand, the old man's fingers encircled her wrist.

For a man whose life was at its end, Mr. Banks certainly had the strength of a person in much better health. Rather than ask, she waited to see what was on his mind.

As his grip tightened, the vessel shuddered beneath her feet. A sound much like a scream rose from somewhere above them. Isabelle put on a smile and willed it to stay thus.

"From the book of Luke, Isabelle, chapter 8," he said. "Wish I could remember how it went."

"Worry not. The words will come to you just when you have need of them."

Isabelle placed her hand over the old sailor's fingers and held on tight as she felt dampness soak the soles of her slippers. In a split second, the dampness became a trickle of water that teased at her ankles and soaked the hem of her skirt.

"Mr. Banks," she said with what she hoped would be a casual tone, "have you the ability to walk if need be?"

"Haven't tried it since we left the docks." He looked past her to where Cookie now helped a sailor climb from the hammock. "Looks like I need to make the effort, don't it?"

Suddenly the water lapped at her knees. The time had come to decide how best to remove Mr. Banks to a higher deck.

"Cookie," he called.

The cook paused in his efforts to drag the sailor away toward the passageway. "Aye. What is it, Banks?"

Rather than respond, Mr. Banks turned to stare at Isabelle. "Wait. I got the words."

Above them, the sound of men shouting had become almost unbearable. She glanced toward the passageway.

"You do?"

"Aye." He closed his eyes. " 'But as they sailed he fell asleep: and there came down a storm of wind on the lake; and they were filled with water, and were in jeopardy.' "

Then came the deafening sound of wood scraping something equally immovable. The wood where only minutes ago she'd banged her head now splintered, and a wall of water poured toward them. In a matter of seconds, the hammocks were hidden beneath the raging sea.

Isabelle bobbed to the surface, still holding tight to the old sailor.

Only a few feet away, a beam fell and took a wall of barrels with it, blocking them from reaching the passageway.

Their only hope was to find a way out of the vessel. "I'm going to get us out," she said, "but you've got to help. Can you swim?"

He didn't respond, so she made the decision for him as the water inched ever higher. Using the beam to propel them, Isabelle held tight to Mr. Banks and shoved him toward the opening. She made to follow, then, with the last of her breath gone, succumbed to the blackness.

CHAPTER 18

"I'll not leave my post." Josiah held his ground against the insistent pleas of those sent to rescue them and claim whatever goods they might haul. "Not until all hands are accounted for."

While the *Jude* slammed against the unforgiving coral of the reef, the wreckers, as they were known, worked quickly to remove the ladies from their cabin below and spirit them away aboard the first of several skiffs. William came next, and to his credit, he showed no fear as he walked across the tilting deck, the wind and rain pelting him.

Josiah knelt to embrace the boy, then pushed wet hair away from his forehead. "I'll need you to be the man in my absence," he said.

William nodded. "You'll be coming along soon, won't you, Josiah?"

"Aye, Sir William," he said as he rose and gave an exaggerated bow. "I will be along shortly, but until I do, you'll be king of the castle, eh?"

The boy returned the bow, then launched himself into Josiah's arms. "But where's the castle?"

"The castle's over yonder a ways at Fairweather Key." A large man with a shock of red hair lifted

William onto broad shoulders. "I'll take care of your son, Captain," he said.

"He's my brother." Josiah reached for the rail, then lost his footing when the cracked wood snapped. When he righted himself, the skiff was gone and another had moved into position.

Anger pounded at his temples, much as his vessel now pounded the reef. He cursed himself for a fool for making the attempt to maneuver the cumbersome vessel through such treacherous waters.

"I see Banks," Harrigan called from somewhere aft. "At least it appears to be him."

One of the wreckers hauled his boat around and headed in that direction. A moment later, Josiah saw what looked like a lifeless body being hauled aboard the skiff.

"He's alive," someone inside the skiff called. "Get him into town quick."

Several others poured themselves into the vessel, and then they were off. Given the fact that Isabelle had gone to see to Banks, surely she now rode to safety with him. He let himself relax a notch.

With passengers and crew evacuated, all that remained was cargo, of which the *Jude* had little. Nothing save the personal items hauled aboard before she lifted anchor in New Orleans, that is.

Behind him, an awful ripping noise echoed.

He turned to see a chunk of the *Jude*'s hull splinter off, hanging by a few boards.

Harrigan raced toward him, picking his way across the debris on the deck like a much younger man might do. "Have you anything in your cabin you wish me to retrieve?"

Josiah thought of the gold coins, then gauged the danger in retrieving them. Finally, he sent Harrigan off with instructions on where to find the treasure.

"Captain Carter, you'll be needing to come with us now."

Josiah turned to see a pair of wreckers heading his way. "She's not long for this world, sir," the taller of the pair said.

"Aye, and what was worth anything has been salvaged," the other, a dark-skinned man with hair as long as a woman's responded.

"Did you happen to find a wooden sewing box?" He used his hands to indicate the size, then described the box in detail.

"Don't sound like anything I found," the dark-skinned fellow said.

Harrigan stumbled toward him. "There's nothing left," he said, "nothing except a hole where your quarters were."

Josiah gave a curt nod. A few items of value would be missed, but most were merely conveniences. The loss of the gold coins, however, presented a different problem.

Still, there was nothing to be done for it.

Someone clamped a hand on his shoulder. A third wrecker had joined them on the deck. "You the captain?"

"Aye," Josiah said.

To his surprise, the fellow reached out to shake Josiah's hand. "I told the boys I wanted to meet the man who could steer this tub so close to shore."

His words stole the speech from Josiah's mouth.

"I'm sure you hoped to get yourself to Key West."

A statement, not a question, yet Josiah nodded. "We had a few sick aboard. I'd hoped to get them help."

"I figured as much." He paused. "With a second storm blowing in so soon after the first, the water's clouded beyond navigating through. Had you gone on with your original plan, it would have meant certain doom, what with the shallows and reefs hidden."

While the man went on in this vein, it did little to allay the guilt Josiah felt at being unable to get ship and crew safely to port.

The long-haired fellow rounded the corner, carrying a soggy length of fabric. As he neared them, Josiah could see it was his mother's waterlogged quilt.

"I figured this might be of some value to

someone," he said. "Perhaps you know the owner, Captain."

He nodded. "Aye, 'tis mine."

The fellow handed it down to a man waiting in the skiff. "With your permission, I'll have my wife wash the seawater from it."

"I'd be much obliged," Josiah said with a dip of his head.

He spied Harrigan and strode toward him. "How fare the crew?"

"All are loaded that have not been lost."

Next came the question he did not want to ask. "And the number of lost?"

"Only two thus far, both from down in Cookie's domain." He paused. "Honestly, Captain, I don't know that they weren't already gone. Cookie seems to think that's the case."

"I see." He watched the men work to secure the items aboard the skiff. "Thank the Lord Isabelle and the others escaped that chamber unharmed."

Silence.

Josiah glanced over at Harrigan and saw his old friend's face go white. "What is it, man?"

"Captain?" This from the red-haired wrecker. "I'm Micah Tate, and I'm in charge of the rescue. I must insist we go. The vessel is on the verge of breaking apart, and I'll not have it take my men down under with it."

"Aye, one moment." He reached for Harrigan's

shoulder and held on tight. "Tell me you've seen to Isabelle's safe departure," he shouted over the sound of the waves beating against the ship.

"I, that is, I think—"

The *Jude*'s hull ripped away and sent them all catapulting into the boiling sea. In short order, the wreckers had all who could be found loaded aboard the remaining skiffs.

"I won't leave until I know Isabelle is safe!" Josiah shouted as he leaped from the vessel and scrambled aboard what was left of the *Jude*.

Refusing to heed their cries, Josiah fought his way up the precariously tilting deck to find a passageway that had not been blocked. Negotiating the narrow passageway proved nearly impossible, yet he continued, all the while calling Isabelle by name.

At one point, he thought he heard someone behind a closed door. When he opened it, sea-water rushed in and nearly filled his lungs. He rose to the top coughing and spitting, only to find an overlarge fish that had been caught in the wreck had caused the commotion.

Bobbing to the top for air, he dove into the water and swam toward the place where his quarters had once been. When he emerged to get another breath, a hand plucked him out of the water and, with the help of several others, tossed him into a skiff.

Blinded by rage, Josiah swung his fist at the first

thing that came near him. Thankfully, he missed, as the man was Harrigan. Somehow, the man had managed to injure himself, as blood covered a good bit of the right side of his face and dripped onto his shirt.

"You're injured."

"Get hold of yourself, Josiah," he said. "It's merely a scratch. Now, if Isabelle's waiting for you on shore, I will be in much trouble should I fail to produce you."

He sat back against the hull of the small boat and sucked in the fresh air. "Perhaps you're right, Harrigan," he said, "but if I should find she does not await me on the shore, I shall stop at nothing to fetch her."

A short while later, the vessel knocked gently against a sandy beach. The wreckers poured out, then helped each passenger aboard to safety with practiced precision. Next came the items salvaged. Each was cataloged and numbered and sent off to a warehouse for safekeeping. Tomorrow the process of reclaiming the goods would begin.

As the *Jude* traveled uninsured and without cargo, the haul would be light and the process a simple one. Had he been carrying cargo, the paperwork would be tied up for months.

Josiah looked around the beach and saw men working together despite the weather. Several had rounded up the passengers and crew and now tallied up their names. By twos, they sent them off.

"Where are they going?" Josiah called.

Micah Tate loped over. "Wrecking's all we do here on Fairweather Key," he said, "so when we get a ship in, everyone in town helps to shelter them." He grinned. "It's a small island, so trust me: No one's going anywhere far."

Josiah spied William and headed toward him. The boy met him halfway to wrap drenched arms around him. "You're safe," his brother said against the skin of his neck.

Josiah held William at arm's length. Out of the corner of his eye, he saw Emilie and the Dumont woman bustling toward him. "Aye, lad, I'm fit and fine, although the *Jude* is not. I fear we must await a new vessel before continuing the trip to England. I hope you're not sore disappointed."

"Begging your pardon, Captain." Viola Dumont tugged at his soggy sleeve. "If I might, I would like a word with you."

Were it not for the present circumstances, Josiah might have been stunned. This was more than the Dumont woman had spoken on the entire voyage.

"Perhaps I could take the boy and find a place for him to settle for the night," Emilie said.

Josiah looked around and saw for the first

242

time that the sun had begun to set. "Aye," he said, "and I'll be much in your debt if you'd see to some dry clothes for the lad."

"There's room at the boardinghouse as well as in the homes of these good men," a female voice called. Josiah watched as a matronly woman hurried over to relieve Emilie of her burden. "I'll put the boy in the wagon; then we must away to the boardinghouse. On a night like tonight, I am sure we will be full as ticks."

Full as ticks. Lovely.

"Captain?"

He'd all but forgotten about Viola. "Aye?"

Her face wore an uncharacteristic look of determination, and her backbone seemed to have found its starch. "I'm bound and determined to fetch Isabelle and Mr. Banks from the *Jude*. Are you with me?"

"Oh, no, Miss Dumont," he said as he led her away from the water's edge. "You see, Mr. Banks was found early on in the rescue. I'm sure Isabelle was with him."

Large eyes threatened to spill over with tears. "No, Captain," she said, "neither has been located, and now the men are done for the night. I cannot let them sleep in the *Jude* alone or, worse, in the sea."

"Then we shall find them together." He strode over to a wrecker who had only just completed evacuating his vessel. "I have need of your skiff," he said. "There are others aboard the *Jude* who must be rescued."

"Sorry, fellow," the man said, "but a thorough search has been done, and there's no one left on that sinking tub."

"Aye, that might well be," Josiah said as he fought his rising anger. "Nonetheless, I have two people missing, and the only place they could be is out there."

The wrecker studied Josiah a moment, then shrugged. "I would like to help you, but heading back out there now would be suicide. I don't think my wife and children would appreciate me taking such a risk."

"Then I shall." He pushed past the wrecker, rage pounding in his temples. If the wreckers refused to help, then he would go it alone.

Josiah spied what looked like a small vessel on the beach a few yards ahead. With Viola Dumont shadowing him, he slipped away from the throng and set the rowboat in the water. The lady climbed in and reached for an oar.

"I shall do this alone, Miss Dumont," he said. "I would suggest you help me look for bodies, or rather persons, in the water."

Her mouth set in a grim line, Miss Dumont gave a curt nod, then held on tight. Josiah pushed the oars through the water until his arms burned while Miss Dumont scanned the waves and called for Isabelle.

After only a few minutes, the water had begun to lap over the sides of the tiny vessel while pieces of the *Jude* pounded it from all angles. Soon Miss Dumont had given up calling and began using any available means to return seawater back into the ocean.

Finally, Josiah knew he must turn back. They would never reach the *Jude* in this small vessel. His only hope—Isabelle and Banks's only hope —was in convincing a wrecker to maneuver his skiff back in the direction of the sinking ship.

Only then could they ascertain the whereabouts of the missing passenger and crewman. Beaching the rowboat, he helped Miss Dumont out, then dragged the vessel back to its resting place. "Have you a plan, Captain Carter?"

He paused to shake his head. "Nothing more complicated than this: I will pluck all from the sea and return them safely to shore. As captain, I've no choice."

Josiah looked toward the area where the wreckers had gathered. Fewer than a dozen crewmen lingered, and it appeared all had made arrangements for a dry place to sleep and a hot meal. Anchored nearby were the wrecking vessels, all of them sturdy and well maintained.

One particularly appealed. Dubbed the *Caroline* as witnessed by the placard on her port side, it sat squat and low in the ocean and looked to be the most reliable of the lot.

The decision whether to spirit away the vessel from under its owner's nose was taken from him when the wreckers parted and joined the group leaving for town. "Go and catch up with them," Josiah told Miss Dumont.

"I cannot. You'll need me to help."

He shook his head. "Should you not arrive at the boardinghouse, you'll be missed. I, on the other hand, will be assumed to have quartered elsewhere." When she continued to look doubtful, he turned her on her heels and pointed her to the wreckers. "Make haste. Your friend's life depends on it."

"I shall pray, Captain," she said before making her way toward the throng of men.

"As shall I," Josiah said. And this time, he knew God would hear him.

A few moments later, the beach was empty, and Josiah had his choice of vessels. He climbed aboard the *Caroline* and set about turning her around and pointing her toward the sinking hulk of the *Jude*. Once he'd moved sufficiently far from the shore, Josiah lit the lantern and aimed it in the direction of the wreckage.

Pieces of the ship littered the water around him and formed a barrier through which it was difficult to navigate. The evidence floating around him seemed to show that when the men's patch had not held, the hull had collapsed and splintered, such was the debris.

Were that he could have fetched Harrigan with him on this mission, but his friend had looked poorly when they had parted. Better Harrigan stayed behind and recuperated. As Josiah scanned the horizon, he said a prayer for the sailor's restored health.

The farther from shore he traveled, the more difficult the going. He'd nearly reached the site of the wreck when a movement in the water caught his attention. Swinging the vessel starboard, he found a piece of wreckage with what looked like people floating atop it.

Let it be them, God. Please, let it be my Isabelle.

Cursing the cumbersome vessel, Josiah made his way to the wreckage. There he found Isabelle and Banks lying atop a piece of wood shorn off from the aft deck.

"Thank You, Lord," he cried. "Now help me if You will to save these two."

Joy turned to fear when he called to them but neither answered. Moving close as he could, Josiah tossed over the anchor and waited for it to catch. This accomplished, he kicked off his boots and dove in.

Due to the pull of the tide, he reached Banks first. Thank the Lord, the old sailor still clung to life. "See to the girl," was his gruff response. "The Lord's not ready for me yet, and the sharks are all afraid of me."

"Aye, Banks," Josiah said. "You'll hold tight for me while I do, won't you?"

"I believe I will," he said as he rested his face on the wood.

Josiah offered Banks a gentle pat on the back, being careful to watch for wounds both old and new. "Once I've spoken to Isabelle, I shall fetch you both back to the boat."

Maneuvering his way around to the other side of the floating rescue barge, Josiah finally held Isabelle in his arms. Water soaked every inch of her, and the braid she'd pinned into a coil had released and now tangled about her like honey-colored seaweed. Her dress had been torn, and one sleeve hung on only by the wrist.

Keeping a tight grip on the boards, Josiah pushed Isabelle's hair away from her face and felt for a pulse on her neck. When he found it, Josiah yelped in victory.

"Isabelle, I will buy a dozen beautiful frocks if you will just live," he said. "Nay, two dozen," he amended when he upended her to see the bruises on her face.

Had he the time, he might have climbed aboard the pieces of the *Jude* that now cradled the woman who'd stolen his heart, for his only wish was to hold her safe against him. But time was not his friend, as witnessed by the waves that seemed to grow larger with each passing moment.

God, You've calmed the waves before. Would You considering repeating that miracle here?

As he saw to securing her atop the wreckage, Josiah watched for signs that Isabelle might awaken. He spoke to her as he worked, making promise after promise and declaring himself to be at her disposal for whatever she might need during the healing process.

"How do you fare?" he called to Banks once he'd satisfied himself that Isabelle was safe.

"I'm an old man who could barely hear all the things you just told that lady, so worry not about me." His chuckle, under other circumstances, would have sent Josiah into a rage.

Now, however, with the first stars twinkling above them and all of Fairweather Key awaiting their return, he merely chuckled.

Reaching the *Caroline* was a more difficult prospect than he expected, so by the time he'd managed to lash the wreckage to the wrecker, he was nearly spent. The moon now climbed past the horizon, and more than a smattering of stars dotted the sky. The only sound other than the pounding of the surf was the creaking of wood against reef as the battered remnants of the *Jude* fought to remain above the waterline.

"Banks, can you hoist yourself over if I bring the wood near to the vessel?" Josiah called.

The sailor lifted up on one elbow to survey the situation. "Nay, Captain, but if you roll me alongside and give me a push, I can manage to find my way onto her deck."

"You're certain?"

" 'Tis a far sight better to land hard on a wrecker's vessel than to sink on a piece of floating debris."

"You've a valid point, Banks." Josiah did as he asked, and in short order, Banks was lying prone on the *Caroline*'s foredeck. "Can you see to yourself now?"

"Fetch the lady, Captain," he said with a sigh. "Knowing I'll have a warm bed and a meal that Cookie didn't make has me content enough to rest a bit. You'll be awakening me should anything exciting happen, eh?"

"I assure you, I shall." Josiah dove back into the water and swam alongside Isabelle. This time when he reached her, he found her conscious and watching his every move.

Thank You, Lord. I'll never ask for another miracle. You've just given me the only one I need.

A bruise decorated her right cheek, and blood was beginning to dry on her lower lip. Still, she looked more beautiful to Josiah than anything he could think of.

"Whatever happened to ladies first?" she said, her voice hoarse.

"Forgive me," he said as he maneuvered her into the center of the wreckage. "Hold tight to my shoulders if you can."

Isabelle made the attempt but could not keep her arms in place. On the second try, she fell backward and slipped beneath the water. Panicked, Josiah dove after her.

Finally, Josiah managed to cradle her to his chest and crawl carefully across the section of decking to reach the *Caroline*. Pausing to catch his breath, he threw his legs over the side and crumpled to the floor of the *Caroline* with Isabelle still pressed against him.

Not caring for propriety, he remained at her side until she made a move to sit on her own. He helped Isabelle into an upright position, adjusting her torn skirts, then doing his best to remedy her water-soaked curls.

"I'm ever so thankful you're not called upon to braid my hair except in dire straits," she said when he'd finally given up.

"Aye, I'd best be left to coil rope and not hair," he said, keeping his tone light as he noted that, in addition to her bruises, she lacked her normal color. Upon closer inspection, she seemed quite unwell.

"Isabelle, how fare you?" he asked as he moved to gather her into his arms again.

She winced, he noticed, when he wrapped his arm about her waist. Touching the middle of her back on either side produced the same reaction.

"You've taken a fall of some sort," he said.

Isabelle remained silent. Her lips had begun to

turn blue, and Josiah cast about for a blanket of some sort. Failing that, he removed his shirt, wet as it was, and wrapped it around her.

Grasping her hand, he brushed her fingers with his lips as he watched her eyes close. "I thought I'd lost you," he whispered. "But God brought you back to me. I'll never lose you again."

Her lids fluttered open. "Josiah, there are so many reasons why we cannot be."

Stung, he shook his head. "You do not love me?"

Her lips bent slightly in a near smile. "Aye, Captain, I fear I do."

Josiah's heart soared. "Then there is nothing that will keep you from me and I from you."

"Yet there is." Sea green eyes peered up at him, and given her soaked state, he could not tell if she cried. "There is the matter of my—"

He stood and began to pace. "I care not for anything save your future, so do not speak to me of your past. You are Isabelle Gayarre, daughter of Jean Gayarre, am I correct?"

"That is what I'm told."

"Then there need not be anything more said." He knelt to offer a quick kiss on her uninjured cheek. "Take care to rest while I bring this vessel to port. I warrant the doctor will be awaiting your arrival." He looked past her to where Banks slumbered. "Both of your arrivals," he amended.

With the wind and waves in their favor, the

Caroline sped to shore twice as quickly as she had left. As he neared the dock, he noted a party of men awaited them.

"Look, Isabelle," he said. "I wager 'tis the doctor come to fetch you."

A glance over his shoulder told him the sea siren now slumbered, as well. At least he prayed it was sleep that overtook her.

Before he could tie the ropes, the men had boarded the vessel. Two he recognized as wreckers. The third, he did not know.

It was this stranger who crossed the deck to reach him first. As Josiah reached out his hand in friendship, the fellow slapped him in irons.

"What is the meaning of this?" he stammered. "There are injured from the *Jude* aboard."

The man called out and several others joined him. None were familiar to him save the two wreckers. While Banks and Isabelle were removed from the vessel, those remaining blocked Josiah's way.

"Tell them who I am," Josiah said. "You know me as captain of the *Jude*. I must see to the injured."

One of them, the burly redhead who had led the wreckers, stepped forward. "Aye, I do know you as the captain of that sinking ship. Have you ownership papers for it?"

"Tate, they are aboard her. If your men rescued my sea chest, they have them."

He nodded. "I'll inquire of it then. Perhaps you might tell me why you took the *Caroline* tonight."

Josiah weighed the question while he studied the irons on his wrists. "I did not take her," he finally said. "I borrowed her to fetch survivors that the others refused to go after."

Tate seemed to give consideration to the statement. "My men swore there was no one left aboard the vessel. Are you contradicting this?"

"Those your men now carry speak the answer."

Tate turned to the stranger. "I wish to press charges. Take him away," he said. "I'll not have thieves about. It's bad for business."

Before Josiah could protest, the stranger knocked him to the deck. A second later, all went dark.

CHAPTER 19

"How fares Isabelle?"

Josiah asked the question before his eyes opened, for thoughts of her permeated his dreams and slipped into his mind even as he tried to awaken. The room was small, dark, and not a place one might expect to offer up as lodging for a traveler.

His stomach complained, and he rolled over in an attempt to settle it. Something stabbed his shoulder, and he sat bolt upright to find he'd slept atop a nail.

The smell of something frying assailed him. Coupled with the scent of salt air, rain, and fresh-caught fish, the odor nearly did him in. Muscles Josiah had forgotten he owned complained as he swung his legs onto the floor and scrubbed at his face with his palms.

His head swam with the effort. When he touched the back of his head, Josiah felt crusted blood. At least that's what he assumed was there.

Then he remembered. This was no boarding-house room.

He was in jail.

Josiah cast about for his footwear, then recalled he had left them aboard the *Caroline*. "Perhaps I could bring a countersuit for theft of my boots," he muttered.

Daylight had not yet touched the barred windows bordering three sides of the cell. It was early, or perhaps late. There was no way of knowing.

Josiah lay back on the bunk and stared into the blackness. Outside, the wind rustled the palms and whistled through the gaps in the walls. A low humming began, and as it neared, Josiah recognized a woman's pleasant voice coming from the hall outside the door. In truth, the sweet singing could have been the voice of an angel.

"Yes, when this flesh and heart shall fail, and mortal life shall cease."

Weak lamplight, the color of fresh-churned butter, spilled under the door and filtered through the boards on either side as the singing halted. Something clanged and rustled; then the singing returned.

"I shall possess, within the vail, a life of joy and peace."

The door flew open, and along with the blinding glare, a woman of great bulk and small height hastened in.

"The Lord has promised good to me. His word my hope secures."

Something clanged again, and he assumed the door had been shut behind her.

"He will my shield and portion be, as long as life endures."

As Josiah's eyes adjusted to the light, he saw the woman had placed the oil lamp, its cut-glass shade proclaiming great value, on a small table made of some sort of intricately carved wood—rosewood, perhaps.

Josiah turned his attention to the matron, who wore her dark hair gathered into a knot atop her head and covered with a white, bonnet-type hat. Her ruddy complexion could have been from too much heat or excessive sun, such was the scarlet on her cheeks. It matched the tiny sprigs of flowers on her plain frock. In sharp contrast, she wore an apron of some sort of fine linen that looked as if it had been a nobleman's tablecloth in a previous life.

"Good morning," she said as she set an elaborate silver platter heaped with breakfast fare on the bunk beside him. "I dare not ask if you slept well, for I'm sure you'd prefer to be lodging elsewhere."

Her manner was too sweet to ruin with a sharp retort, so he said nothing.

The woman fussed with setting out the serving pieces, all of the finest silver and decorated with a coat of arms that vaguely resembled that of the Duke of Willingham. Beneath the platter of food was a gold-rimmed china plate. It matched the cup the woman now filled with coffee.

She set the cup on its saucer and stood back to admire her handiwork. In truth, had he not been dining in the dank confines of a prison cell, he might have been impressed at the splendor laid before him. Instead, he merely felt confused.

Confused and suddenly famished.

"We don't have many prisoners here."

He looked over at the woman, who now stood with her hands on her hips. What sort of response did a man give to such a statement?

She moved a step closer and seemed to be studying him. "You don't look like a thief."

Josiah lifted a fork and studied it. "And you don't look like the Duke of Willingham's wife."

"Mercy, no." She clutched her hands to her chest, and Josiah noted her bejeweled fingers. "My Clarence, he's a wrecker. At least that's his main job."

"Well, that certainly explains the splendor of my breakfast tray." He stabbed at the most bland-looking item on the platter and held it to his lips. "Although I'm sure the duke is wondering where his silver has gone."

Clarence's wife giggled. "You don't know about wreckers, do you?"

"I know a bit." He willed his parched throat to swallow.

"All we have's bought and paid for," she said. "There are no thieves among us." She blanched. "Forgive me, sir, but it's the truth. I'm sure the duke was well paid by his insurers for the loss. Clarence and the others, they were paid when the items they salvaged were auctioned. Sometimes we are rewarded in coin, and other times it's in the bounty of the vessel."

"I see, Clarence's wife." The bite slid down and stayed, and, to Josiah's surprise, it was quite tasty. "So it's legal stealing. Interesting."

Her back straight, she affected a stern look. "Look here," she said. "This isn't stealing. Not at all. Besides, who would save the people off these vessels if it weren't for the wreckers? Our men risk their lives every time they leave port. You don't think these ships sink in fair weather, do you? No, it's most always in the storms."

She seemed to be waiting for him to agree. A nod would have to suffice.

"I'll come to fetch the tray when you're done." Her bluster eased, the woman sighed then made for the door. "And my name is Rosemary," she said. "Rosemary O'Mara."

"Wait." Josiah set the tray aside. "I would have news of my passengers and crew. In particular I'm concerned about a young lady."

"A young lady?" She gave him a sideways look. "Is she your wife?"

He paused. "I am as yet unmarried."

"I see."

"Aye, the lady was grave injured. In fact, these wreckers you're so fond of had gone and left her for dead in the wreckage of the *Jude*. My man Banks was also abandoned to the elements." He fisted his hand but kept his temper. "In order to fetch them, I appropriated the *Caroline*. 'Tis this act of desperation that landed me in your hospitality."

Perhaps it was wishful thinking, but something in her face told Josiah that Mrs. O'Mara believed him. "I'll inquire on your behalf, but I cannot make any promises. Your fellow is Banks?"

"Aye."

She nodded. "And the woman, what is her name?"

"Ah, the woman." He looked away. "She is

called Isabelle. You will know her by her eyes, which are the same color as the sea that devoured my vessel." He shifted positions. "And, Mrs. O'Mara?"

"Yes?"

"I would like very much to petition for my release. How and when may that be done?"

Mrs. O'Mara shrugged. "That's up to the judge. I'm sure when he's weighed the evidence he will make his decision."

"Surely he will speak to me before that decision is made."

"I don't know, Mr. Carter," she said. "We rarely have prisoners here."

The door shut behind her, and Josiah was alone. With the pale light of the morning sun filtering through the palms and dancing across the dust motes of the small cell, he resisted the urge to gobble the fare placed before him. Did Isabelle yet live to enjoy a meal today?

And what of the others? How many of his men awoke to see daylight this morning?

He held his head in his hand and willed it to stop throbbing. Perhaps a few bites would be in order to keep up his strength and stave off the hunger that caused his stomach to rumble and complain.

By the time he heard Mrs. O'Mara coming, his belly was satisfied, and his head had nearly ceased its pounding. The worry over Isabelle, however, had increased. A different verse of the same song greeted him.

" *'Twas grace that taught my heart to fear, and grace my fears relieved."* The door swung open, and Mrs. O'Mara stepped inside the cell, a folded blanket in one hand and a bucket in the other. *"How precious did that grace appear, the hour I first believed!"*

She set the bucket before him and peered down at the tray, cradling the blanket in her arms. "Well now, I figured a man of your size would have a better appetite."

"My appetite would be greatly improved were I dining in my own rooms."

Mrs. O'Mara chuckled. "And my singing would sound much better in the Royal Hall, but it weren't to be."

Josiah leaned gingerly against the wall and shrugged. "Perhaps if you sang the verses in their proper order, the odds might improve."

"What would be the fun in that?" She moved the tray to the end of the bunk, then set the bucket in its place. "Anyone can sing the verses of a song in the order they were written. I prefer to sing them as the Spirit leads."

"You have a point." He gestured to the bucket. "Are you intent on washing me?"

"Surely you jest, Mr. Carter," she said as she set the blanket beside him. "You'll be doing your own washing, or you'll go without."

He sobered. "Do you bring news of my Isabelle?"

Mrs. O'Mara sighed. "I'm afraid I do not. I've brought a set of Mr. O'Mara's clothing wrapped in that blanket." She gestured to the bucket. "Get yourself presentable for the doctor. He'll be here soon. Perhaps he will have word of your woman."

Once his hostess was gone, Josiah peeled off the shirt that had stiffened and molded to him and tossed it aside, then did the same with his trousers.

Reaching into the bucket for the sponge, he sluiced water over his arms, then went to work on his chest. Where last week he had worn the marks of his fall from the yardarm, now they were only pale scars.

The memory of Isabelle doctoring those wounds made him smile. Then it made his knees buckle.

He fell to his knees and threw the sponge. It hit the opposite wall and landed with a splat on the floor.

How did I get here, Lord? What happened? How do I repair this damage I've caused?

Head bowed, Josiah waited for an answer. How long he remained there, he could not say. Finally, he rose and fetched the sponge.

When he was done, Josiah made haste to step into the borrowed trousers. Next came the shirt, which pinched a bit across the shoulders but was otherwise serviceable.

Mrs. O'Mara had even thought of leaving a length of leather with which to tie back his hair. Dunking his head in the bucket, Josiah emerged to shake off the water and make use of the leather.

His bath complete, Josiah lay back on the bunk to await the doctor. He closed his eyes for a moment, and when he opened them again, the sun rode high in the sky. By his reckoning, it was noon or thereabouts.

No meal came to him, nor did the doctor visit. The cell was bathed in shadows when the familiar sound of Mrs. O'Mara's song slid beneath the door.

"Amazing grace! How sweet the sound that saved a wretch like me! I once was lost, but now am found." The door opened and the light poured in. *"Was blind, but now I see."*

"Starting your hymns at the beginning, are you?" Josiah swung his legs over the side of the bunk and pulled himself into a sitting position.

"That I am." She set the tray beside him, then took two steps back. "I regret the doctor cannot see to you until tomorrow at the earliest."

"Truly there's no need," he said. "I am more interested in the fate of my crew and the passengers whose lives I endangered."

Mrs. O'Mara bustled about removing covers from the plates and seeing to the coffeepot. When she stopped, she looked him in the eye, her expression uncharacteristically serious. "The way I hear it, you saved all those people by getting the ship as close to shore as you did."

"Yes, well, you heard wrong. I took a ship that wasn't seaworthy into treacherous waters during the height of a raging gale." He waved away any further conversation. "Thank you for the food and the clean clothes. They are much appreciated."

She looked him over, and a smile broke. "I'm glad to hear it. I'll do all I can to see you're taken care of." She reached for his stained clothes and tossed them into the bucket. "The way you rescued those people, well, I think it makes you a hero."

Josiah's chuckle held no humor. "Some hero." He leaned back against the wall and toyed with the linen and lace napkin, so out of place in this dim and dirty cell. "I wonder if I might impose on you for something, Mrs. O'Mara. Something I'd ask to be brought to me, if possible."

"If it's an imposition, I'll say no." She lifted the bucket with ease and held it with both hands. "What is it you'll be wanting?"

"A Bible and a lamp to read it by."

"Now that I believe I can do." She bustled toward the door. "Clarence just brought home a crate that may have that very thing in it. You eat, and I'll go take a peek."

"Thank you," he called.

She returned several hours later, or at least that was Josiah's estimation of the passage of time. No traces of the day remained, and the night sky had faded from orange to purple to black.

Having given up on the woman's returning that night, Josiah had already folded his blanket into a passable pillow and was searching for a way to sleep that did not force the nail into him.

"He rules the world with truth and grace, and makes the nations prove." Again the keys jangled as lamplight spilled around the door. *"The glories of His righteousness, and wonders of His love, and wonders of His love, and wonders, wonders, of His love."*

Josiah lifted his head and grinned in spite of himself. "Have I slept till Christmas, Mrs. O'Mara?"

She chuckled. "You're a funny one, Mr. Carter. Forgive the late hour. Mr. O'Mara was busy with a meeting until a bit ago. The good news is I've found a Bible." She set the lamp on the table. "Mr. O'Mara says you may keep this, long as you're careful."

He swung his legs over the side, being careful to avoid the nail. "Careful?"

Mrs. O'Mara pointed to the ceiling. "This whole place is made from driftwood. Should you care to send yourself to glory, all you need do is mishandle that lamp."

"I see." He spied the book in her hand. "Is that the Bible you've brought for me?"

"Oh," she said as she looked down, "yes, it is." She set it beside the lamp and reached for the tray. "A little damp, it is, but then in this climate, that's to be expected."

Josiah nodded. "The double curse and blessing of living near open water. I know it well."

She eyed him a moment. "I reckon you do, Captain Carter."

"Oh, so I'm *Captain* Carter now, am I?"

The older woman grinned over her shoulder as she made her exit. "As I said before, I've heard stories that tell me you've earned the title. Now don't stay up too late reading. Breakfast comes early to Fairweather Key." The door shut, the lock clanged, and once again, Josiah was alone.

"Joy to the earth, the Savior reigns! Let men their songs employ."

Josiah tested his legs by standing and stretching; then he rolled his shoulders in an attempt to rid them of the ache that seemed unending. Finally, he walked the four paces to the table and picked up the Bible.

True to Mrs. O'Mara's warning, the book was damp. It was a Bible, nonetheless, and he gave a quick prayer of thanks for having received it so quickly.

Help me find strength here, Lord, he added, *and if You please, would You get me out of this place? Until I can watch over William and Isabelle, would You do that for me? I'm afraid I didn't do such a good job of the responsibility You gave me, but if You please, I'd be grateful for another chance.*

Josiah went on in this vein for another moment, then felt guilty for piling all his burdens on the Lord at once. Isabelle would call him foolish, of course, for in her estimation, the Lord had heavenly shoulders broad enough to lay any burden upon.

How he missed her tonight. The absence of her good company was worse than any prison cell. And William. The plan to spirit him away from their father had never included depending on the kindness of strangers to shelter him.

"Enough," he said to the dark shadows that taunted him. "I've a Bible and oil sufficient to light this room for a few hours. That makes today better than yesterday."

In order to read comfortably, he moved the table and lamp nearer to the bunk. That accomplished, Josiah settled on the only place he could sit, the bunk, and held the small black leather Bible in his lap. It opened to the flyleaf; then the breeze caught the thin paper and turned the page. Inscribed in an elegant and feminine hand were words that made his knees buckle.

He read it aloud, tracing the script with his forefinger. "To Isabelle, from your sister Emilie, on the occasion of your nineteenth birthday, December 24, 1833."

Josiah closed the Bible and held it to his chest. Welling up from the depths of his soul, the tears came.

CHAPTER 20

Hezekiah leaned against the rail of Dumont's schooner and cursed himself for a fool, then thought better of it. The Lord had given him two sons, and like it or not, he'd been called to love both of them equally.

The truth be told, he did love both boys with the same measure of affection and the same depth of parental duty. Josiah, however, Hezekiah had spent most of his adult years trying to like.

Oh, he admired the lad's courage, his ability to puzzle out a solution to the most difficult of problems, and a myriad of other things. What drove him to distraction was Josiah's ability to discern exactly what his father did *not* want him to do and then do it to perfection.

It was a trait that started early. Hezekiah chuckled at the memory of a barely toddling Josiah leading his governess on an obstacle course through the neighbor's newly plowed field. One might argue that the governess should have dissuaded the tot from the excursion, but Hezekiah knew too well the low chance of success in making that sort of attempt.

"And yet you continued to try," he muttered as he made his way to his stateroom.

Perhaps Mary should have accompanied him on this voyage. When no one else could, Mary seemed to find the words to soothe the savage beast that was their son. But then she had the same effect on her husband.

Hezekiah turned the latch and let himself into his stateroom. "Perhaps my son is more like me than I want to admit."

Two days passed with only Isabelle's Bible and Mrs. O'Mara for company. Each time the woman brought the heavily laden silver tray, Josiah begged for any scrap of information she might give him on the well-being of his brother, Isabelle, and the others.

Much as she seemed to try, Mrs. O'Mara could find little in the way of news. The boardinghouse was full to the brim with sailors and passengers from the *Jude*, but she could only ascertain that there were no more casualties and that those who had not been injured were slowly leaving the island on other vessels.

She also discovered there were at least two unmarried women and a boy living there. Whether any were named Isabelle, she did not know.

By the third day, the hymn that announced Mrs. O'Mara didn't even cause Josiah to lift his head from the pillow. *"Dear name, the rock on which I build, my shield and hiding place."* The door opened. "You've visitors, Mr. Carter," she said. "Ladies, they are. I'm sorry it's not the doctor or the judge."

Josiah scrambled into an upright position and looked beyond Mrs. O'Mara to the door. "Isabelle?"

"I'm afraid not." Emilie Gayarre stepped into the cell, followed closely by Viola Dumont. Both ladies looked as if they'd slept in their clothing.

Unlike the timid woman he'd allowed aboard the *Jude*, Viola Dumont now seemed to have found a measure of confidence. It was she and not Emilie who walked over to greet him.

"I'm sure Isabelle would be with us if she could, but it's impossible for her to leave the infirmary just yet," Viola said.

Just yet. "So she's not seriously injured." Josiah sank onto his bunk and covered his face with his hands. "Thank God." He looked beyond the ladies to the open door. "I must go to her."

"That's not possible, Captain Carter." This from Mrs. O'Mara. "You'll be seeing the judge soon enough to clear up the matter. In the meantime, you're to stay right where the Lord and those men put you."

"I seriously doubt the Lord had anything to do

with me being jailed like a common criminal."

Viola touched his sleeve. "I feel responsible, Captain Carter. If I hadn't insisted you go after Isabelle and Mr. Banks, none of this would have happened."

He looked down at the Dumont woman. "You saved Isabelle," he said. "I'll not allow any apologies over that fact." Josiah turned his attention to the jailer. "Upon my honor, if I might just have a look at Isabelle, then I could return and serve whatever time I'm due." He thrust his hands toward her. "Clap me in irons if you must, but I vow I will not attempt escape."

"I can vouch for the captain's sterling character," Emilie said.

"As can I," Viola chimed in.

Mrs. O'Mara's face softened. "I'm truly sorry. If it were up to me, well . . ."

Emilie reached to pat the jailer's hand. "Perhaps you will join us in praying for the captain's swift release."

The thought occurred to Josiah that he could easily make his way past these women to Isabelle and freedom. This time, if necessary, he would appropriate the first vessel that would allow him to spirit Isabelle away from the island. He'd send payment, of course, and double whatever the ship's worth.

It was a grand plan provided Isabelle's health allowed her to leave. If he'd managed to

271

maneuver the ancient and unwieldy *Jude* through the reef, a smaller and more seaworthy vessel would make the going quick and easy.

They could be to Key West before morning, then on the first ship to anywhere but New Orleans. Only the knowledge that he was innocent kept him still. Surely God wouldn't allow this injustice to continue.

Viola stepped forward and offered a shy smile. "I've been caring for Isabelle myself," she said. "The doctor has much need for assistance, and I find I've a talent for nursing."

"I see." Josiah tried in vain to tame his restlessness. "So this doctor, he's a man of skill?"

"I'll just leave you to him while I fetch his dinner, ladies, but do call if he becomes unruly." Mrs. O'Mara winked as she stepped out and closed the door. *"The Lord has promised good to me. His word my hope secures,"* she sang as she walked away.

"Yes indeed," Viola said. "He's been quite busy, what with the number of injuries that came in with the sinking of our ship." When Josiah winced, she quickly added, "The men are faring well."

"She's very good at tending the sick," Emilie added. "In fact, she's only just now left Isabelle."

Josiah's heart thudded against his aching ribs. "What is her condition?"

Viola shook her head. "The doctor cannot yet say. Not until she awakens."

"So," Josiah said with care, "she has not yet . . ."

"Awakened?" This from Emilie. "No, I don't believe she has. Am I correct, Vi?"

"You are." Viola knelt before Josiah and grasped his hands. "She's young and strong, Captain, and the Lord is not done with her yet. I know this."

"You know this." He repeated the words, numb. "She had a wound here." He pointed to his face. "Is it yet healed?"

"Yes," Viola said. "Already the bruises are fading. Her beauty is intact."

He rose and stepped past Viola. "Think you that beauty is what has bewitched me? Isabelle Gayarre is much more than a beautiful woman. She is . . ." By degrees he became aware that the women were staring. "Forgive me. I am unable to be anything but passionate when discussing this topic." He took a deep breath and let it out slowly. "And what of my men? How fare they?"

"Some are quite well," Viola said. "There's a ship heading to Charleston on the morrow, and many have signed on as crew."

"Excellent." Josiah paused. "And the others? I wonder about Mr. Harrigan and Mr. Banks."

The women exchanged glances. "Mr. Banks is still with us, but there is little hope of a complete recovery. He is, however, a strong man. The doctor has not given up on him."

"I see." Josiah studied her face. "And my friend,

273

Mr. Harrigan. As I recall, he was injured about the head or face. He claimed it merely a scratch, but I doubted him."

Neither woman spoke.

Josiah's heart sank. "He did not survive."

"No," Viola said softly. "I'm afraid he succumbed to his injuries three days ago. A funeral and Christian burial were held for him."

So his old friend was gone. The idea did not yet register.

Somehow, he found the bunk and sat on it. So many lives had depended on him; so many were lost. "Are there other casualties? I would know names."

"Yes, Captain." Emilie stated the names, and with each one, more guilt was heaped atop the pile. There were seven in all.

"And what of the others? Would that I could pay the salaries they were promised."

Emilie offered a weak smile. "Actually, those who could work were quite fortunate in that a schooner bound for Baltimore had need of men. A few men sailed this morning, and others have pledged to sail on the morning tide."

"Including the lads?"

Viola nodded. "Despite the fact that Emilie offered to take them in and add them to her growing list of students."

"So they elected to take their education at sea rather than in a classroom." Josiah chuckled. "I'm afraid I understand that decision all too well." He paused. "And what of those who are not sailing tomorrow?"

"Two found work as wreckers," Viola supplied. "Cookie, however, decided to hire out on a mail packet headed for New Orleans. He says he's done with life at sea."

Emilie nodded. "He visited with us after Mr. Harrigan's service and asked that we give you a message."

"Oh?"

"Yes," Emilie said. "He wanted us to be sure and tell you how very much he admired you, Captain."

"His exact quote," Viola interjected, "was 'the Carter lad could find safe port for a bucket in a hurricane, but he's harder on himself than anyone else would be. Tell him I'm going home to my grandchildren with great stories of sailing with him.' "

"Thank you for your honesty," he said when she finished. Odd as the sentiment sounded, being told the truth—the complete truth—was a refreshing change to Mrs. O'Mara's hedging and avoidance.

Emilie ventured forward two steps. "Captain Carter?"

He turned to face her. "Aye?"

"I bring news of William." She smiled. "He's a wonderful boy. Very bright."

Josiah's emotions calmed at the mention of his brother. "I've always found him to be an apt pupil." He paused. "Although I fear I might soon be surpassed by him should I attempt to continue giving him his lessons."

Isabelle's sister chuckled. "Indeed you describe him well. With your permission, I will continue instructing him until you're able to take over."

He nodded. "I am in your debt, Mademoiselle Gayarre."

"No," Emilie said, "it is I who am in your debt. It has not gone unnoticed that the presence of women on your vessel was not a comfortable state for you and your men. Had I the ability to do things differently, I might have chosen to remove Isabelle from her situation in another manner." She paused. "Although I am convinced that the Lord put you and your vessel in our path because none but you could see to Isabelle's escape."

Josiah let the idea settle in his bones.

"Perhaps I could bring William to visit you," Emilie suggested.

"No." His response was quick, abrupt. "I'll not have my brother seeing me in this place."

Eyes downcast, Emilie nodded. "I hadn't considered that."

"Forgive me," he said, "for my rudeness. I'm in your debt for the care you've given my brother." He turned his attention to Viola. "And also for your attention to Isabelle. I cannot repay you now, but I vow someday I shall."

Emilie shook her head. "It is I who must protest now, Captain Carter. There is no balance sheet for things done among friends."

Josiah thought for a moment, then nodded. "Aye, 'tis true. Ladies, I wonder if you might have news of my vessel and the status of the salvage operation."

Viola nodded. "Just yesterday, I overheard the doctor speaking to someone about the *Jude*. He said there was nothing to salvage."

Josiah pointed to the Bible. "Yet I have Isabelle's Bible. How came my jailor to have it unless someone found something to salvage?"

Emilie reached for the book and, after reading the flyleaf, held it to her. "Indeed, this is Isabelle's. I would ask the judge, Captain Carter."

"If I ever see that man, I shall," he said. "As yet, I have not had the pleasure of his company." Josiah shook his head. "Forgive my interruption. What other news do you have, Miss Dumont?"

A strange look crossed the woman's face. "I am reluctant to say, Captain. These things are unfounded and thus . . ."

"And thus?" He rose. "I cannot refute what I do not know."

She nodded. "Yes, well, there is some question as to the provenance of the vessel."

Josiah inclined his ear. "Go on."

"The vessel was uninsured," she said.

"I carried no cargo, thus no insurance was needed." He shrugged. "I fail to see how this fact would be cause for conversation."

"Yes, well," Viola hedged, "there's more."

"What else?" When Viola seemed reluctant to continue, he looked to Emilie. "Do you know what she won't say?"

"Yes," Emilie said slowly. "A few of the wreckers are claiming that the *Jude* was, well, that the vessel was used to carry slaves."

Josiah nodded. "Aye, 'tis possible it was. I would wager the man I purchased her from would have had no qualms about carrying human cargo. I, on the other hand, find the practice detestable." He crossed his arms over his chest. "Were I a slaver, how can you account for my feelings for your sister, Miss Gayarre?"

"So she's told you of her background," Emilie said. "I was unsure whether she'd mentioned it."

"Aye."

Both women looked relieved. Viola spoke first. "Then you only have to produce the receipt for the vessel's purchase, and the issue will be solved."

He sighed. "I cannot."

"You must." Viola touched his sleeve. "Until you prove the vessel is newly purchased . . ."

"I will be considered a slaver?" he supplied.

"It is a conundrum, I'll warrant, but there's nothing to be done for it."

A few hours later, Josiah had a similar conversation with three gentlemen from the town council, including the judge on whose decision his freedom rested.

Judge Benton Campbell, whose wife ran the only boardinghouse in Fairweather Key, took charge of the meeting the moment he entered Josiah's cell. Flanked by two of the men who'd seen to the rescue of those aboard the *Jude*, the judge pushed his spectacles into place and began reading the charges against Josiah.

"Now that I've read all that, I've got one question." Blue eyes peered at Josiah from the space between bushy gray brows and wire spectacles. "What say you to the charges of theft of a wrecking vessel and of importing slaves, young man?"

Josiah looked the judge in the eyes, his backbone straight. "I am not guilty, sir."

The judge looked over his shoulder at the men who stood behind him. "You boys hear that?" When the pair nodded, he returned his attention to Josiah. "Your plea has been duly noted and witnessed. I'll figure up your bail and set a trial date."

Josiah did not move a muscle until the door clanged shut behind the men. Only then did he allow his shoulders to sink along his hopes of freedom. Raising bail of any amount would be impossible unless he wrote to his father for help.

"About as likely as snow falling on the wreckage of the *Jude*."

Hezekiah would greet any request for help as confirmation of all the things he'd believed true about his son. He might even come down to Fairweather Key and tell Josiah this himself—right before he laughed all the way back to whatever ship brought him there without paying a cent of the bail.

Josiah looked out at the palms rustling, listened to the sound that had become the background music of his imprisonment, and wondered why God continued to allow him to live like a caged animal.

"It has been two weeks since I sent a letter to Father. I'm sure he's received it by now," Emilie said. "The captain of the *Redfoil* promised he would deliver it straightaway. A very nice man, he was, and I'm certain a man of his word."

Isabelle heard Emilie's words as if they were being spoken from somewhere far away. She spent the last of her energy trying to open her eyes, only to have the effort fail yet again.

"Honestly, Emilie." This voice sounded very much like Mademoiselle Dumont's. "I know your father loves you dearly, but even he might balk at being asked to convey a sum of money under these circumstances. Imagine if he knew the funds were to bail out the man who made it possible for us to escape New Orleans."

Isabelle tried again to open her eyes. Had she misunderstood, or was Josiah in need?

"Vi, dear, be practical. My father loves me. He will help."

. "Well, mine loves me, too," Viola said. "But if I dare write him, I have no doubt he would be on the first ship out of New Orleans to fetch me home."

"Going back to New Orleans is not an option for me, Vi. Not after what I've done to free Isabelle."

Much of what Isabelle heard soon disappeared into the white froth of her mind like so many clouds on a windy day. One moment, they were right in front of her; then the next, they'd drift to a point beyond the horizon, never to return.

She gave in to the blankness for a time. Then came the happy sound of laughter.

Viola's giggle was unmistakable and a welcome change from the sullen and withdrawn woman who'd rarely left her bunk aboard the *Jude*. "So I told the doctor I would help him until he can find a proper nurse. It makes me feel useful, and truly, I am in no hurry to leave."

"I understand," Emilie said. "I am also reluctant to consider leaving the island once Isabelle's health is restored. I find I am enjoying seeing to the lad's schoolwork."

The lad. Isabelle struggled to remember.

"I do find William a dear to teach," Emilie said. "He is such a bright boy. Did you know he's quite adept?"

Yes, William. The boy. Water. The *Jude*.

Isabelle lost interest in the conversation. Perhaps if she concentrated, she could turn the darkness to light.

CHAPTER 21

The stranger's messenger reached Andre Gayarre at a most inopportune time. Fresh from his disastrous voyage to nowhere, he was in no mood to suffer the company of fools. His regular table had been prepared at La Grison, and several ladies awaited his presence.

Yet here he stood in the shadow of the Dumont warehouses with nothing to show for his evening but an empty belly and a clear head. He checked his watch. Five more minutes, and he would give up the venture.

The offer he'd been sent was too profitable to ignore; the details too personal to dismiss. Finally, though, it was the letters of recommendation for John Miller that had garnered the stranger an interview.

At either end of the narrow avenue, Andre's

men were stationed. Another had taken a position just inside the warehouse door. All had weapons that had been fully loaded and tested.

No chances were ever taken when it came to his safety, not after the rumblings that had come back to him through his men. It seemed his future father-in-law had grown weary of waiting for Andre to produce his runaway bride. Only last night, word had arrived that Monsieur Dumont was considering taking action against Andre for, among other things, the damages to the *Perroquin*.

Thus far, nothing had been mentioned regarding the missing captain of that vessel. The few who'd witnessed the man's trek from the deck to the waters of the gulf had been paid well to disappear. Of course, Andre had paid others even more to seek these exiles and eliminate them altogether.

A sign from his watchman told him someone approached. Andre nodded, and a dark-cloaked man of compact stature was allowed to pass the first guard unimpeded.

"Monsieur Gayarre." He offered his hand in a firm handshake.

Andre noted the thick accent and decided the man was from Spain or perhaps Cuba. Caution suddenly became more important. "I don't believe we have been formally introduced."

"I beg to differ," he said as he raised a dark

brow. "I sent letters of introduction that should suffice."

Andre made eye contact with the guard stationed inside the warehouse and saw the man nod before returning his attention to the stranger. "The letters you offer list a name that does not seem to fit, sir."

The man stared at him, then shook his head. "You are right, and for your safety, it is preferable we keep my name out of this. I assure you the letters are authentic." He paused. "But then, I am sure you know that."

He did, having personally contacted each man whose signature appeared on a letter. All said the same thing: John Miller was a man of great means and infinite discretion.

"Shall we walk?" Miller said.

Andre glanced past the stranger to his guards. "I've a better idea. My carriage awaits, and it will afford a measure of privacy that a walk will not."

The stranger considered the idea. "I, too, have a carriage nearby. Several, actually. I'm sure you understand that I will require my men follow us."

"Of course." Andre fell in step beside the man, trying to memorize his features in case the information was needed later.

Once inside the carriage, the man wasted no time making his proposition. "It has come to my attention that you are in need of a vessel."

Andre leaned back against the seat and feigned indifference as the carriage lurched into motion. "First a question. How did you find me?"

"I was apprised of your situation." The man shrugged. "Beyond that, there is nothing you need know."

"My situation?" Andre forced a laugh, yet he wondered what, if anything, the man actually knew.

"My friends are your friends, although I am sure you understand the need for discretion in any dealings you might have with me."

The carriage made a turn onto the broad avenue leading away from the docks. "What sort of fool does business with a man who will not identify himself?"

The stranger gave him an even stare, his dark eyes barely blinking. "A desperate one."

There was no good response to the statement. *You depend on me, Andre. Without me and my money, you have nothing.* His father's words. Andre swallowed hard, yet the bitter taste of the truth remained.

Until Emilie stood in his father's parlor with the dreaded Bible and letters, there was nothing to do but beg for crumbs from his father's table.

John Miller made to reach inside his cloak, and Andre reacted immediately. Before the stranger could blink twice, Andre beheld a pistol inches from his nose.

The man's laughter stunned Andre, as did the folded paper Miller removed from his cloak. Disregarding the weapon, the stranger tossed the document into Andre's lap.

"What is this?" Andre said as he holstered his pistol.

"An offer of sale on a ship much faster than the tub you last attempted to give chase in." He looked away, gazing out the window as if dismissing Andre altogether "By the way, my price includes a second ship. Perhaps you know of it." He paused. "It is called the *Jude*."

The deal struck, Andre ordered the coachman to stop and let the stranger out. "On the morrow, then," Andre said.

"On the morrow," the stranger replied as he disappeared into the darkness.

Andre's evening plans no longer appealed. Rather, he would use the time to prepare for the journey he would take very soon. "Home," he told the coachman.

The lamplights still burned when Andre burst through the door, but his father was not about. "All the better," he mumbled as he traversed the distance between the hallway and the tray of bottles in his father's study.

In keeping with Father's newfound desire to abstain, the tray was nowhere to be found. Andre was about to call for the help when he spied the letter on the desk.

"The handwriting," he said as he lifted the page and began to read, "is undeniably Emilie's."

A moment later, he set the letter down and smiled. "England is cold this time of year," he said with a grin. "And Fairweather Key sounds like a lovely place to visit."

According to Mrs. O'Mara, the month of May had arrived. The woman set such stock on May Day, as she called it, that she prepared a special breakfast and added an arrangement of golden blossoms she called tickseed to the tray.

To Josiah, they looked like the yellow cone-flower that grew alongside the herbs in his mother's cottage garden back in Virginia. The thought sent an uncharacteristic pang of home-sickness through him.

Rather than consume the bounty set before him, Josiah reached for Isabelle's Bible. The pages had dried to a wrinkled mess, but the words were clear and readable. On more than one occasion, his hostess had offered to replace it with one in better condition, but Josiah refused.

He turned to a page and opened it, knowing not where the text would lead. "Honour thy father and thy mother," he read, "as the Lord thy God hath commanded thee; that thy days may be prolonged, and that it may go well with thee, in the land which the Lord thy God giveth thee."

And so it went once again, an exhortation to honor the one man who deserved no such respect. Reaching to the Bible for comfort had instead provided a challenge.

Josiah shut the book and set it back on the table. How easy to argue that when the Bible was written, Hezekiah Carter did not yet exist. It was fool's logic, of course, but trying to believe it gave him a measure of relief.

The door opened with no hymn preceding it. A vaguely familiar red-haired man in working-man's clothing stood in the threshold. He looked as if he had grave doubts whether to enter or leave.

"Land sakes, Mr. Tate," Mrs. O'Mara said, "get on in there and stop wasting time."

He nodded to the jailer, then ducked to step inside, removing his hat to clutch it against his chest. When the door swung shut, he jumped as if he'd been shot.

"You get used to it," Josiah said. "Sorry, it's a poor joke."

The man's face flushed, but he looked Josiah in the eyes as he thrust his hand toward him. "Micah Tate," he said. "I'm the owner of the *Caroline*."

"I thought you looked familiar." The man's handshake was firm, his face honest-looking enough. Josiah gestured toward the bunk. "Won't you sit?"

"Thank you, but no," Tate said. "I'd rather speak my piece standing up."

"All right then." Josiah leaned against the bunk and nodded. "Go on."

"The men and me, well, we feel bad about what happened to you." He looked over his shoulder as if checking to see if they were alone. "Not a one of us believes you're guilty of what you're accused of. I've personally met your family and some of your crew, and they're good folks."

"My family and crew?" He sighed. "Aye, thank you. I hired good men where I could find them, and William is a good lad."

"And the ladies . . ." The scarlet in his face flamed deeper. "Well, anyway, I just wanted you to know we're working on Judge Campbell to let you go." He paused to study the toes of his well-worn boots. "I reckon every once in a while the judge needs to prove there's crime enough to keep him on the payroll."

"I see."

Tate's gaze swung up. "Miss Gayarre says there's no money for your bail."

"Had I any money, Mr. Tate, I would use it to pay for the funerals I've caused and the men who no longer have work." His heart lurched. "So Isabelle Gayarre has awakened?"

The wrecker looked confused. "No, it's Miss Emilie Gayarre I speak of."

"Ah." He nursed the disappointment for a moment longer before extending his hand to Micah Tate. "I appreciate your visit, Mr. Tate, and I would ask that you tell the other men I am in their debt."

So much debt. Lord, only You can repair this damage.

Slowly, the red-haired man stepped back. Strange, but it almost seemed as though he had more to say. Finally, he spoke. "There's a man in town. Just rolled in with the tide. Heard some of the men down at the docks saying he's been asking about the *Jude*. I figured you ought to know that maybe someone's come to see to getting you out."

So Hezekiah had found him. Josiah affected a casual attitude. "Is that so? Did he happen to mention his name?"

"Don't know, but the boys said he acted like he knew you. Said he mentioned you by name." Tate jammed his hat back on his head. "I haven't seen him, but if I do, I'll ask."

"No need," Josiah looked down at his bare feet and borrowed clothes. "I'm sure he will find me. I'm certainly a captive audience."

Tate gave him another awkward look, then knocked on the cell door and called to Mrs. O'Mara.

Josiah shrugged. "I seem to be making poor jokes today."

After the wrecker made his exit, Josiah sat on the bunk and closed his eyes.

"Lord, I know what you say about honoring your father, but I'm not so sure you've ever met Hezekiah Carter." He looked up at the water-marked ceiling and spoke to He who was not bound by such limitations as jail cells. "Were I to admit it, I am no saint either. Therein lies the conundrum."

Isabelle stretched and opened her eyes. A room came into view that was at once cozy and unfamiliar. Near a window that framed a view of an undertaker's office beside a harbor full of boats at anchor and men laboring, a woman worked with needle and thread.

Moving her head to the right, Isabelle could see the other side of the chamber. A curtain of dark velvet had been drawn together to cover what might be a door. On either side of the curtain were tables of some elaborately carved style. Each had been situated with a tall vase filled with flowers in a riot of colors.

Turning farther, she spied a bookcase where every sort of volume seemed to rest alongside strange objects and tiny, framed silhouettes of men, women, and children. Just beyond the bookcase was a desk of massive proportions that held an assortment of papers in neat and orderly piles, each topped with something to keep the sea breeze from whisking it to the floor.

The oil lamp burned on the desk, casting a golden glow across the pages and disappearing into shadows behind the overlarge leather chair. Remnants of the lamplight poured through a prismlike paperweight and speckled the quilt that lay atop her with rainbow dots.

A movement caught Isabelle's eye. She turned to follow it and found it was Viola Dumont who sat near the window. The needle in her hand caught the light each time she pulled it through the snow-white fabric in her lap.

Outside, wisps of white clouds slid along the horizon and disappeared from view. The sky, so blue it hurt to look at it, was otherwise clear and bright. A man dressed in the fine clothing of a gentleman strode across the docks, his cane tapping a rhythm she could almost hear. Several men stopped their work as he passed, but none greeted the dandy.

Isabelle watched for a moment, unsure whether she dreamed. There had been so many dreams.

Fire.

Water.

The smell of sickness and death.

Emilie.

Viola.

Someone referred to only as *Doctor* who never seemed to have good news.

Another named Mrs. O'Mara who spoke of Josiah in hushed terms.

Mrs. Campbell who laughed much.

Mr. Tate who didn't.

All of it she'd surely imagined. Or had she?

Her fingers traced the pattern on the quilt. Vaguely familiar, it was, yet she knew she'd never been in this room until now.

But when was now? She glanced out the window and guessed it must be nearing midday.

Her attention returned to Mademoiselle Dumont. She wore a look of peace and contentment and even hummed softly as she tied the knot and began to rethread the needle. Once the deed had been accomplished, she stabbed the needle into the pincushion and sighed.

She held the fabric up as if to study it, and Isabelle could see the garment was a man's shirt. "The man has exceedingly broad shoulders," she muttered as she rose and headed for the velvet curtains. "I do hope it fits."

Parting the curtains, Mademoiselle Dumont stepped out and called to someone whose name Isabelle could not quite hear. "See that this is ironed and sent to Mrs. O'Mara along with the other clothes immediately, please," drifted through the small opening in between the panels of velvet.

A moment later, the mademoiselle returned and took up her seat by the window. She reached into a basket near her feet and pulled out another piece of cloth. This one was smaller and pale green in color, and it might have been the bodice to a dress. As Isabelle looked closer, she could see that the fabric was sprigged with pink flowers.

Isabelle watched a moment more, then cleared her throat. "Mademoiselle Dumont, what are you sewing?" She must have spoken aloud, for her companion nearly fell from the chair.

The mademoiselle tossed the garment into the air, seemingly heedless of where it landed. "Did you truly speak, Isabelle?"

She tried but could not respond.

CHAPTER 22

On the morning of the second day of May, the now-familiar voice of Mrs. O'Mara sounded in the hallway. *"Dependent on Thy bounteous breath, we seek Thy grace alone."* The key turned in the lock but did not open. "Captain Carter, might I ask you to help?"

Josiah jumped off the bunk and padded to the door. "Help you how, Mrs. O'Mara?"

"By opening the door, of course."

"Of course."

He turned the latch, and the door swung open. Before him stood the jailer, her arms full with what looked like a set of folded clothes. Atop the clothing was a shiny pair of boots. Upon closer inspection, he recognized them as his own.

"What is this?" he asked as she pressed past him to set the items on the bunk.

" 'Tis an interesting thing, this bond of friendship," she said. "You seem to have already found many here on the key."

Many friends? He, the man who ran the *Jude* aground and failed to save so many lives?

"I fail to understand."

He reached for one of the boots and lifted it up. The leather was polished with great care, and the soles newly shod. Upon inspection, he found the other had received similar treatment.

"What is there to understand, Captain Carter? Much as my husband's shirt pulls and strains at the shoulders, I warrant you'd be judged indecent should you try to work in it." She looked down at the trousers he wore and shook her head. "And my Clarence, he's not near as tall as you, though that might be to your advantage should you be forced to go wading."

"But what sort of thing is this?" he said as he laid them back on the bunk. "It appears someone has restored my footwear to its former glory."

Josiah sat back on the bunk and picked up the shirt. Someone had taken fine linen and fashioned it into a garment that would have stood him in good stead at the president's table.

In fact, he had once worn a shirt much like this when President Monroe and his wife had shared the dinner table with the Reverend Hezekiah Carter and family.

"I'm sorry, but your other clothes were beyond repair," Mrs. O'Mara said. "Except for the boots, that is. I reckon you already figured that out."

He touched the mother-of-pearl buttons someone had sewn at the neck. An expensive touch for a garment given in charity to one who could not at present repay.

"Who would do this?"

"Your friends, Captain Carter." She turned to make a *tsk-tsk* sound at the sight of the still-full tray. "I'll not take this just yet, as it's obvious you've forgotten to eat." She strolled to the door, then paused to glance over her shoulder. "I have it on good authority you'll not be dining here tonight."

"Is that so?" He smiled. "Then I suppose I should return Clarence's clothing. Please convey my sincere thanks."

The door closed, and Mrs. O'Mara walked away singing some hymn he did not recognize. He threw off the old clothes and donned the new, then sat on the bunk to pull on his boots.

It was the first time he'd worn shoes in almost a month.

Josiah stood and walked the perimeter of the room. Gathering his things would take no time at all. All he had was Isabelle's Bible, and even that was not truly his.

Not at all the state in which he had expected to greet his father when this adventure began.

Exactly how he would respond to Hezekiah's gift of bail would depend on the manner in which the gift was given. *No.* Josiah sighed. *It would not.*

Some time later, the door latch opened, and the judge stepped inside. "Your bail's been posted, Mr. Carter," he said. "A decision will be made in a week or two as to whether or not we'll be prosecuting you for slaving."

Josiah squared his shoulders and tamped down on his temper. "I am not a slaver, and I challenge any man to prove I am."

"I reckon if we can't, then you'll be free to go," the judge said without looking Josiah in the eye.

"Then I'll look forward to discussing this with you further as soon as possible." Josiah nodded toward the door. "Am I free to go?"

"For now," Judge Campbell said, "but don't leave the island unless it's for work purposes."

Work. He would need something to employ him and fill his time until Isabelle's health was restored.

Indeed, once the pleasantries were exchanged with his father and the words that needed to be spoken were said, Josiah would make haste to see Isabelle. Perhaps he would do that first and speak to Hezekiah later.

He tested his freedom by stepping over the threshold into a small hallway. To the right, the smell of food being prepared enticed him, and he realized he hadn't touched a bite on his breakfast tray. To the left, however, was daylight and with it, freedom.

He would go hungry before he stepped back into that jail cell again.

"She spoke to me, Doctor," Viola Dumont said. "She sat right up and asked me what I was sewing."

"Calm down, Miss Dumont. It's likely you imagined this, given the length and seriousness of her illness."

Isabelle lay very still and listened while the debate over her health raged on just outside the barrier of the velvet curtains. She thought of calling out to them, but the idea of ending the conversation so soon did not appeal. Rather, she liked the idea that Viola Dumont might stand up to a man, even if it was over an issue as trivial as this.

"I know what I saw, Dr. Hill, and what I saw was Isabelle Gayarre with her eyes open and speaking just as if she'd awakened from a nap."

The temptation to aid the mademoiselle in her endeavor was too strong. "I'm afraid she's right,

298

Dr. Hill. I did speak to the mademoiselle, although I must say I don't feel rested at all." The pair barged through the curtains and nearly tumbled atop her. "So, as for the claim of my speaking as if I'd just awakened from a nap, that part is false. The rest, however, is true."

The doctor, a rather bookish-looking man with a pleasant face and a shock of dark hair, raced to the desk and opened a drawer. A moment later, he pointed some sort of odd instrument at her eyes, temporarily blinding her. When she opened her mouth to complain, he stuck something inside. Through the ordeal, Viola Dumont stood at the man's side.

Seemingly satisfied, Dr. Hill leaned away and nodded. "She seems fit and well."

"Indeed she does, Doctor," Viola said. "Why, honestly after all this time for Isabelle to merely awaken with no obvious trauma cannot be explained in any other way than to call it a miracle."

Dr. Hill gave Viola a sideways glance. "Be that as it may, I would like to do further tests to see the nature of the illness and possibly prevent any complications."

Viola looked skeptical. "Do you think that she might have complications?"

Isabelle crossed her arms over her chest. "Would both of you please stop talking as if I am not in the room?"

"Yes, dear," Viola said. "Do tell us how you're feeling, other than tired, of course."

"Well, I'm a bit hungry."

The doctor smiled. "A good sign, indeed. I wonder if you might wish to try and sit, Miss Gayarre."

Isabelle attempted to lean forward and rest her weight on her elbows, but the effort did her in. "Perhaps not just yet," she said.

"Indeed, rest is what I prescribe," the doctor said. "And I'll have Viola fetch something for you to eat from the boardinghouse." He peered down his nose at her. "Do you feel up to a bit of lunch?"

"I do."

"That's a good sign." He reached for a pen and began making notes in a notebook. When he looked up, he seemed concerned. "Tell me, Miss Gayarre, what do you remember about the accident?"

"Accident?" Isabelle thought hard. Bits of memories jolted her. Water. A piece of driftwood. Then Josiah scooping her up and bringing her to safety. All this she relayed to the doctor, who seemed to be trying to write down each word.

Sleep threatened, but Isabelle was not yet ready to give in. "Josiah," she said as she stifled a yawn. "I would like very much to see him."

Viola and the doctor exchanged a look. "Of course," Viola said. "You rest, and I shall see if I can find the captain when I fetch your lunch."

●●●

Josiah had not felt sunlight on his face in what seemed like years. The moment he stepped away from the squat building that obviously served as a jail, a courthouse, and a home to the O'Mara family, he paused to close his eyes and let the sun warm his face.

It was May, and with the month came the brisk wind that made for fine sailing. The thought pained him. What good was a sailor with no vessel?

The thought disappeared as he considered what awaited him in port. What sailor would want to set sail with Isabelle Gayarre waiting on shore?

"Isabelle." Where would she be? In a town the size of Fairweather Key, there should be no problem finding the infirmary.

For that matter, where was Hezekiah?

Josiah glanced behind him, thinking perhaps his father had chosen to wait to present himself. Only the lonely facade of the jailhouse greeted him.

"So he's going to make me wait before confronting me. How very much like my father." Josiah strode toward the main street when, to his astonishment, a thought occurred. *'Tis you who are very much like your father. What say you to this charge?*

For a man only just tasting freedom after weeks

behind bars, any indictment was poorly timed. This one, with such a powerful truth at its core, was particularly painful.

Unlike the accusation of slaving and theft, which were patently false, he could name any number of ways that he very much resembled Hezekiah Carter. Thankfully, there were just as many ways in which they differed.

Still, the accounting left Josiah with a sobering thought: Forgiveness worked both ways.

He shrugged off the thought and concentrated on his search for Isabelle. He could peer into the doorways of every home in the key, or he could go down to the docks and find Micah Tate or one of the other wreckers. They would know where to find her.

A tap on his shoulder stopped Josiah in his tracks. He whirled around to find a well-dressed man. Though the day was temperate, the man wore a heavy coat and gloves.

"Monsieur Carter, we meet at last," he said. "Perhaps you know of me?"

Josiah shook his head. "Should I?"

The man looked disappointed and then, by degrees, dangerous.

Were it not for the sinking of the *Jude*, he'd be properly armed and ready to do business with the fellow should the need arise. Without his knife, Josiah knew the issue might require settlement with his bare hands.

He clenched his fists and waited. If need be, Josiah was ready.

Never had he backed down from a fight.

The fellow's smile seemed genuine enough, so Josiah relaxed a notch.

"New Orleans," he said. "Our fathers are acquainted. Perhaps you did not know this."

Again, Josiah felt his senses send out a warning. "Did my father send you?"

The man seemed to consider the question before nodding. "I'm sure you understand he cannot be associated with such an endeavor as seeing to the release of his son from prison."

"It was a jail, not prison," Josiah corrected. "Nonetheless, I'm certain my father would not know the difference. His humiliation would be the same in either case."

"I've been sent to fetch you aboard that vessel." He pointed to a fine, three-masted schooner. "Have you any bags or possessions that need delivery to it?"

Josiah stopped short. In his haste to leave, he'd forgotten his sole possession of value. "Only one, but I'm afraid I've left it back at the jail. Wait here."

He turned to retrace the path back to the jail only to find his father's man had fallen in step beside him. "Allow me to accompany you," he said.

Something in the way the fellow spoke the words shouted a warning. Josiah curled his fists and picked up his pace. He'd not start any fights that might land him back in jail, but he certainly would not be set upon by whatever manner of con man or thief Hezekiah's man was without defending himself.

If the incident happened within sight of judge and jailer, all the better. He'd not be falsely accused and sent to a cell again.

The jail loomed ahead, and only the desire to fetch Isabelle's Bible could override the strong need to avoid the place altogether. "Perhaps you will want to wait here," he said as he reached the door.

"I wouldn't think of it," the man said.

Josiah stopped and drew himself up to his full height. "So my father has paid you to shadow me."

An accusation, not a question.

He waited for an answer, only to see the man staring at something behind him. Josiah turned slowly and saw nothing out of the ordinary.

"Whatever my father has paid you, go back and tell him it wasn't worth it. And you can tell him this is a small island. I will be easy to find should he desire to do so."

The man studied him a moment, then gave a curt nod. "Perhaps you are right," he said slowly. "I've other errands to run."

"Then you'll want to be off." Josiah watched the man stride toward the docks and disappear into the crowd. With a sigh, he stepped inside the long hallway leading to the cell. Without looking back, he strode into the dark room and found the Bible on his bunk.

No, this was no longer his bunk.

Josiah lifted his gaze to the heavens. *Thank You for getting me out of here. Please, would You work a similar miracle with my father?*

A knock on the door behind him alerted Josiah to the fact he was not alone. "I told you not to—"

When he turned around, Viola Dumont stood in the doorway. "She's awake," the woman said. "Isabelle is awake."

"Tell me how to find her." Josiah shook his head. "No, better yet, take me to her."

"I cannot. I'm to fetch a meal for her." She smiled. "Can you feature it? She is hungry." A giggle followed. "You'll find her with the doctor. His office is three buildings past the boarding-house."

"Three buildings past the boardinghouse." He snatched up the Bible and followed Miss Dumont out the door. "So you'll be fetching Isabelle's lunch then?"

"I will." She glanced up at him. "Might I bring you something, as well?"

"Oh, no. But thank you all the same." Josiah headed quickly into the sunshine and breathed deeply of the fresh salt air, then paused to allow

Miss Dumont to catch up. Once they reached the main street, he turned to his companion. "How is William?"

Sidestepping a pair of rough-looking fellows deep in conversation outside the courthouse, Miss Dumont touched the pocket of her skirt and frowned in their direction. A moment later, her smile returned. "The boy is quite well, Captain. We've enjoyed his company these past few weeks, and he has blossomed into quite a scholar under Emilie's tutelage."

"Excellent. Does he ask about me?" He looked over at Miss Dumont, who seemed frozen in place. "Are you unwell?"

She seemed not to hear him. Rather, her face went pale, and she swayed a bit. Josiah steadied her with a hand to her elbow. "Perhaps you should sit for a moment. I'm sure the strain of—"

"Oh no," came out soft as a breath. "Andre."

She turned and ran.

"Miss Dumont, wait!" Josiah headed after her only to find his path blocked by the two ruffians they'd just passed outside the courthouse.

He watched Miss Dumont hurry past the boardinghouse, but the number of people milling about made it impossible to know if she'd been followed.

"You'll be needing to stay right here, mate." This from a greasy-haired sailor whose last bath must've been months ago.

"Easy there, mate." A second less-fragrant fellow stepped forward and pressed his finger into Josiah's shoulder. "You just got out of jail. Wouldn't want to be thrown back in for accosting a law-abiding citizen."

There. Josiah spied the man shadowing Miss Dumont. Conspicuous for his formal clothing, the man still seemed to be trying to call no attention to himself. Three buildings past the boardinghouse, Miss Dumont slipped inside.

Three buildings past the boardinghouse. *The infirmary.* His father must know about Isabelle.

"He's not listening, Reginald."

Josiah returned his attention to the thugs. "Tell Hezekiah Carter his man is chasing the wrong woman," he said as he pressed past them and headed for the infirmary, the Bible tucked under his arm.

"Hezi-who?" one of them said.

"I don't know," the other responded. "I think he's trying to trick us."

Greasy Hair raced up and tried unsuccessfully to tackle Josiah. Reginald found slightly more success reaching to grab Josiah by the arm, causing Isabelle's Bible to tumble out of his reach.

When Reginald raised his fist to throw a punch, Josiah beat him to it. A second punch, and Reginald hit the ground and rolled onto his stomach just inches from Mrs. O'Mara's flower garden.

"You can't follow the boss." Greasy Hair threw his shoulder into Josiah's midsection.

He went rolling backward, the air whooshing from his lungs. As Josiah fought to breathe, Greasy Hair helped Reginald up. The sailor landed on his feet cursing and ordering Greasy Hair to finish Josiah off.

A pair of matrons skittered by, shock registering on their faces. Josiah held his position, unwilling to risk drawing helpless women into danger.

"He's down now," Greasy Hair said. "Let him be."

Ignoring his companion, Reginald stalked toward Josiah. Rage contorted his features and his fists. Josiah remained still, waiting. From his vantage point, he saw the well-dressed man nearing the entrance to the infirmary.

Reginald yanked Josiah up by the collar, and he rose swinging. Greasy Hair joined the fray and, in a matter of seconds, both sailors were down. Josiah lingered a moment longer to be sure his assailants wouldn't follow, then sprinted to the infirmary.

As he reached the door, a single shot rang out.

CHAPTER 23

Josiah burst through the door, heedless of the fact he went in unarmed. Sprawled in the middle of a sparsely furnished room was the well-dressed man looking well and truly dead.

Miss Dumont wept in the arms of a man Josiah assumed was the doctor. A dueling pistol with an ivory stock lay on the floor between their feet. By contrast, the dead man's weapon was still in its holster.

"Are you injured?" he asked Miss Dumont.

"No." She pointed to the man on the floor and backed up until she brushed against a broad expanse of velvet curtains. "But he's dead. I know he's dead."

The other man held Miss Dumont at arm's length. "I must see to him." He looked to Josiah, then knelt at the man's side. "Name's Dr. Hill. I figure you must be Josiah Carter."

Josiah nodded.

A few steps behind Josiah seemed to be half the men and most of the women in Fairweather Key, among them an irritated-looking Judge Campbell. The judge yanked the napkin from his collar as he pressed his way through the crowd.

"Somebody better tell me why I had to leave a perfectly good lunch to come over here." He looked down at the dead man. "Anybody know who he is?"

"Andre Gayarre," Miss Dumont said.

"Gayarre?" The name hit Josiah harder than any punch. Was this man a relative of Emilie and Isabelle? Surely his father would not stoop to such a level. He searched the man's face for some sign of similar parentage and found none.

The judge pointed. "Seeing as this is your office, Dr. Hill, you want to tell me what's going on here?"

Dr. Hill rose and gave Miss Dumont a reassuring look, then turned his attention to the judge. "Miss Dumont and I were having a discussion about a patient when this ruffian barged in without announcing himself and began acting in a menacing way to Miss Dumont. Seeing a threat to the ladies, I had no choice but to protect those under my care."

Josiah rubbed his sore jaw as he watched the man carefully, looking for deceit. At least part of that story was completely untrue, and both he and the doctor knew it.

Miss Dumont knew it, too, for her lip quivered, and she buried her face against the doctor's shoulder. "No, he came after me," she said, "and I shot him."

Dr. Hill rose and gathered Miss Dumont into an

embrace, making soft sounds as she wept on his shoulder. Looking over the woman's head, the doctor addressed the crowd. "She's distraught and has no idea what she's saying."

"I had to shoot him else he'd never have left me alone." Miss Dumont swallowed hard. "He was an awful man who would have killed me with his fists had I not found the doctor's gun."

The judge glanced over at Josiah. "Funny how this man got shot the same day you were let out of jail." His look became a glare. "And looks like you were the first one on the scene. You getting this pretty lady to lie for you now?"

Miss Dumont gasped, and the doctor protested. Josiah, however, stood firm and forced himself not to react. Micah Tate's words of warning had been well timed.

"And I saw him fighting with two men right in front of the courthouse," someone called from the back of the crowd.

Another shouted an agreement while a third said something about the *Jude*. "Maybe we ought to set up a jury right here," the judge said. "We got plenty of able-bodied citizens of Fairweather Key in attendance."

"You do that, Judge Campbell, and I'll be forced to tell everyone who will listen that you condemned an innocent man." The doctor pointed to the man on the floor. "This man is Andre Gayarre, formerly affianced to Miss Dumont. She left home because she feared his violent nature. As you all can see, her fears were not unfounded."

So this had nothing to do with Hezekiah. Josiah let out a long breath. Much as he hated to see a man die, even a bad one, it was a relief to know his father hadn't sent the fellow. The judge stared at Josiah a moment longer, then nodded. "I can see how it might have been like you said, Doc."

Judge Campbell cleared his throat. "Doc Hill, is it your professional opinion that this man is dead?"

Dr. Hill nodded. "It is, sir."

Affixing his dinner napkin to his collar once more, the judge looked over his shoulder. "Did I see Bert the undertaker back there?"

"Yes, sir, Judge Campbell," someone called.

"All right, let's get this over with. In my official position as judge of this island, I do hereby pronounce this man—what's his name?"

"Gayarre," Miss Dumont supplied. "Andre Gayarre."

"Andre Gayarre," the judge continued, "deceased by way of gunshot." He gave Josiah a hard look. "I'm taking the doctor's word for the fact this man died at his hands and not by the devices of anyone else in this room." When no one contradicted him, the judge continued. "Cause of death is self-defense. I declare this case closed. Now if anyone else gets shot before I finish my lunch, they can just wait."

The crowd began to part, and Emilie Gayarre walked into the room, her head held high. "I understand there's been an unfortunate incident with my brother." Her eyes lowered, and she gasped. "Oh, Andre," she said as her knees buckled.

Josiah went to her but knew not what to say. Instead, he knelt beside her and allowed her to lean against him.

"This is your brother, young lady?" the judge asked.

When Emilie did not speak, Miss Dumont came forward and joined her. The ladies embraced as Josiah rose. "I'm so sorry, Emilie," she repeated as she broke into sobs.

"Yes," the doctor finally said. "Andre is Emilie's younger brother."

"That's all I needed to know. Everyone out," the judge called. "And Bert?"

The undertaker wove his way through the departing townsfolk. "Right here, sir."

"Here's your customer," the judge said as he headed for the door.

"Yes, sir." Bert removed his hat to reveal close-cropped blond curls that made him look more like an angel than an undertaker. "I'm real sorry, miss," he said to Emilie.

Josiah placed his hand on her shoulder. "Perhaps I should escort you from here so the gentlemen can see to him."

Ignoring him, Emilie leaned over the body of her brother, tears falling one after the other onto the man's dark waistcoat. He could see the resemblance now, the tilt of the nose and the shape of the chin. Beyond those physical things, this man obviously bore no resemblance to the kind woman Josiah had entrusted with his brother.

The undertaker ducked his head. "I'll just wait outside until you're ready for my men and me to remove the . . . that is . . . your brother." His face flushed, Bert made haste to follow the crowd out onto the street. "I'm real sorry," he said again as he left.

"So am I." Emilie kissed her forefinger and touched it to her brother's lips. "Oh, Andre," she whispered.

Rather than look at the ladies, Josiah watched the townspeople file out. When Dr. Hill reached for the weapon, he noticed the man did not handle it like one who had experience in firearms. Rather, the man held the dueling pistol between his thumb and forefinger as if he found it distasteful.

Interesting.

Josiah turned his attention to Miss Dumont. The woman who had stepped aboard the *Jude* was a pale and delicate creature with frightened eyes and blood on her wedding dress. Having worked for her father, Josiah had no doubt the old man would have tutored his daughter in all she needed to make her way in the world. Including wielding an ivory-handled dueling pistol with deadly precision.

Emilie embraced Miss Dumont once more, then rose, her back straight. "I should see to William," she said. "I'm sure he's wondering where I am."

She gestured for the undertaker to return. Bert nodded and headed inside to kneel beside the body. A moment later, another man joined him.

Josiah stepped in front of her and reached for her hand. "Emilie," he said, "you have taken care of William, and I am in your debt. Let me see to your brother's arrangements. Now that you've said your good-byes, it might go easier on you if you don't have to shoulder that burden, as well."

She stared at him as if debating, then finally nodded. "Your brother has been a delight, and I'll not allow you to think you owe me anything for his care. It is I who am grateful that I had him for company. I will, however, be the one to write to our father and to speak to the undertaker regarding Andre. I am most grateful that you thought to offer. You're a good man."

He nodded and followed Emilie to the door, shielding her view as the undertakers began to see to the dead man. They got as far as the street before Emilie stopped him.

"William will be asking for you." She shielded

her eyes from the sun as she looked up at him. "Do come around to the boardinghouse after your visit with Isabelle."

Isabelle.

His breath caught.

"Aye," he said. "I am anxious to see my brother."

"And my sister, as well, I'm sure." Emilie touched his sleeve. "You've just seen how fleeting a life can be. Do not take a moment of it for granted. Go to Isabelle."

Josiah ducked his head. It seemed shameful to talk about good things with a woman who'd just left the side of her dead brother.

"Go," she repeated.

He nodded and walked back inside, carefully avoiding the undertaker and his assistant. The doctor and Miss Dumont were deep in discussion, but their words ceased when they caught sight of him.

No doubt that pair had plenty to talk about.

"Doctor," Josiah said slowly, "I'd be much in your debt if you would tell me where I can find Isabelle."

"Captain," Miss Dumont said, "a word with you first, please."

The doctor blinked hard, then sighed. "If you'll excuse me, I'll go and check on the patient before Mr. Carter goes in."

The patient? Josiah watched the doctor disappear behind the velvet drapes. "Isabelle?"

Miss Dumont stepped between Josiah and the curtains. "Yes, she's been recuperating in the doctor's study. It seemed the only proper thing to do as she certainly couldn't stay upstairs. That's where the doctor sleeps."

"Of course." He stared at the slight gap between the panels. "She's been this close, and I didn't know," he said under his breath.

Something touched his hand, and Josiah looked down to see that Miss Dumont had placed two letters there. Josiah grasped the pages, both of which had broken seals, and shook his head.

"What's this?"

She leaned close. "I found them in his jacket pocket, already opened."

Josiah looked down at the spidery handwriting and saw Emilie's name. He moved that letter to see another below it addressed to Isabelle.

"Why give them to me? Shouldn't you be delivering these to the ladies?"

"Possibly," she said, "but I wonder if Emilie's letter might need to wait a few days. I'm sure the events of today have come as a shock to her."

He looked down at the Dumont woman, searching her face for any sign of guile but saw none. "I'm sure," he echoed.

She frowned and touched his jaw. "What happened to you? It looks as if someone hit you."

When Josiah did not answer, a look came over her. "Those men on the sidewalk, they were with Andre, weren't they?"

"Aye," Josiah said. "But I doubt you'll find any trouble from them. Men of that ilk don't keep loyalties past the grave. I'll warrant as soon as news arrives that their employer is no longer breathing, they'll be shipping off on the next tide."

"I pray you're right," she said. "Now about those letters. Give them to Isabelle. She can choose the proper time for her sister to read them."

"Captain Carter?" Josiah looked up to see the doctor standing between the parted curtains. "Miss Gayarre will see you now."

He held the letters to his chest and willed himself not to run.

In truth, the anxiety of facing a mob of angry headhunters in the Spice Islands paled in comparison to walking into the room where Isabelle lay. While the headhunters had been after his body, Isabelle Gayarre had stolen his heart.

Josiah stepped into the room where Isabelle lay, intent on telling her how much he'd missed her. But when he caught sight of the woman who had dominated his thoughts and stolen his dreams lying beneath the quilt his own mother had fashioned, Josiah forgot how to speak.

For a moment, he also forgot how to walk.

Standing there like a fool, all he could do was fist his hands and wait for his senses to return.

The doctor busied himself at a desk in the corner of the room, providing Josiah with something to look at other than Isabelle, yet Josiah found his attention would focus nowhere but on her.

Her illness had chiseled Isabelle's full cheeks into more sculpted angles, and she still bore the lightest of shadows under her eyes. When she smiled, the shadows disappeared.

"Isabelle," he managed.

"She's still quite weak, and I've given her another dose of laudanum to keep her calm, so she may soon be sleeping again." The doctor rose, a length of what looked like toweling under his arm. "But under the circumstances, I think a visit is in order." He headed for the curtained exit, then paused. "Oh, and I conveyed our apologies for the disturbance in the foyer."

"The disturbance?"

"I seem to have dozed through all but the crash of thunder," she said in a voice still thick with sleep. "Odd, how the weather can look sunny yet portend rain. What a blessing that the doctor could offer his foyer for shelter from the lightning."

"Yes," Josiah echoed. "I don't expect we shall see any more thunder today. What say you, Dr. Hill?"

The doctor peered into the foyer, then turned to meet Josiah's stare. "No," he said slowly, "all is quite clear. Now, Miss Gayarre, if you need me, I shall be just outside."

"Thank you."

Josiah approached slowly, the letters held down at his side. While his heart demanded he scoop Isabelle into his arms, his head told him to wait.

I missed you demanded to be spoken. "This is a comfortable room," he said instead.

Sea green eyes looked his way. "Yes, it is, although I must confess I'm a bit tired of it already."

"I understand completely. Say," Josiah said lightly. "I believe that's my quilt." He touched the fabric. "Aye, my mother made this with her own hands. I'm glad it was not lost with the ship."

"Yes. It's beautiful. Perhaps you want to fetch it home with you."

"I have no home." Josiah cringed. "What I mean is, at present I have no need of the quilt. Please continue to enjoy it."

Why are we discussing blankets?

He crushed the letters in his palm and stuffed them into his pocket. Miss Dumont could see to the delivery of these items. It was all Josiah could do to keep the conversation going. He'd not explain the bloodstains on the pages or the broken elaborate wax seals marked with the letter *G*.

Not now.

Not today.

"You're injured."

Isabelle touched his cheek. "An inconvenience caused by slow reflexes and a trusting nature," he said. "Do not trouble yourself."

"I see." Isabelle watched him intently, her fingers worrying with the edges of the quilt. "Might I ask you something, Josiah?"

She said his name. He swallowed hard and managed a nod.

"I have many questions. I remember little of how I got here." Her gaze dropped to the quilt. "I do not even know where here is."

But do you remember your feelings for me?

Pulling a chair near the bed, Josiah offered a smile he hoped would pass for genuine. "Here is Fairweather Key. As to how you got here, well, you were fetched here by boat some three weeks ago."

"The *Jude*?"

"No," he said gently. "Suffice it to say that the locals have a double meaning in the name they have given their island."

Isabelle released her grip on the quilt and began to toy with the ruffle at the neck of her bed jacket. "Oh?"

Put your hand in mine, sea siren.

"Aye." He inched the chair closer. "As it happens, a vessel can only negotiate the reef in fair weather. As the main occupation of the men here is wrecking, it's a fine day when the rain begins to fall."

She seemed confused, yet a smile dawned. "I see," she said. "The *Jude*. Did it arrive in fair weather or foul?"

"Foul, I'm afraid. It is no more." *Are we?*

Closing her eyes, Isabelle looked as if she were attempting to conjure up a memory. "Mr. Banks." Her eyes flew open. "He was ill." She shook her head. "No, he was injured."

"Aye. Burned in a fire upon our exit from New Orleans. You were his nurse," he said.

"I was?" She seemed genuinely surprised, then supremely disappointed. "I don't remember."

His heart sank. *Nor do you recall your love for me.* "Perhaps it's best, then."

"No. I mustn't forget. Something important happened."

Aye, that it did.

Josiah reached across the quilt to touch Isabelle's hand. "Mr. Banks is no longer with us, Isabelle. Hard as you tried to save him, the injuries from the fire were just too severe. 'Tis my understanding that Mr. Harrigan succumbed, as well. On the morrow, I intend to see to the welfare of the remainder of the crew. As their captain, 'tis I who am responsible, and I take that responsibility seriously."

"Banks and Harrigan."

Her eyes welled with tears, and he reached to wipe them away. "You're remembering now, aren't you?"

CHAPTER 24

If the truth were known, Isabelle had never completely forgotten. While her memories of the voyage were hazy and fraught with holes where pieces had been removed, she knew the important things.

The fire at the docks, a storm near the reefs, and Mr. Banks recalling scripture in the hold of the *Jude* were recollections still as real and present in her mind as if they'd just happened.

So was the kiss she shared with Josiah Carter.

He called her a sea siren, and she'd wondered what that meant but had never dared ask. He had also taken to reading her Bible, yet never had he admitted on which side of the Lord's favor he rested.

Asking him now was quite tempting, as was requesting just one more kiss. Neither was possible, however. Not if she were to go ahead with her plan to release him and flee to England. To stay was a fool's dream, as was the idea that she might try and pass for someone she was not. She stared past Josiah to the scene unfolding outside the window and felt a wave of dizziness. Focus became impossible for a moment; then her mind cleared.

A group of men stood in a half circle outside the undertaker's office across the street. Several women and children milled about. It seemed as though they were waiting for something.

Someone, perhaps.

"A penny for your thoughts, Isabelle."

"My thoughts," she said, "are scattered, truly."

Isabelle watched a wagon pulled by a sway-back mare stop in front of the collection of townsfolk. Two men made short work of carrying a body wrapped in what looked to be toweling.

Isabelle tried to make out the faces, but suddenly her eyes seemed to rebel. They wanted to close, and she let them.

"Isabelle?"

Opening her eyes, Isabelle tore her gaze from the goings-on across the street to seek out Josiah. She found him and forced herself to focus.

He reached across to grasp her hand. "I don't want to press my suit until you're well and able to respond," he said, "but I do wonder how much you recall of our conversations at sea."

I would have you kiss me.

Yes, she knew that statement quite clearly. The kiss, she would never forget. It would have to carry her all the way to England and the farmhouse where she would surely call it up on lonely occasions as she quietly lived out the remainder of her days.

Or would it? Be it from the elixir Dr. Hill gave her or the presence of Josiah Carter, her ability to imagine that life began to fade.

The Virginian's broad shoulders slumped. "Your lack of response leads me to believe either you do not recall or you've had a change of heart."

A tear welled up, and she quickly made the attempt to swipe it away. On the second try, she managed the feat. "Neither."

"Neither?" Josiah ducked his head, then looked up to reveal the smile that turned his face from merely handsome to unforgettable.

"I fail to see there might be a third option, Isabelle. Either you love me, or you don't; you want a life with me, or you do not." He rose and returned the chair to its spot by the window, lingering a moment. "Forgive me. I had not intended to speak so freely. I know you're only just beginning to recover, and I'll not trouble you further on this matter."

He made to leave, and Isabelle almost let him go. "Josiah?" she said as he reached the velvet curtains.

Josiah froze but did not turn around. "Aye?"

Isabelle spoke before good sense could prevent it. "Before you go, I would have you kiss me."

" 'Tis the laudanum speaking," he said.

"Perhaps." She had to concentrate to see him clearly, an endeavor quite worth the effort. "But perhaps not. Are you willing to take the risk?"

He turned and moved toward her slowly, deliberately. "The risk?"

Her bravado began to fade. "Yes," she said with more courage than she felt.

"Isabelle, Isabelle," he said, his voice low, husky with emotion, and his smile ripe with promise.

Her heart did a flip-flop even as she fought to keep her eyes on him. What had she done?

Josiah reached the end of the bed and, without looking in her direction, began to run his hand across the quilt at her feet. "I am not a man to be trifled with."

Indeed.

Abruptly he stopped.

Their gazes collided. His smile was gone. "Rest assured that once the laudanum has run its course, you will not find you can make such an offer and see me walk away from it."

How the man did vex her, even as his image swayed and righted itself. "Perhaps I am under the influence of some sort of truth serum. What say you to that possibility, Captain Carter?"

Josiah closed the distance between them yet did not touch her. He smelled of soap, sunshine, and salt air, and his overlong hair had been captured with a single leather cord. Where once his face bore the signs of good health, he now appeared a bit gaunt.

"You need a haircut. And something to eat. You're too thin." She giggled. "But otherwise your appearance has not suffered in the process. You smell nice, too."

Isabelle inhaled readily, willing her fractured senses to memorize the moment as her fingers captured his face. Running her hand across the stubble of his cheek, she tried to smile.

"Isabelle, open your eyes."

She complied, not having remembered closing them.

"Listen carefully."

Isabelle placed her forefinger on Josiah's lips, and he captured her hand in his.

"Are you listening?"

Somehow she managed a nod.

"Good, because this is important." He released her hand and took a step back. "Never have I wanted so much to believe you speak the truth, yet never have I been so uncertain of it."

"But, Josiah, I—"

"I am also uncertain of my ability to remain a gentleman in your presence; thus I shall not

327

return to this place lest I once again find you in this condition."

Her focus fell from his lips to his starched white collar, then rose again. "I am not in a condition," she said.

"No," he responded, "perhaps not, but I am, and I'll not allow it to happen again. Perhaps the next time we meet, you should be the one to find me."

"But how shall I find you?"

"You managed it once; you can manage it again, I. M. Gayarre."

Swift as a jungle cat, he stalked to the exit and disappeared between the velvet curtains, leaving Isabelle to wonder whether she ought to be relieved or disappointed.

"How did you find her, Captain?"

Josiah turned to see Viola Dumont standing in the foyer, an apron covering a dress more suited for the theater than the sickroom. "I found her quite, well, *interesting*."

"I see." She looked down at her gown, then back at Josiah. "My wardrobe is limited and, well, after cleaning, I—"

He held his hands up to stop her. "There's no need to explain. I wonder, however, about Emilie. Perhaps I should fetch William."

"No, don't do that." She smiled. "That boy has done wonders for Emilie. The Lord gifted her with the ability to teach, but other than working with Isabelle, she's never done anything with her talents."

"Working with Isabelle?"

Viola nodded. "It's my understanding Emilie spent the last year tutoring Isabelle."

Until then, he hadn't thought of what Isabelle's life must have been like before the day she appeared on the dock. Perhaps he hadn't wanted to.

Perhaps he knew he couldn't abide the details.

Details. Yes, the letters. He thrust the blood-stained pages toward Viola. "I could not broach the subject of the late Monsieur Gayarre with her for several reasons, not the least of which was the laudanum. I think it better that you choose the proper moment to bestow these on the ladies."

She took the letters and tucked them into her apron. "Perhaps a bit of time should pass before either of them is ready to read these."

"Perhaps." He cast a glance at the floor that only a short while ago had been stained by Andre Gayarre's blood. "I should go and see to William."

Viola studied the ground a moment. "Did you know Andre Gayarre or his father, Captain?"

What an odd question. "I did not."

"No," she said slowly, "I don't suppose you would."

He studied Viola a moment. "I wonder if you might remind Isabelle of something I've told her today."

The change of topic seemed to bring some measure of relief to Viola. "Of course."

"I won't be returning to visit her here. The laudanum makes proper conversation impossible."

Viola worried with the pocket of her apron. "Does she know this?"

"I told her, but I wager she'll not remember." He paused. "When her mind is clear, I would like it very much if she would seek me out."

She nodded. "I will tell her. When her mind is clear."

"Thank you," he said as he made haste to leave the infirmary before his resolve crumbled.

Isabelle's words chased him all the way back to the boardinghouse.

I would have a kiss.

Perhaps I am under the influence of some sort of truth serum.

He picked up his pace lest he turn and run back to her side.

Isabelle must have slept, for when she opened her eyes, the lamps were burning and the curtains had been closed. She stretched and leaned forward on her elbows. The dizziness was gone, ravenous hunger taking its place.

Vague and splintered thoughts of Josiah Carter tried to form, each fading to nothingness before it could be reached. Had he paid her a visit?

Something about thunder seemed important as did the offer of a kiss. She shook her head as if the motion might dislodge the cobwebs binding her thoughts.

The curtains parted, and Emilie stepped inside with her dinner tray. "You're awake," she said.

Odd that Emilie would be the one to see to her this evening. "Where's Viola?"

The tray in her hands wobbled a bit, and Emilie slowed her pace until the dishes were back in place. "I sent her off to enjoy her evening."

"I see." Isabelle watched her take great care to place the tray on the desk. Even in the shadowed room, Isabelle could see something was terribly wrong with Emilie.

She reached out to catch her sister's hand. "You've been crying."

"Don't be ridiculous, Isabelle." Emilie's backbone went stiff, her face suddenly stern. "The doctor says you're making excellent progress. There seems to be no more water in your lungs, and the other injuries you suffered are all healing nicely. We're all very grateful the Lord has spared your life."

"In truth, I do feel quite well."

Isabelle watched Emilie set the tray on the desk, then endured her sister's brisk plumping of pillows and adjustment of bed coverings. What Emilie lacked in nursing skills, she made up for in enthusiasm. Finally, she placed the tray before Isabelle.

"Thank you," Isabelle said. "Won't you sit with me awhile?" She looked down at the tray, the platters overflowing. "Oh my, this is much more than I can ever eat. Do join me."

When Emilie did not respond, Isabelle nudged her. "A penny for your thoughts, Emilie."

A penny for your thoughts.

Had someone said that to her recently? Josiah, perhaps? When Viola returned, she would ask if the captain had yet been to visit.

She sighed. No use in asking anyone. Early on, she'd learned that all who came into her sick-room must have pledged to remain silent on the topic of Josiah Carter.

Emilie shook her head. "The doctor insists you finish your meal without help, dear, and don't forget to take your medication. You have your health to consider, and I don't know what I would do if something happened to you."

Once again, Emilie looked as if she were about to cry as she handed Isabelle an embroidered napkin. "Now do enjoy your food. If you like, I can read from the newspaper while you dine."

"Yes, please."

Feeling more like a dutiful child than an adult,

Isabelle complied, although she refused to take even a sip of the awful medicine. When she could eat no more, Isabelle set the napkin across the tray and waited until her sister finished reading a story from the monthly newspaper about the president's latest battle with Congress.

"Do take your medication, dear," Emilie said.

Isabelle reached for the cup and held it to her lips. "Would you continue reading, please?"

Suspicion showed on Emilie's face as she lifted the paper. With Emilie hidden behind the paper, Isabelle quickly poured the laudanum over the remains of her dinner, then replaced the napkin.

"Might I interrupt you, Emilie?"

The paper crinkled as it lowered. "Of course."

Affecting an innocent expression, Isabelle gestured to the tray. "Might I ask you to remove this? I'm afraid I'm done."

Emilie glared at the half-eaten food and, for a moment, Isabelle thought she might investigate the soggy mess further. "Does Viola require you to finish everything?"

"Oh no," she said quickly.

"I see." She stared another moment as if trying to detect any guile on Isabelle's part, then removed the tray. When she returned, she picked up the paper, stifling a yawn.

"You're tired," Isabelle said. "I assure you I

would not be offended if you were to retire early."

Her sister almost looked grateful. Almost, but not quite.

"No, I must discharge my duties as caretaker to you, Isabelle." Hiding her yawn behind the newspaper, she quickly recovered to shake her head. "I've given Viola my word."

"And what of William?"

Emilie lowered the paper and peered down her nose at Isabelle. "He is in the care of Mrs. Campbell for the evening."

"I see." Isabelle settled against the pillows and listened to a story on the upcoming birthday of Fairweather Key's eldest citizen, the launch of a new vessel into Fairweather Harbor, and finally, the arrival and departure list of vessels for the month of May.

The departure list of vessels for the month of May.

"Emilie, excuse me, but would you mind terribly reading that last sentence again?"

Her sister sighed. "The paper stated the *Amberjack* is to arrive with its monthly load of supplies and will set forth for Key West and ports east on 5 May."

Isabelle's mind began to reel with the possibilities this vessel's departure might bring. "What day is this?"

"May 2," she said. "Why?"

"No reason." Isabelle threw back the quilt and stretched her legs. "I wonder if I might have a bath."

"A bath?" Dark brows rose. "Are you daft, Isabelle?"

"No," she said, "I'm perfectly sane and desperately in need of a hot soak." She paused. "I'm certain it would help speed my recovery."

"Are you now?" She folded the paper. "Isabelle, I'm no fool. What are you planning?"

"I am planning a long bath." Isabelle folded her legs beneath her and leaned toward Emilie. "I'm well, Emilie. I assure you I have no more need of bed rest or that vile laudanum. In fact, I submit I might have been up and around weeks ago had I not been medicated thus."

Emile rose and set the paper down. "You didn't take the laudanum as instructed, did you?"

Isabelle swung her legs over the side of the bed and tested her ability to stand. After a moment, she succeeded. "No, I did not, and forgive my impertinence, but I do not intend to take another dose."

"But your lungs, your hysterics." She sighed. "You do look fine, dear, except that perhaps you seem a bit pale."

"As do you," Isabelle said. "Might I speak in confidence?"

"Yes," she said. "Please do."

"I recall little of today." Isabelle shrugged.

"Actually I recall little that has happened since I left the captain's quarters aboard the *Jude*."

A shocked expression crossed Emilie's face. "You were in the captain's quarters? Isabelle, I thought we discussed the fact that once you left New Orleans you—"

"Emilie, do hold your tongue." She paused. "Were time not of the essence, I might be offended. However, I know you only want the best for me, so please understand that you have no need to worry."

"I believe you," she said slowly.

"Did anything of great import happen while I was under the influence of the doctor's concoction?"

She seemed to consider the question a moment. "Nothing I wish to discuss tonight. Perhaps tomorrow I can speak of it. You did have a visit from Captain Carter."

So her memory hadn't completely failed her.

"I see," Isabelle said. "Good. Now, I must depend on your help. Might I call on you to purchase passage on the *Amberjack* for William and me? I assure you I will see the boy safely to school before making my journey to Clapham."

"But dear, that vessel leaves three days hence."

"Exactly." Isabelle held tight to the bedpost and nodded. "All the more reason I will need your help."

"I won't help you," Emilie said. "I cannot lose another sibling. Not today."

"What are you talking about?" Isabelle shook her head. "Wait, your brother? Has something happened?"

Emilie nodded and between sobs shared the story of Andre Gayarre's demise. "So you see, this is not the day to tell me you're leaving. Not with my only brother awaiting burial."

Isabelle wiped away her tears and stepped carefully toward her sister, gathering her into an embrace. For a moment, they cried together.

"Come with me," Isabelle said when she could manage it. "You've nothing tying you to this place, and going home to New Orleans seems out of the question now. When you and Viola arrived on the dock together, I assumed the plan was for the three of us to escape together."

"Actually, there was no plan." Emilie sighed. "Andre and Vi were to have been married that day. I was to have accompanied Vi to the church, but Andre arrived. He was not a man to be denied his wishes." She paused and looked as if she were reliving the moment. "He is—was—a violent man."

"Why did he come here?"

"Somehow he learned Vi's whereabouts. I assume he wanted to exact revenge." Emilie shivered. "He was always very careful to exact his revenge."

Did she misunderstand, or did Emilie's statement go beyond any association with Viola Dumont? "Emilie?" She looked up. "Is there more?"

"More?" Emilie squared her shoulders. "Whatever do you mean?"

"Oh, I don't know. It just seems as though a man like that would, well, never mind." She looked away. "Perhaps he came to fetch me home. Or to exact revenge for my being taken from your father."

"Our father, Isabelle."

"Our father," she repeated.

"Let me think on it. Tonight I must write to Father, and I have no idea what I'll say. I'll leave anything else, including my future plans, for another day."

"There's time," Isabelle said, "but not an overabundance of it."

"True." She stepped out of the embrace. "What of the captain? I understood there was something between you."

"I think there might have been, but I cannot hold him to it now."

"Cannot or will not?" Emilie shook her head. "The two are not the same."

"I will not cause him to suffer the consequences that an association with me would bring upon him." She paused. "And upon his family."

"Whatever are you talking about?"

"I was born a slave, Emilie. A slave." Her voice

caught, and she paused. "Property to another. By law, a man cannot marry property."

"No one on Fairweather Key treats you like property." She reached over to touch Isabelle's sleeve. "You could easily live out your days here without anyone suspecting. I don't think I'm speaking out of turn here to say that it certainly doesn't seem to be an impediment to the captain's affections."

"I've considered that, although I'm ashamed to admit it," she said. "Prayed about it, actually. I just cannot imagine living a lie, and I don't think the Lord would bless that. Do you?"

"So you will leave him without giving him a choice in the matter?" Emile sighed. "That seems a bit unfair, don't you think?"

A salt-tinged breeze rustled the curtains and blew across the room.

"Emilie, I stopped being concerned with what was fair long ago."

"Still, you must understand this is not going to be well received by the captain. He loves you, you know."

"He thinks he does, but the Lord will provide someone else for him. Now, about that bath . . ."

Emilie put herself between Isabelle and the door. "You're forgetting to consider something. What if the Lord provided you for Josiah Carter?"

Isabelle sidestepped her sister. "Then the Lord will provide a way."

CHAPTER 25

"Josiah!" William launched himself into his brother's arms and held on tight. "Miss Emilie said you were coming back, but I didn't know it would take so long. I missed you terribly." He leaned back to peer into Josiah's eyes. "How was your voyage? Did you fetch us a new ship?"

"My voyage?"

He looked to Mrs. Campbell for guidance, but she wore a blank face. Rather than address the first question, he settled on responding to the second.

"Well now, I wasn't on a voyage, and I haven't exactly worked out all the details, but I assure you there's a trip to England in your future."

"I don't care about England anymore. I just want to be with you." The boy nestled against Josiah's neck. "Don't go away again unless you take me with you. Promise me."

Josiah patted his brother's back and tried to ignore the scowl of the boardinghouse owner. "I cannot promise never to leave you, William," he said, "for what school would take an old man like me as a student?"

The boy began to giggle and, after a while, so did Mrs. Campbell. Josiah seized the moment to begin tickling his brother. Soon the pair were sprawled in the middle of Mrs. Campbell's parlor with William seated firmly atop Josiah's chest.

"I've bested you, Sir Josiah," he said. "Now fetch yon pillow, and we shall duel."

"Oh no, you don't," Mrs. Campbell said through fits of laughter. "I'll not have this sort of mischief in my home. Now upstairs the both of you, and be on your best behavior."

"Aye, Mrs. Campbell," Josiah said with a smart salute. "Off with you, Sir William, for 'tis past your bedtime, and I'll not be answering to Miss Emilie for your departure from her schedule."

"Yes, but now I'll be staying in your room and not with the ladies, because I'm a man." He gave Josiah a defiant look. "And since I am a man, I shall keep man hours like you."

"Indeed you will be a man someday." Josiah scooped the lad up on his shoulders and hauled him up the stairs. "But tonight, you are a boy, and boys need their rest." He feigned a yawn. "And so do men. So whichever category, there shall be sleep in the Carter room momentarily."

But sleep did not come for Josiah. He lay awake listening to the soft, even breathing of the boy he loved enough to move heaven and earth for, enough to steal away from a father Josiah thought would do the lad harm.

"Only to prove I am not capable of caring for him, either."

Josiah leaned over on his side and watched William sleep. Silver rays painted his hair a ghostly pale hue and cast shadows across his childish features. Had he ever been so young?

Tonight the prospect seemed impossible.

Back in Virginia, his mother kept a painting in her bedchamber of him by a fellow named Sully. While his father wished for a dignified portrait of the heir to the pulpit, his mother allowed for one sitting with his favorite playthings. Josiah had run to fetch the toy sailboat that only the week before he had sailed holding to a string along the banks of the New River while his father talked politics and religion with men far too important to be bothered with a lad still in knee pants.

He'd christened that vessel the *Pegasus*, and as Mr. Sully painted, Josiah had told the fellow everything he'd learned about the constellation from the book he'd found in his father's library. When Mr. Sully offered to paint the vessel's name on both the portrait and the actual vessel, Josiah was thrilled.

Not long after Mr. Sully completed the painting, Hezekiah caught sight of the name and broken the vessel in two, tossing it into the river while delivering a lengthy diatribe on the blasphemous name he'd chosen. Many years went by before Josiah discovered there was another Pegasus, this one a winged creature from mythology. By then, his impression of his father and what was blasphemous had suffered serious damage.

William stirred, and Josiah patted his back until the boy settled again. Now that he was free to do so, he'd have to write a letter to his mother.

But what would he tell her? That William's classroom was not inside the venerable gates of the Willington School as she'd planned, but rather in whatever place he and his untrained tutor might choose?

That he'd lost the *Jude*, leaving him with a debt he could not pay on a vessel that no longer existed?

That he had a room for tonight only due to the good graces of the woman whose husband had seen him jailed for three weeks?

That his heart was hopelessly lost to a woman he could neither support financially nor marry legally?

He sighed and shifted positions to stare out the open window at the moon reflecting off the now-calm sea. How easy it would be to wonder where they would all be had the ocean not churned the night he made the attempt to reach the harbor.

How futile.

He closed his eyes and let the ghosts of Harrigan, Banks, and the others follow him into his dreams. After a fitful few hours, Josiah climbed out of bed and cast about for Isabelle's Bible. Perhaps there would be something between its water-damaged covers for the dilemma in which he found himself.

It took only a moment to realize he no longer possessed the Bible, and another moment beyond that to remember why. The following morning, once William had been fed and handed off to Emilie, Josiah set off toward the last place he'd seen it.

Taking the steps of the courthouse two at a time, Josiah stepped inside. A desk cluttered with papers and bearing a sign saying BACK LATER filled the room. Beyond the desk, an open door revealed the one man he'd hoped to avoid for the remainder of his brief stay in Fairweather Key.

Josiah turned to leave. Better to give the volatile Judge Campbell a wide berth.

Unfortunately, the judge saw him and waved him over. "I see the wife sent you over just as I asked." He set his pen down. "I love her, but sometimes she can be forgetful."

Not daring to respond, Josiah merely waited for the judge to get on with whatever conversation he intended to have. Like as not, he'd be doing more jail time over whatever unknown offense he'd committed.

"Actually, I was only hoping to inquire as to the whereabouts of a lost Bible."

The judge looked at Josiah with what seemed to be equal parts surprise and disbelief. "Sit down, Mr. Carter."

The judge pointed to the lone chair, a carved masterpiece with water-stained silk that looked as if it belonged in some society matron's drawing room. The desk it sat before was of the same ilk, finely carved and likely expensive. The contrast to the rough-hewn floors and simple construction was striking.

And very much reminiscent of the dinner trays Mrs. O'Mara had delivered to his jail cell.

Josiah complied, albeit reluctantly. Better to humor the judge and leave quickly than irritate him and remain indefinitely.

"One never knows what the wreckers will find," Judge Campbell said as he pushed back from the desk. "In case you were wondering about the furnishings."

"They did catch my attention." He touched the arm of the chair, then gave the judge his full attention. "The quality is quite nice."

Judge Campbell rose to walk around the desk and rest his hip on the edge. "What do you know about wrecking, son?"

"Very little, actually."

Nodding, the judge crossed his arms over his chest. "You planning to stay long?"

Not if I can help it. "I had not intended to do more than deliver an ill crew member to the doctor for attention." He forced himself to pause and keep his expression neutral. "With the loss of my vessel, I'm afraid I'm not certain what my next move will be."

"Yes, well, it's that ship of yours I'd like to talk to you about. One of the things, anyway."

"I see." *Here it comes. Fetch the handcuffs.* "I'll tell you what I can, sir, but I only possessed the *Jude* for a short while."

He nodded. "So you say."

Josiah's temper flared, but he forced himself to ignore it. "Had the vessel not been lost, I would offer proof. At the moment, the only thing I can give you is my word."

Judge Campbell seemed to be considering the statement. "For now, I suppose that'll do."

A thought occurred, and Josiah decided to act on it while the judge seemed in a decent mood. "As I mentioned, I know little about the process of wrecking," he said slowly, "so I wonder if you might help me understand something."

"I will if I can." He shifted positions. "What is it you want to know?"

Help me say this the right way, Lord. "When a vessel is wrecked, there is compensation to the owner, correct?"

The judge nodded. "Whatever's brought in is sold at auction. The owner gets half the proceeds, and the wrecker gets a third."

"Who gets the rest?"

"Me and the state," he said matter-of-factly.

"I see." Even in wrecking there was a payoff. "And if there's an item of sentimental value offered at auction, might the owner be allowed to purchase the item at a fair price before it is shown to the public?"

Judge Campbell gave him a sideways look. "What're you wanting off that boat, boy?"

"A gift I purchased for my mother while in the Orient." He paused and tried to look as nonchalant as possible. "A painted sewing kit with ivory thimbles and thread holders." He paused. "I looked long and hard before finding just the right one." *The truth.* "Of course, 'tis a small item, so it may well be lost with the ship."

"It was a gift for your mother?"

"Aye," he said.

"Tell me what it looks like, and perhaps if I find the time, I'll search the warehouse for it."

Not the answer he'd hoped for, yet perhaps there was hope. "Might I see what's been brought up from the *Jude*? I vouch for the fact we carried no cargo other than the passengers and crew who are currently here. I could then point out the item if I were to see it."

"I doubt it." Judge Campbell shrugged. "But I suppose I can look into the possibility. You going to be at the boardinghouse for a while?"

"That remains to be decided." He rose and

347

looked the judge in the eye. "I'm not a man who takes charity."

"No," the judge said slowly, "I didn't figure you for a man who would."

Josiah offered his hand, and after a moment, the judge shook it. "Thank you, Judge Campbell," he said. He turned on his heels and left while the judge's mood was still good.

"Oh, wait, boy."

Josiah's heart sank when he realized the judge had followed him outside. "Yes, sir?"

"I nearly forgot to tell you the most important thing."

More important than salvaging the *Jude*? "What's that, Judge?"

"The charges against you have been dropped."

"Is that so?" Josiah lifted his eyes to give a quick thanks to the only One who could have changed the grumpy old man's mind. "Well, thank you," he added.

"No thanks needed," the judge said as he disappeared inside the courthouse.

Rather than return to the boardinghouse, Josiah headed to the docks. The combination of sunshine and salt-tinged breezes always seemed to lift his spirits.

A familiar vessel loomed ahead, and Josiah picked up his pace. Aboard the *Caroline* was Micah Tate. His red hair was unmistakable, even covered with a workingman's cap while Tate applied himself to some sort of repair on the aft deck.

"Ahoy, Tate," Josiah called. "Permission to come aboard?"

The wrecker rose. "Don't need permission here" was his terse reply.

Josiah picked his way across the uneven deck to meet Tate halfway. "I appreciated your visit in jail, Mr. Tate."

The fellow shook his head and turned back to his work. "If you're thinking to thank me, you're wasting your time. I represented all the wreckers."

"I understand," he said as he looked around, taking in the shabby condition of the vessel. Funny how he hadn't noticed any of this the night of the *Jude*'s sinking.

But then, he'd been focused on Isabelle and Banks, and nothing else took heed.

"Tate, I owe you an apology."

"An apology?" That got the man's attention. Micah Tate set down his tools and rose. "What for?"

Josiah shrugged. "This is your vessel. I shouldn't have taken it. I was wrong, and I would ask your forgiveness." He thrust his hand toward Micah Tate. "If you're amenable, I'd like a fresh start."

A gull's cry split the silence, and Josiah watched it land atop the vessel's wheelhouse on a bucket most likely holding the wrecker's lunch. For a moment, Tate seemed more interested in the bird than Josiah.

Finally, Tate turned his attention to Josiah. He lifted his cap and swiped at the sweat on his brow with the back of his hand, then replaced the cap. All the while, Tate never took his eyes off Josiah.

"You're serious," he finally said.

"I am."

The wake from a two-masted schooner beat a rhythm against the peeling paint of the *Caroline*'s hull and caused the deck to roll. Josiah barely felt it. Rather, he stared at Tate and kept his back straight. He could wait as long as the wrecker wanted; he had nowhere else to go.

Finally, Micah Tate extended his hand to shake Josiah's. The man had a firm grip and a decent smile when he tried.

The smile faded as Tate stepped away and returned to his work. "Takes a big man to admit he's wronged someone, Carter," he said. "I appreciate that."

Josiah stepped over a tangle of rope and, by habit, reached down to work the knots out. Squatting, he completed the job, coiled the rope, then rose.

"I can't help but notice you've got a big job here." He paused to choose the correct words. "I wonder if you might need some help."

"I reckon I'd be lying if I said I didn't need

some help." Tate looked up from his work. "Trouble is, I can't pay you."

"Truthfully, I'd be grateful for something to fill my time." He nodded toward the wheelhouse. "Today I'll work for half of whatever's in that lunch bucket. Tomorrow we'll see if I think it's worth coming back for. Deal?"

Tate grinned. "Deal."

That evening, Josiah returned to the boardinghouse tired, dirty, and in better humor than he'd felt in weeks. The work was hard, and Micah Tate was sorely lacking as company, but the feeling of a job well done made up for it all.

He thought of breaking his vow and going to visit Isabelle but fell asleep before he could manage even a trip downstairs to supper. The next morning, Josiah awoke before the sun with his muscles complaining and his neck red and paining him. His fine linen shirt and smartly tailored trousers would not last long under the punishment of the Florida sun, yet it was all he had.

Josiah donned them in the dark and yanked his boots up from the place where they'd fallen last night. With William still fast asleep, he crept downstairs, then sat on the porch and stepped into his boots.

"You thought you'd be getting away from me, did you?"

He turned to see his landlady standing behind

him. "I thought not to wake you," he said. "Forgive me for doing so, anyway."

"Aw, pshaw," she said. "I've been cooking for an hour. Now come and eat. A workingman won't last in these parts if he doesn't see to his belly first."

Despite Josiah's protest, Mrs. Campbell sent him off with a hearty breakfast, a pot of fresh coffee, and a pail containing a lunch fit for two.

The wrecker smiled as Josiah approached. "You look as if you're moving in," he said.

"Now that's not a bad idea." Josiah chuckled as he handed Tate a mug, then steadied himself before pouring black coffee. "What do you charge for a room here?"

Tate sobered. "You know, that's not a bad idea at all."

"What's not a bad idea?" Josiah set the coffee-pot down on the wheelhouse and settled Mrs. Campbell's bucket next to Tate's.

He shrugged. "Never mind. I've got some thinking to do before I say anything."

"All right." Josiah reached for the hammer. "Speak up when it's time for lunch. I tend to get wrapped up in my work and forget."

The redhead laughed. "Well, I don't miss a meal, so you're safe with me."

Later, in the shade of the banyan tree nearest the spot where the *Caroline* was docked, Josiah nursed a full belly and the intense desire to take a nap. He glanced over to see that his companion was of a like mind, so much so that he'd set his cap down over his face.

Leaning against the bark of the gnarled tree, Josiah closed his eyes. He might have stayed there all day had a bell not shrieked through his sleep.

"What's that?" Josiah said as he scrambled to his feet.

Tate turned to stare out at the horizon, shading his eyes with his hands. "Looks like we got trouble." He turned his attention to Josiah. "Forget any work on the *Caroline* this afternoon."

Josiah dusted the sand off the back of his trousers and adjusted the cap Tate had loaned him. "Why's that?"

Before Tate could respond, the call of "Wreck ashore!" answered for him.

The wrecker bolted for his vessel and stopped short to turn around. "You just going to stand there, Carter, or are you coming with me?"

CHAPTER 26

To be back at sea after so long ashore would have been exciting enough, but to be chasing time and tide to save lives made boarding the Caroline even more gratifying. As the vessel plowed through the warm green water, Josiah placed the spyglass to his eye.

"There," he said to Tate. "See, she's listing to starboard."

He handed Tate the spyglass and took the wheel. "I see her," Tate said. "Looks like we've got ample time to work." He lowered the spyglass. "It's not always that way."

Josiah thought back to the night he had tried to bring the *Jude* into the harbor. "It isn't," he echoed.

Tate slapped Josiah's back, then stepped into position behind the wheel, handing Josiah the spyglass. "That tub of yours was going down well before you aimed for Fairweather Key, wasn't it?"

"Aye." He turned his face to the wind. "We'd breached the hull, but the crew thought it patched."

"But the patch didn't hold." The wrecker shaded his eyes against the afternoon sun. "Where were you coming from?"

"New Orleans. Headed for London."

"I see." The wrecker seemed to be thinking on something. Finally, he spoke. "I don't know you that well, but I would guess it wasn't bad navigation that brought you in so close to the reef."

"No," he said. "One of my best men was injured. I aimed for the first place where he could be properly cared for."

The wind brought them near the wreck in short order. Already, several other boats had arrived and were laying anchor. At Tate's orders, Josiah did the same for the *Caroline*.

"See that fellow over there?" Tate gestured toward a man in a dark hat. "Name's Sanders. He got here first, so he's in charge."

Josiah swiped at his forehead and let his gaze scan the wrecked vessel. "What do we do?"

"We do what he tells us." Tate yanked on his cap. "There seems to be more boats than people, so I'm guessing once Sanders gets all the passengers off, he will use us and a few others to haul back whatever goods we find."

Josiah leaned against the rail and shook his head. "Let me get this straight. We're to board that sinking vessel and comb it for valuables, then take whatever suits us?"

Tate looked amused. "Basically, yes."

"And you make a living doing this?" Josiah shook his head. "If I didn't know better, I'd call this organized piracy."

"Don't let the others hear you say that. We wreckers don't take kindly to pirates." Sanders called Tate's name. Using some sort of signals that Josiah couldn't quite decipher, the men communicated for a moment. "All right, we've got permission to board the wreck just as soon as those two vessels pull away."

"All right."

"And Josiah?"

"Yes?"

"We're wreckers, not pirates. We're on the right side of the law, strictly legal. You understand?"

He nodded. "I do."

"All right then." Tate turned to focus on the wreck. "Just remember, I don't know you so well that I wouldn't search your pockets when this is over."

Josiah stepped into Tate's line of sight. "I welcome that search." He shook his head. "No, I demand it."

The next hour flew by as Josiah worked alongside other men to haul out furniture and other valuables and load them onto the vessels ringing the wreck. The *Caroline* made several trips, as did most of the other vessels. Finally, the call of all clear was made, and the last of the wrecking ships pulled away.

It was backbreaking work, yet Josiah hadn't felt this good in weeks.

Years maybe.

As the *Caroline* pulled into her place at the docks, Josiah jumped out to see to her mooring. When she was secure, he gave Tate the sign. Together, they hauled off the last of the items and placed them with the other goods on the dock.

Off in the distance, the shell of the wrecked vessel could barely be seen. By tomorrow, Tate assured him, the water would claim her completely.

"Come on, Carter," the wrecker said. "We're needed to help get all this into the warehouse."

"Not yet." Josiah stepped in front of Tate and slowly pulled the lining from his pockets.

The wrecker nodded. "All right."

Together, they walked over to join the other wreckers.

"You didn't have to do that, you know," Tate said as he took his place in line.

"Yes, I did," Josiah responded. "Trust is earned."

"It is at that." The wrecker glanced at him. "You're a natural at wrecking. Ever give thought to making this your livelihood?"

"No," he said. "I can honestly say I never have."

Micah Tate nodded. "Well, maybe you'll think on it after you hear my proposition."

Isabelle found the prospect of moving from the infirmary to the boardinghouse exciting, to say the least, although it appeared it would not happen for another day. At least Dr. Hill had given up on dosing her with laudanum. The result was that Isabelle could now think and remember. This she gave thanks for and despised in equal measure.

Someone found her Bible at the courthouse

and had given it to Viola, who delivered it to her that morning. Now Isabelle could sit beside the window and read God's Word instead of merely gazing out to sea. It was a welcome change.

Staring out to sea only made her wonder when the supply ship would arrive. Until she broke the news of her plan to Josiah, she would look but not anticipate.

After the deed was done, she could see for herself that Josiah Carter was not the least bit worried about any feelings he might have once claimed in regard to her. After all, she'd been here three weeks and had no memory of any sort of visit from the man.

Three weeks.

Isabelle sighed. It was a blessing, for sure, yet it was not. Indeed, the Lord must want her to continue the journey she had set out upon, for He had done nothing as of yet to deter her from it. Other than this brief side trip, that is.

Her lunch tray remained on the desk, the food picked over and a fanciful embroidered and embellished napkin covering the remains. Emilie set great stock in Isabelle's appetite, while Viola had long since declared her well and fit.

Yet she remained at the infirmary. Had Isabelle not known better, she might have wondered if Viola Dumont was using her as an excuse to continue spending each day with the handsome Dr. Hill. Viola certainly blushed when the doctor appeared in the room, and she hung on his every word when the man made his daily visits to Isabelle's sickroom.

A bell rang, and Isabelle set the Bible on the bedside table. The call of "Wreck ashore" drifted through the open window, setting off a flurry of activity. One by one, the wrecking vessels raised anchor and sped toward the horizon. Before long, the harbor was nearly empty.

From her vantage point, Isabelle could not see the wreck, but she managed to spy the spot where most of the vessels were clustered. She began to pray for the unfortunate folks aboard what was likely a sinking vessel, adding a prayer for the safety of the wreckers, as well.

Before long, the boats began to return. The first vessels deposited drenched but visibly thankful passengers and crew on the docks, then headed back to the fray. Next came the sloops and schooners heavily laden with crates, trunks, and odd pieces of furniture. The last to return were those carrying pieces of the ship itself: a bell, coils of rope, a carved figurehead of a scantily clad woman, and other odd items.

After a fashion, a sort of bucket brigade was set up. The items went from man to man in a line of humanity that spanned the space between the vessels and a long, low, warehouse-type building. A man who looked very much like Mrs. Campbell's husband the judge stalked around like a banty rooster giving orders and taking notes on a length of paper.

Isabelle raised the window and peered out to get a closer look at the excitement. She saw no familiar faces among the passengers and crew, nor did she recognize any of the men who worked to get the bounty to safety.

Then she spied Josiah.

His formal white shirt and trousers set him apart from the others, whose working clothes seemed much more suited to the labor they performed. Yet the captain looked to be quite unhindered as he passed each heavy burden to the next man in the line.

A red-haired man stood next to him, and occasionally Josiah and the fellow seemed to share a few words of conversation or exchange a friendly nudge. When the last item had been unloaded, a bell rang, and the men shouted a loud, "Hurrah!" They gathered in a tight knot, and much celebrating occurred.

From the relatively hidden viewpoint of the infirmary window, Isabelle could watch without fear of being caught. And watch she did, never taking her eyes off Josiah as he laughed and shook hands with each man.

Two fellows approached him, and Josiah's smile disappeared. Some sort of serious conversation occurred, for at one point, Josiah crossed his arms over his chest and nodded. After a few moments, the men shook hands with Josiah. Finally, the red-haired man joined the trio, and more backslapping and celebrating occurred.

Isabelle leaned back in the rocker and, for a moment, allowed herself to imagine Josiah Carter as her husband. No doubt, she would be the envy of the other ladies in Fairweather Key, for the captain was quite a handsome fellow and had displayed a fine character.

Until the truth of her escape from New Orleans was known. Then what would become of them?

The answer was simple. As long as Josiah Carter was associated with her, he would be a fugitive. Even if he found safe haven in England along with her, Josiah would never see his home and family again. Likely, William would grow to adulthood believing his brother to be a criminal.

And then there was the impossibility of any marriage between them.

"No," she whispered. "The penalty for aiding a slave to escape is too high. I cannot allow Josiah to pay it."

As she watched Josiah step away from the group and sprint toward the boardinghouse, she touched her finger to her lips and remembered their kiss. That memory would have to suffice, for she would soon be pretending she had no recollection of it.

It was the only way.

CHAPTER 27

Josiah whistled a tune all the way to the boardinghouse. This day had certainly been an eventful one. "Afternoon, Mrs. Campbell," he said as he left the empty bucket beside the kitchen door, then stomped the sand from his boots before stepping inside.

The scent of stew made his mouth water. "I declare that was the best lunch I've ever had, and I should remind you I've dined at both the White House and Monticello."

"You have not," Mrs. Campbell said with a giggle, "but I'll take the praise all the same." In truth, he had, but he'd not correct her. "It is praise well deserved. Micah Tate sends his compliments, as well."

"You tell him I'm most happy he enjoyed it." She looked up from her work. "What's that you've got slung over your shoulder?"

"That," he said, "is a set of clean clothes given to me by Micah Tate."

"Well, now." The boardinghouse owner rested her hands on her hips. "Is that so?"

"Aye." Josiah grinned. " 'Tis my first day's pay as helper to Micah Tate. As of tomorrow, I'll not be troubling you for a roof over my head, either."

"Well now." The older woman reached for a length of toweling and mopped her brow. "That part of your pay, as well?"

"It is." Josiah leaned against the door frame and watched Mrs. Campbell turn to stir the simmering broth. "Until the proceeds from the *Jude*'s auction are distributed, I cannot pay for the hospitality you've shown to my brother and me, but rest assured, you will be fully compensated when that occurs. I also intend to reimburse you for the cost of hosting the ladies." He paused. "I insist."

"Do you now? I reckon a man of your character would insist." She draped the towel over her shoulder and studied Josiah for a minute. "However, I also figure a man like you isn't one to disagree with a lady."

A disagreement with Isabelle over whether to kiss her came to mind. Once again, Josiah did not contradict Mrs. Campbell.

"So, Josiah Carter, I'll come right to the point. I love my husband, but he's not perfect. In fact, in all the years we've been married I can't recall a single time that the judge apologized for anything."

Josiah shook his head. "Really, Mrs. Campbell, it's not necessary to—"

"I'm not done, young man." She pointed in his direction. "I may just be a woman, but I know my husband used the unfortunate sinking of your ship to his own gain. What you don't know is that you very likely saved my husband's job."

"I don't see how that's possible."

"No, I don't suppose so. Still, I'd say we're more than even, Mr. Carter, since the judge is a mite less irritable now that his job is safe again." Mrs. Campbell went back to stirring the stew. "So I've decided in addition to you taking your meals here, your brother and the ladies will be welcome under my roof as long as they would like to stay. You, too, although I do have concerns about the propriety of Miss Isabelle staying under the same roof with you after what I hear is quite the romance you two have struck up."

Isabelle. His heart did a flip-flop at the thought of seeing her again. Yet that was not under his control. Not since he vowed it was she who must come to him.

I am an idiot. "I would argue," he said.

"But you won't." She smiled. "Go on now, and get yourself cleaned up. That girl's worth the effort, least that's what I'm told."

"Who told you that?"

"Now never you mind," she said with a wink.

"Aye, well, that she is," he said as he raced out of the kitchen. "Oh, and thank you," he called. "Thank you very much."

Josiah reached his room and thankfully found a note from Emilie saying that she and William were out working on a study of the constellations. Any other time, Josiah would have been sorely tempted to join them.

Tonight, however, he counted the moments alone as a blessing. Working alongside Micah Tate had given him a new perspective on what could conceivably be his future.

And the thought of a day's worth of hard work and a night spent with Isabelle did have its appeal. Josiah frowned.

Still, Josiah washed quickly and dressed in the clothes he'd earned with the day's hard work. Odd, but he looked forward to the next time he could use his skills and work alongside the other wreckers.

Tate had boasted to the others that Josiah was a natural as a wrecker. He'd also offered lodging aboard his vessel in exchange for helping to make her seaworthy. It was a daunting proposition but one Josiah looked forward to.

At least until Isabelle accepted his offer of marriage.

The thought made him smile. He couldn't ask her tonight; she was still weak. And so was he.

No, another week or two, and Isabelle would make a full recovery. Then he could make his proposal.

That thought carried him down the street and to the steps of the infirmary. Before Josiah could knock, the door flew open.

Viola Dumont offered him a wide smile. "Good evening, Captain Carter. To what do we owe this visit? I thought you weren't coming back for a while."

"Just Josiah now," he said. "I'm afraid my days captaining a vessel may be behind me."

Unless it's a wrecking vessel.

The thought took him by surprise, yet it held an appeal that could not be denied. There would be plenty of time to consider such things later. Tonight, he sought only to think of Isabelle.

"And I know what I said before." Josiah returned his attention to Viola. "But I am here to pay a visit to Isabelle. How fares she tonight?"

"She fares quite well, actually," Isabelle said.

Josiah looked past Viola to see Isabelle standing a few steps behind. Unlike the last time he visited, Isabelle did not seem to be under the influence of any sort of medication.

"You look lovely," he said.

She touched her hand to her throat, then smiled. "Thank you."

Viola cleared her throat. "Excuse me, won't you? I'm just going to go and see to the . . . well, I'm going to see to something. But I won't be far."

Though Josiah felt shy as a schoolboy, Isabelle's smile emboldened him. "I thought perhaps we might discuss the future tonight."

An expression Josiah could not identify crossed

Isabelle's face. "I suppose tonight is a good night for that type of discussion. You see, I've made some plans."

He took a step toward her. "As have I."

Isabelle gestured to the front door. "It's a lovely evening. I wonder if we might sit outside."

Josiah escorted her to the front steps, then helped her get comfortable on the topmost step. A moment later, he sat beside her. The last rays of the sun sparked across her golden hair and lit her smile. Any traces of ill health were gone from her visage.

Still, he needed to be sure. "I should ask, Isabelle, whether you've taken anything today."

"Taken anything?" She gazed at him with what looked to be a truly astonished expression. "Of course not. I put my foot down and told that doctor I'd rather be ill than medicated. You wouldn't believe the things Viola told me I said while medicated. It's rather disconcerting, actually."

That settled it. He would never tell her of the things she said to him.

Unless she asked.

"What's so funny, Captain Carter?"

"Just Josiah, please." He restrained himself from reaching out to touch her. "And nothing is funny. I am merely happy to be with you tonight."

His admission seemed to trouble her. "I'll get right to the point, Josiah." She looked past him rather than at him. "I understand there is a mail packet, the *Amberjack*, due soon. I intend to be on it. Emilie told me William was to start the new term at school in England. I propose to see to his passage and his safe arrival at school before completing the rest of my journey. The deed to the house in Clapham was lost with the *Jude*, but Emilie has agreed to write letters of introduction that should suffice until her attorney in New Orleans can handle the transaction."

She smiled sweetly, acting for all the world as if she hadn't just destroyed the happy life Josiah had planned for the two of them. The life he intended to tell her about tonight.

"So," she said, "what was it you wished to discuss with me?"

"I, well, that is . . ." Josiah rose. "It wasn't anything nearly as exciting as your news. When does that ship arrive?"

"Soon," she said.

Soon. His heart nearly stopped at the thought. "I see." *Don't let it happen, Lord.*

"So, what's your news?"

"My news?" Josiah looked as if he'd forgotten for a moment, then shook his head as if remembering. "I will be, that is, I am employed as a wrecker."

"Is that so?" The thought of him working alongside the men this afternoon intruded on her thoughts. She gently pushed it away. "How did that happen?"

He told her without enthusiasm of his work alongside Micah Tate. "So after today's adventure, I decided this might be the job for me." He shrugged. "I can't complain. It comes with a place to stay and all the fresh air and sunshine I can stand."

She said nothing for a moment.

"Are you surprised?"

"No," she said, then thought better of it. "Yes, actually, I am. I thought you would always captain some sort of ship."

"And I thought you would always be with me." Josiah's expression told her he hadn't intended to speak the words.

It would be so easy to give him the answer he wanted. The answer she wanted. Instead, she said what she felt would give them both lives of ease and comfort rather than prosecution and persecution.

"What do you mean?" she said, choosing her words carefully.

"Us," he said. "I thought perhaps . . ." His expression changed. "You don't remember, do you?"

Rather than give an answer, she remained silent. *Let him think what he will. I am only protecting him.*

Josiah rose abruptly and helped Isabelle to her

feet. "I shouldn't keep you out long. You've got your health to guard."

"My health is fine," she said, "but I appreciate your concern."

He ducked his head, then looked away. "Have you already purchased your tickets for the voyage?"

"Not yet," she said slowly, "although I understand Emilie will be taking care of that soon."

He swung his attention back in Isabelle's direction. "And you remember nothing of the journey to this place?"

She would not lie, yet Isabelle could not admit all the memories that plagued her. "I wouldn't say that."

Josiah moved close, too close. She did not move. "What do you remember?"

How much to tell? *Guard your heart, Izzy. No, guard Josiah's future. Your heart will heal.*

"I remember your great kindness at allowing the ladies and me aboard the *Jude*. I recall a fire on the docks in New Orleans and your fall into the river along with your miraculous return."

"*Miraculous.* You use that word deliberately."

"Don't you believe it?"

"Aye," he said softly, "I do believe."

Isabelle's heart soared, but at the sight of his forlorn expression, it sank once more. "Perhaps you could let Emilie know whether William will accompany me."

"Yes," he said, "perhaps."

"Of course," she said as casually as she could manage, "if you prefer, you could see him to school yourself. I'm sure there is ample room aboard the *Amberjack*."

"I'll give that some thought, as well." Josiah reached out to shake Isabelle's hand. "It's wonderful to see you looking well. I would love to show you around before you leave. After tomorrow, I shall be staying aboard the *Caroline*. William, too."

A thought occurred. "It is not necessary for you to move out of the boardinghouse. I'm perfectly content to stay here. I'm sure Viola and the doctor would prefer it."

"Isabelle." His voice caressed her name. "This has nothing to do with you."

"I see."

"I am a man," he said as he inched forward. "And a man provides for himself and his own."

Her heart thudded against her chest. "Perhaps I shall see you before my departure then."

Josiah ran his hand through his hair. "And when is the vessel to leave again?"

"At any moment," she said.

Three days later, the vessel *Amberjack* had not yet arrived, much less left with Isabelle or anyone else aboard. Isabelle took to watching the docks in between helping Emilie with William's lessons and assisting Mrs. Campbell with light housekeeping at the boardinghouse. When the vessel did not arrive on time, she refused to panic. Instead, she wondered whether the Lord or the devil was the cause.

Certainly, arguments could be made on both sides.

One week after the funeral, Andre Gayarre's vessel headed back to New Orleans carrying two notes to his father: one from Judge Campbell detailing the manner in which Andre died, and the other from Emilie.

Isabelle never asked her sister what she'd written to their father, nor had Emilie offered to tell her. Rather, she'd handed off the letter to Mrs. Campbell one morning before breakfast with the request that she give them to her husband for inclusion in the packet being sent back to New Orleans.

As the vessel's sails caught wind, Isabelle watched from the safety of the dock. Viola had chosen to accompany the doctor on his morning rounds rather than join them, but Emilie stood beside her.

"I'm sorry," Isabelle said as the vessel seemed to grow smaller.

Emilie's dark brows rose. "Whatever are you talking about, Isabelle?"

She linked arms with her sister. "If not for me,

you could have been on that vessel, heading for home."

"That's ridiculous," she said. "Because of you, I've found a purpose for my life." As if embarrassed by her uncharacteristic show of emotion, she shook her head. "We do have to be mindful of one thing. When that vessel arrives in New Orleans, certain persons will be apprised of our location—if, indeed, they do not already know."

Isabelle nodded.

"While Viola and I are not completely safe from concern, you, dear, are in great danger." She turned toward the horizon. "Perhaps your choice to take passage on the *Amberjack* is a wise one after all. Thanks to Mr. Wilberforce, you'll find safe haven in England."

One of Emilie's great passions had been to follow the course of the abolition of slavery in England through the many newspaper accounts and scholarly books on the subject. Many of these had become fodder for Isabelle's course in learning to read, so she knew well the legacy of William Wilberforce, who had just died the year before.

"I am blessed to have a refuge in Clapham," she said, although blessed was the last thing Isabelle actually felt.

Emilie did not raise her voice in agreement. She did not, however, disagree.

● ● ●

Hezekiah Carter's plan to make his way slowly toward the Keys was beginning to wear on his nerves, as was the tiny stateroom to which he had been assigned. While there were obvious benefits to letting the lad stew in jail, he'd come to know more than a few drawbacks were also associated with the plan.

First and foremost was the length of time Hezekiah must lie on a bed that rocked with the tide and caused an ache in his bones. Then there was the matter of the less-than-sumptuous meals he had endured. Finally, he found he actually missed his wife.

Perhaps leaving Mary off this trip was not a wise choice. "There's nothing to be done for it," he said.

He'd posted a letter to her in each city where the vessel docked. With Mobile behind them and St. Petersburg at least another day's sail ahead, Hezekiah knew Mary would find yet another long letter had been written.

Likely the woman thought him daft for spending so much time putting pen to paper. Hezekiah had long since given up on gaining his sons' interest, so keeping some sort of journal seemed a pitiful waste of time. At least with letters, he could be certain that Mary would read them.

Adapting his steps to the rolling of the floor beneath him, Hezekiah shifted from the bunk to his writing desk. Made of solid and serviceable rosewood, the small, portable desk had traveled with him on many journeys.

Hezekiah carried the writing desk back to his bunk, lifted the tray, and reached for his writing paper, only to have something else inside the desk catch his attention. There, hidden beneath the blank pages, was the document he'd carried with him for nearly two decades.

He reached for it, abandoning any idea of writing. The edges on the bill of sale were beginning to yellow, such was its age, but the writing was still legible despite the miles it had traveled inside the desk.

So were the signatures: his and Jean Gayarre's.

Hezekiah folded the page and tucked it back into its place, then thought better of it. Retrieving the page, he crumpled the document between his fists and opened the porthole. With a flick of his wrist, any trace of his involvement in a wrong that might never be righted could be gone.

Instead, he closed the porthole and stuffed the crumpled page back into his writing desk. Much as he dreaded it, the time for telling the truth had come. "Perhaps now the Lord will hear my prayers."

CHAPTER 28

Sanding the deck of the *Caroline* was proving quite therapeutic for Josiah. Rather than fighting the constant urge to find Isabelle and talk some sense into her, he found that the labor caused him to focus his thoughts elsewhere.

For the hundredth time since he walked William to the boardinghouse, Josiah reached for the spyglass and scanned the horizon. Satisfied no vessels approached, he set back to work.

"Ahoy, Carter."

Rocking back on his heels, Josiah looked over his shoulder to see Micah Tate approaching. "That best be lunch you're carrying. I'm famished."

Since Isabelle moved into the boardinghouse, Josiah had elected not to take his breakfast there. As there were no cooking facilities aboard the *Caroline*, he was forced to wait for lunch.

Perhaps the next repair should be to the galley. Then, at least, he could have his eggs in peace.

The wrecker set his lunch pail down and made a wide circle around the spot where Josiah had been working. "Looks like you're going to sand her down to the waterline."

"I'm just being thorough." He set his tools aside and stood, then followed Tate to their customary spot beneath the banyan tree.

"So how's your brother like life aboard ship?" he asked as he uncovered the lunch.

Josiah's stomach growled as the scent of fried chicken rose from the bucket. "William's had his sea legs since birth, I believe. He's quite at home here."

"And his education. Is it suffering at all for the tutoring he gets with Miss Gayarre?"

"Not at all, actually." Josiah smiled. "Emilie is a wonderful teacher. I understand she's already found several other protégés to teach along with William. Soon there will be a regular classroom full."

"That would certainly be a blessing for Fairweather Key, and who knows? Perhaps one day there will be a school here."

"Perhaps."

They ate in silence for a moment, and then Tate pointed at Josiah. "And what about you? Are you at home here?"

"Aboard the *Caroline*?" He tossed the chicken bone into the water. "Aye, I find the vessel to be a comfortable home."

The redhead helped himself to a boiled potato. "Actually I meant in Fairweather Key. Do you find it to your liking?"

"Aye, very much." He set down his plate.

Might as well let the fellow speak his mind. He'd not get any peace until whatever was dogging the wrecker was said. "Get on with it."

Tate shook his head. "Get on with what?"

Josiah reached for another chicken leg. "I know you're bound to be considering whether to say something, so I'll help you with the dilemma by telling you to get on with it."

He smiled. "You sure?"

Nodding, Josiah settled back and bit into his lunch.

"All right, I was just thinking that you don't know much about me, just as I don't know much about you." He shifted positions. "And most times, that's fine by me. All I need to know about a man is whether he's honest and whether he's a hard worker. I've found you are both."

"I appreciate that," he said.

"Just a fact, that's all." Tate met his stare. "That boat there, she's named after my wife."

This wasn't where Josiah had figured the conversation would head. "I didn't know you were a married man, Tate."

"*Was* a married man." He looked past Josiah to the ocean, or perhaps it was the sky the wrecker studied. "Know that part in the Bible where it talks about our lives being like a vapor?"

He didn't but would not interrupt the man to say so.

"Well, it is." Micah's face went serious. "I

thought Caroline and I would be together forever. Raise a family, the works." He paused. "The
fever got her and took the babe she carried with
her. That was back in '29."

Five years he'd mourned the woman, and yet
Micah Tate seemed as struck by the loss today
as if it had just happened. "I'm sorry," Josiah
managed to say.

The wrecker nodded, and they fell into silence
until the food was gone. Josiah rose first and
stretched. He had a full afternoon ahead, and
he'd best get to it. He bid the wrecker good-bye
and headed back toward the *Caroline*.

"Wait," Tate called.

Josiah slowed his pace to allow his friend to
catch up. "Something you'd like to add to my list
of chores?"

"In a way." The wrecker shrugged. "I watched
you risk your life to save your woman out on
the reef."

His woman. Josiah's jaw clenched, as did his
fists. Had Isabelle ever been his?

Sadly, he could not say with any certainty.

"It was something any captain would do for
passenger or crew." As he said the words, he
found he could not look the wrecker in the eye.

"Perhaps." He paused. "The *Amberjack*'s never
been late before, yet it's now two weeks behind
schedule." Tate stepped past him to board the
Caroline. "Makes a man wonder whether the

Lord's trying to make His will obvious to someone too dense to see it otherwise."

Josiah feigned irritation. "Surely you're not speaking of me."

"Surely you're not going to allow this brief reprieve to pass without taking action." The wrecker situated the lunch bucket atop the wheelhouse. "Or perhaps you are. It's of no consequence to me, except that if you were to ask my advice—"

"Which I have not."

"Which you have not," he echoed, "yet if you were, I would tell you that though I only had a few short years with Caroline, I would do it all over again, even knowing how it would end."

The wrecker made to turn and leave, but Josiah called him back. "And if I were to ask your advice?"

"I might give it," Tate said with a grin.

Josiah nodded. "This is in confidence, you understand."

"I do."

"Yes, well," he said as he pondered the correct way to state his dilemma. "There are impediments to our relationship." Josiah paused. "Financial impediments."

He gave Josiah an odd look. "Such as?"

"I had only recently purchased the *Jude*, and the note on her had not been paid when she sank." He thought carefully before continuing, his voice lowered. "The funds that were to settle the debt sank with the vessel."

"I see." The wrecker paused only a moment. "Yet you've got a new source of income in wrecking. It looks as if God meant for you to have a means to settle that debt and any others you might have."

"Like passage for my brother and the ladies to England." He looked away. "That was to be our destination before this unplanned change of course."

"I see." They watched a schooner drift past and waved at the familiar faces aboard. "And you think you've got to be willing to see the ladies and the boy to that destination, even if it's not where you intend to settle?"

Josiah nodded.

"I suppose I understand how you would feel obligated. I can tell you that the folks around here generally will allow you to sign a note paying for passage, so if you've a mind to, that's an option you can consider." He shrugged. "Any other impediments?"

"Aye. Legal impediments."

His red brows shot up. "She's married?"

"No."

"You're married."

Josiah's gaze swept the surrounding boats to see if anyone had heard, but none seemed to have noticed. "No! I've never married."

"Well, I think we can safely remove the only other impediment I can think of. She's definitely a *she*."

"Aye," he said with a grin, "that she is. Most definitely."

The wrecker shrugged. "Does she profess a faith in God?"

Josiah leaned against the wheelhouse and watched a lone gull circle the vessel. "She does."

"Do you love her?"

He thought a moment, then braved a look at the wrecker. "I might."

"You might, eh?"

"Yes, I might."

The redhead broke into a grin. "Then I fail to see what impediment there might be, legal or otherwise."

Crossing the deck, Josiah reached to shake Micah Tate's hand. "You've given me plenty to think on. You're a good friend."

"Some might say I'm not." He paused. "After all, I've very possibly caused a good man to give up his status as a bachelor."

Josiah noticed the lookout climbing the tower over near the courthouse. "Might be trouble brewing," he said. "Grab the spyglass."

Tate reached for the instrument and held it to his eyes. Lowering it, he handed the spyglass to Josiah without comment.

"Ship ahoy," the lookout called.

Josiah didn't have to ask. He knew it was the *Amberjack*.

"Where are you going?" Tate called.

"To do the right thing," he said. "And pray I'm wrong."

It seemed as though the whole town had come out for the arrival of the *Amberjack*. All, that is, except Viola Dumont and the Gayarre sisters. Even as the ship's sails lowered, Josiah continued to scan the crowd for signs of them, to no avail.

The moment the vessel was docked, Josiah headed aboard the *Amberjack* to find the captain. He located the fellow, a stout, bald-haired fellow, on the aft deck, barking orders to men who rushed about trying to unload cargo from the hold.

It was a scene he knew well and strangely did not miss.

"A word with you, Captain," Josiah called.

The man held his hands out in front of him. "Before you start complaining about our tardiness, please understand I did the best I could. We had a bit of a problem with our mainmast and had to lay at anchor in Mobile until she was seaworthy again."

"No, no," Josiah said. "No complaints here. I just wondered if we might discuss business."

The captain called to a fellow standing a few yards away. "Keep them moving at a fair clip," he said. "We've no time to waste if we expect to turn this vessel around as planned." He gestured to Josiah. "Come, walk with me."

Josiah fell into step beside the captain.

"What business is it you have with me, son?" he finally asked.

"I'm Josiah Carter, and I seek passage for three ladies and a lad." Josiah paused to swallow the lump in his throat. "Their destination is England. London, actually."

The captain shook his head. "Sorry, son, I can only fetch them as far as Cuba. From there, they should have no trouble finding passage to London. Would that suffice?"

"Aye."

"Very well, then. I suppose the only thing we need to discuss is payment." A crewman halted their progress, and the captain stopped to correct him. "Now, as I was saying, payment." He slid Josiah a sideways glance. "Cash is preferred, Mr. Carter."

CHAPTER 29

Payment in cash is an issue," Josiah said. "Until the auction is settled on my vessel, I've nothing but my word to offer."

The captain laughed, then mopped his brow

with his handkerchief. "And why would I take your word as payment when I've got empty berths that could be filled by passengers who pay in coin?"

"I was captain of a vessel until recently," Josiah said, "and I had occasion to ask that same question."

"Is that so?"

Activity swirled around them, but Josiah kept his focus on the captain. "Aye."

"What did you do?"

"I took those passengers aboard with the promise of payment." He shrugged. "And now I ask you to see them to the completion of a voyage I have been rendered incapable of completing."

He seemed to be thinking, then suddenly turned away. "What happened to your vessel? You mention an auction."

"Aye, she developed a leak that we thought was patched. I sought help for a gravely ill crew member only to find the patch did not hold. The *Jude* was lost, although there is some hope the wreckers salvaged enough to bring a decent sum at auction."

"A pity, that."

"Aye."

The captain made an abrupt turn and headed back in the direction they'd just traveled. "Have you anything to offer as promise of payment should the auction not be successful?"

Josiah nodded. "I am now employed as wrecker on the *Caroline*."

His thick brows went up. "Micah Tate's vessel?"

"Aye."

The captain grinned. "Well, why didn't you tell me so? I make a monthly trip to this lovely locale, barring any unforeseen delays. Are you amenable to making payments each month until the sum is settled?"

"I am."

He dared not add up the total of his debt. Better to pile one atop the other and give no heed. All were his by rights to settle, and settle them he would. He shook hands with the captain and made to leave.

"Son?"

Josiah turned. "Aye?"

"We sail at dawn."

"So soon?" He felt like a fool as soon as the words were out. "What I mean is, I figured you'd be in port a day or two."

"Generally we are, but seeing as we've been delayed, we'll make an exception this month."

"Of course," he muttered as he wove his way through the crowd milling along the docks.

By the time Josiah reached the boarding-house, he had decided what to say when he saw Isabelle. Just to be sure, he circled the block, then returned to the steps. One more moment to practice, and then he knocked.

Isabelle opened the door, and he promptly forgot every well-rehearsed word. Instead, he stood on the steps like a fool, his only thought being to notice how well her green dress matched her eyes.

"Josiah?" Mrs. Campbell's voice cut through the fog of his thoughts. "Come in, come in. Is it dinnertime already? I was so excited about the *Amberjack*'s arrival that I must have lost track of time."

"Oh, no," he said to her retreating back. "It is early yet."

It was then he noticed that Isabelle was not looking at him but past him toward the harbor. "So the vessel has arrived?" she said.

"Aye." He felt his breath catch but made an effort to force the words.

Isabelle closed her eyes for a second, and he dared not think of what that meant.

"Isabelle, do invite the captain in." Emilie appeared in the door behind her. "Forgive me, but I couldn't help seeing you round the corner. I was just reading with William. Are you already here to fetch him?"

Josiah shook his head.

"He's come about the *Amberjack*, Emilie," Isabelle said.

"Indeed?" Emilie smiled. "I heard the commotion and thought perhaps the vessel was in port."

"Only just," Josiah said. "I wonder if Miss

Dumont is about. I'd prefer to have this conversation only once, and I need to speak to all three of you."

"She's making rounds with the doctor. I can fetch her." Isabelle reached for her bonnet and stuck it on before hurrying past Josiah, leaving the distinct scent of lavender in her wake.

"Josiah!" William ran toward him and launched himself into his arms. "You're early. Can we go fishing?"

Mrs. Campbell peered in from the back porch. "A pity you want to leave. I've got a batch of sweets out here in the kitchen that I need some help with."

The lad scampered away without so much as a good-bye, leaving Josiah smiling. The smile faded when he caught sight of Isabelle coming up the steps with Viola behind her.

Was that a tear she swiped away?

That settles it. I cannot let her leave.

Yet he could not force her to stay.

Viola burst through the door, her face flushed. "It was the most amazing thing. I just helped the doctor deliver a baby. I—oh, hello, Captain Carter." She shook her head. "I mean, Josiah."

"Vi, dear, whose baby did you deliver?" Emilie asked as she positioned herself on the settee and pulled the Dumont woman down beside her. "Two of the children who come for lessons have siblings on the way."

Josiah stepped back to let the ladies chat. Soon enough, they would remember he stood in the room, and he would be forced to deliver the news of their swift departure.

Isabelle met his gaze, then quickly looked away as she sought out the chair nearest the door. Finally, the ladies tired of their talking and looked to Josiah. "Do tell us why you've gathered us here," Emilie said. "And please, sit with us. There's a comfortable chair next to Isabelle."

"Thank you, but I prefer to stand if you don't mind." He focused his attention first on Emilie, then on Viola. Looking at Isabelle while he delivered the news was impossible. "As you've noticed, the *Amberjack* has arrived. Since I was charged with the responsibility of delivering you to England, I have purchased passage for the three of you and William aboard the vessel as far as Cuba. From there, the captain has assured me he can assist you in finding a London-bound vessel." Josiah paused to take a breath. "The problem is the vessel sails at dawn, so you must decide soon. Actually, now."

His speech duly delivered, Josiah punctuated the statement with a forced smile.

"Well, now," was Emilie's reply as she leaned back against the settee's horsehair cushion.

"Indeed," Viola softly added, her fingers cradling her chin as if in thought.

Neither would look at him.

"Isabelle?" Emilie said, turning to face her sister. "What say you of the kind gift Josiah has bestowed on us."

"No, Emilie," Josiah corrected. " 'Tis not a gift."

"I see," she said. "Then you'll not take offense if I do not accept it?"

"What?" Josiah shook his head. "But I thought . . . that is . . ."

"Josiah," Emilie said gently, "I've come to love it here in Fairweather Key. Honestly, I think the Lord sent me here to teach these children. Besides William, there are a half dozen others in my care on most days. Were it possible, I might take on more." She paused to offer what seemed to be a genuine smile. "So you see, while I am forever in your debt for your kindness, I cannot accept it." Her smile faded. "Oh, but if you wish William to attend a proper school, I will understand completely. I know I am not as qualified as the teachers in—"

"Don't make me go, Josiah! Don't make me go!" William burst through the door and latched onto Josiah's leg. "Miss Emilie says I am an apt pupil. Isn't that right?" When Emilie nodded, William pointed to Josiah. "You said you wanted me to get a good education. I have that here."

"Caught with my own words." He shrugged. "Fine, I shall not require it." He put on a serious look as he pried the boy off his leg and knelt. "I shall not require it yet," he added. "But I reserve the right." He glanced over the boy's head to Emilie. "What say you, Miss Emilie?"

"I think it's a fine compromise."

"There," Josiah said, "we've compromised, William. Perhaps you'd go and help Mrs. Campbell now?"

"Aye, Sir Josiah," he said with a mock salute before skittering away.

Viola cleared her throat and rose. "I, too, greatly appreciate your offer of passage to England."

"But?" Josiah supplied. "You'll not be wanting a ticket, either?"

She shrugged. "I'm afraid not. You see, I've just helped deliver a baby."

"Yes, I heard," he said.

"And there's the matter of Dr. Hill." She blushed. "What I mean is, he's never had a proper nurse, and I've been learning for weeks now. It would be a shame to throw all of that learning away, don't you think?"

Josiah chuckled. "Indeed."

This was going quite well. Two of the three ladies had declared themselves ready to remain in Fairweather Key. Now to speak to Isabelle.

"So," he said as he planned his reaction to her decision to stay, "Isabelle, what say you on the matter of passage aboard the *Amberjack*?"

"First, I must echo Emilie and Viola's thanks. I

know this must have been an expensive purchase."

He withheld his smile, waiting. Rather, he shrugged.

"It was a grand gesture all the same, one I will not soon forget."

She ducked her head, then lifted it again. Outside, Josiah could hear William's laughter mixed with the cry of a gull.

"And?" This from Emilie. "Really, Isabelle. Do not keep the man waiting."

"And . . ." She paused to worry with the hem of her apron. "I wonder if you might tell me what time I should board the vessel?"

"Vi, dear, I wonder if you might come upstairs a moment. I've been thinking of teaching William about medicines, but I'm uncertain as to which plants are used for what. Do you think you can help me?"

"Of course."

Their chatter continued until a door closed upstairs. Finally, he and Isabelle were alone.

"So," he said as he watched her rise, "you will finally see England."

"Yes, I will." She walked toward the door and reached for the knob. "I'm sure you'll understand if I tell you I must see to preparations."

Josiah moved in her direction, intent on brushing past her to make his exit. Like a moth to a lantern, however, he felt drawn to her, even as he knew it would only bring disaster.

She is leaving.

He paused, so near he could once again smell the jasmine scent of her.

She refuses to admit she loves you.

As if he could not help himself, Josiah reached to capture her wrist. He expected Isabelle to protest.

She did not.

She would have me kiss her.

So he did.

Isabelle could have spent the rest of her life lingering in Josiah's arms. It was as if this place, this protected safe place, was where she was meant to be.

Reality forced itself upon her.

Without a word, she broke the embrace and raced up the stairs. Bypassing the room where Emilie and Viola chatted about herbs and poultices, she slipped into the darkness of her own bedchamber. With nothing to pack but the dress Viola had found for her, Isabelle was left to fill the hours until dawn.

The sound of the door closing downstairs drew her to the window. From her vantage point, she could see Josiah cross the street and head for the docks. He lived on the *Caroline* now, this she knew from William; and he'd been working hard to bring the vessel back to its original glory. He had also been accepted into the community of wreckers. This she'd learned from the doctor, who often made trips to the docks after a salvage operation was completed.

His shoulders slumped and his head down, Josiah walked briskly. Still, Isabelle mentally calculated how long it would take to catch up with him.

Or she could call to him through the open window. Even now with the breeze and the sound of the surf, he was not too far away to miss hearing her call his name.

All the more reason to close the window, which she did.

"I'm doing this to protect you, Josiah," she whispered as the man she loved disappeared into the evening's shadows. "And I won't cry. I just won't."

But she did.

CHAPTER 30

Josiah was on the docks when the wind caught the *Amberjack*'s sails. He remained carefully hidden in the crowd, although he almost gave away his hiding place when he spied Isabelle marching toward the gangplank, her backbone straight and her attention focused ahead.

She carried a small satchel and wore a cloak

that must have been loaned to her by Mrs. Campbell, such was its vintage. Her golden curls were hidden under a proper traveling bonnet of sky blue, and she held her Bible against her chest as if it were precious gold.

What a contrast to the woman he'd met on the docks in New Orleans such a short time ago. Then, she'd been a mystery to him, a sea siren who caught his attention and set him on guard.

Today, she was all that and more, except that she had captured his heart and seemed intent on taking it with her to Cuba, then on to London, eventually settling at Clapham, where no doubt she would waste away without him.

"Probably not, but I would like to think she would miss me."

"Oh, I'm sure she will."

Josiah jumped at the sound of Mrs. O'Mara's voice. He searched about for something clever to say. Failing that, he merely shrugged. "I can hope so," he added.

"I understand the charges against you were dropped," she said, though he barely heard her for watching Isabelle climb the gangplank.

"Aye." She disappeared onto the deck, and he could focus on his former jailer. "Judge Campbell was kind enough to rethink the charges." He saw Micah Tate's red hair across the plaza and waved. "Forgive me, Mrs. O'Mara, but I must be off."

She grasped his hand and held him in place a moment longer. "You're a good man, Josiah Carter. Someday, if the Lord decrees it, she will find her way back to you."

"Thank you," he said. "I hope you're right."

"And I hope 'tis sooner rather than later," she replied.

For a week, Josiah started and ended the day at the docks, certain Isabelle would find a way back to him. Sooner became later, and then later became not at all. Eventually, Josiah stopped looking for Isabelle to return.

With William busy learning, Josiah was free to throw himself into turning the *Caroline* into a vessel Micah Tate could be proud of. When the auction that would include items from the *Jude* was announced, Josiah decided funds leftover from purchasing the *Jude* and Isabelle's ticket on the *Amberjack* would be used to purchase new sails for the *Caroline*. Tate protested, but he placed the order all the same.

The morning of the auction, Josiah walked William to the boardinghouse, as was their custom. Since Isabelle's presence was no longer a distraction, Josiah joined the ladies for breakfast some mornings. Today, however, he elected to hurry William to the steps, then turn for home.

"Josiah," William called, "I wonder if I might bid on something at the auction today."

He leaned down to give his brother a hug. "You're too young to bid. Besides, how do you know what's down there? The judge hasn't let anyone in to see what's in the warehouse."

William smiled. "Miss Emilie convinced the judge we could use the practice for our counting skills. Yesterday we tallied up the items, and I found one I must bid on."

"Tell me what it is, and I shall place the bid."

He looked downcast. "I wanted it to be a secret. Miss Emilie said she would place the bid for me."

Josiah reached into his pocket and pulled out three coins. "If Miss Emilie can get the item for this much, so be it."

"Wreck ashore!" the lookout called.

Josiah gave his brother a swift hug. "Off with you, now. I must go."

He sprinted to the *Caroline* and waited for Micah to arrive.

Working in tandem, they headed the vessel toward the horizon, where a ship lay smoldering.

"That's a nasty one," Tate said. "I don't like it when fire's involved."

Josiah thought back to his swift departure from New Orleans and nodded. As they reached the reef, Tate maneuvered the *Caroline* around and set her anchor near the other wreckers.

"Tate and Carter, board the vessel and help

O'Mara and Simpson search for survivors," the fellow in charge called.

The leap from the *Caroline* to the wreck was easy for Josiah, but Tate nearly missed. Josiah grabbed his arm and yanked him onto the slanting deck, then waited for instructions.

"Hey, thanks," Tate said. "Looks like the others are heading for starboard, so let's go aft. I'll take everything on the right, and you look to the left."

"Aye." Josiah followed Micah Tate across the vessel, looking over and under any space capable of hiding a human. When he reached the rail, he signaled to Tate. "Nothing. You?"

The wrecker shook his head. "I'm going below. Why don't you head over there to the passengers' quarters? I know they've been searched, but it never hurts to make a second pass, seeing as how that's where people usually are this early in the morning."

Josiah did as he was told, searching three cabins and finding them empty. In the fourth, however, he spied a crumpled form in the corner behind an overturned stool. With the smoke thick in the cabin, he had to crawl across the floor to reach the man.

He rolled the man onto his back, then sat back on his heels, stunned. It was his father.

"Are you an angel?" The man's eyes opened wider. "Josiah," he whispered. "It's you."

"Aye," Josiah said, "so I warrant your question as to whether this is an angel has been answered."

He gave the man a yank and pulled him from the corner. "Tate, anyone! I've got someone in here," he called. No one answered.

"Well, Father," Josiah said before dissolving into a fit of coughing. "The great irony is I am about to save you."

His father grabbed Josiah's hands and held them. "William? Is he safe?"

"Aye, he's quite safe."

Nodding, he rested his head on the floor, then closed his eyes. "Father, it will go well for you if you'll remain awake. Can you do that?"

"Thank you," he said, "for standing up to me."

Josiah shook his head. "Now I know I'll be fetching you to the infirmary. You're not a well man if you're thanking me for taking your son away."

Hezekiah smiled, and Josiah nearly dropped him in shock. "No, I'm thanking you for forcing me to see what I was doing to both of you. I'm an idiot. I've had time lying on this floor to contemplate that."

"Would that I could give you more time to contemplate how wonderful I am, Father, but this vessel is about to burn to the waterline, and I doubt you'll want to be aboard when that happens."

Flames erupted on either side of him as Josiah

dragged his father out of the cabin, then hoisted him over his shoulder. At the rail, Tate loped up to help load Hezekiah aboard the *Caroline.*

"Where did you find him?" Tate asked as he made to lift anchor.

"In cabin four."

The anchor landed on deck with a thud, and the wind caught in the sails. With Tate at the wheel, they made quick time.

"Do you know who he is?" Tate asked as they neared the shore. "The doc always likes us to get a name just in case."

"Aye," Josiah said. "Micah Tate, meet my father."

"Your . . ."

"Aye." Josiah glanced over and saw his father motioning to him. "Excuse me." He made his way to where Hezekiah lay. "What is it, Father? Some water, perhaps?"

"No, a word with you," he said. "I must ask about Isabelle."

"Isabelle?" Josiah's guard went up, and he said nothing.

"Don't waste my time, son," Hezekiah said. "I know you took her, but I also know it wasn't your idea."

"How do you know this?"

He looked up at Josiah. "I know many things, son. For instance, I know more about your Isabelle than you do."

"My Isabelle?"

Hezekiah nodded. "It's hard to miss the look of a man in love, son. Although I must wonder if you know what sort of trouble you're getting with that one."

"I don't want to talk about Isabelle." He rose, but Hezekiah caught him by the wrist. "You'll listen." He paused, his defiant look turned pleading. "You'll want to listen."

"All right." Josiah glanced up to gauge the distance to shore. "You've got five minutes. After that, we will have arrived at the docks."

"Five minutes is plenty of time." He leaned his head back and seemed to stare up into the sky for a moment. "Jean Gayarre has been my friend longer than Mary has been my wife, but there are many things he does—or rather did—which I neither agree with nor condone. While his was not a happy marriage, neither should he have taken her as a mistress." Hezekiah rapped the deck with his fist. "I don't care if it was the custom. *Is* the custom, actually. The Bible says it's wrong."

"Aye," Josiah said. "As is slavery, yet many tolerate it."

"Ownership of Isabelle was arranged at the time of her birth." He shook his head. "No, that's not right. She came into the world on the twelfth of December, if I recall, and he snatched her up from her mother's deathbed on the fourteenth. I remember that because the Brits were at our doorsteps, and he was a fool for leaving his house."

"Wait, what are you saying?"

Hezekiah shook his head again. "No, that's not right. She was a Christmas Eve baby, Isabelle was. Her mama, Sylvie, well, she passed on three days later. Same day Jean's wife was giving birth to Emilie."

Josiah leaned against the rail and tried to make sense of the tale. "So you're saying Isabelle was taken from her mother after she died?"

"Childbed fever, I was told. He gave the babe to Delilah, a house servant of his, to raise. Set them up in a nice little place outside of town. Plantation was owned by a widow woman who needed the money and didn't ask any questions. It all worked out just fine. Isabelle was none the wiser until Emilie found out about her."

He paused to take a breath, then dissolved into a fit of coughing. When he captured his breath, Hezekiah continued. "It was all arranged. Jean, he could hardly purchase his own slave. You see, he owned Sylvie, thus he owned Isabelle and the other, as well."

"The other?"

"Sylvie had a son by him. Jean hired him out to a family in New Iberia by the name of Arnaud. Jean told me recently that the boy died at sea."

Josiah took a deep breath and let it out slowly.

"What was your part in all this, Father?"

"My part"—he offered a weak smile—"was to purchase Isabelle the same way I purchased her brother. Once she was mine, I would free her. It was a simple solution. Unfortunately, she disappeared before it could happen."

Something was not setting well with Josiah. The solution was too easy, his father too unlike the kind man he saw now. "I don't believe you."

"The proof is in my pocket." When his father couldn't manage it, Josiah retrieved a paper from his coat pocket. "Read it," Hezekiah said.

He scanned the page, holding it tight lest the wind take it flying. There in a masculine handwriting was the bill of sale for one Isabelle Marie Gayarre, born December 24, 1814. Freed April 10, 1834."

"Freed?" Josiah folded the paper and attempted to return it to his father's pocket, his mind reeling.

"Keep it," Hezekiah said as the vessel bumped gently against the dock. "I've an idea you may yet need it."

"You're serious?" Josiah shook his head. "You helped your friend by doing this for him? By freeing Isabelle?"

"And her brother, rest his soul."

It took a moment for Josiah to adjust his image of the venerable Hezekiah Carter. When he did, it rendered him speechless.

The doctor boarded the vessel, followed closely by Viola Dumont. His father recognized Viola immediately, and from the look on her face, Viola recognized his father.

"Josiah, do you have a name for this man?"

"Aye," Josiah finally said. "This is Hezekiah Carter. My father." He paused. "Take good care of him, Doc."

Josiah looked up to see Judge Campbell racing toward him. "About time I found you, Carter."

The idea of being arrested again held no appeal, especially when it could happen in front of his father. "What did I do this time, Judge?"

Hezekiah looked up sharply. "Are you the judge who incarcerated my son on trumped-up charges?"

The judge looked down at Hezekiah and shrugged. "Guilty. Although I'm here to make it up to him. That rascal who paid his bail isn't around to fetch the money back, so I figured it ought to go to him."

Josiah shook his head. "No, it should go to Emilie."

"What would she want with it?"

"Why don't you ask her?" Josiah said. "I believe she mentioned something about a proper school for the town." He smiled. "You know, that would really get you some positive attention, what with you being responsible for a new school being built here."

The judge grinned and shook Josiah's hand, then turned to Hezekiah. "You've got a smart boy here, Mr. Carter."

"That's Reverend Carter," he said, "and yes, I do."

The doctor returned. "We've got to take you to the infirmary now, sir," he said to Hezekiah.

"Just a moment more," Josiah said.

"Only that," Dr. Hill responded.

"Father," Josiah said when the doctor had moved on to the next patient. "I must ask what's happened to cause such a change in you. I know I haven't been the easiest son to love, but, well . . ."

"I haven't been the easiest father to love, either." He chuckled. "To say the least. As for what happened, that would be a combination of things. First, your mother made me see the error of my ways and sent me on the journey that would end out there on the rocks. Then there's the matter of finally telling someone the truth." Hezekiah paused to draw in a ragged breath. "Never underestimate the power of telling the truth."

"Aye," Josiah said. " 'Tis a powerful weapon."

"As is fear." He pointed to the burning vessel out on the horizon. "Before you snatched me out of the fire, I was lying on the cabin floor, knowing I was about to die and meet Jesus face-to-face. I don't mind telling you I was terrified."

Josiah tried to imagine his father fearing anyone or anything and found it impossible.

"I'm an old fool, but not so old or so foolish that I don't know when I'm wrong." He tightened his grasp. "Forgive me, Josiah?"

"Aye," he said as the doctor arrived to pry his father from him.

He helped Doc Hill haul his father onto the back of the same wagon that had carried Andre Gayarre to the undertaker, then followed them to the infirmary. Viola had gone ahead and met them at the door.

"His bed is ready, Doctor," she said. "A word with you, Josiah," she added.

Josiah stepped aside to allow his father's transport into the room where Isabelle had so recently recuperated. He remained on the other side of the velvet curtains until Viola emerged and bade him follow her.

"All right," she said when they were outside on the front steps, "explain yourself."

Josiah shrugged. "I don't know what you mean."

"Is that not the man you took your brother from?"

"It is." He tipped his hat to Mrs. Campbell, then returned his attention to Viola. "He has reformed, it seems. He also told me a most interesting story about Isabelle."

"Oh?"

"Aye." He looked around to be certain they were alone. "It seems as though Isabelle's father made arrangements with my father to purchase

Isabelle and free her. It was done, but she disappeared before she could be told."

"Really?" Somehow Viola did not seem surprised at the news. "You must go and find Isabelle. She needs to know this."

"I doubt it would make any difference." Josiah looked away.

"You don't understand. It would make all the difference." She bit her lip and seemed to consider whether to continue. "She loves you, Josiah, enough to let you go."

"I don't understand."

Viola shrugged. "In the eyes of the law, Isabelle is an escaped slave. What life would you have together?" She paused. "That's the only issue keeping you apart, and with the story you told me, it is no longer an issue."

"Still, I can't go, Viola."

"Why?" She shook her head. "Emilie can certainly look after William for the few days it would take you to catch up with her in Cuba, and I will be sure your father stays right here."

He lifted a brow, skeptical. "How can you do that?"

She smiled. "Laudanum, Josiah. It's good for keeping a patient right where you want them."

"I see," Josiah shook his head. "There's the matter of a vessel. I've got much to ponder."

"Don't ponder too long," Viola said, "or she'll find a ship to England and be gone."

CHAPTER 31

As it turned out, he had little to ponder. Five minutes of conversation with Micah Tate led to the offer of the *Caroline* for transportation and Tate as crew. At daybreak, they set out for Cuba, and the next morning Josiah began his search for Isabelle.

At the customhouse, he located the sailing log for vessels headed to England since Isabelle's arrival on the island. Only three were listed, and none had left port yet, so he went to each of them and searched their passenger lists.

Nowhere did Isabelle's name appear.

It made no sense.

Heading back to the customhouse, he gave the log another thorough look and found the same results. Only those three vessels were to depart, and none had left since the *Amberjack*'s arrival in port.

Only two possibilities remained: Either Isabelle was sailing under an assumed name or she remained somewhere on the island. He made his way back to the docks, pondering the situation.

"Did you find her?" Micah asked when Josiah stepped aboard the *Caroline*.

"No," he said, "and frankly I'm stumped. I don't

know what to do or where to turn." He leaned against the rail and looked over the sea to where the spires of a church showed above the trees. "I think I might know who does, though."

Making his way off the vessel was easy. Finding the way to the little church he'd spied from the water was not. The avenues in Havana were not broad like those back in Fairweather Key, and they twisted and turned, too often ending abruptly. As he was about to give up, Josiah spotted a sign that read simply *CAPILLA DE JESÚS.*

"Chapel of Jesus."

He smiled and headed up the narrow alley to the front steps of the stone church with the double spires. Once inside, he had to stop and wait for his eyes to adjust to the light. As he waited, he heard a soft sound not unlike crying.

The air was hot and muggy, and the candles were poorly made and stingy with their light. As his eyes adjusted, Josiah spied a woman at the altar, her head bowed. Unwilling to intrude on the woman, Josiah slipped into the back pew and sat waiting for the proper words to come.

To petition the Lord for Isabelle's swift return seemed a bit presumptuous considering he'd been sparse in his prayers thus far. *I know I only seem to come to You when I am in need, but this time it's for Isabelle. She must know she's free. That she's been redeemed.*

The thought occurred that he, too, had been redeemed. Josiah closed his eyes. *And others save with fear, pulling them out of the fire.*

"Josiah?"

His eyes flew open. Before him stood Isabelle Gayarre. "I have surely died and gone to my reward," he said as he reached out to touch her sleeve. "No, you're real, aren't you?"

"I am as are you." Isabelle smiled. "I prayed, and here you are."

"As did I." He rose to gather Isabelle into his arms, and to his great joy, she allowed it. "I feared you were lost," he said, "and there's so much you need to know."

She rested her head on his shoulder, the tears coming afresh. "I was so afraid. The ships were full, and the *Amberjack* was already on her return trip. I've been sleeping in this church and praying someone would find me." She shook her had. "No, I was praying you would find me."

"I have much to tell you," he said as he rested his head atop hers. "So much is not as we thought."

"Not now," she said.

Josiah lifted her chin with his index finger so that she looked into his eyes. "Isabelle, my father came to Fairweather Key with papers regarding you."

"Papers?" She shook her head. "What sort of papers?"

"Sit with me." He settled on the pew and waited until she did the same. Then he told her the story his father had shared with him aboard the *Caroline*.

"How can that be? Emilie told me he was to purchase me for his personal use." She covered her mouth with her hands.

"What?" He gave her a sideways look. "You knew my father was your protector?"

Isabelle sighed. "Emilie knew. I'm sure she overheard her father discussing it. Once I knew the name of my protector, it was a simple matter to find you and get passage out of New Orleans."

"Wait—you chose me because of who my father was?"

"No." She entwined her fingers with his. "Emilie instructed me to listen for anything that might be said about the Carters. I overheard things about your father but also about you. Things I know now are wrong."

"Like?"

She studied the pew in front of her. "Like how you were an infidel."

"Ah, that would have come from my father." He paused. "Did he also characterize me as stupid, lazy, and dangerous?"

Her look answered the question. "I'm sorry. He was wrong, and thus, so was I."

Josiah sighed. "It is in the past. I prefer to look to the future." He swiveled in the pew to face her. "Without you, there is no future, Isabelle. Tell me you love me, for you know I've never stopped loving you."

"Yes," she said softly, "I know, and I do."

He moved closer, bringing his lips near her ear. "Say it, Isabelle."

When she turned, their lips almost brushed. Almost but not quite. "I love you," she said.

Josiah leaned back a notch to better see her. "Anything else you'd like to say?"

A broad smile dawned. "Yes, I would have you kiss me."

So he did.

"What is this?" a man called out in heavily accented Spanish. "Get out of here, you two. The chapel is no place for this kind of behavior. I warrant you are not even married."

Josiah rose and pulled Isabelle out of the pew behind him. "Josiah Carter," he said. "And you're correct. We are not married—yet. Might you be a padre?"

"I am," the old man said.

He turned to Isabelle. "Before God, I would have you as my wife. Will you marry me, Isabelle Gayarre, and heed not what anyone save the Lord says about it?"

"But, Josiah," she said, "what if—"

He ceased her concern with a kiss, then offered a quick apology to the cleric. "In the eyes of God, you and I are free to marry. I ask you one last time and never again thereafter: Will you marry me, Isabelle Gayarre?"

"Yes," she said as she fell into his embrace. "I will."

The wedding was held by candlelight in the Capilla de Jesús that evening with Micah Tate and the padre's sister as witnesses. While Micah kindly brought a hammock onshore and stood guard, the newlyweds spent their honeymoon night together aboard the *Caroline*.

Josiah opened his eyes before dawn and knew the day was going to be fine. Rather than awakening to William's foot in his ear, he held Isabelle Gayarre in his arms. "No," he whispered against the jasmine scent of his wife's hair. "Isabelle Carter is in my arms this morning."

"Aye, Captain," she said, then yawned.

By the time the sun shone through the windows of the *Caroline*, Josiah had been fed his breakfast and had weighed anchor. "You were right, Tate, when you recommended married life. I must say it does agree with me."

To his credit, the wrecker merely laughed as they set sail across the sea to reach Fairweather Key before dusk. The lookout must have announced their arrival, for the *Caroline* docked to quite a reception.

The docks and adjoining town square were ringed with torches, chasing away the shadows of the evening. Mrs. Campbell had thrown open the doors of the boardinghouse, and people milled about. When Josiah emerged onto the deck with Isabelle in tow, a cheer went up.

Micah brushed past them and chuckled. "I'm fairly certain this is not for me," he said as he made sure the vessel was properly moored before stepping onto the dock. "Ladies and gentlemen," he said as he made a grand bow, "may I present Mr. and Mrs. Josiah Carter."

Mr. and Mrs. Josiah Carter. Isabelle had been a bride for a full twenty-four hours, and still she could not believe it. The thought of the ceremony made her smile.

The memory of their night aboard the *Caroline* made her blush and smile.

To think, it was only the first day among many.

The reception had been a surprise, all of it coordinated by Viola and Emilie along with help from Mrs. Campbell and Mrs. O'Mara.

"How did you do all of this so quickly?" she asked Emilie and Viola when they managed a moment away from the crowd. "I wanted to have you as attendants in the wedding," she added, "but Josiah deemed it improper to wait."

Viola giggled. "Improper? Like as not he was afraid you would change your mind."

"Excuse me, ladies." Isabelle looked up to see the object of their discussion along with his brother and father. "William has a wedding gift he would like to present to us." He glanced over at Hezekiah. " 'Tis my understanding that he and our father conspired to present the gift to us together."

"Well, someone had to bid on it at auction." William pointed to Emilie. "She was too busy making all these plans, so I had to have Papa help me." He shook his head. "It wasn't easy, either, what with the medicine Papa took—well, he did say the silliest things."

Josiah's glance collided with hers, and Isabelle felt herself blush. "Aye," he said, "it will do that."

William thrust the gift toward Josiah. "You'd better open it, 'cause it's too heavy for Isabelle."

He accepted the gift. "Aye, 'tis heavy. Have you brought me pirate's treasure, William?"

The boy looked stricken, so Josiah quickly opened the gift. Inside the wrapping was the Chinese lacquer sewing box he presumed had been lost with the *Jude*. As he moved the box, he could feel the coins inside slide.

"The drawer is stuck," his father said, "but I'm sure with a bit of work you can get the thing open."

"Aye." Josiah lifted his brother into an embrace. "A fine gift, Sir William," he said. "I'm much pleased."

"As am I," Isabelle added.

"Isabelle," Viola said, "could you spare a moment? I've something I'd like to share with you." She glanced over at Emilie. "You, too," she said.

"Of course," Isabelle said. "Will you excuse us, Josiah?"

Josiah captured her fingers and held them to his lips. His eyes held a promise that sent her heart galloping. Had Viola not wrenched her away, Isabelle might have remained happily at her husband's side.

"What was so important that you had to bring me up here now?" Isabelle sat at the end of the bed and stared into the hearth, where a small fire burned.

Viola produced two folded papers. The one on top had Isabelle's name on it, and Viola handed it to her.

"What is this?"

"One of two letters," Viola said, "from Jean Gayarre. Both were entrusted to me when they were found inside Andre's coat after his untimely demise." She paused. "I thought to give them to you that day, but circumstances intervened. I felt this was the appropriate night for reading them."

Isabelle lifted the seal, and it came up easily. "This has been opened," she said.

Viola hung her head. "The seals were broken when I received the letters. I confess I read

416

yours, Isabelle. I thought to destroy it. After seeing what it said, I decided against it."

Isabelle unfolded the paper, dotted with what most surely was Andre Gayarre's blood, and began to read.

These are the words of Jean Gayarre, father of Isabelle Gayarre, and the testament of the events of December 27, 1814. Upon leaving my home that night, I thought to visit Sylvie, my dearest love and the mother of my daughter born three days prior. I found Sylvie in a most distressing state, and while I was there, she did expire.

Isabelle looked up from the letter. "None of this is new to me."

"Read all the way to the end," Viola said softly. "I wager there will be something you do not know."

It was a time of war, and the enemy was near to storming the gates, so I did what I now know was an act of desperation. I took that baby girl from Sylvie and brought her home with me. That very night, my wife gave birth, and as fate would cruelly have it, that infant, too, was a girl child. Faced with two daughters born a mere three days apart, I knew not what to do.

Married to a woman who despised me and mourning for a woman who loved me, I made a choice, Isabelle, that I find hard to justify, lo, these many years later. The newborn daughter born of my wife and the three-day-old daughter of my concubine lay in the same cradle side by side with only Delilah as witness. There was no honorable debate among choices that night, though I wish it were so. Rather, I snatched up Sylvie's three-day-old daughter and returned to my wife's chambers claiming her as our newborn. You, the daughter of my marriage, were sent away to be raised by Delilah, always protected and always intended to one day be free.

Isabelle crumpled the paper and held it to her chest while she willed her heart to stop racing. The truth unfolded gently in soft cascading pools.

Daughter of the wife who despised me.

Two girls in one cradle.

There was no honorable debate among choices made that night.

She, Isabelle Gayarre, had never been born into slavery but was the legitimate daughter of Jean Gayarre and his wife. This meant Andre was her brother. It also meant Emilie was—

Oh, no.

She read the name on the letter Viola still held: Emilie Gayarre. Isabelle snatched it away and tossed it into the flames, along with her own.

Emilie squealed as she rose and darted to the fire. Too late to save the documents, she could only watch them burn. "Isabelle, whatever did you do that for?" she asked.

Isabelle exchanged smiles with Viola. "Some things are not fit for a lady to read," she said. "Will you forgive me for sparing you?"

Emilie's smile was slow to appear. "Of course," she finally said as she headed for the door. "Isabelle, you've kept your guests waiting long enough. Do come, and let's rejoin the celebration."

"And of some," Isabelle whispered to Viola, "have compassion, making a difference."

About the Author

Kathleen Y'Barbo

Kathleen first discovered her love of books when, at the age of four, she stumbled upon her grandmother's encyclopedias. Letters became words, and words became stories of faraway places and interesting people. By the time she entered kindergarten, Kathleen had learned to read and found that her love of stories could carry her off to places far beyond her small East Texas town. Eventually she hit the road for real, earning a degree in Marketing from Texas A&M before setting off on a path that would take her to such far-flung locales as Jakarta, Tokyo, Bali, Sydney, Hong Kong, and Singapore. Finally, though, the road led back to Texas and to writing and publicizing books.

Kathleen is a bestselling author of twenty-eight novels, novellas, and young adult books. In all, more than half a million copies of her books are currently in print in the U.S. and abroad. She has been named as a finalist in the American Christian Fiction Writers Book of the Year contest every year since its inception in 2003, often for more than one book.

In addition to her skills as an author, Kathleen is also a publicist at Books & Such Literary Agency. She is a member of the Public Relations Society of America, Words for the Journey Christian Writers Guild, and the Authors Guild. She is also a former treasurer of the American Christian Fiction Writers. Kathleen has three grown sons and a teenage daughter.

You can read more about Kathleen at www.kathleenybarbo.com.

Center Point Publishing
600 Brooks Road ● PO Box 1
Thorndike ME 04986-0001 USA

(207) 568-3717

US & Canada:
1 800 929-9108
www.centerpointlargeprint.com